PETINA GAPPAH

Rotten Row

FABER & FABER

First published in 2016
by Faber & Faber Limited
Bloomsbury House
74–77 Great Russell Street
London WC1B 3DA

Typeset by Faber & Faber Limited
Printed and bound by CPI Group (UK) Ltd, Croydon, CR0 4YY

A CIP record for this book
is available from the British Library

ISBN 978–0–571–32418–7

2 4 6 8 10 9 7 5 3 1

For three legal eagles and the dearest of friends:
Munyaka Wadaira Makuyana, who pushes me to be better,
Victoria Jane Donaldson, who pushes me to do more
and Silas Xaverio Chekera, who fired the starting gun.

Contents

A Note on Rotten Row

In London, Rotten Row is a wide, untarred road that begins at Hyde Park Corner and ends at the Serpentine Road. Established in the time of William and Mary to provide access to the new palace at Kensington, the name is a corruption of 'Route de Roi', French for King's Road.

In Salisbury, the capital of the Crown Colony of Southern Rhodesia, initially administered from London – and the only colony in Africa to be founded by a private company, Cecil John Rhodes' British South Africa Company – the name Rotten Row was given to the road that was created to begin at the intersection of Prince Edward Street and Jameson Avenue. As the city grew, Rotten Row expanded to become a busy thoroughfare linking the city centre to those of Rhodesia's famed industries that were based in Salisbury, and to Harari Township, the city's first black township, home for the men who provided the cheap labour that powered those industries.

Rhodesia is now Zimbabwe, Salisbury Harare, Jameson Avenue is Samora Machel, Harari Township is Mbare, and the industries have all but collapsed. For now, at least, Rotten Row remains Rotten Row, or, to give it its colloquial, Shonglish name, Roton'ro.

It is a street redolent with remembrance. From its middle section, you go right to reach the kopje, where Rhodes' invading force, the Pioneer Column, first raised the Union flag on 13 September 1890, the act that established Rhodesia. At the top end of Rotten Row, just before it merges into Prince Edward Street, stands the towering building nicknamed 'Shake Shake'. This is the headquarters of the Zimbabwe African National Union (Patriotic Front) (ZANU PF), the political party that, together with the Zimbabwe African People's Union (ZAPU), fought the Rhodesian white minority regime and led the armed struggle for a free Zimbabwe.

The approach to Mbare is dotted with colonial bungalows that now house funeral parlours, car breakers and colleges of further learning. They make an incongruous backdrop for the thundering traffic, but are protected by the legislation and by-laws that make it difficult for the Harare City Council to destroy buildings older than fifty years without considerable hoop-jumping.

Also on Rotten Row is the 'Civic Centre', comprising the Harare City Library, formerly known as the Queen Victoria Memorial Library, the Museum of Natural History and the Criminal Division of the Harare Magistrates' Courts. The Civil Division is not on Rotten Row but some metres away on Fourth Street, in a building that was used to stable government horses before the widespread use of cars. For that reason, this building is and is likely to be forever known to all solicitors, magistrates and other court officials as 'The Stables'.

It is of the Criminal Division, the criminal courts, that most people in Harare think when they hear the name 'Rotten Row'. It is these criminal courts that have given this story collection its name. The stories in this volume are not all set in or at Rotten Row but are about the kinds of strife, tensions and conflicts that sometimes end up finding their only resolution at the courts.

Any coincidences between real life and the fictional lives of my ill-fated characters is only further proof that, as is written in the Book of Ecclesiastes, that which has been is what will be, that which is done is what will be done and there is nothing new under the sun.

Petina Gappah,
Geneva, June 2016

CAPITAL

Out of the crooked timber of humanity
no straight thing was ever made.

– Immanuel Kant –

The Dropper

Avenge not yourselves, but rather give place unto
wrath: for it is written, Vengeance is mine;
I will repay, saith the Lord.

– The Epistle of Paul the Apostle to the Romans –

Musatsiva, vadikanwa, asi mudzivurire kutsamna;
nokuti kwakanyorwa, kucinzi: Kutsiva ndokwangu,
ini ndicaripira-ndizo zinoreva Ishe.

– Nwadi yaPauro kuvaRoma –

Never believed all that blather in all the adverts, all that Rhodesia is super and all that. The first five drops at the end of my rope were as white as I am. Rhodesia wasn't super for them, that's for'shore, or for the poor buggers they popped. Misfits and madmen, odd-balls and nobodies, the lot of them. Like my first drop, the Wankie train murderer. Bloody big he was, neck like a bull in heat. Needed more rope than I thought. Give a drop enough rope, I always said.

It all comes down to the rope, man. It's all about the rope. Always preferred sisal to nylon myself. One inch thick, no more, no less. Sisal is strong. Natural. Nylon blisters the hands. You spend a helluva lot of time tying the knot. Have to get it right. Eight turns is what I used though I know some used thirteen. Much prefer the Hangman to the Gallows Knot myself. Breaks the neck, you see. I reckon it's cleaner all around. Easier for everyone. Gallows Knot strangles.

Callous bastard and thick as two planks, he was, the Wankie train drop. Kept wringing his hands just before I dropped him, wringing and wringing his hands. I promise you, I don't know who was more nervous, him or me. One of the medics up at the Maximum put a bottle of *dop*, Bols brandy it was, in my hand. Strong stuff. Told me to take five swigs to steady my nerves.

The Americans and them won't drop an 'oke who is a little soft in the head. Well, they don't drop them *drop them* but you know what I mean. He was like that, the Wankie train drop, a little soft. Come to think of it, the next one was a bit soft too. Had one of those hangdog faces, like life had served everyone else oranges and only he got the lemon, and not even a full lemon either, but a quarter lemon and rotting with it. Up from Umtali he was. Don't mind me. I slip into the old names every now and again. Mutare, I mean.

Gave his wife six of the best for breakfast and six of the best for lunch and then six more just for the hell of it. Had a load of snot-nosed kids too, one after the other, place was simply crawling with *laaities*. Poor as *munts* they were. Then when she said, 'I've had enough of you, I am outta here,' he took out a gun and popped her along with thirteen other buggers, just like that. Pop pop pop. One after the other. Fourteen times. Said he didn't know what came over him, he was out of himself.

Funny that. They all say that. I was out of myself.

Came close to dropping a woman once. Bit loose she was. Shot the 'oke who was giving it to her. Not her old man. Some sort of boyfriend who had used her up and dumped her. She was one of those Stickistuff types; she stuck and stuck and stuck to the poor 'oke, refusing to be dumped then she shot him. She was out of it too, she said. Didn't know what came over her. Got fifteen years instead of the rope. Pretty thing, she was, man. All eyes. I reckon that's what saved her for'shore, being a pretty chick.

Next six drops were *terrs*. Well, they didn't think they were terrorists, obviously. Called themselves guerrillas, didn't they, comrades and freedom fighters and such like. Wanted to bring socialism and communism and the this ism and the that ism. Socialism. What a fucken joke. Britain had said no more droppings, they had abolished their own and wanted the same here but Smith and Dupont and Lardner–Burke and them said to the Queen and all those 'okes up in London: fuck you. We have UDI now; we have our own country and our own government and you can't fucken tell us what to do. We do what we fucken want and we drop who we fucken want to drop when we fucken want to drop them.

Phoned me on one of those party lines. Crossed lines with that Bridget van Tonder, old bitch who ran the General Store next to the Chipinga Hotel. Fucken do-gooding Nosey Parker, up in everyone's business. When she got off the line, the Salisbury lot was saying, 'Come now, man, you are dropping six two days after tomorrow.'

A bloody bad business that was, that's for'shore. My first mass dropping. Helluva mess afterwards. Made a few mistakes, I won't deny that. Couple died hard, man. Necks didn't break cleanly when I sprang the trap. Twitched and twitched as they swayed and down their legs flowed rivers of shit and piss. Never did much understand the local lingo. Tricky language. One word can mean six different things, but I know a couple cried for their mothers. Couldn't shoot them or anything. Had to wait it out. Twitched and twitched, they did. Dead man's dance. Drank my first full bottle of Bols afterwards. Stopped using the Gallows Knot.

No dropping is ever like the one before. Some of them walked themselves there. Stood above the door, all straight you know, though they trembled a helluva lot. But most had to be dragged along, screaming out of their senses and shitting and pissing themselves. Some even got a stiffy. Angel lust, one of the medics said. That's what they called it in what do you call them, Middle Times or Medieval Ages or whatever you call them.

Funny term for it. Angel lust.

Never had much schooling myself, man. Always had common sense, though, that's all you need, bloody common sense, only it's not that common now, is it? Tried to tell the 'okes and them up in Salisbury, it would make a helluva lot more sense if you gave them *muti* or *dop* of some kind, that local *kachasu* stuff would do it. Cheap as a Chipinga *hure* and will make them drunk enough to handle. But no, they wouldn't have that. Had these electric whatnots, these taser things to move them to stand above the door.

'73 to '75 were my busiest years. Eish, man. It was hotter than Kariba in October, I promise you. War was raging everywhere and they were dropping like flies, man. Their lot was shooting our lot. Our lot was shooting back and bombing. That fucken coward Smith sent all those boys and them to war, the Call Up and all that and for what? What did they fucken die for? One of my drops that time was a *laaitie*, bloody shame that was. They said it was all right because he was nineteen but he can't have been more than sixteen. Could smell the fear dripping out of him with his sweat. Even after I covered his face with the hood, his eyes were still burning into mine. Taught me something, that one did. Never look directly in the eye before a drop, man, not even when you're hooding.

By the time I dropped my fiftieth, I had the hang of it, so to say. I could have dropped with one hand, that's for'shore. I had the hang of it, but something was shifting inside, you know. And I couldn't do a drop without the Bols. Got *dopped* before each drop, then again after.

It's all a bit of a blank, to be honest with you.

People around here knew well enough what I did; it's a small town, Chipinga. A no town, really. An 'oke can't swing his cock in the direction of the local *hures* without hitting the likes of that fucken Bridget van Tonder. I promise, I would not let my fucken dog piss on the fucken bitch if she was on fucken fire.

When I was not dropping, I ran the cafe up at the Chipinga Country Club. Place wasn't short of people who came just to stare. Nothing like a dropping to sharpen the appetite, particularly when you are served your burgers and chips by the dropper himself.

Had this chick once, well, girlfriend I suppose, maybe even, what'd they call it in all those novels, fiancé. Asked her to marry me. Chuffed like hell I was when she said yes. I was that taken, man, I promise you. Wheat farmer's daughter with tits as big as the

Bumi Hills and legs like an answered prayer. She was almost Miss Gatooma but she got rubella, a sort of German measles, she said, and she had to pull out. Stacey, she was called. She'd have won too, beautiful singing voice she had. Really gave it to her. Never was one to turn down free milk if you put it before me in a jug.

Broke it off after a year. Chipinga wasn't good enough for Almost Miss Gatooma, was it. She was on at me all the time about the *dop* and that fucken Bridget van Tonder was on at her all the time about the this and the that and the *hures* and then she ran off with an 'oke from Fort Vic who was with the railways, he was one of that Bridget van Tonder's nephews, wasn't he. Saw her fifteen years later up in Melsetter, kids crawling all around her and the Bumi Hills down to her armpits.

Lost her chance, didn't she?

Gave up dropping round about that time, after the war. But they called me back six years later. Needed a dropper, they said. Thought they'd bin the whole thing, to be honest. Tried to tempt me with my own record. 'You've dropped ninety-seven,' they said. 'Don't you want to make a clean hundred, at least? Go for the century.' Heard from my connections up in Salisbury that after I said no thanks, they got a couple of 'okes from South Africa and another from Swaziland. Gave up after one or two years.

They have had a hard time getting a local. *Engozi* and all that, the fear that if you kill a man, you will be haunted forever by his dead spirit, that sort of thing, haunted down to the next generation and the one after that.

Never had much truck with all that sort of crap myself. But sometimes, I swear, I hear sighs and whispers all around the hills. I promise, the hills come alive. And no, it is not the *dop*, that's what they said, up at the hospital, the useless pricks. I asked them, what did they want me to do about it when the *dop* is the only thing that stops it.

And now the comrades and freedom fighters and whatnots are coming for the farms. Started down in Mashonaland, didn't it, and now they are here. It's all this indigenisation, isn't it. The land must go to indigenous people they say, it must all be indigenised, and the likes of me must just bugger off to England. As if I could live on fucken Mud Island. Never even set foot there in my life, born here, wasn't I, down in Enkeldoorn.

Well, they can indigenise this farm all they want, and they can indigenise my Zesa electricity bill too if it comes to that and my phone company bill while they are at it and good luck to them. It is no skin off my nose if they take this place, that's for'shore.

Got the job after the Country Club collapsed. Manage this farm for some Pommies who know nothing about tea. Come down from Mud Island a couple of times a year to braai and toast themselves in the sun. Couple of 'okes down the road destroyed their machinery and all their this and all their that before they left, but I won't do that. Not got much to destroy that's for'shore and besides, I reckon that debts have to be paid. They will be paid one way or the other, man. Debts have to be paid. It's the way it is, life goes up and down, goes round and comes round again, and that's just the way it is.

So when they come, I will go sit up on the terrace overlooking the tea. I'll finish this novel I'm reading, *Hold the Dream*, it's called. I like those chick writers, Jackie Collins and Judith Thingummijig and Barbara Taylor Whatshername. They are the only things that Miss Gatooma left behind her.

So I'll read this one and get *dopped* as I watch the sunset. It's something else, man, the sun sinking behind the hills and the crickets sounding and the birds flying against the red and orange sky. That's the last thing I want to see, the sky lit up with fire above the rows and rows of tea. Then I will do my last drop.

I reckon I might as well end with myself.

Copacabana, Copacabana, Copacabana

Execute ye judgement and righteousness;
. . . neither shed innocent blood in this place.

– The Book of Jeremiah –

Tongai zakarurama nezakatendeka, vuye musatevura
ropa risinemhosa panzimbo ino.

– Buku yaMuprofita Jeremia –

It is just after nine o'clock in the morning. Gidza will die in exactly forty-three minutes and thirteen seconds. At this moment, he is leaning out of the open window of a *kombi* omnibus that plies the route between the suburb of Chisipite and the city centre. A flea-market Liverpool shirt ripples on his reed-thin body. 'Copacabana, Copacabana, Copacabana,' he shouts. 'Copacabana!'

He follows this with a piercing whistle. At the wheel, Prosper blows the horn in counterpoint. In the days when Leopold Takawira was Moffat Street, Copa Cabana, two words, was a nightclub. What *kombi* touts like Gidza and *kombi* drivers like Prosper now call Copacabana, one word, is the area around the former club. Where once the air rang with tunes from the Devera Ngwena Jazz Band, the Pied Pipers, the Bhundu Boys and the Ocean City Band, it is now a cacophony of hooting horns and yelling touts.

Their *kombi* is a death trap. A woman named Shupikai Mukono who lives in Cambridge, close to Grantchester on the River Cam, and who works as a psychiatric nurse at Addenbrooke's Hospital, imported it from Japan. Her life, nasty, British and short of happiness, is lived in the hopeful expectation that she will give it all up one day and never again have to minister to minds diseased. She has seen first hand the terrible hurts that come when the mind, so fragile, oh how fragile, turns in on itself and poisons everything.

She saw the *kombi* as part of her investment strategy for the day she would return home, but there has been no return, either for her, or of her investment. The brother in whose care she left it spends nothing at all on its maintenance. And so it is that the legally mandated fire extinguisher under the seat is nothing but an empty red can with a nozzle and fading lettering. Thick sheets of semi-transparent plastic sheeting have replaced the glass windows. The factory-made sign says '12 PASSENGERS ONLY', but extra wooden benches have been built in to make room for an additional eight. Travelling calls for posterial dexterity, the most comfortable position for any passenger is to sit on one buttock. Passengers are usually so tightly packed that they do not need seatbelts, which is as well because those are as distant a memory as the front indicator lights. By the end of the journey, they will know each other more intimately than is, perhaps, proper for strangers.

The first thing that Gidza noticed about Prosper when he met him was that the outside of his right arm was much darker in complexion than the rest of his body; no small wonder as it is the arm that is always out in the open so that he can indicate his intention to turn. Prosper's own seatbelt is no longer adjustable to the size of its wearer. Whenever they approach a police checkpoint, Prosper has to sit on the extra length. The *kombi* has passed police inspection at every roadblock.

Spray-painted on the outside, in the vivid colours of the national flag, is the legend '100 PER CENT TALIBAN'. This was Gidza's idea. His real name is Groblar Khumbulani Bhajila. He was born in the weeks after the giddy moment in which a son of this soil had spurred Liverpool to victory over Roma in the European Cup and a nation roared with him. Gidza's father had been an early fan of Bruce Grobbelaar, The Jungleman, and of his first club, Highlanders, the lauded 'ama Bosso'. He had followed The Jungleman's rise from the heat and dust of Bulawayo to light up Anfield. It stood to reason that he would name his first child in honour of his favourite footballer, in the natural hope that his son would follow where The Jungleman had led. An indifferent clerk had registered the name as he thought it should be spelled, and thus Groblar his son became.

The illogical order of Shona slang names for English and sort-of-English first names means that the minute Groblar moved from Bulawayo to live with his mother's uncles in Harare, his name became Gidza, just as all Philips become Fidza, all Ryans Ridza, all Davids Divha and all Jonathans Jonso. He has not followed his father's dream for him. A big-time dream without the talent and the money to go with it can only ever be a wish, and so here he is now, at ten past nine on a Wednesday morning in September, a small-time *hwindi* in a battered *kombi* on Enterprise Road, driving to his death.

The term *hwindi* is a double pun. Not only do Gidza and his fellow touts hang like limpets from the windows of their vans, they also hang out into the wind. Gidza has mastered the skills of a good *hwindi*. He, for it is always a he – it is no suitable job for a woman, this – is more than a tout. He is a necessary part of the driving – because he does his job so well, Prosper can concentrate on driving, knowing that Gidza will shout out their destination to attract passengers, collect the right amount of money for fares, and, with the brusque command, '*Garisanai* four four,' bully the maximum number of people into squashing next to each other in the small interior space.

'Copacabana, Cop'c'bane, Cop'c'bano!'

It is monotonous to call out the same destination every few metres, so he makes things lively for himself by varying it a little. He chants it – 'Copacabana' – sings it – 'Cop'c'bane' – gives it a little zip – 'Cop'c'bano'. Having called out the destination, he manoeuvres himself back into the van, checks his phone and shrieks with laughter. '*Iyi yakapenga manje iyi* M'koma Prosper,' he says. 'Ah gosh! Listen to this one. Congratulations, you have been awarded the amount of $0.00 dollars for calls to any destination at any time on this network.'

Prosper laughs with him. In his laughter, Gidza leans into a smartly dressed male passenger of proportions that would be more comfortable in a more capacious and less occupied kind of vehicle. 'You are squeezing me, *shamwari*,' the passenger says.

'Sorry, Big Dhara,' Gidza says. 'For sure, you are extremely squeezable. Sorry, biggest.'

Just after they pass the Congolese embassy sign just before Arcturus, Gidza leans out of the window again. 'Copacabana, Cop'c'bano, Cop'c'bane!'

A frail looking old white man holds out his arm to stop them. He extends a liver-spotted arm to Gidza. '*Gemu rachinja*, M'koma Prosper,' Gidza says as he pulls him in. '*Shiri yabata rekeni*. This is a reverse land invasion this one.'

Before Prosper can respond, two policemen, one fat and the other thin, wave them down. They eject the passengers in the front seat so that they sit next to Prosper. The two ejected passengers look sullen, but say nothing as they squeeze their way into the back. '*Ko, vana va*Mambo,' says Gidza with insouciant cheer. '*Matitsika vakuruvakuru*. How about doing something unusual today?'

The larger of the two turns to him, frowns and says, 'What are you talking?'

'How about paying your fare today?' says Gidza.

'Watch your mouth,' says the smaller one.

'Okay, okay, you have worn me down,' says Gidza. 'I will give you a discount. Only one of you will pay.'

They both ignore him and speak to each other in low voices. Unable to get a rise out of them, Gidza leans out of the window again. 'Copacabana, Cop'c'bane, Cop'c'bano!'

The van slows down as a woman runs up.

'Are you going to Fourth Street?'

'If we are going to Fourth Street,' says Gidza, 'I will say we are going to Fourth Street. Have you heard me say we are going to Fourth Street? Copacabana!'

As Prosper drives off, a woman dressed in the long white garment and veil of the Apostolic Faith church runs up. She has a baby on her back, is leading a child in one hand and holds a suitcase in the other. Her white garment billows behind her as she runs. Prosper does not stop completely, but maintains a slow crawl while beeping the horn. She pants with effort as she runs alongside them. As she clambers in, she hands the suitcase to Gidza, and takes the baby off her back.

Gidza helps the little boy in and slides the door closed. 'If he sits on a normal seat,' Gidza tells the woman, indicating the child, 'then you have to pay for him.'

The woman tries to balance both children and her suitcase on her knee. The boy slips off. '*Chigara pa*Kadoma, biggest,' Gidza says to the boy and directs him to a seat on the metal casing above the engine.

'Mhamha, it's too hot, it's too hot, mhamha,' the child says as he shifts one leg after another.

'*Wotojaira zvako m'fanami*,' Gidza says with callous cheerfulness. 'That's what happens when your mother cannot afford to pay for a seat for you.'

Under her white veil, the Apostolic woman scowls. 'What kind of talk is that?' she says. 'What do you know about what I can or cannot afford?'

'Where did I lie?' says Gidza. 'Copacabana!'

'Mhamha, it's hot,' the child says again.

The woman fishes into her suitcase and hands a half-full plastic bottle of Cascade juice to her son, which consoles him. He finishes it in four large gulps. He burps and hands the empty container to his mother. 'You had better not be thinking of leaving that bottle in here,' Gidza warns.

She sends it flying out of the window where it almost hits a sleek, latest model Mercedes with diplomatic plates that is moving in the opposite direction on the Enterprise Bypass. The Cascade bottle falls on the side of the road under a Forestry Commission sign that says, 'Nine Million Trees Planted This Season! Thank You Zimbabwe!'

'*Hesi* baby, *hesi nhanha*,' Gidza says as he pokes the baby's cheek. The baby rewards him with a stony stare. Gidza smiles and clicks his tongue against the roof of his mouth. The baby glares back.

At the sculpture market on the Enterprise Bypass, the old white man and the two policemen get off. Gidza's attention is diverted from the baby by a seemingly endless row of headless, armless and legless sculptures with disproportionately large breasts and buttocks.

'M'koma Prosper,' he says as he points to the sculptures, '*mari inenge yawanda sei kuti mutenge zvidhori izvi*? Your money will be truly burning a hole in your pocket if you are going to be spending it on this stuff. Just look at that. These are monstrous horrors these are, M'koma Prosper! *Munenge mazvitengera* horror! Copacabana!'

At the traffic lights at the Newlands shops, they stop to let a blind man pass. He wears torn blue overalls while the boy leading him wears a shirt and a pair of shorts belonging to two different school uniforms. '*Bofu rafamba iri*, M'koma Prosper,' Gidza says. '*Ndariona nhasi makuseni chaiwo elokhuzeni, kuKuwadzana.*' To the street kid he says, '*M'fanami*, why aren't you in school like others your age? Here's a dollar. If I see you again today, don't ask for more. Copacabana!'

They have left the Bypass and are almost at the end of Enterprise Road. The rains of the night before have dropped petals from the Jacaranda trees at the edge of the road. The *kombi* moves over a carpet of crushed purple blooms. The city centre buildings in the near distance are Gidza's cue to start collecting the fares of those who are still to pay. He shouts, '*Ngatibatanidzei tione vabereki nevaberekesi.*' As he cannot move around himself, the passengers pass him their money in a relay.

'Wait a minute,' he says. 'Who has given me ten rand?'

The passengers look sullen. No one says a word.

'I said who paid ten rand?' he says again.

'Just give the money back and each will take what they had,' Prosper says.

A woman in a blue woollen hat looks up from her phone.

'Ten rand?' she asks.

'Yes, mothers,' Gidza says. 'I have seventeen dollars here, I should have eighteen, but someone has paid using ten rand instead of a dollar.'

'But ten rand is one dollar,' she says.

'*Imi* mothers,' he says, his voice laced with impatience. 'How many times do we have to say we no longer take Zuma's tumbling *zuda* money? It's Obama all the way. If I am to change this, I will only get seventy cents or sixty, and that's if I'm lucky. I don't get a full dollar, okay? So just pay me your dollar and stop wasting my time.'

'But it is ten rand from Avondale,' the woman argues.

'Are we coming from Avondale? Do we look like we are coming from Avondale? When you look out of the window, are you seeing Avondale? And do you not see that sign?'

The blue-hatted woman looks at the signs above the driver's head. In addition to the one specifying the optimum number of passengers, there is another that says JESUS IS MY DRIVER and another that says NO RANDS ACCEPTED BY ORDER MANAGE-MENT. She mumbles angrily as she reaches into her blouse to produce a dirty dollar bill from her bra. She hands it to the man sitting in front of her, who passes it on to Gidza.

'*Pa*corner,' says a voice.

Gidza bangs the roof to stop the van.

'Copacabana, Cop'c'bane, Co'p'c'bano!'

Two passengers jump out to be replaced by three more. The *kombi* moves off again in a cloud of petrol and exhaust fumes. Among the new passengers is a young woman in a bright red top and leopard print skirt. She wears a perfume of such pungency that it almost defeats the exhaust fumes that fill the van.

As she gets in, Gidza clutches his heart in mock shock. 'Ah, ah, *hi hi hi*!' he says as he pushes against the man in the front seat next to him to let her pass. It is the same passenger with whom he has already collided. He stumbles and collapses into the man.

'Sorry *zvakare* Big Dhara, *nhasi ndinemi*,' he says as he brushes past the man's jacket pocket. He turns back to the woman and says. '*Ko sisi vakapfeka mbada kunge dindingwe*, as smart as you are, where are you off to today? *Handeka kupungwe kusvika kwati ngwe*!'

The woman ignores him and takes out her mobile phone as it rings.

'Alcohol you letter,' she says. 'I am going to Boledale.'

'M'koma Prosper, did you hear this leopardess of ours?' shouts Gidza. '*Sisi vembada vanoza wena*!'

'What did she say?' says Prosper.

'Boledale. Do you mean Borrowdale? She is going to Boledale. This is what we mean when we say someone is talking like they are chewing water. Boledale, she says. Too embarassed to be associated with us! Maybe one day, if you are very lucky, sister, you will have a shiny car to match your accent then you won't have to use *kombis* like you are one of-us *povo*. Boledale. *Hela*. But I bet that if I stepped on your right foot right now, or even your left one, you would say *maiwe-e*, like M'koma Prosper, or *umama wami* like me, not *oh my mummy*. Boledale! *Hela!*'

His body out of the window once again, he shouts 'Copacabana!'

As he settles back in, he says, '*Eish*, but you smell so nice. She smells so nice, M'koma Prosper, *regai zvavo vativhairire* sister *vembadilo.*'

'I can smell her from here,' Prosper says.

Gidza sings, '*Ndirege ndifare usandikanganisa! Chinamira! Tarira mhandara dzinoshereketa! Kunge kutsombora tsombo, kana kutakura dombo!*'

In the second row, an old man lets out a sneeze that startles the stony-faced baby into crying. '*Maiwe-e* sister,' Gidza says in mock horror, 'look what you have done now. This poor old man is sneezing and that baby crying and it's all from your perfume. Maybe it is the ancestral spirits that do not like modern times. *Svikai zvenyu bho kulez.*'

The sneezing man scowls and shouts, '*Munataura zwamunoziva mhani mazwinzwa.*' He sneezes again. The words are spoken in the sing-song voice associated with Malawian farm labourers and domestic workers. It is the cause of much laughter for Prosper and Gidza, who says, 'You had better watch out. *Hona manje watsamwisa ava* Sekuru MuChawa. You have made him angry. Now you won't hear the end of it. You will probably find a little Malawian tokoloshi waiting for you at home.'

'*Amalume,*' Gidza says to the old man. 'This is how the city women smell, *achimwene*, you had better get used to it, this is not the reserves.'

'Who said I have come from the reserves?' the old man says. 'And who said anything about Malawi? You should know what you are talking about before you just start to talk talk for nothing. You *hwindi*, that is all you know how to do, you just talk talk for nothing.'

Gidza's mind has moved on from the leopard-skirted, perfumed woman and the Jah Prayzah song that he was singing. He now entertains Prosper with a story of a *n'anga* from Mufakose, a man of Malawian origin who specialises in restoring lost property and removing the male organs from adulterous men who sleep with women that are not theirs.

'Havaiti kani,' Gidza says. 'This other man in, *elokhuzeni*, in Chitungwiza was with this other man's woman, M'koma Prosper, but what he did not know is that the man had fixed her good and proper with Sekuru MuChawa's help. Central locking proper proper, it was proper central locking, M'koma Prosper, he had locked her all tight so that any man who was with her would suffer, *maona manje*. So this man is with this woman, and afterwards he feels this strong urge to urinate, so he goes to the toilet and there is nothing there, can you imagine? Nothing at all. He was smooth as *ilokhuzeni*, as a doll down there, M'koma Prosper, just smooth, like a *m'postan'a's* head.'

The woman whose perfume has triggered this conversation raises her voice to speak up. 'Holeday Urn,' she says.

But Gidza is concentrating on describing just how the smooth-as-a-doll man with the missing appendage reacted to his missing appendage and his newly minted smooth-as-a-dollness, and he does not hear.

'Ah sad Holeday Urn,' the woman says just at the moment the van drives past the Holiday Inn.

'Why didn't you ask me before?' Gidza says. 'You know we can't stop here now.'

'She did ask you, but you were not listening,' the large man over whom he has twice fallen says.

'And who made you the invigilator of this examination?' Gidza retorts. 'What are you, the *kombi* prefect?'

Gidza does not fully take in the look of pure loathing that the man directs his way. The *kombi* stops just before the traffic lights. The leopard-skirted woman gets off, leaving behind the smell of her perfume. As she crosses Samora Machel Avenue she shouts, 'You are as ugly as your mother's cunt.'

Gidza makes as though to go after her, but the light changes and the *kombi* moves. He contents himself with shouting after her, '*S'febe! Mazigaro! Kuda kutamba nemadhaka pasina vhat*'! *Ndinokushagada ukashisha semashakada*! You think you are so special, but your funeral will not even be open casket. Ugly bitch.'

Gidza now abandons the story of the man with the missing genitalia to describe in graphic detail just what he was going to do to the departed woman if he got the chance. 'A woman like that', he concludes, 'just needs a good seeing to, that's all she needs, M'koma Prosper. Copacabana!'

As the *kombi* passes Second Street, Gidza spots a face he knows behind the steering wheel of a *kombi* that has stopped on the other side of Samora Machel Avenue.

'*Mwapona*!' he shouts to the driver.

To Prosper he says, 'Wait a minute, M'koma Prosper,' he says. 'There is that *mufesi* I have to see.'

He jumps out and weaves his way through the traffic, a fleet-footed blur in his Liverpool shirt. He stops at the driver's window. The passengers cannot see him; his back is to them as he talks to the driver. They wait, two, then five, then seven minutes while Gidza talks to his friend. In the eighth minute, he is back, running through the traffic.

'*Kahwani*!' he says to Prosper and bangs twice on the roof. He seems even more cheerful than before.

To the passenger he fell over he says, 'Why so glum, Big Dhara? Are you still sore because I fell on you? Sorry *zvenyu m'dhara, inotambika*.' He laughs without knowing that this will be his last real laugh. He will laugh again in the seventeen minutes that he has left to live, but it will be the nervous laughter of a man close to his death. He picks up the song he was singing earlier, '*Pungwe, kusvika kwati ngwe. Pungwe, kusvika kwati ngwe!*'

The sound of a ringing phone cuts into Gidza's singing. It belongs to a young Coloured man who is right at the back. 'I'm by town now,' he says. 'But I got no juice, you check.' The man seated next to Gidza, who had put his hand to the inside pocket of his jacket when the phone started to ring, now pats his jacket pockets.

'My phone,' he says. He tries to stand up and fails. With difficulty, he pats his trouser pockets. 'I don't have my phone,' he says. His voice begins to rise in panic.

'My phone,' he says again. 'My phone.'

Gidza shakes his head. 'It will not come because you call for it,' he says. 'A phone is not a dog, you know, or a cow.'

'Maybe you left it at home,' Prosper calls out from the front.

The man turns an accusing eye on Gidza.

'It was you,' he says.

'What?'

'It was you who took my phone.'

'You must be mad,' Gidza says.

'Yes, that's right,' says the woman in the blue woollen hat. 'He brushed against you and pretended to fall, I saw him.'

'And me,' says the man with the Malawian accent.

'And me too, I saw the whole thing,' says the Apostolic woman.

Another voice comes from the back and says, 'All these *vanahwindi* are thieves, we all know they will take anything if given an opportunity. He must have taken it when he brushed against you.'

Amid Gidza's protests, Prosper drives into Copacabana. As soon as the *kombi* stops at the rank, the passengers get out and crowd around Gidza. 'I did not take your phone,' he says. 'I don't have your phone on me. Look.'

He holds out his empty hands.

'I have nothing in my hands or pockets apart from the money I collected from you all, and this phone, my own phone.' He takes his own phone from his pocket, a battered Samsung, and holds it up. Then he holds up his arms in submission to an inspection. The owner of the missing phone searches him roughly, particularly in the groin area, but finds nothing.

'He must have given it to someone,' the woman in the blue hat says.

'Yah, that's what happened,' the man with the Malawian accent says. 'He gave it to that man, the one he talked to on Samora. I saw him pass something.'

Gidza's eyes are round with fear now, his thoughts run confused in his mind, faster than speech allows.

'It was nothing,' Gidza says.

'I saw it all,' says a voice.

'We are going to the police.'

'It wasn't a phone, what I gave him. It was, that is, it wasn't. It wasn't a phone. It was . . . I took . . . I took nothing. I swear on the grave of my mother, *ngiyaphika lomama wami*, I did not take your phone.'

The man with the missing phone takes Gidza by the upper right arm and begins to march him away. His grip on Gidza is tight. The commotion has now attracted a crowd to the rank. What has happened, what has happened, what has happened? The answer sweeps across the rank. A thief has been caught, a *hwindi*, you know how they are, such thieves, every last one of them. He was caught red-handed, actually just imagine caught with his hand in someone's pocket, no, he filched money out of a woman's bra, no, it was a child's school bag, imagine and it happened just like that. As the news distorts itself across the taxi rank, Gidza faces a hostile crowd.

'M'koma Prosper,' Gidza pleads.

He is no longer the cocky brazen Gidza of a few moments before. His stammer, long conquered, comes back. 'M'koma Prosper, please, tell them. I- I- I- have not taken a, a, anything. I- I- I- swear on my mother who is buried at Serima Mission. I- I- I- did not take a- a- anything from a- a- anyone. *Vele handina.*'

Prosper tries to prise Gidza out of the arms of the man pinning him.

'*Vakuru,*' he says, 'we will go to the police and sort it out.'

The man with the missing phone rounds on Prosper. 'You are in it together. He took it, you know he did.'

'But how can you be sure, can you prove he took it?' Prosper asks.

'He has to prove he did not take it,' the phone's owner says.

'I- I- I- did not do it,' Gidza says. 'I- I- I- swear on the dead. I- I- I- I swear o- o- o- on the grave of my mother, I- I- I- swear on her grave. *Vele nyiyaphika.*'

'*Ari kuti a- e- i- o- chii chacho,*' says a voice. '*Kutokakamira nhema* nechi*Ndevere*! He is stammering for nothing. Take him to the police, they will beat the a- e- i- o- u- out of him.'

Gidza laughs a nervous laugh.

A voice shouts out, '*Ari kutoseka futi,* he is actually laughing.' It comes from a bald, stocky man in a green dustcoat who has been watching from the door of a barbershop on Cameron Street. He is so incensed by Gidza laughing at such a moment that he approaches him and gives him a ringing slap across the face. Prosper tries to intervene but is pushed away. He turns and flees in the direction of the police station. Three men in the crowd chase him, but he outruns them. They go back to the real matter before them.

Gidza breaks free and tries to follow Prosper. Two vendors selling different ice-cream brands abandon commercial rivalry as they join forces to grab him. They shove him against a pile of rotting vegetables and ice-cream wrappers. It is not certain where the next blow comes from, or the third, or the fourth. More and more people join to kick him again and again as the news of the captured thief streams across Copacabana. It reaches Kaguvi Street and Kwame Nkrumah Avenue and all the way to the flea market, as people rush to see the thief.

'Watch my box,' a woman called Ma'Nelly says to her teenage daughter Shylet. She arrived that morning from a funeral and is late to go to her stall at Mbare Musika, but that can wait. She heads to where everyone is headed, brow perspiring with the effort of running, and joins a crowd that swells now with everyone who ever had a grudge against a *hwindi*, anyone who has ever had anything stolen, and anyone who has nothing to do but enjoy the spectacle of a man being beaten by a crowd.

Ma'Nelly pushes her way to the centre. She has to fight to get in, her face is scratched, and the sweat of other bodies almost defeats her. But she is built like an East German shot putter, Ma'Nelly, with extra padding too, she is what her ancestors would have called *chitsikapanotinhira* – when she walks, the earth shakes. She pushes through until she is within sight of Gidza. Just as Gidza raises his head she kicks him back with her left foot. His head strikes the ground. There will be more kicks to his poor broken and bruised body, but he will not feel them. It is seventeen minutes to ten o'clock.

Her effort almost costs Ma'Nelly her balance. She rights herself, and, with a surge of triumph, lets others take her place. The assault on Gidza continues until there is a shout of '*mapurisa, mapurisa*' followed by blasts from three police whistles. With the police is a bare-chested Prosper holding his shirt to his bleeding head. As quickly as it had gathered, the crowd melts. The angry horde becomes individuals again.

Ma'Nelly walks across to her daughter, eager to recount to her friends the kick she gave the thief. She finds Shylet flirting with a *hwindi* and scolds her for smiling at thieves. She scolds Shylet almost all the way to Mbare until the incident is forgotten as she tells the story of the beaten thief. At the market, the story of Ma'Nelly and the kick she gave the thief is the sensation of the morning.

The large man with the missing phone also walks away from the crowd. He is afraid that he will now be late for his meeting. He has seen the thief beaten up, he saw him lying, bloodied and unconscious, but that's not enough. He wants him dead, he hopes that he is dead. He heads up Speke Avenue. As he walks past Cleveland House, he hears a voice call his name.

'Bam'k'ru'Ba'Selina.'

He turns to recognise his *muramu*, his wife's young sister Makanaka, walking quickly and out of breath. She has clearly been running. 'I am coming to your office,' she explains. 'Maigur'-Ma'Selina sent me. She said you would not be happy unless you had it with you so she sent me to get you thirty minutes after you left the house.'

'Unless I had what?' he asks.

'Didn't I say,' she laughs. 'Here.'

She holds out his phone. 'Did you know,' she says, 'someone said there was a thief who was beaten up just now at Copacabana. I always miss these things.' Now he has to buy her a pie and a Coke, she says, or maybe she should have a Cherry Plum and Nandos, no, she would much rather have a Stoney Ginger Beer and Steers. Not in a plastic bottle, though, but in a can because isn't it funny how the drinks in cans always taste better than the drinks in plastic bottles? And she will need money to go back home. As they cross the flyover above Julius Nyerere Way, he puts his phone where he always keeps it, in the inside pocket of his jacket where it rests next to his heart.

The News of Her Death

Even so the tongue is a little member,
and boasteth great things. Behold how great
a matter a little fire kindleth.

– The Epistle of James –

Saizozo vo rurimi mutezo muduku, runozirumbidza
zikuru. Tarirai, mnoto muduku unotungidza huni
zhinji sei!

– Nwadi yaJakobo –

By the time Pepukai emerged from the *kombi* at Highfield, it had just gone half past eight. She was thirty minutes late. Kindness had said she should come at eight or just before. She had followed the directions in the text message: take *kombi* to Machipisa, get off at Gwanzura, cross road, walk past Mushandirapamwe Hotel, go left after TM, go past market, saloon (that is how Kindness had spelled it) is next to butcher.

She found the salon with no problems. The name 'Snow White Hairdressing' appeared below a painting of a woman with hair that flowed and curled into the letters around her. From the butchery next door came the whirring sound of a saw on bone. Everything about the salon spoke of distressed circumstances, the peeling paint outside, the worn chairs and dirty walls inside, the faded posters for Dark and Lovely and Motions Hair Relaxers.

Snow White Hairdressing made her usual hair place in Finsbury Park look like the Aveda in Covent Garden. Then again, none of the Nigerian and Kenyan women at her salon in London would have done her hair in long thin braids that lasted four months and cost only fifty dollars. If they had, it would have cost £500 and lasted two days or more, if she was lucky.

There were five women inside. Four were standing talking together in a huddle, while the fifth swept the floor. They could have been a representative sample of the variegated nature of local womanhood. One was large with a big stomach and bottom and skin like caramel; another was her opposite, thin and sallow with long limbs and dark gums; the third was medium-sized in everything – height, breasts, bottom, complexion – while the last was short and slight with delicate hands and bones, and skin so light it was translucently yellow.

The one thing they all had in common was their hair. It was dressed in the same weave, a mimicry of Rihanna's latest style with dark hair tumbling to the shoulder, and reddish hair piled up over one eye so that they had to peer out of the other to look at anything. It was a hairstyle that neutralised features rather than enhancing them; it suited none of them, giving them all the same aged look. Pepukai thought back to the Greek myths she had loved as a child. They looked like the Graeae might have done, had they had one eye each and had there been four of them.

Away from the group of four, the youngest of the women, not a woman at all, Pepukai realised, but a teenage girl of maybe sixteen or seventeen at the most, was sweeping the floor, leaving more hair behind her than she swept before her. Her hair was not in the Rihanna weave of her workmates, but was half done, with her relaxed hair poking out in wisps from one side of her head, while the other half was in newly plaited braids.

All five looked up as Pepukai entered. She was the only customer. She felt their eyes on her, giving her that uniquely female up and down onceover that took in every aspect of her appearance and memorised it for future dissection.

'Can we help,' the largest of the women said.

'I am here for Kindness.'

'Kindness?' they exclaimed together. The large, caramel-skinned woman threw a hand to her mouth. The sweeping girl stopped, her hands on her broom, and looked at her open-mouthed.

'Yes, Kindness, I had an appointment with her at eight.'

Almost simultaneously, they turned to the right to look at a hair dressing station above which the name Kindness was written in blue and red glitter. Pepukai's eye followed theirs. There were bottles and brushes and combs, but no Kindness.

'Kindness is late,' said the large woman.

'I am also late, quite late in fact,' Pepukai said. 'How late do you think she will be?'

'No, I mean late *late*. She is deceased.'

'I am sorry?' said Pepukai.

They did not hear the question in her tone.

'Yes, we are all very sorry,' the black-gummed woman said. 'She passed away last night. We are actually waiting to hear what will happen to the body.'

'She has gone to receive her heavenly reward. She is resting now, poor Kindness. May her dear soul rest in peace,' intoned the small slight woman.

All five of them came to her and, one after the other, offered her their hands to shake, as though they were condoling with her. As she shook hands with them, Pepukai did not know what to say. Things were now more than a little awkward. She was sorry, of course, that this woman that she had never met was so suddenly dead, she was about as sorry as she could be at any stranger's death, but, after all, she had not known Kindness. She had never even talked to her – she had only exchanged a series of texts arranging the appointment.

The truth was that she was feeling slightly panicked at this news. Her flight to Amsterdam was at ten that evening. Her afternoon was to be given to a whirlwind of last-minute shopping at Doon Estate and Sam Levy's and farewells that would see her criss-crossing the city. She had only this morning left to get her hair done, and, according to her sister, the now late lamented Kindness was one of the rare hairdressers in the city who had both the skill and the willingness to do the kind of braids she wanted.

Even as these thoughts pressed on her, she did not think that she could be brutal enough to say, effectively, that the death of this unknown woman was a major inconvenience, but she need not have worried because the women came to her rescue.

'What did you want done?' said the black-gummed woman.

'Braids,' Pepukai said. 'I would like long, thin braids like this.'

On her phone, she showed them her Facebook profile picture.

'Oh, you are the one who wants the Shabba?'

'The what?'

'Kindness told us that there was someone who had sent a text to say she wanted those Shabba Ranks braids. We could not believe it, they are so old-fashioned, why not just get a weave like this?' The black-gummed woman caressed her own hair as she spoke.

'Well, I like my hair done that way.'

'We can do it for you that way if you really want,' said the large woman. 'We would have finished off your braids even with Kindness here, she would never have finished alone in one day. It would have been the five of us doing your hair at the same time. It will be eighty dollars, and it will take all of us three hours. Do you have your own extensions?'

This was not the fifty dollars and two hours that Kindness had promised her, but Pepukai did not have the heart to argue. She handed over the five packets of hair extensions she had bought at Daks in Finsbury Park. They settled her into a chair at a station belonging to Matilda, who, Pepukai gathered, was the largest woman. The others introduced themselves. The black-gummed woman was Ma'Shero. The small, slight one was called Genia, and the medium-sized everything one was Zodwa. As Ma'Shero combed out Pepukai's hair to prepare it, the other three separated and prepared the extensions.

Pepukai broke the silence by asking what had happened to Kindness. Even as she asked, she knew what the answer would be. It would be the usual long illness or short illness, the euphemism for an HIV-related disease. Wasn't it one in four dying, or maybe it was slightly less now that cheap anti-retroviral drugs were everywhere. Kindness, who had gone to receive her heavenly reward, would probably be another death to add to the national statistics.

'She was knifed by her boyfriend,' said Matilda.

'Not knifed,' said Genia. 'She was shot.'

'That's right, sorry,' said Matilda, 'at first they said she was knifed but it turns out that she was actually shot by her boyfriend.'

'You mean to say by one of her boyfriends,' added Zodwa.

This exchange was so entirely unexpected that the only thing that Pepukai could ask, rather feebly, was, 'Where?'

'Northfields,' said Zodwa.

'Northfields?' Pepukai asked.

'You know, Northfields, those flats opposite the sports club where they play cricket when the Australians and South Africans come,' said Zodwa.

Ma'Shero said, 'It is that expensive complex where they pay three thousand dollars a month for rent. It's close to State House.'

'Three thousand, who has that sort of money?' asked Matilda.

'Obviously dealers, just the type Kindness would go for,' said Ma'Shero. 'She was killed right there in one of those expensive flats. They have lifts that open up to the whole place. She will probably be in that *Metropolitan* paper tomorrow.'

'You mean you go from the lift straight into the flat? You don't say?' This was Matilda.

'It is called a paint house-sweet but I don't know why,' said Ma'Shero. 'They are actually bigger in size than many of those houses in the suburbs, you can have a whole floor just for yourself alone. The only thing you won't have, being so high, is a yard.'

'You don't say,' said Matilda.

'Well,' Ma'Shero continued, 'the cleaner came at six this morning, got in the lift, went to this paint house-sweet, and there she was, Kindness, just lying there, all shot, with bullets and blood everywhere.'

'You mean she was shot with a gun?' said Pepukai.

'She can hardly have been shot with a spoon now, can she?' retorted Ma'Shero.

'All the dealers have guns now, all of the ones in Northfields anyway, they need the guns for their mega deals and, well, you know,' said Genia.

From the doorway came a loud voice, '*Ndakapinda* busy mai mwana, but listen, I have no more airtime. No more airtime. I said no more . . . *ende futi* Econet.' The voice belonged to a woman in her fifties who wore the blue-cloaked uniform of the Catholic Church, with a white headscarf covering her head. In one hand, she had her phone, and in the other, a roasted maize cob. Her overloaded handbag seemed to drag down her left shoulder.

'*Hesi vasikana,*' she greeted as she entered.

'*Hesi* MbuyaMaTwins,' said Matilda.

'*Hesi Mati,*' MbuyaMaTwins said. '*Ko, kuita chidhafinya kudaro, kudhafuka kunge uchaputika? Hee? Kuita dhafukorera kudai!* Why are you so fat now, Matilda, honestly? Are you pregnant or something?'

As she spoke, she poked at Matilda's stomach with the pointy end of her maize cob.

'*Mukawana nguva mundikwanire, ndinonhumburwa nani* Steve *zvaari ku*South?' said Matilda. 'How could I get pregnant when my husband has been away this long?'

'There are those who are able, it is not just husbands and Steves who can do it. *Varipo vanotumbura nokunhumbura!*' MbuyaMaTwins gave a coarse, leering laugh that shook her chest and the rosary beads around her neck.

'Besides, I have been on Depo how long now, since my last born, you know, the one who was born legs first,' said Matilda.

'You know how Depo makes you gain weight.'

'Depo?' said MbuyaMaTwins.

'Yes, Depo Provera. You know, the contraceptive, the one you inject.'

'So it is injections that are making you so fat? Better to be pregnant in that case, at least you get something out of the fatness. *Ndigezese musoro* Mati, I want just a shampoo and set today.'

'Shylet will do that for you. *Handiti* you know she is now my junior?' said Matilda. 'Shylet!'

The sweeping girl came over.

'Do MbuyaMaTwins. But mind, I'll be watching you.'

Shylet walked with MbuyaMaTwins to the sinks.

'Did you hear about Kindness?' Ma'Shero said, 'She is now late.'

MbuyaMaTwins, who was about to sit down and lower her head into a sink behind her back said, 'What do you mean?'

'She was killed by her boyfriend.'

'What are you talking? What are you telling me?' MbuyaMa-Twins forgot that she had been about to sit and remained crouched above the seat in a half squat, her face twisted into a rictus that was almost a caricature of disbelief, the maize cob in her hand stopped just before her mouth.

'How is it that this came to be?'

'She was shot by her boyfriend.'

'What are you telling me? Do you mean the boyfriend who drove a silver Pajero, the junior doctor who worked at Pari?' MbuyaMaTwins said.

'What do you know about her boyfriends, MbuyaMaTwins?'

MbuyaMaTwins stretched to stand as she said, 'Who did she not tell about her boyfriends? Everyone in Highfield, from Egypt to Jerusalem, knows about her boyfriends. She told me about him when he picked her up after she did my hair just the other week. *Hanzi ndirikudanana nadoctor vangu varikutoda kutondiroora.*

– 37 –

Hede! His name is Dickson and he is going to marry me. I said to myself, *haiwa mahumbwe ega ega*, what kind of a doctor, even a junior one, would want to marry a saloon girl?'

'Ha, MbuyaMaTwins, are we saloon girls not women also?'

'No, Genia, you know what I mean, there are saloon girls and then there are saloon girls. You and Kindness are very different types, she was her own type, that one.'

'Anyway, myself I think this boyfriend is the one who drove a red Mercedes and not a silver Pajero,' said Matilda.

MbuyaMaTwins heaved herself into the chair below with an exclamation and laid her head on the sink. Shylet opened the taps and put a finger under the water to test its temperature as she asked, 'Are you talking about the man who bought lunch for us the other day? The one she went shopping with to Joburg? Because that one did not drive a silver Pajero. And he was not called Dickson.'

'No, that was someone else. He did not drive a red Mercedes either,' said Ma'Shero. To Matilda, she said, *'Iwe udza mujunior wako kuti azive zvekugezesa musoro kwete kungopindira nyaya dzaasingazivi.* Tell your junior to stop interfering in news that does not concern her.'

'You mean she had three going at the same time?' said Mbuya-MaTwins. As Shylet ran water over her hair, she continued to chew at her maize cob, almost absent-mindedly, her face still frowning her disbelief.

'Kuda zvinhu, Kindness,' said Matilda.

'Makwatuza!' said Ma'Shero.

'Makwatikwati,' said Zodwa.

With MbuyaMaTwins's quizzical prompting, the four women speculated over which of the three boyfriends could have been her killer. It could not be Dickson the junior doctor, said Ma'-Shero, because he did not live in Northfields.

'But imagine if he followed her there, Ma'Shero,' said Zodwa.

'This is you, Dickson. *Ndiwe uyu*. You follow her there and you find her with another man, what would you do if you were him?'

Ma'Shero said Kindness had been seen two nights ago in the red Mercedes. But the night before, she had been in the silver Pajero. 'Maybe,' said MbuyaMaTwins, struck by a charitable thought, 'maybe it is the same man. You know these dealers, they all have different cars. Maybe it was the same man, just in different cars.'

'Then,' said Ma'Shero, 'he must have changed his body type too, because I saw the men and they looked different from behind. *Ndisingazivi kumberi uko*, maybe they are alike in the front area.'

'*Makwatuza!*' said Genia.

'*Makwatikwati!*' said Ma'Shero.

At that moment, a young man came in through the open door. The wide smile on his face was almost as big as the large box in his arms. '*Hesi vana*mothers,' he said. 'Today I have crisps, doughnuts, maputi, sausages, fish, belts, Afro combs, phone chargers and cellphone covers. I also have something very special for you, in addition to my usual Tiens Chinese herbs, I have a new one, a proper *hevhi musambo* that can cure period pain, that is good for teething babies and that can also remove bad luck.'

'Let's see the fish,' said Ma'Shero. 'Is it fresh, Biggie?'

'It is very fresh. Fresh smoked fish just for you,' said Biggie. 'Just five dollars for four fish.'

'Biggie, you are back with that smelly fish of yours, when will you learn we don't want it. It's that Lake Chivero fish that swims in people's faeces and urine, isn't it?' This was Zodwa.

'From Kariba straight, mothers,' said Biggie. 'This is fresh fish, fresh from Lake Kariba. Do I look like I would sell you fish from Chivero?'

'But what is to say that it really is from Kariba?' Zodwa pushed him. 'Did you go yourself to catch it yourself with your own two hands *nhaiwe* Biggie?'

'Mothers, when have I ever sold you something that was not really real? You know I get the fish direct from Sekuru Fish himself, he is the one who supplies all the civil servants at Mkwati and Kaguvi buldings.'

'Sekuru Fish or no Sekuru Fish, Biggie, where do I even start? You once sold us relaxing cream that made the hair even harder after you relaxed it.'

'You could say it was an unrelaxing cream,' boomed Mbuya-MaTwins from under the hair dryer.

'And there was that soap that he said had glycerine in it but it produced no suds, *yaisapupira kana* one day,' said Zodwa.

'And what about . . .'

'Okay, okay,' said Biggie. 'Why can't you just forget some of these things? Even Jesus made mistakes. But maybe the clients are interested?'

He thrust the box before Pepukai who shook her head.

'Don't shake your head,' said Matilda, 'I am planting the braids now.'

'Ko, what about you, MbuyaMaTwins?' said Biggie.

'*Undikwanire semari yebhazi wanzwa?*' she said. 'Last time, you sold me those batteries that didn't run. You still have not given me back my money.'

'What about you, Shylet? A smoking girl like you needs something to make you even more smoking. How about some smoked fish for a *chimoko*?'

Shylet giggled and said 'Ah, you also, Biggie.'

At Shylet's giggle, the four women around Pepukai eyed and nudged each other.

'I will take the fish,' said Ma'Shero. 'I am thinking maybe Ba'Shero might like it.'

'If Ba'Shero can eat that fish,' said Zodwa, 'then he is a man among men.'

'Biggie,' said Ma'Shero, 'I will give you a dollar a week until it is paid off.'

'*Kahwani* mothers,' he said. 'No problem at all. That is how we do business. Any excuse to come back.' He grinned at Shylet as he spoke. She smiled behind her hand. He was about to say more when his phone rang. He answered it on speaker. Into the salon, a tinny voice shouted, 'I have no airtime. *Ndiri paMebaz naGi . . .*' before the phone cut.

As he pocketed his phone, Biggie asked, '*Ko, imi. Nedza*Kindness. Someone in the butchery says Kindness was axed by some man?'

'She was shot, not axed,' said Zodwa.

'There was no axe? Are you sure? I heard it was an axe.'

'But even if there were, she is still late, Biggie.'

'So what is going to happen?'

'We are waiting to hear where the mourners are gathered, as soon as we are done with this one, we are off.'

'But mmm, that Kindness, well, I shall not say, but mmm, she was special that one. *Mai Muponesi chaivo.*'

'*Iwe,*' Zodwa rebuked him, 'you should concentrate on selling your smelly fish, what do you know about Kindness?'

'Sorry mothers, *pa*later.'

'Ma'Shero,' Zodwa continued as Biggie left, 'how can you buy that smelly fish? You can't keep it here otherwise we will all end up smelling of fish. You had better ask *uyu mu*junior to take it to the butcher next door.'

'Shylet,' Ma'Shero called.

The junior had finished washing MbuyaMaTwins' hair, setting it in rollers and had settled the client under the hair dryer. She abandoned her chair near the sink where she had been plaiting her own hair and came over.

'Take this to the butcher. I will pick it up when I go home.'

They watched the girl shuffle out.

'I bet you she won't come back in a hurry,' said Genia.

'That one? *Pane basa.* You saw how she was with that Biggie. She has been making eyes at that butcher boy too, next door.'

Making her voice louder to be heard over the sound of the dryer, MbuyaMaTwins boomed, 'You mean that pimply boy who looks like he has not had a shower since nineteen *gochanhembe*?'

'Ah,' said Matilda. 'She would even go with a *hwindi* this one, she is not fussy. *Anonyengwa kana nefreezit uyu*, she will drop her pants at the sight of a Coke. *Muchamunzwa*. These are some of the Kindnesses in the making.'

'*Makwatuza!*' said Ma'Shero.

'*Makwatikwati*,' laughed Zodwa.

'*Kuda zvinhu*,' said Genia.

Shylet returned as they laughed and Matilda immediately turned the conversation. '*Imika imi*,' she said. 'Imagine people like Biggie, of all people, are now commenting on Kindness, can you imagine?'

'*Iwe*, who did not know about Kindness?' said Genia.

'Even in Engineering, even in Five Pounds, they know about Kindness,' said MbuyaMaTwins. 'I bet you even people as far as Gazaland know.'

They looked up as a sleek, silver car pulled up to park outside. The woman who emerged from the driver's seat wore a dark grey suit, elegant heels and sunglasses. Her cropped hair framed her face. As she entered, she pushed up her glasses to her forehead.

They looked at her in silence.

In a low, pleasant voice, she said, 'Afternoon, ladies, I am looking for Judith.'

'Judith went to Dubai two weeks back,' said Zodwa.

'Oh yes, she did say she may be going,' the woman said. 'When is she back, do you know, because I have been trying to reach her?'

'She comes back Thursday.'

'Oh, thank you, I will call her then.'

'Is there anything we can do?' Ma'Shero asked.

'No, that's fine,' she said with a smile. 'I have to take one of my children to play in a tennis tournament this afternoon. I could have stayed if it was not for that, so I will just wait for Judith.'

'Thank you, ladies,' she added.

Their eyes followed her to the door and to her car. Even before she had driven off, MbuyaMaTwins was asking, 'And who is this Tennis Tournament one?'

She had poked her head from under the dryer, and was trying to scratch her scalp with the rollers on her head. Shylet jumped to attend to her and reset the rollers.

'That is one of Judith's clients, you know Judith goes out more and more these days, she is making herself exclusive to a few clients,' said Ma'Shero. 'She goes to their homes in the surbubs, *uko kuma*Dale-Dales, they don't have to come here.'

'*Hoo*,' said MbuyaMaTwins, '*Ndoosaka kufinyama finyama*, is that why she was looking at us like we were something under her shoe? Because she is a special Tennis One from the Dale-Dales who gets her hair done at home?'

'I thought she was nice,' said Shylet as she shifted the rollers.

'Nice *chiikowo iwe*, you should talk what you know about,' said Ma'Shero.

'*Nhai zvako*,' said MbuyaMaTwins. '*Ndivo vakadzi vanoshereketa ivava*. Did you see that car? How did she buy it? With money from where? Do you think such money is clean? There must be something behind it. Harare *yabata-bata vasikana*.'

'*Vanobata-bata!*' said Ma'Shero. 'You read that story in *Metropolitan* about that small house in Borrowdale Brooke. She slept with that mad man to get a love charm to trap her lover. This is exactly the sort of thing women like that do, you think it is money from just working?'

'Ah,' said MbuyaMaTwins, 'are you saying that woman is a small house?'

'She isn't at all,' said Shylet. 'Judith said she has a very good job, she runs a big bank in town.'

'Then she will have a young Ben Ten stashed away somewhere, some young man whose services she has bought with dirty money,' said Ma'Shero.

'Exactly what I mean,' said MbuyaMaTwins. '*Ndivavo vakadzi vemuma*bank. *Ndivo chaivo vanobata-bata*. You would not believe the things that go on in banks. *Bvunza isu*. My own husband once wanted to take a job in a bank. I said to him, and this is what I said, no thank you, I said to him. *Mari yacho ngaigare*. I know those bank women. I would rather we suffered, yes, I would rather eat plain vegetables, even cooked with no cooking oil than have you work with women like that. Even up to now, he is not working.'

'She probably got into the bank through being a small house,' said Ma'Shero.

'She is a widow,' said Shylet. 'Her husband died in a car accident three years back.'

There was a silence until Ma'Shero said, '*Manje* some of these widows, you would never believe they are widows. There was this funeral I went to last week you won't believe. It was at the church of BaShero's cousin brother and can you believe the widow wasn't even covered in a wrapper cloth or headscarf or anything, she wore a smart dress, *ka*shift*so*, and it was not even black-black but blue-black. She had high heels on can you imagine, high heels at a grave site, just like that woman, and sunglasses too like that one.'

'*Achitoti akatopfeka* sorry?' said MbuyaMaTwins. She was back in the dryer, her face aghast with shock at what she was hearing. 'What sort of mourning outfit do you call that?'

'*Imi*, it was like she was going to a wedding, she even had make-up on, and a black hat.'

'There will be something there,' said MbuyaMaTwins. 'Mark my words, *pane chiripo*. Before the year is out, you will have heard something. *Kana kunzwa kuti vanobatabata. Kushereketa chaiko!*'

'Ah,' said Matilda, 'it would not surprise me at all.'

A sharp-eyed woman in a TM supermarket cashier's uniform entered, bringing with her the strong smell of the orange she was peeling and eating. Her TM nametag indicated that her name was Plaxedes. She had the mismatched hands and face and the patch-patch giraffe skin of different shades of brown that was typical of a woman *anozora*, one addicted to skin-lightening creams. As she greeted the others, she approached Pepukai to admire the now almost completed braids. Pepukai could smell the orange on her hands as Plaxedes gathered up the plaits to examine them closer.

'This is nice, girls, *inga* this is nice,' Plaxedes said. 'Maybe I should have this next time, what do you think?'

Without stopping for breath, she said to Pepukai, '*Ende vhudzi renyu rakareba*. Is your hair natural?'

She pulled at the little of Pepukai's hair that still remained to be braided. Again, Pepukai was hit by the smell of oranges.

Pepukai said, 'Yes, it is, it is natural.'

'*Hoo. Ende futi makazochena. Kabhutsu kenyu karibhoo manje.* Perfume *yenyu inonzi chii*? What perfume are you wearing?'

'It's called Jardin Sur Nil,' said Pepukai. She was now being suffocated by the smell.

'*Jadan chii*?'

'Jardin Sur Nil,' said Pepukai. The smell of oranges was threatening to overpower her.

'*Chirudzii*? What language is that?' asked Plaxedes.

'Erm, French, I think.'

'*Hoo, saka munotochitaura chi*French *chacho*?'

'Not really, no,' Pepukai said. 'I don't speak French.'

'*Hoo nhai, saka inodhuraka*? It smells expensive. It must be expensive. Is it expensive? How much is it? Where do you live?'

'*Ndeve*London *ava*,' said Genia, with proprietary ownership.

'London! *Zvenyu*! *Kuchiri kupindika ku*London? But why is your skin so dark? You don't look at all like you live in London. When do you go back? *Munoita nezveyi ikoko*?'

Pepukai did not know which of this medley of questions to answer, so she only said. 'My flight is tonight. I work in a field called transitional justice.'

'*Zvenyu!*' said Plaxedes, but without paying much attention. 'My sister went there only seven months, she was in London but not London exactly, she was in Men Chester, do you know it, and she was almost as light as a Coloured when she returned. *Akadhipotwa* together with her husband, my Ba'mkuruTryson, they were both deported. Luck'enough, they did not yet have their son Kuku. Do you have a white man? But you don't look like the *ngoma kurira mbira dzenharira* type, you are too polished, you are not the type they like. My sister MaiKuku says white men like black women who just look rough and who wear *zvechi*Rasta Rasta*so*.'

'*Ngoma kurira chiikowo iwe*,' said Ma'Shero. 'Stop going on about white men, Plaxedes, have you not heard about Kindness?'

'Kindness?'

'Kindness is late. She has passed away.'

'*Haa*?'

In her surprise, Plaxedes pulled at Pepukai's hair.

Pepukai winced, but the other woman did not notice.

Plaxedes pointed to Kindness's empty station. 'Do you mean this Kindness, this one right here?'

'That Kindness,' MbuyaMaTwins called out from under the dryer.

'*Ichi chitekete ichi*? *Uyu* Kindness *wekuzvinzwa uyu*, who walked like her feet did not touch the ground and talked like she was chewing water?' said Plaxedes.

'That very one,' said Ma'Shero.

'That Kindness?'

'That Kindness.'

'How?'

'She was shot by her boyfriend.'

'She was shot by her boyfriend?'

'She was shot by her boyfriend.'

'But that one had so many boyfriends!'

'That is just what we were saying,' said Matilda. 'She wanted to be upper class that one, and she thought the way to be upper class was to go out with an upper-class man, now look at her.'

'*Ii*, I should let my sister know,' said Plaxedes.

For Pepukai's benefit, she added, 'That's MaiKuku, the one who was deported from Men Chester, but she is quite well up now. They live in Mebryne, in Hedgepark and my Ba'mkuruTryson even has relatives in Ballantyne Park.'

Into her phone, she said, 'Hello. Hello, Kuku. *Ipa mhamha* phone. *Ipa mhamha* phone. *Ipa mha* . . . Hello, MaiKuku? . . . *Ende futi*! *Iwe*, you won't believe it. Kindness is late . . . Kindness! . . . Kindness *mhani iwe, wekunoku*Fiyo . . . The hairdresser . . . Don't you remember Kindness? . . . You met her that time at the Food Court at Eastgate, remember? . . . We had gone with BabaKuku to watch that film, what was it called? *Rabbit, Habit* something, the one about those creatures who look like *tokoloshis* but walk and talk and act like normal people even though they are not actual people . . . Yes, *Hobbit*. That's the one. We had gone to watch *Hobbit*. And she was walking in front of us and I said to you, MaiKuku, I said, I know that bottom . . . Yes . . . Yes . . . Very big . . . *Chivhindi-kiti so* . . . Yes . . . That's the one. She wore a tight red trouser and a white blouse . . . Yes . . . *Nekabhutsu kake ke*blue*so* . . . *Ende aichena zvisingaiti mwana iyeye, asikuzvinwa. Hanzi* she died . . . Shot . . . I said shot . . . Yes, shot . . . Yes . . . Shot with a gun. . . . *Ufunge* . . . Yes

. . . Some boyfriend . . . I don't know, *mira ndivhunze.*'

She turned to Matilda, 'Where did this happen?'

'Northfields, in town,' said Matilda.

Plaxedes turned back to her phone. 'Northfields . . . Northfields. In town. I said North . . . Ah, I have run out of airtime.'

'*Ii vasikana, inga i*horror,' she said. '*Manje* I have to go. My break is over but I will be back in an hour to find out more. If you are not finished with the braids, I will even come and help.'

Pepukai breathed at last.

Plaxedes's phone rang as she left, and they could hear her say, 'Northfields . . . Northfields . . . Yes . . . She was shot at Northfields.'

As soon as she was out of hearing, Ma'Shero said, 'Is there a bigger gossip than that Plaxedes?'

'You know, don't you,' said Zodwa, 'that her husband's sister and aunt actually beat her up once because of her gossiping?'

'Serves her right,' said MbuyaMaTwins. 'She is not the type that you can tell anything.'

As she talked, MbuyaMaTwins moved from under the dryer to a dressing station. Shylet stood behind her to unroll her hair from the curlers and style her hair. MbuyaMaTwins admired her reflection in the mirror. Pepukai thought the wash and set made her neck and head look like a very small mushroom on a particularly bulbous stalk. As Shylet sprayed liberal doses of a smelly moisturiser over the finished hair, Pepukai tried not to cough.

'*Ende machena zvekwa*MaiChenai *chaizvo,*' said Ma'Shero. 'That looks so nice.'

'*Ndachenaka?*' said MbuyaMaTwins. She preened in the mirror as she turned her head, the tips of her spread-out fingers lightly tapping her new hairstyle. 'I am going to the First Lady's rally on Saturday. Then we have a function at Feathers Hotel in Mebhuraini. This time, *bambo vekwangu* will have to come, I won't hear any more of his excuses. What sort of golf is it that is played at all hours?'

The women nudged each other. MbuyaMaTwins, unseeing, continued to admire herself in the mirror. They all looked up as a voice came from the door. '*T'ookumbirawo rubatsiro vanhu vaMwari. T'ookumbirawo rubatsiro vanhu vaJehovah.*'

It was a blind beggar who was led by a small boy of no more than seven or eight years of age. The man wore tattered blue overalls while the boy wore a shirt and shorts that belonged to two different school uniforms. They were both barefoot.

Matilda said, 'Does anyone have a dollar?'

MbuyaMaTwins rummaged through her overstuffed bag. Pepukai opened her purse. Genia let go of Pepukai's hair so that she could dig into her trouser pockets. Ma'Shero and Zodwa went to their stations to get their handbags. As the boy went from woman to woman collecting money, the old man dropped to his knees in thanksgiving, raised his voice in blessing and clapped his hands in gratitude.

'*Mwari wenyu vakukomborerei, vakukomborerei, vakukomborerei. Mugare kure kwemoto vakukomborerei, vakukomborerei, vakukomborerei.*'

They left the salon.

MbuyaMaTwins took twenty-two dollars from her bag and handed it to Matilda. 'I will give you an extra two dollars for a drink,' she said.

'Thanks, MbuyaMaTwins,' said Matilda. 'Shylet!'

Shylet's face brightened.

'Go and give this to Plaxedes at TM, I owe her thirty for the relaxer. Tell her the rest is coming.'

Shylet's shoulders drooped as she walked out.

'Right, girls,' said MbuyaMaTwins, '*bofu iri rabata mwoyo wangu mufunge*. I have to go, but before I do we need to pray.'

Without further prompting, the women melted from Pepukai to gather around MbuyaMaTwins in the middle of the salon, their heads bowed. Unsure of what to do, Pepukai joined them.

MbuyaMaTwins' face became twisted with effort.

'Bless, Lord, everyone in this salon, Lord, and especially this daughter who is taking a flight today. Send her journey mercies, dear Lord. Do not put evil thoughts in the mind of the pilot, Lord, *bvisai utsinye mupfungwa mapilot, bvisai mweya wetsvina* Baba *mupfungwa dza*pilot, *itai kuti* pilot *amhare ndenge zvakanakisa, zvinokomborera imi*, let the pilot land the plane with no incident, let him not crash it deliberately.'

'Amen,' said Genia.

'We ask you to receive into your loving arms our sister Kindness, take her into your glory, Mwari Baba to you she has come to rest Lord. *Ndimi* Mwari Baba *vemasimba, ndimi* Mwari Baba *munopa nekutora, munopa ndimi* Mwari Baba, *ndimi* Mwari Baba *munogona*, Mwari Baba *munogona*, Mwari Baba *munogona kani*, Mwari Baba *munogona!*'

'Amen,' the women chorused.

'We ask you to guide us today in everything we do, so that all that we do may be to honour your holy name, *mutiponese panjodzi, muve nesu mumabasa, tingwarire zvatinotaura, tirumbidze zita renyu nguva dzese, tidadise pane zvese.*'

'Amen,' said Genia.

'We ask for your special blessings on the First Lady, Mwari Baba, as she travels around the country sharing her deep and educated wisdom with the nation, watch over her and over all the Members of the Women's League, Jehovah, *muvasvetutse panjodzi.*'

'Amen,' moaned Matilda.

'This we ask in Jesus's name. *Muzita ra*Baba, *nere*Mwanakomana, *nere*Mweya Musande. Amen.'

'Amen.'

MbuyaMaTwins crossed herself and kissed her rosary. She picked up her bag off the floor, stuffed her white headscarf into its capacious depths and with a radiant smile said to Pepukai, 'Wofamba mushe dhali, travel well, my dear', and to the others, 'Ndiyoyo vasikana, see you next week.'

'Inga vakatozvipengera zvavo mothers ava,' said Genia as soon as the client was out of hearing. 'So she is really serious about this Women's League stuff? And isn't she supposed to be a Roman Catholic?'

'You know she is,' said Matilda. 'You saw what she is wearing, so why do you ask?'

'Because she prays like a Pentecostal, that's why, zvechurch yemweya chaiyo,' said Genia.

Shylet piped up from the sink. 'She apparently wants to set up her own church. She is doing it with that other fat one, her best friend from Mbare, Makorinde. They are setting up a women's Ministry. That's why she is working with the Women's League, to get all the permits.'

'That is a smart move,' said Genia. 'If she does not make money from the Women's League politics stuff, there is plenty money to be made in these new churches.'

'And she will need all the prayers she can get with that husband of hers,' said Ma'Shero. 'He is the busiest unemployed man in the city.'

'And he is never alone either,' laughed Genia.

'Makwatuza,' said Matilda.

'Makwatikwati,' echoed Zodwa.

'Kuda zvinhu!' said Ma'Shero.

They laughed and clapped their hands to each other.

It took a little more talk of Kindness and another hour before Pepukai was done. The braids fell beautifully and lightly from her head, in hundreds of long thin ropes that were perfectly even. The last thing was to soak the ends in hot water to seal them and make sure that they did not unravel. Genia held up a mirror to the one before her so that Pepukai could see the back of her head.

The women beamed as they admired their handiwork.

'You are so right,' Matilda said, 'this is very old-fashioned but it really suits your face.'

'Perfection *sipo yekukwizira chaiyo*,' said Ma'Shero.

'*Maworesa nhunzi ye*green,' agreed Genia.

Shylet approached, shaking the can of the stinky spray. Pepukai held up her hands as if to ward off evil. 'It's really okay, thank you, Shylet,' she said. 'I do not need the spray, I will do that later.'

She paid the eighty dollars that Matilda had requested, and gave her an extra twenty. 'This is my *chema* for Kindness,' she said. 'I hope it all goes well.'

As she spoke, Matilda's phone buzzed out a new message.

'It's from the cousin sister of Kindness. She has no airtime, but she says we have to come now,' said Matilda. 'The mourners are gathering at their house in Mebhoreen.'

'Is it okay if I just wait here for my hair to dry a bit?' Pepukai asked.

It was fine, Matilda said, Shylet would stay to lock up. They said their goodbyes and bustled out. Pepukai continued to hear their voices until they turned the corner past the butcher's. In thirty minutes, her hair was dry enough for her to leave. The last Pepukai saw of Snow White Hairdressing was Shylet sitting at Kindness's station, plaiting the rest of her hair. That night, on her flight to Amsterdam, Pepukai chose the chicken over the fish. Nor did she eat any of the orange segments in her fruit salad, choosing to eat, instead, the grapes and cubed melon and the delicate slivers of apple.

The Death of Wonder

But let judgement run down as waters, and
righteousness as a mighty stream.

– The Book of Amos –

Asi kururamisa ngakuyerere semvura, vuye
kururama sorwizi runongoramba rucidira.

– Buku yaMuprofita Amosi –

In the newspapers, they called him the murdered man who got his own justice. They said he fought his own battle. When I talk about his case, particularly in a drinking setting when the shadows of the night are lengthening and the beer and talk are flowing and we take a turning to the supernatural, I will often do a bit of grandstanding, you know, making light of it all and hamming it up for effect, but if I am to tell you the truth, Wonder's case shook me up in a way that no other case had ever done. These days, I am no longer as secure in myself as I once was. I am no longer as certain in my beliefs.

Three facts, at least, are beyond dispute. The pathologist who handled Wonder's autopsy is indeed mad. If you ever have reason to go to the psychiatric hospital at Ingutsheni in Bulawayo, and I hope, for your sake, that you never do, you will find him there, but whether he is there because of his handling of the post-mortem, I cannot say.

It is also true that the two cousin brothers who were the killer's accomplices have departed this life. But did they die simply because it was their time, or was it, as all of Gokwe would have you believe, the wrath of Wonder reaching out from the grave to bring them to him? And it is true that in his cell at Whawha Prison, the man who killed him is now blind. That was Wonder, says Gokwe, using his own mother's blindness to close forever the eyes of his murderer.

Without ever actually using that word, I always thought that I was an atheist. As a policeman, you see enough raped children, battered women and murdered men to doubt that God exists. Or else you conclude that if this is what the world looks like with a supposedly All-seeing and All-knowing Being in charge of it, such a Being is not one in which you want to believe.

I used to love that book by Stanley Nyamfukudza, do you know it, *The Non-Believer's Journey*? It was one of my O level set books. I thought it a particularly apposite title for my own life. But it is an awkward position to be a non-believer when the companions on your life's journey are all believers for whom even the slightest whiff of disbelief is enough to brand you the leader of one of those Satanic sects that always seem to be popping up in Mufakose. So I kept my disbelief to myself. I went to church every Sunday with my wife and children. I sang the hymns. I said the prayers.

My disbelief went the other way too, in the direction of what my mother called Chivanhu. Until Wonder's case, I did not believe at all in the world of traditional beliefs and all that goes with it, you know, the naked witches flying in the night, the talking snakes that spit out cash, the owls and omens. I do not recall when it was that it seemed preposterous to me that people could believe that women, and they only ever seemed to be women, could fly naked in the night on winnowing baskets, or sit astride hyenas as they travelled to eat the flesh of the dead.

At the most basic of levels, it struck me as a stupid waste that witches would expend such marvellous abilities on such pointless activities as flying to cemeteries to eat rotting corpses, when they could have gone anywhere in the world that they chose to go without the trouble of applying for visas or purchasing air tickets. They could have transformed aviation as we know it. Those Wright brothers would have had nothing on them.

My mother managed to believe in both ChiKristu, Christianity, and Chivanhu. When close family members died, she and the family elders would go to a *gata*, that supernatural autopsy in which a *n'anga* is asked to determine how the deceased met his death. My late father succumbed to a combination of lung cancer and cirrhosis of the liver when I was twenty-five. My mother wanted us to attend a *gata*. As she put it, 'Yes, it may very well be that the doctors are right that it was this lung liver disease that killed him, but we need to find out who it is that gave it to him in the first place, who it was that allowed this to happen.'

Considering that my Old Man's liver had finally given out on him after he spent two days drinking non-stop in a township shebeen, a death preceded by a lifetime of smoking three twenty-packs of Kingsgate every day and drinking his wages away with every hooker between Zengeza 4 and Seke before coming home to use his fists on his wife and children, his death under those circumstances should have been a surprise to absolutely no one. And as you can probably tell, I have no fond memories of the man. We were like the family in that Oliver Mtukudzi song, what is it called, '*Tozeza baba, baba chidhakwa*'; we were a family ruled by fear and alcohol. It's probably why I became a cop, come to think of it, to get over that sense of helplessness, that constant feeling of powerlessness.

But back to the main point. After my passing out parade at Morris Depot and I was posted to police villages across the country, I took the lead from my superiors in how the law dealt with witchcraft. Incidentally, it was usually the same sort of person accused, an unpopular in-law, the usual family conflicts spilling out into accusations of witchcraft. It was striking that the young and the beautiful were never accused; *shavi reuroyi*, that pestilential spirit of witchcraft, it seems, chooses to possess only the old and unpopular, the lame and the halt.

In such cases, we ignored all the mumbo jumbo and the superstitions. We concentrated on what the law could actually touch. We focused on the actual harm caused, and punished that, and on threats to do harm and punished those. The Witchcraft Suppression Act helped keep things in check. A colonial statute from about 1895 or thereabouts, it gave us powers to arrest anyone who accused any other person of witchcraft. In their reforming zeal, our colonial overlords took the view that the belief in witchcraft was a primitive superstition best suppressed by punishing any native who talked of it.

But as with all things that are driven by punitive legislation and not genuine social change, the act did nothing to suppress witchcraft. It only served to drive underground the work of the many witch-hunting *tsikamutanda* around the country who never went away. When it was finally repealed a few years ago, I almost choked on my tea when I read the headline in the state paper that trumpeted: 'GOVERNMENT LEGALISES WITCHCRAFT.'

Now, I hope that I am not giving you the impression that I am a scientist of any kind, because that is the last thing I am. I cannot claim to be of a particularly scientific bent. I did Core Science in school, of course, like everyone. I remember some of the periodic table, you know, hydrogen, helium, lithium, beryllium, boron, carbon, nitrogen and all that. I remember my biology lessons about Mendel's experiments and Pavlov's dogs and the peppered moth. I know the difference between an atom and an amp. At least, I think I do. I have just always been suspicious of things that cannot be proved. So I placed value in things that could be demonstrated as truthful without needing to have faith, and without having to believe the say-so of a man who knows a man who knows a man who knows another who saw a ghost. I considered both ChiKristu and Chivanhu to be equally irrelevant to my life, because as far as I was concerned, they were both superstitions and I believed in neither. This is who I was, until the death of Wonder.

❖

Wonder Pasipanodya was just twenty-one years old when he died. It is a great thing to be a young man of that age. I remember my own early twenties with extreme nostalgia. At that age, you have not only discovered the delectability of girls, but you have also realised that some of them, with the right inducement, can be taken to bed. You have discovered the pleasures of beer. You are probably in your first job, or if you are really lucky, you are learning a trade or, if you are luckier still, you are at college or university. You have a bit of money, but are not yet weighed down with the turgid responsibilities of being a full adult. The world seems yours to conquer. Unless, that is, you are living in a place like Gokwe or any of the other shitholes in this country.

What can I tell you about Gokwe that you don't already know? Keeping with the religion theme that I have started, there are places so beautiful that they are considered God's own countries. The kindest thing you can say about Gokwe is that it is a place that the Devil once called home until he abandoned it altogether as he ran shrieking from its ruins.

Back in the 1890s when Cecil John Rhodes and his band of merry marauders established Rhodesia by taking over the fertile land on the Mashonaland plateau, they dumped the people who lived there in places they called native reserves. It is where the term *kumaruzevha* comes from, and it is generally agreed that such a life, *hupenyu hwekumaruzevha*, is one of unremitting hardship. Gokwe was one of the first native reserves. The keen injustice of it was that this abandoned land onto which people were dumped from their fertile land had been abandoned for a reason.

With a harsh and unforgiving terrain, bad harvests and worse roads, Gokwe's other claim to fame used to be that it was one of the main tsetse fly base stations for Midlands province. I suspect that many of the tales of witchcraft deaths there arose from plain old sleeping sickness. Its recent elevation to town status has not changed it much from the days it was a reserve, apart from the addition of a bank or two, a small dusty branch of the country's biggest supermarket chain and the requisite mobile phone steel towers. It is still the same poor community in the middle of nowhere that it has always been, only now it has a Town Council, complete with a chairperson, a secretary, an administrator and a clutch of other councillors who earn salaries running it when there is really nothing to run.

I can hear you ask, why, then, it is that I find myself here. It is important that you believe me, so I will tell you the truth about myself. I will say right away that I am here because I took bribes. There. I took bribes. Or, perhaps I should say that I took too many bribes. I got careless. I got caught.

No one in the police gets fired for corruption any more. If they did, all that would be left would be some skinny bald-headed recruits from Chendambuya who don't know their docket-books from their traffic-books. So bent cops like me are not removed from the force. We just get sent to places like Gokwe, like Checheche, or the aforementioned Chendambuya. And there we stay until we can plot our return to the streets of Harare that are full of drivers to milk.

There was a curious symmetry to my career, such as it was, in Gokwe. Wonder's case was my last case. My very first case also involved the supernatural. A week after I got to Gokwe, I was informed by my new private, Phiniel Zuze, that we had to look into a case of missing women's underwear. I was still smarting from my transfer, and thinking of the half built house that I had left at Mainway Meadows and that I could have completed in a few more months of collecting traffic fines and keeping them for myself if I had not been caught. So when this underwear case came to me, I was not in the best of moods.

I thought at first that there had been a breaking and entering at one of the two clothing shops in what passes for the town, but Phiniel soon put me straight. By the way, before I had even arrived in Gokwe, Phiniel had somehow ferreted out my totem title. Instead of addressing me by my name, as Mafa, my official title, Chief Inspector, or even as just 'Chef' as is normal, he addressed me as 'Mwendamberi.' This, combined with his self-effacing and over-confiding manner always made him sound like a man touching up a recalcitrant son-in-law for a loan when he still owed on a previous one. Indeed, he had asked to borrow money within two days of meeting me, spelling out his request in an elegant note written on a page torn from the Charge Book and signed Constable Phiniel Zuze, Gokwe, just in case I mistakenly gave the money to another Phinel Zuze not in Gokwe. Don't let the gentle exterior fool you; when Phiniel places his unforgiving hands on a criminal, it is all we can do to restrain him. So fearsome is his reputation around these parts that his nickname is Boko Haram.

Someone, Phiniel said, was taking the underwear off women at night all across the outlying village of Nembudziya. 'The women go to bed at night all there, but in the morning, Mwendamberi, they have no underwear. It just vanishes. Disappears. Like it was never there. They suspect it is a *chikwambo*.'

Now, in a full demonstration of the limitations of the English language to capture fully the fetid inventiveness of the Shona imagination, a *chikwambo* is usually translated as a goblin, when in fact it is a combination of a familiar, a good luck charm and a sort of unpaid messenger. Sure enough, our *chikwambo* soon made its debut in the papers as the 'Gokwe Goblin'. I became the butt of jokes among my old colleagues. Any time I went back to Harare and stopped for a drink at the Police Club and went into the officers' mess, I would get slaps on the back and questions about whether I had caught the goblin yet.

In Gokwe itself, I was inclined to ignore the whole thing, but the matter became serious when the female teachers at the local school demanded that I do something at once or they would all of them leave, en masse. This was followed by angry calls from the provincial head of the education ministry in Gweru. The goblin appeared undiscriminating: old women, young women, fat women, thin women, tall women, short women, all had their underwear removed.

Phiniel muttered darkly about *mubobobo* spells, he believed that someone in the village was using the goblin as a succubus to have virtual sex with all the women in the village. I did not believe a word of it. I told him that while I admired this mysterious man's ingenuity and redoubtable stamina, there were surely more pleasurable ways to be with a woman than by remote control.

I considered the whole thing to be a big waste of my time, to be honest with you, and did not always listen to Phiniel's witterings about the latest developments. I did attend a few village meetings, and found myself in the middle of accusations that flew faster that an Air Zimbabwe plane taking the President to his annual Asian holiday. Talk about long memories. Someone remembered a grandfather saying that person's grandmother had said something about a *chikwambo* to that other person's *tateguru* in the time of Hitler's war; another's mother-in-law had done this to that one's great-aunt two years before the mission school was built and this person had been told she was to inherit her aunt's witchcraft *shavi* spirit and it had been passed on to her children. But so it is with people who do not ever leave the places they are born in until they are eventually buried there. All they have are memories, petty strife and grudges handed down along with the inherited clothes of the dead.

In the end, it apparently took the combined effects of both ChiKristu and ChiVanhu to restore nocturnal dignity to the women of Nembudziya. A local sikamutanda joined forces with a Harare prophet of the fire and brimstone variety. They called an assembly of all the villagers. Together, they pointed to a cluster of men. One of them fell in a heap to the ground and confessed and produced the goblin, which apparently chose to make its entrance in a pair of moth-eaten underwear belonging to the village headman's wife. On seeing it, she immediately had the vapours. After she had been restored to her senses, and the *chikwambo* burned and buried, the matter was considered closed.

But as I pointed out to Phiniel, who narrated these events to me in a breathless voice, it was astonishing that the journalist from the *Metropolitan* newspaper who reported the *chikwambo*'s exposure, or even Phiniel himself, for whom separation from his phone for more than an hour is enough to declare national mourning, had had no eye on posterity. They had not thought to actually record the creature with their cameras.

For a man who claimed to have laid eyes on the thing, Phiniel was suspiciously vague in the details. In his placid, confiding tones, he said, 'It was not quite human, Mwendamberi, but not quite animal, maybe a little bit birdlike but it had no wings. It was half and half, yah, half and half, Mwendamberi, with a head larger than a rooster's but smaller than a very small baby's, but a different shape, a bit like a mouse, not a house mouse as such but a field one, yah, that sort of shape but not quite. It also had quite a lot of fur, but not too much.'

And clearly, I added, the goblin's bottom must have been quite sizeable if it was able to fit into the underwear of the wife of Nembudziya's village headman. She is not, by any means, a small woman.

✿

This, then, was the Gokwe in which Wonder and his friends came to young adulthood, a backwoods hotbed of superstition, gossip and grinding poverty. If they had been in Tsholotsho or Beitbridge, the youth of Gokwe would have hot-footed it across the border to South Africa or Botswana, braving the crocodiles of the Limpopo just to get away. A few did leave, mainly to go to relatives in Gweru, Harare or the resort town of Victoria Falls, but they soon came back. Those cities soon spat them out; they have unemployed youths of their own.

Wonder wanted the three things that any young man of that age wants: a job that gave him a bit of money, a girlfriend and a smartphone. The latter two obviously depend on the first of those. But in Gokwe, there are no industries, no farms, no jobs, no hope. Like many other young people, he and his friends saw their future as coming from the elections. With the right government, they believed, all things were possible. Poor deluded bastards. The one bit in the Bible with which I agreed with all my heart is that bit that says, how does it go again, put not your trust in princes and the sons of men.

Wonder and his friends were burning for change. They joined the opposition party and went around in party regalia. They drank the free beer at rallies where they sang and chanted slogans. They stuffed themselves with opposition food. But the ruling party is strong in Gokwe. There were soon what the papers called skirmishes between youth groups of the rival parties.

It was a busy time for us, I can tell you. In the run-up to the elections, my men and I got frequently called out to hear cases of tit-for-tat assaults, hut burning and that sort of thing. There were sporadic attacks across Gokwe North and South, from Kuwirirana Kana all the way to Zumba, and from Nembudziya all the way to Gandavaroyi, which was Wonder's village. Mostly though, the youth gangs limited themselves to insulting songs and dances after their rallies and meetings. There is nothing as amusing as rival gangs trying to out-dance each other. It was like that video of Michael Jackson's 'Beat It', I tell you, only with bare feet and ragged clothing, better moves and serious intent.

As the police, we could afford to ignore most of it. It helped a lot that both parties were equally responsible. I know that the standard line is that opposition activists are a helpless lot who do no more than turn the other cheek meekly when presented with ruling party violence. Well, cry me the Zambezi at flood time, will you, because nothing could be further from the truth. Give a bunch of idle youths a bit of beer and a burning cause of whatever stripe and as sure as cows have calves, you can create your very own militia. Our only saving grace was that none of the parties could actually afford to arm their youths with guns.

As I say, both parties were responsible for the mayhem that followed. Where we could not ignore it, we took a few of the more boisterous opposition activists into our custody, to keep them safe, we said, but of course the truth is that we would have had blue murder on our hands if we had so much as cast a glance in the direction of the ruling party youths. When you are in the police here, you know whom to arrest. And better still, whom not to arrest.

Then came the two big rallies, one after the other. Without the distinction created by the differing party colours and empty slogans, you would have thought the politicians from both parties were the same people visiting on two consecutive weekends. The same big men from Harare in their four-by-fours came to promise the earth, along with their orange-toned women in big hats and vertiginous shoes. They sat on the same sort of tent-covered platform, in plush seats of violent colours while the poor women of Gokwe baked in the sun and ululated and the young men danced in the dust and chanted from the trees they sat in to get a better view. Then the politicians drove off in their air-conditioned vehicles, leaving behind them inflamed tempers and painful hope, leaving nothing for the young to hold on to beyond their hate and their rage.

Three days after the second rally, Wonder was found beaten to death. I had, to say the least, a knotty problem on my hands.

°

Police work is not like you see it on television. I would say that in eighty to ninety per cent of the normal cases, it is easy to identify the culprits. One of the things they teach all would-be officers during training at Morris Depot is that the first and most import-ant question to ask the victim of any crime is: 'Who do you think did it?' I can see you are looking sceptical, but it is much more effective than you would think. Of course, you get your armed robberies and stranger rapes and so on, but crime is, for the most part, an intimate matter, particularly in places like Gokwe.

Even in this case, it did not take long to identify the killer. Wonder had last been seen in a fight with three youths, who were then seen dragging him towards the field in which he was found dead. There was no doubt at all as to who those three were. They were Takura, the youngest son of the local Member of Parliament, and Dakarai and Rangarirai, two cousin brothers who served as his unpaid minions and acolytes. The word was that all three had been heard boasting that they had fixed Wonder, the cousin broth-ers had held him while Takura beat him. So I had on my hands an opposition party activist killed by ruling party activists. And they were not just any old raggedy-taggledy activists either, one of them was the son of the local Member. I was in what you might safely call a quandary.

I won't lie to you, I thought if we did nothing for long enough, and gave a few soothing assurances to Wonder's family along the lines that we were pursuing several avenues and soon a number of people would be called in to help with our inquiries, it would all die away. But the opposition sensed that they could make a meal out of this case.

The newsmen soon descended, with their screaming headlines. Wonder's death was a gift to the opposition, their strategy before each election was to trumpet any such deaths because, of course, they needed to discredit the government and the outcome of the election. The aspiring Member for the opposition raised a hue and cry. He even made an appearance on the BBC, his subtitled grief beamed to all the world. The president of the party wept for him like he was his own child. Overnight, Wonder was transformed from being just another ragtag youth who occasionally sang and danced at rallies in exchange for booze to the lynchpin of the entire opposition movement in Gokwe.

The government, for its part, was doing its damndest to discredit itself without opposition help. I soon received instructions from Harare to do nothing at all. The Governor of Midlands Province himself summoned me and told me in no uncertain terms that if I or any of my men made as much as a move towards the Member's son, I would know what it was that caused a dog to have the ability to snarl when it was unable to smile. As I had neither the burning curiosity nor desire to solve that particular riddle, I did nothing. It didn't hurt at all that he followed up the stick with a carrot that came in the exceedingly pleasing faces of several dead American presidents.

The most I did was to issue the usual anodyne statement that we trot out in domestic violence disputes, 'Members of the public are urged to refrain from using violence to resolve family disputes', crossing out the word *family* to suit the circumstances. The trouble began three weeks after his death.

❖

After Wonder was found, I ordered that his body be taken to the mortuary in the government hospital next to the police station in Gokwe Town, where it was to stay until the post-mortem. I received instructions from Harare that I was to call the Provincial hospital in Gweru to speak to a government pathologist called Dr Ananias Rixon Ngabi. I spent the better part of the day calling him. He eventually called me back a day after I had tried to reach him.

'So tell me about this Never,' he said.

'Wonder,' I said.

'What do you wonder?'

'His name is Wonder.'

'Ah. Tell me how you found him.'

I described the finding of the body and how the body looked. As I talked, chewing sounds came down the line to me, and I imagined him at his desk, chewing whatever it was he was eating as he listened to me. The injuries to the front of his body appeared to be defensive wounds, I explained, but the real damage seemed to have been done by the blow to the back of his head that had cracked his skull.

'That is what probably killed him,' I added.

'Now, now, Officer Mafa,' Ngabi said as he took a gulp of whatever it was he was drinking. 'Officer Mafa. Let's see, Mafa, Mafa, Mafa, I know that name. Are you one of the Mafas who come from Mberengwa? Was your father a headmaster?'

'I am a Mafa from Shurugwi,' I said.

'Mberengwa, Shurugwi, same same *fananas*,' Ngabi said. 'Now then, Officer Mafa from Shurugwi, all these things you are telling me about this Clever . . .'

'Wonder,' I said.

' . . . all these defensive wounds and so on and so forth, who here is the pathologist precisely? Is it you, Officer Mafa of Shurugwi and not Mberengwa, or myself, Dr Ngabi?'

'Will you send a car to pick up the body?' I asked. 'Or will you come down yourself? We have no transport and we are not likely to have any for a while as we do not have enough cars or fuel to get him to Gweru.'

'That is not at all necessary,' he said. 'Your description of the body is detailed enough for me to go on.'

'Are you certain you can reach any sort of conclusion without actually examining the body?' I asked.

'Oh yes, yes,' he said as he chewed, 'the rest is just detail, and so on and so forth.'

He then spent the rest of the conversation not talking about Wonder at all but trying to establish whether I knew every Mafa who had ever crossed his path.

Ngabi duly issued his report. Wonder, he found, had died from self-inflicted wounds. The burial could go ahead with no inquest. Indeed, confirmed Harare, there was no foul play. Now, I won't lie to you, I have participated in a cover-up or two in my time, but even I thought this was going a bit far. At a minimum, there should have been even the most basic kind of inquest to record a verdict of foul play by a person or persons unknown, if only to give the semblance of, well, a bit of integrity to the whole thing.

Speaking of foul play reminds me of one of my first trials as a police offer. There was this particular interpreter who became a little confused when the prosecutor asked if a witness had suspected foul play. The poor chap obviously confused foul with fowl, because he translated it as *makafungira here, changamire, kuti kungangova nekutambatamba kwehuku*, upon which the irate magistrate said, what playing chickens are you on about now. You really see a lot in the courts, I tell you.

But back to Wonder. I informed one of his uncles that the body could now be released for burial. When no one had come to collect him by the end of that day, I again sent word that they should come and pick him up. The answer was a short and uncompromising no. So I ordered my men into a truck and drove to his family homestead.

We arrived just after 3 p.m. As usual in these villages, word of our intentions had preceded our arrival. We found a group of Wonder's relatives. In their ragged clothing, they radiated hostility. The women among them immediately started keening and wailing. I waited a bit until the worst of it was done, but just when I thought I could finally speak came a keening so sharp it was like an animal in pain.

Supported by two young women, his mother emerged from her hut and was led to where we stood. There is that saying, isn't there, that a grieving person is not one you look full in the face. I averted my eyes. To be honest with you, I would have done so anyway, even if she had not been grieving. I have never been able to look a blind person in the face, there is something not quite right about being looked at by a blind person, okay, I know it is not a look exactly, but you know what I mean, there is something unsettling about knowing that the person looking at you cannot see you but you can see them. There is a sort of nakedness in looking at eyes like that, eyes that look at you without seeing you.

Her voice, when she spoke, was heavy with surrender. 'These tears on my cheeks,' she said. 'My eyes have not cried tears for the ten years that I have been blind, but every evening I weep for my son and the tears run down like rivers.'

I was touched, I have to say, I would have to have been made of stone not to be moved, but my path was clear. They were to bury the body, I said. If he was not buried by the next day, I would arrest them all for the crime of refusing to dispose of a dead body in an appropriate manner. I quoted the relevant section of the Criminal Codification Act. I drove back to Gokwe with my men.

The next day, I came late to the station. The coffin was still there. It remained there for another two weeks. All this time, the opposition people were crying to anyone who had a microphone or notebook, and orders were being barked to me from Gweru and Harare. It is obviously not the business of the police to bury bodies, but that was the order that came from Harare. We were to bury him at the first opportunity that presented itself, preferably at night. I ordered a fearful Phiniel to go with three other men to the hospital.

'He will not like to be buried, like this, by strangers and not his own people, Mwendamberi,' Phiniel said. 'This is why this country is cursed. All those boys who died in the independence war, lying like wild animals in Mozambique and other places, buried by strange hands, all away from home. Wonder will not like it.'

'Wonder', I said, 'will just have to lump it.'

I went off to get my lunch.

It was a baking afternoon with not a single cloud above, in other words, a true Gokwe day. By the time I got inside my house, I was sweating from the heat and boiling with rage. I would arrest all the male members of the family, I swore. They needed to know who was the law. But I had to face the reality that if they chose to riot, I did not have enough men to arrest all of them. I was contemplating whether it was worth it to request back-up from Gweru, or even to get some army reserves called in when Phiniel ran up. His eyes were wide and fearful.

'It won't move,' he said.

'What?' I asked.

'The coffin, Mwendamberi, it just won't move.'

He was right. The coffin would not move. It was as though the wood had joined with the steel of the mortuary cabinet. I ordered them to pull it out. Then I tried it myself but I too had to give up. It was at this point that doubts began to enter my mind, but I clung to the possibility that there was a perfectly reasonable explanation. Perhaps there was something that caused the wood to stick.

After that, none of my men would go near the coffin. I eventually had to tell Harare that if they wanted Wonder buried, they just had to come to Gokwe to do it themselves. I would hear from them what the next steps in the matter would be, I was told. But there were no next steps. The coffin remained in the mortuary for almost a year.

In that year, the talk in Gokwe was that Wonder was haunting Gokwe, and that he was being seen everywhere but in the one place that I most wished him to be, six feet under with grass growing over him, as far away from my jurisdiction as it was possible to be.

✿

He was first seen outside the mortuary. '*Anga akatobhara* four *zvake* Wonder, Mwendamberi,' said Phiniel. 'Cool as anything he looked, sitting there cross-legged and all, like it was the most normal thing in the world to be sitting there all cross-legged, Mwendamberi, when he was actually dead.'

He was then spotted on a moonless night, outside the Member of Parliament's kraal, counting the Member's herd and repeating the names of all the cows. Then he was seen outside the bottle store owned by the Member. A teacher at the school claimed that Wonder had stopped her to tell her he was tired. A bus driver claimed he almost had an accident because Wonder stood in the middle of the road.

Then came the animal deaths. Three of the governor's cows died in calf. A goat belonging to the Member drowned in shallow water. A dog at the homestead of the parents of the two brothers went mad and killed six chickens. It was at this point that Phiniel, who, until now, had been content to recount the things that others had told him they had seen, gave himself a starring role in the drama. He claimed that one of his she-goats had given birth to a creature with a humanoid form, something no one could verify as he and his brother had burned it before anyone could see it. He had touched the coffin, he said, and this was the result. He asked for leave to consult a woman in Chipinge who could intercede for him with Wonder. When he came back, he told me that he would sooner be fired than touch that coffin again.

Then followed a series of car accidents. There was even a car accident in the family of Wonder's murderer's brother in England. I was sceptical that Wonder's reach was extraterritorial. At this point, you will understand, I was becoming more and more uncertain, but I still scoffed at all the strange happenings.

Then I received the phone call from my wife. She had taken one look at Gokwe and turned her heel. She had chosen to stay in our house in Harare. She was one of the reasons I so frequently left the area. There had been an accident at school. My son is one of those township boys who took to cricket like a duck to water. His room is papered with cuttings and posters of Hamilton Masakadza, Tatenda Taibu and Chris Gayle and with the Manicaland Mountaineers and Mashonaland Eagles. Now, my wife informed me, he had been hit in the head by a cricket ball. He had turned his head at just the wrong time and the ball had felled him to the ground. It was a freak accident, but now he was in a coma.

I rushed to Harare, but there was nothing to be done. We had only to sit and wait. I have vivid memories of that day. We managed to get him into the Avenues, thank heavens for my wife's health insurance. In the next bed a group of people sang over a small child. I will always remember that song. From the lugubrious melody of the song, I could tell they were members of my mother's church, a church she continued to call Dutch Reformed long after it dropped that name. The words of the song were a familiar tune. *'Makakomborera vamwe, musandipfuure.'*

As I sat and watched my son's still face, I found myself saying the words of the song: 'You, who have brought blessings into the lives of others, don't pass over me.' I even found myself praying. I hedged my bets and addressed both God and my son's ancestors on both sides. And I bargained with Wonder.

I did not stay in Harare long because I was called back to Gokwe. Things were boiling over. Harare was thinking of sending out a riot squad.

The governor's daughter had died in a car accident in South Africa. All Gokwe was now whispering with the news that all of us who had been afflicted with misfortune had stood in the way of justice for Wonder. Everyone wondered who would be next. As it turned out, it was the pathologist. Reports came from Gweru that he had been struck mad, and was eating from bins. He could not stop chewing, even when he was not eating, his jaws moved up and down in momentary spasms.

When the two accomplices heard this news, they attempted to flee the jurisdiction. They left Gokwe without anyone knowing where they were going. The next we heard of them was that both cousin brothers had perished in the Beitbridge Bus Disaster. You must surely remember that one, it was the bus disaster of the year. Two buses racing each other on the Masvingo Road collided with a haulage truck and half the passengers in each perished. The brothers were in the bus that was going to South Africa.

Two days after the bus accident, Phiniel came running to my office. He is confessing, he said without preamble. And indeed, Takura sat in the Charge Office, his father and mother on either side of him, all three looking drawn and desperately ill.

This was one case we did not need to torture out the confession. I did not need to set Phiniel on them for the full Boko Haram treatment. Takura was clearly more afraid of what Wonder could do to him than anything Phiniel could have done. I really should not say poor Takura, because of course he killed Wonder. But I think of him as poor Takura because, as I said earlier, he developed an eye infection in Hwahwa Prison and went blind. He is still in prison, the death sentence spared only because he made a full and remorseful confession.

That was the beginning of the end of the matter. On the day after Takura was sentenced, the Member and his senior relatives went to Wonder's homestead. Phiniel and I accompanied him, to keep a watching brief. The Member took off his shoes and approached the homestead on his stomach, while his elders clapped their cupped hands as they rested on their knees. Wonder's mother came keening from her kitchen hut. She felt her way to him, raised him, and the two, the mother of the murdered and the father of his murderer, embraced and keened and staggered in supportive sorrow.

✲

The negotiations followed. The Member pledged to give a hundred head of cattle. The families held a ceremony to the spirits of Wonder's ancestors to beg them to intercede with Wonder and soften his heart. Things became a little tense when they began to talk about a bride for Wonder. The tradition, of course, is that the family of the deceased has to pledge a young girl to the family of the victim, to bear sons to replace the dead.

Every man has his sticking point, and this was mine. I can overlook a lot but crimes against children will see me move heaven and earth to effect an arrest. I have never accepted a bribe in any crime against a child. *Ngozi* or not, I said, there would be no girl exchanged. Cows and cloths were all well and good and they could trade those to their hearts' content, but, even with all that I had seen, I felt it had to stop somewhere. What justice was there in using a young girl to appease a crime she had nothing to do with, thus blighting every chance of a better life of her own?

'The minute any young girl is sent from your homestead to this one,' I told an emissary of the Member, 'I will arrest your Chef for facilitating a kidnapping.'

I repeated the same message to Wonder's family.

'It is up to Wonder,' they said.

'Actually,' I said, 'this one is up to me.'

Wonder or no Wonder, I was not going to let some child miss out on an education just so that she could be married off to God knows which of Wonder's many unwashed male relatives. On this point, I am pleased to say, they listened to me.

They finally buried Wonder a year after his death. When his brothers lifted his coffin from the mortuary, it moved lightly to their shoulders. They buried him on the *churu* where his grandfathers also lay. Throughout the night of his long wake, Gandavaroyi rang with drums and rattles. The air trembled with the sharp keening and ululating of women. And after that, Gokwe saw Wonder no more.

Now, I don't expect you to believe me, people outside the area rarely do. After all, animals die all over the place. The number of road accidents is no surprise given the potholed roads and the decrepit cars that are driven by drivers in possession of bought licences. And can it really be that Wonder killed a whole busload of people just to get at the two brothers? Perhaps Ngabi would have turned mad anyway. Perhaps my son just had concussion, as the doctors said. And prison conditions are bad enough to throw up all sorts of illnesses, including eye infections. Perhaps the sightings of Wonder were some species of mass hysteria, a manifestation of collective guilt.

But I still remember the cold panic when my wife called me about our son. And I remember my bargain with Wonder. If my son became well, I had vowed, the arrest of the man who killed him would be the last thing I did in the force. I would never take another bribe; a vow that I could keep only if I left the force.

It has been hard but I have kept my word. There are no more road traffic fines for me, no more conveniently misplaced dockets. My wife and I set up an auto-parts company on Rotten Row. We travel to Zambia and Botswana to buy parts to sell. The house in Mainway Meadows is still not finished. But my son is in the First Eleven at school, they get beaten more than they win. It is enough to see the joy on his face. We struggle and we get by. It is a life.

I had just one thing to do before I left Gokwe. I took the two thousand from the governor and gave half of it to Phiniel. A nobler-minded man would probably have given the money back to the governor, but I have never claimed to be such a man. Money is money, after all. Wonder, I figured, would surely not begrudge the man a new donkey, and maybe an extra cow or two. Phiniel's overwhelmed smile cracked his face in two as he took the money with both hands. I gave the rest to the family of the deceased brothers, to put headstones on their graves. Every man deserves some dignity in death.

I said earlier that three facts are undisputed, the pathologist's madness, the two brothers' deaths, and the killer's blindness. Here is a fourth one. Since the death of Wonder, there has not been a political killing in Gokwe. No young man has ever again killed another in the name of politics. And I am willing to stake my life on it that none ever will. You could say that this was Wonder's gift to Gokwe. In the terror of his death, he taught us all a new respect for life, for all our lives.

The Old Familiar Faces

Execute true judgement, and shew mercy and compassions every man to his brother: And oppress not the widow, nor the fatherless, the stranger, nor the poor.

– *The Book of Zechariah* –

Ruramisirai kwazo pakutonga, mumne nomumne aiitire hama yake vunyoro netsitsi.

– *Buku yaMuprofita Zekaria* –

The Old Familiar Faces are unhappily gathered at a once-elegant four-star golf resort and conference centre to which tourists no longer come. In the reception area and in their workshop room, the Jacaranda room on the second floor, banners proclaim the theme of their workshop: 'Assessing, Analysing and Evaluating the Impact of Political Violence on the Coming Election: Problems and Perspectives from a Problematic Past.'

The banners are emblazoned with the Vision Statement of Umbrella, the organisation that has convened this workshop. 'Our mission is to passionately partner human rights organisations in Zimbabwe in improving their competitive performance by professionally supporting and actively encouraging a professional and active human rights environment in Zimbabwe underpinned by a record of achievement, professionalism and excellency.'

The Vision Statement was developed painstakingly by Umbrella's senior staff at a four-day Strategic Planning workshop in Victoria Falls, with the assistance of a highly paid motivational speaker slash pastor and a donor-provided management consultant.

After the opening prayer and the introductions, after the pam-pam of appreciation for the moderator and the resource persons of the morning session, after all protocol had been observed and after the welcoming of the Special Guest, who is the new First Secretary at the European embassy that is the sponsor of this event, the Familiar Faces cluster to bemoan their fate over Choice Assorted biscuits, lukewarm tea and instant chicory coffee.

They know each other well, the Old Familiar Faces. Since the beginning of the Zimbabwe Crisis more than a decade ago, they have spent many hours together at seminars, workshops, conferences, colloquiums and other outreach programmes. But they still wear around their necks bright red lanyards that identify their names and organisational affiliations. That, by the way, is one of their favourite phrases. Not where do you work or who are you with but what is your organisational affiliation. They are very educated, the Old Familiar Faces. They pride themselves on their Excellent English.

To one side, within comfortable reach of the biscuits, stands Mrs Maudie Chikombe, the convenor of the workshop and Mr Collins Dube, the moderator of the morning session.

Mrs Chikombe, a well-known Feminist Activist, is a flamboyant woman who favours loud prints and dirty-blonde wigs. She long ago lost a half-hearted battle against middle-age spread, but underneath her layers of lurid clothing, artificial hair and excess body weight are glimpses of the loveliness that used to transport Mr Dube into delight on the many nights they spent together at NGO gatherings around the country. Such had been her comeliness that it had induced Mr Dube to launch her career in the NGO sector just after her Master's degree in Rural and Urban Planning.

Their affair burned out many years before Mrs Chikombe was married. It goes without saying that Mr Dube was already married, but that is by the way, and more importantly, it was before Mrs Chikombe was Born Again, a mercifully releasing process that involves the erasure of sinful pasts without necessarily requiring a concomitant commitment to a sinless future.

Though he has become broad before and broad behind, Mr Dube has aged significantly better than his former paramour, for what he has lost in hair he has gained in girth and bonhomie. His penchant for wearing cowboy hats made from khaki canvas, taken together with his comfortable padding, give him the look of a benevolent politician about to hand over buckets of donor maize in exchange for rural votes. He has made much of being in the small category of men specialising in Women and Gender, and indeed, in addition to Mrs Chikombe, there are other women in this sector in whom Mr Dube has personally specialised.

They have taken different paths to leadership. While Mrs Chikombe has had a simple and upward trajectory to the top, Mr Dube's path has been slightly more meandering. Having ascended the ladder both early and quickly, he came down a few rungs after he defrauded an Unnameable Embassy when he was its Chief Project Officer, but as he was not prosecuted, he was able to cast it in subsequent job interviews as a simple misunderstanding among friends, a mere matter of the wrong figures inadvertently appearing in the wrong column and besides, most of it was owed to him in expenses. In the intervening years, though a cloud of suspicion has followed him, he has clung to the highest point of elevation that he has managed to reach in the sector. Though he is unlikely to scale the dizzy heights of which which Mrs Chikombe is assured, he is comfortably high up enough that he is not unduly threatened by her success. And so there they are, two of the most glittering stars in the civil society firmament, gossiping and complaining as they munch bourbon creams, custard creams and lemon creams.

'You know those people are becoming very stingy,' Mrs Chikombe says. 'What do you call this now? We suggested Leopard Rock or Elephant Hills, but they said absolutely not.'

'For sure, they are on a mission,' Mr Dube says. 'I hear they have cut the funding at about ten NGOs now.'

Mr Dube is partly right: the number is actually seventeen. The more the country's democracy crisis drags on, and the recession bites in Europe, the less their donors are willing to fund their seminars, workshops and conferences, colloquiums and other outreach programmes. Even their usually-to-be-relied-upon European sponsor of a Benelux Slash Scandinavian persuasion, usually committed to fully meeting the international pledge to give a defined percentage of GDP in development aid, has cut back funding.

The global recession coincided with the posting, four years before, of an ambassador from the Belt-Tightening, Scrimp and Scraping, Corner-Cutting school of Donor Funding. Unlike his three predecessors, who had all been sent here as their last posting, he was a young Ambassador, in his first posting, in fact, and he was not content to be seen to be doing things. He actually wanted to Do Things. He wanted to Make Waves.

Why, for instance, the Ambassador had asked, as he looked at the applications that his mainly local staff had approved for funding, should the embassy fund the Centre for Human Rights (CHR), the Human Rights Organisation (HRO), the Institute for Human Rights (IHR), the Human Rights Initiative (HRI), the Human Rights Agenda (HRA) and the Association of Human Rights Agencies (Umbrella), six human rights organisations that all had the same mandate and seemed to exist only to compete for funding?

And why, the ambassador asked, as he pored over a budget that would have seen him give 200,000 Euros to a year-long 'Awareness and Outreach Programme', is it necessary that the country's human rights problems and democratic deficit should be discussed exclusively in holiday resorts?

Why, he had asked further, should the embassy take people who saw each other daily in the city to tourist resorts such as the resort town of Victoria Falls to discuss these problems in overnight accommodation? And why was it that, having carted them halfway across the country, paid full board for them, the taxpayers of his country should, in addition, give each participant a *per diem* of 100 dollars a day for the four or five days that they were in the holiday resort? And why should the embassy then pay for mementos emblazoned with the name of the event they were attending, two different styles of T-shirt, one with a collar and the other collarless, ballpoint pens and caps, key-rings, lanyards and laptop bags?

These decidedly undiplomatic questions, to which there were no diplomatic answers, had resulted in the Ambassador cutting the funding of four of the human rights organisations, and for the remaining three, taking his pen to the budgets, circling a few line items and reducing their budgets by two thirds. He had then directed his reforming zeal to fifteen election support organisations, seven Peace and Reconciliation through Art organisations, and five voter registration initiatives. Only the organisations supporting Victims of Domestic Violence, Girl Children, Orphans and Other Vulnerable Children, Released Convicts and Recent Drop-Outs had proved immune to the cuts. 'And it is not even,' complained Mrs Chikombe bitterly, 'it is not even as though some of these organisations even applied for funding.'

After wreaking this havoc on the sector, the Ambassador had gone on to Do Things and Make Waves in another posting. Afghanistan, the Old Familiar Faces heard with some satisfaction – *vachasotana ikoko ne*Taliban, Mr Dube chortled – but by then, the belt-tightening philosophy seemed likely to be entrenched at the embassy.

Things are a little better since his departure. This workshop is a Big Push. As Mr Dube confirms to Mrs Chikombe over the coffee break that there are indeed no *per diems* at this conference, she glowers in the direction of the Special Guest. The Special Guest catches her eye and smiles in their direction. Mrs Chikombe and Mr Dube transform their faces immediately into beaming smiles of such high wattage that they confirm for the Special Guest everything she has heard about the charm and disarming friend-liness of the locals.

The bell goes, the coffee break is over and they head back to the Jacaranda room for their workshop. It is not just any work-shop, this one. It is necessary to collate the results of the research from the previous years to justify a pitch for more funding for this year. Unless the sector gets funding for salaries and educa-tion, fuel and domestic servants and security guards, they will be helpless against the political violence that they are sure will engulf the country. That the Special Guest is here, and more, important-ly, that she is new, gives them some hope. The Ambassador has not been appointed yet, and this is a chance for the human rights organisations to restate their case.

In the Jacaranda room, the chairs and angled tables are cov-ered with a lacy, white net cloth more suited to a bridal party than a hard-hitting seminar on the political violence they predict will engulf the country. Next up is Mr Magaba, Mrs Chikombe's dep-uty director. He likes his watches, Mr Magaba, and, by the simple stratagem of being ignorant of Segal's Law, has chosen to wear a watch on each wrist, thus always showing off at the same time two of the watches in his, at present, ten-watch collection. He also has the distinction of being one of the clutch of thirty-seven-year-old Born Frees who were named after the one and only president, as well as having a last name that sounds like the president's. They are an excellent team, he and his boss, the Born Again and the Born Free.

He uses his name as the ice-breaking joke in every presentation he gives, as he does now. 'As you may appreciate,' he begins as he raises his lanyard, in the process revealing his right-hand watch, 'the name is Robert Gabriel Magaba. One might say Magaba is just two vowels short of State House.'

The Old Familiar Faces have heard this before but they give their customary titter. They each have their own style of presenting. Mr Magaba has trained himself to speak of himself only in the third person, and to lay stress on the last phrase of each sentence and to smile as he does so. He has also taken seriously the advice that he should pick just one member of the audience and address only him. He zooms in on the Special Guest and stares into her grey-blue eyes as he continues.

'As Magaba will show in a moment, especially concerning is the likely prospect of a surge in political violence, particularly the many cases reported last time of torture, murder, and punitive aggravated rape.' His eyes opening wide in emphasis, he gives the Special Guest a beaming smile on 'punitive aggravated' that lasts all the way to 'rape'.

'And unfortunately, we are likely to experience the same retrogressive unwillingness on the part of the police to prosecute the panoply of criminal cases that are likely to be rupturing like a cancerous boil. In effect, the police force of this country is guilty of such gross misconduct that you might call their conduct, not just a dereliction of duty but also a defecation on democracy.'

The smile that starts on 'defecation' lasts all the way to 'democracy'. On he continues, Mr Magaba, evaluating the matrixes and assessing the democratic deficits, evaluating the overarching frameworks, and smiling and stressing and fixating his gaze on the Special Guest. Only when he says, 'Ladies and Gentlemen, last but not least,' does he break the connection. After the applause, Mr Dube, who is the moderator for this session, says, 'With that presentation, Mr Robert Gabriel Magaba, I would say you are closer than two vowels to State House.'

The Familiar Faces titter.

Mr Dube then summarises Mr Magaba's presentation; the summary, in fact, is half as long as the actual presentation, for Mr

Dube, with a microphone in hand, is inclined to be a little expansive. The eyes of the Familiar Faces flicker restlessly to the large Africa-shaped olivewood clock whose copper hands are ticking precisely towards lunchtime. 'Let's have another pam-pam for His Excellency,' says Mr Dube.

The Familiar Faces applaud.

Mrs Chikombe presents after Mr R. G. Magaba. Her Power-Point presentation is a straightforward statistical summary of political violence per province. She has neat graphs and pie charts that show the incidence of political violence in each of the ten provinces. Mashonaland Central, East and West are represented with slices in three different shades of green, Matabeleland North and South are orange and ochre, Manicaland is red, Midlands pink, Masvingo blue, and Metropolitan Harare and Bulawayo are purple and mauve. The green slices take up the largest portion of the chart.

As she moves to Masvingo Province, the trailing edge of the lace tablecloth catches on the heel of a young woman who has just entered the room. The cloth drags as she moves her leg, almost toppling the little jars of Mazoe orange crush and the bowls of white Endearmints on the table. Three Familiar Faces grab the jars before they fall over. The entrapped woman frees her heel and gives a smile of apology in the direction of Mrs Chikombe who has stopped talking.

Mr Dube is much more taken by the new arrival than Mrs Chikombe. She resumes her presentation to recount the instruments used per province while Mr Dube fixates on the Unfamiliar Face. Mrs Chikombe moves to a series of slides showing photographs of victims of violence in states of undress. The Special Guest gasps as a slide comes up that shows a young man, his back to the camera, with dark purple welts on his back and buttocks as well as a pattern of marks all over his buttocks that look like they were made by . . .

'. . . teeth,' says Mrs Chikombe. 'A lot of the youth groups were known to have used their teeth on their victims as we see here.'

Her laser pointer circles the young man's right buttock. 'This is in addition to the plethora of other instruments like sjamboks, belts, whips and iron rods both heated and unheated.'

More pictures follow, women with their buttocks beaten, a man with his skin sliced off, two opposition activists with their eyes closed in their coffins. Only the Special Guest seems to experience distress at any of the images. Mr Dube surreptitiously checks his phone and forwards a joke on WhatsApp. Mr Magaba's phone vibrates on the lace cloth. 'Magaba,' he whispers as he answers and walks out, his shadow briefly obscuring the picture of a dead opposition activist in his coffin. They hear his raised voice as the doors close behind him. 'No, no, I think it is just the brake lights, not the brakes themselves,' he says.

Mrs Chikombe winds up her presentation. She is a good speaker, Mrs Chikombe. She also gave the opening prayer that morning: it had just the right amount of passion, and she made sure to cut it off when she saw that some of the more exhibitionist, and Pentecostal, female Familiar Faces were beginning to moan, rather than speak, their Amens and Hallelujahs and had started to sway slightly and breathe more shallowly than was called for in a brisk morning prayer.

As the head of Umbrella, she runs a tight ship, particularly when it comes to the conduct and clothing of her female staff. One of her first acts when she moved from the Human Rights Organisation to head Umbrella was to decree that none of the female staff were to wear trousers or skirts above the knee. A workplace, in Mrs Chikombe's view, was not the right place for distractions. Mrs Chikombe's brand of Feminism is very big on Personal Reponsibility, very big indeed, but curiously only for women. Her brand of Feminism decrees that it is up to women to ensure that men are not distracted. It is also strongly rooted in her Born Again-ness. She is, if you like, a Born Again Feminist, which means that when she worked for a domestic violence NGO, she managed to persuade many women that they were beaten by their husbands because they did not pray hard enough.

On her clothing decree, a young and attractive Project Officer had been heard to snigger that their new Director had only banned those items of clothing that she could not wear herself. She had been dismissed on the spot, and when the organisation's Human Resources Officer had tentatively suggested that the Labour Relations Tribunal might have something to say about the unlawful dismissal of the Project Officer, Mrs Chikombe had sim-ply responded, in her best Born Again Feminist voice, that they would see who was the Director here, her or the Labour Relations Tribunal. In the event, the Project Officer had had no money to pursue her case for unfair dismissal and Mrs Chikombe's next act was to ban Trésor, a pulchritudinous French perfume that Mrs Chikombe had first smelt on her secretary Mandi and immediate-ly decided was just the one for her.

She had asked what the perfume was, her secretary had handed it to her, and she had sniffed it in appreciation. 'Iyi *yatova ya-*Director Mandi *iyi,*' Mrs Chikombe said. 'Only the Director can wear this one.' With the memory of the fired assistant in mind, Mandi had complied. The perfume continued to linger on her own clothes until it was completely washed out and she found a new perfume, though not one she liked as much, and her job, for now at least, was safe.

If all this seems contradictory with Feminism, it is because Fem-inism is an activity, not a philosophy, it is club or clique; it is a civil society activity that requires workshopping and resourcing, mon-itoring and evaluation. It is an income-generating activity in the NGO sector, just as human rights is an income- generating activity in the NGO sector, election support is an income-generating activity in the NGO sector, and voter education is an income-generating activity in the NGO sector. And as an income generating activity in the NGO sector, it has its gatekeepers and sentinels who stand guard at the gates to Feminism, to make sure that Unsuitable Women do not enter. The Old Familiar Faces have quite enough Feminists to be going on with, they do not need new ones, thank you.

In the Jacaranda room in the middle of Mrs Chikombe's lecture, a phone has the audacity to ring. Mrs Chikombe stops talking to give a glare in the direction of the offending Familiar Face. She looks closer with a frown, this is actually an Unfamiliar Face, the phone belongs to the same young woman who had caught her heel in the tablecloth earlier. The Unfamiliar Face switches off her phone with an apologetic wave. The wave catches Mr Dube's eye who sits up a little straighter the better to see her. His attention is momentarily diverted and he does not immediately realise that Mrs Chikombe has concluded. He then thanks her and summarises her presentation, invites a pam-pam, but even now has his eye on the clock. It is ten minutes to one when the group goes to lunch.

Over lunch, Mr R. G. Magaba, who has also noticed the newcomer, makes his way to the Unfamiliar Face. 'The name', he says, 'is Robert Gabriel Magaba. In fact you might say . . .'

' . . . that you are just two vowels from State House,' she says with a smile. 'I saw your presentation.'

She introduces herself as a postgraduate student. Her name is Pepukai. She has almost finished writing her Master's dissertation, she explains. Transitional justice is her subject. Over lunch, they have a choice of three starches – rice, potatoes and *sadza* – three different types of meat – chicken, beef stew and pork chops – and two salads – coleslaw, and lettuce and cucumber. The Familiar Faces do not believe in choice. They take all the options.

Mr Dube moves to stand behind the Special Guest who is helping herself to salad, and in a loud voice says, 'We Hard Mashona Types don't eat these leaves.' The Special Guest, surprised by the address coming so loudly from behind her, turns with a startled smile.

'Don't mind me,' says Mr Dube. 'I am high voltage.'

He laughs loudly.

He follows the Special Guest to a seat, but his eye keeps moving to Mr R. G. Magaba's companion. He has gotten to know in a special way five of the women in this room, in fact, he has gotten jobs for three of them after coming to know them well, and he would like to extend his knowledgable assistance to the young lady. He invites her and Mr Magaba to sit with him, much to the displeasure of Mrs Chikombe, who looks a little sour. He is unable to make much headway, not only does Mr Magaba monopolise the Unfamiliar Face completely, Mrs Chikombe also monopolises him, and instead of discovering more about the Unfamiliar Face, Mr Dube finds himself listening to the all too familiar talk of budget cuts and the scandalous conduct of Mrs Chikombe's female staff, female domestic servants, and some of her female relatives.

After lunch they go into break-out groups to discuss the 'take-aways' from the day's session. Mr Dube had planned to use that time to nap after his heavy lunch, but the new colleague fascinates him. He is afraid that beside the polish of the younger RGM, he might not look as shiny. Mr Dube calculates that he will only have a chance if he can offer the young lady a job. As it happens, a position for a Programme Officer is soon to become available in his organisation.

MaiWashington, his mother-in-law's niece has been pestering him to employ her daughter-in-law. 'These Beijing Beijing things', she had said the last time they saw each other at a family funeral, 'and all this Gender Gender Business is just the sort of thing for

Washington's wife. She is a real dunderhead, that one, without five O levels to her name, just imagine. But she would do very well in this Gender Gender Business.'

To Mr Dube, this Pepukai person is a much more attractive prospect than Washington's wife. He decides to forgo the nap and use the break-out session to press his advantage. But first, he returns a call from his wife to discuss a funeral she is on her way to.

They go into the wrap-up plenary session where the day's presenters open the floor to questions. Pepukai asks Mrs Chikombe, 'I wanted to question your statement that political violence is the biggest killer of women in this country. If the violence is cyclical as you say, how does it manage to beat the statistic for deaths from domestic violence, high numbers of which occur almost weekly? And the state media, which has dedicated court reporters, documents that at least five women are killed every week, so surely women are more likely to be killed by their intimate partners than they are to be murdered for political reasons?'

Mrs Chikombe says, 'When you have been in the field long enough, you will know that it is best not to take any statistics from biased media.'

The young woman presses on. 'But what is the state media's interest in inflating figures for domestic violence?' 'And what about road traffic accidents? Given the state of our roads, and the condition of our ageing fleet of motor vehicles, surely more people, whether men or women, die in road traffic accidents than from politically motivated violence? The police indicated that just this last Christmas alone . . .'

'You surely cannot take seriously anything the police says,' interrupts Mrs Chikombe.

'I am not saying the problem is not serious. Not at all. I just want to understand it in a proper perspective.'

'Perspective is academic,' Mrs Chikombe says sharply. 'It is academic and we have no time for academic questions here. Look at this, look at this.' She goes back to her slides and her pointer moves frenetically over the maimed, the beaten and the dead. 'Tell me if these people know anything about perspective. Tell me if they would rather not have died from road accidents or domestic violence.'

That last statement makes no sense at all, but in the face of the wounded and the eloquent dead, the young woman can only retreat. A few more questions follow, to which Mrs Chikombe responds with the prologue, 'Now *that* is a constructive question'. Mr Dube asks for one final question. Pepukai raises her hand.

Mr Dube looks around the room before reluctantly indicating that she has the floor. 'What will happen if the ruling party learns that it has other ways to steal an election without using violence? What is the strategy then?'

In the silence that follows her question they hear a squeaky trolley moving outside. A waiter pops his head round the door and waves towards the top table. Mr Dube announces this is an opportune moment to break for tea, but they would think about the question over the break. After tea, there are no more controversies, just final statements mapping the way forward and more pam-pams of appreciation. No one answers the last question

A cocktail follows. In the background, a band plays Bee Gees covers. Mr Dube watches as Mr Magaba and Pepukai dance energetically to 'Tragedy'. The Unfamiliar Face is no dancer, but her joy is infectious. He cannot remember the last time he saw anyone as animated as she looks. After the song, she moves to the bar, where she is approached by the Special Guest. They sit at the bar stools. He cannot hear what they are saying above the music. Mrs Chikombe comes to him and says, 'Now look at that.'

They watch as the Special Guest hands over her card.

'I found out during the tea break that that one has a sister who is married to a Tarumbga,' says Mrs Chikombe as she nods her head towards the Unfamiliar Face.

'A what?'

'Tarumbga. There is an Assistant Commissioner of Police with the name. She has her own agenda I am sure. Probably CIO. In fact, I am certain she is. And frankly, she has no professionalism, none at all. Her skirt is much too short for a gathering of this nature.'

Mr Magaba joins them. 'She is quite a dancer that one.' As he says this, they notice the presence of a second Unfamiliar Face, a dreadlocked young man in a black leather jacket and very tight jeans. The Unfamiliar Face makes her excuses to the Special Guest, jumps off the bar stool and embraces him with abandon. The three Familiar Faces watch as she leaves the room, talking animatedly to her companion. A cocktail glass drops to the floor and shatters. A waiter comes scurrying up to clear it. 'Well,' says Mr Dube, 'I think that's it for me. I am turning in.' Mrs Chikombe follows suit. Mr Magaba waves them off. The band strikes up the introduction to 'Staying Alive'. The remaining Familiar Faces dance.

A Short History of Zaka the Zulu

Wherefore came I forth out of the womb to see
labour and sorrow, that my days should be consumed
with shame?

– The Book of Jeremiah –

Ndakabudireiko pacizaro, kuti ndivone
kutambudzika nokucema, kuti mazuva angu apere
nokunyadziswa?

– Buku yaMuprofita Jeremia –

He was always a bit of an odd fish, Zaka the Zulu, but he is the last boy that any of us thought would ever be accused of murder. According to the boys in his form, from his very first days at school, he had worn his school uniform every day of the week, even on Sundays. Not being a wit, a sportsman or a clown, he was not a popular boy. We could, of course, have admired him for his brains. In the high-achieving hothouse that was the College of St Ignatius of Loyola, the annual winner over a consecutive fifteen-year period of the Secretary's Bell for Outstanding Results, we admired any boy we labelled a Razor. Zaka, though, made such a song and dance about his sharpness that you would have thought that he was the only Razor in the school.

He became most unpopular when he was made head prefect. In a school like St Ignatius, where everyday order is outsourced to the prefects, being head can bring out the tyrant in even the nicest sort of chap. Zaka brought to that office an obnoxious and big-headed self-importance that made him absolutely insufferable.

As head prefect, he took off demerits for the slightest offences, marking down boys who did not wear ties with their casual khakis at Benediction, making unannounced spot-checks for perishable goods in our tuck boxes and trunks, sniffing to check for beer on the breath of every boy who had snuck out to Donhodzo, the rural bottlestore in the valley below our school and, from the strategic-ally placed Prefects' Room, making forays at unexpected times to see if he could catch anyone smoking outside the library.

It seemed to us that he would not be happy until he had taken away as many of our pleasures as he could. We were sure that it was Zaka who made the suggestion to Father Rector that the Middle and Junior House boys should have an extra period of prep on Friday afternoons. He wanted us out of the way on the days when the Institute of the Blessed Virgin Mary girls took their weekly swim. We called them Mary Wards, pronounced Merrywards. We felt the injustice of this edict keenly.

The swimming pool was set in a quadrangle with the Junior House common room at one end, and at the other, the Middle and Senior House dormitories. From the vantage points offered by the common room's high windows and the dormitories' balconies, the whole school had a good view of the swimming Merrywards.

They were sylphs in our eyes, every single one of them from the fattest to the thinnest, from the tallest to the smallest, not because they were particularly beautiful as girls went, but because they were the only girls that we saw on a daily basis. Imagine four hundred boys with their storming, raging hormones, locked away for three months at a time at a boarding school deep in rural Mashonaland and you will understand that even our choirmaster's wife, with more hair about her chin than her husband, was, to some of us anyway, a vision of beauty.

There were forty Merrywards in any one year. They came to the school for A levels, but lived separately, at Mary Ward House, under the authority of Sister Hedwig and her fellow Sisters of Loreto. The presence of the Merrywards was considered necessary to tame the older boys. The thinking of the Jesuits was that the boys should get used to seeing and being around girls, so that no boy went demented at the flash of a breast or a bare leg in the world outside Loyola. In return for their civilising influence, the girls got the best Jesuit education that the country could give. The Loreto nuns' passion for education was matched only by the Jesuits'. The

Merrywards also got the guarantee, for even the least attractive of them, of at least one besotted boyfriend in their lifetimes.

Only the Senior House boys who shared A level classes with the Merrywards saw them at close range. They even touched them. For one hour every week, at the Social Dance after Mass and Sunday breakfast, with the smiling approval of Father Rector and Sister Hedwig, the Seniors and Merrywards waltzed, mamboed and cha-cha-cha-ed to records on a scratchy gramophone. When we heard Dobie Gray longing plaintively for the freedom of his chains, we knew that some lucky Senior had a Merryward in his undeserving clutches for the three and a half minutes that the song lasted.

As for the rest of us, we watched them as they moved in small groups, neat and trim in their white blouses, grey skirts and shining legs. We strained to hear their voices above the drums and rattles at Mass, and to catch their perfumes above the incense at Benediction. Only their weekly swimming lesson allowed us to see them at something approaching close range, and to see them too with only the thinnest, wettest Lycra hiding the best things about them from our eager eyes. Zaka's officiousness ended it all for us.

Watching the girls swim had been one of the few activities that brought together Junior and Middle Houses. In the hour in which we watched the Merrywards crawling, butterflying, back- and breast-stroking, we were of one mind. The Juniors jostled on the benches in their common room, pushing and shoving and whistling while from our balconies in Middle House, we clutched our crotches in mock agony. We paid no regard to Brother Peter, our housemaster, who lectured that, for our own good, we had to sublimate to the superior governance of our minds the fleshly wants of our bodies. Recovery from the state of simulation could cause such permanent damage, he said, that it was always to be avoided, unless there was the possibility of consummating the act. But this could only happen, he stressed, within the sacrament of a fully blessed Catholic marriage.

The Senior Boys were abject hypocrites. They pretended that their strolls from their dorm to the balcony were for no other reason than to hang up clothes, which, curiously, only ever seemed to want hanging up during the Merrywards' swimming hour, or to admire the view of the kopje in the distance. The best view of the swimming Merrywards was from the Prefects' Room, which was at pool level. You could see almost every pore from that close range, but the prefects, rare beings in their cream blazers with sleeves striped red with sporting colours and academic honours, pretended to be too sophisticated for this. They made it a point of honour not to go into their own room when the Merrywards were swimming.

The rumour at the time of the Swimming Decree was that Zaka had become the boyfriend of the curviest of the Merrywards. He had instituted the ban because he did not want the junior boys to see her in her glistening glory. It turned out to be untrue. The curvy Merryward had the good taste to involve herself with a different Senior. The ban was, as a consequence, attributed to his general joylessness, to his ZakatheZuluness.

We boys may have disliked Zaka but Father Rector and the Fathers considered the doctrine of Zakal infallibility almost as important as the Papal one. They approved him as a model for us all, particularly when it came to spiritual life. He took seriously the Jesuit philosophy that even our most mundane tasks were for the greater glory of God. He wrote 'AMDG', for *Ad Maiorem Dei Gloriam*, in the upper right-hand corner of all his schoolbooks. He was one of a handful of boys to take communion twice a week, at Mass on Sundays and again at Benediction on Thursdays.

In the two years before he became a prefect, when he could have been a hooligan denizen of Middle House like his fellow form-mates, he was an altar boy. He was even more solemn than

Father Rector as he swung the thurible to waft the incense over us at Benediction and rang the bell at the Elevation of the Host. We knew better than to stand in line behind him at confession because it took him at least twenty minutes to confess. Yet he did not break a single school rule in the entire six years that he was at Loyola.

The only thing he enjoyed outside the classroom and the chapel, the only thing he did with anything approaching passion, was chess. On the evenings that he chose not to be in the Prefects' Room or out swooping on smoking boys outside the library, he would sit in the main common room, frowning over a set with a headless queen and two missing pawns that were replaced with fifty-cent coins.

Until he stopped playing chess after he struck up that curious friendship with Nicodemus, he had become so good that there were only two people in the entire school who could give him any sort of challenge, Father Rector himself, and a small Junior with a photographic memory who had at birth been burdened with the unfortunate moniker of Kissmore Mateko. Mercifully, he lost his natal name and was forever after known as Kasparov.

Zaka played sport only because he had to. Chess aside, he had a cold, bloodless discipline that made him pursue only those things that directly related to his academic success and spiritual purity. He even begrudged the literature set books that he had to read. He saw them as frivolous, unnecessary and entirely unworthy of his attention. 'Such petty things as novels, plays and poetry,' he said in his strong accent, 'are an abject waste of time for those of us who have aspirations to higher, scientific ambitions.'

From that accent came our nickname for him. We called him Zaka, after the village in Masvingo Province, because he had the thickest Karanga accent that any of us had ever heard. We could just have named him Masvingo, but that name was already allocated. And we could have called him Gutu which is where he was actually from in Masvingo, but as his real name was Zacharias, we thought it rather clever to pun on his name in this way. The junior boys added the rest. When a group of Form Twos did a history lesson on Shaka Zulu's cruelty to his subjects in the same week that Zaka not only banned us from watching the girls but also made all of Junior House clean every toilet in the school because he had caught two of them measuring their erections with the blackboard ruler, they started to call him 'the Zulu.' The name met with the approbation of the whole school.

If he knew that he was universally loathed, Zaka did not show it. Having achieved all As for his O levels and the slight blemish of a B in English literature, Zaka had chosen for his A levels the killer combination of maths, physics and chemistry. As expected, he got the top fifteen points at the end of the school year, clearing his path to reading engineering at university and to a secure and certain future.

So you can imagine our surprise when we heard that he had not only flunked out of Engines in his first year, but had taken up a job as a temporary maths teacher at St Peter Claver, the upper-top secondary school in the valley. And you can imagine our even greater shock when we read, fifteen years later, that he had been not only accused of but also found guilty of murdering Nicodemus, the boy who had been his best friend at school.

✢

The friendship between Zaka and Nicodemus was unusual because Nicodemus was two years younger. Even if those two years had not proved an impassable gulf, there was Nicodemus's Middle House status.

It was not uncommon for a Senior House boy to make something of a pet of a boy in Junior House, or for a Junior to follow a

Senior about in worshipful admiration as Kasparov did with Zaka, but there was a longstanding enmity between the Middle and Senior Houses.

Caught between the bottom and top ends of the school, the Middle boys were disliked by both Juniors and Seniors. The Juniors hated us because, not to put too fine a point on it, we bullied them. We hated the Seniors because when we had been in Junior House, and they in Middle House, they had bullied us. We hated them, they hated us right back, and so rolled the endless cycle of age-based enmity that was as old as St Ignatius.

We had other reasons for despising the Seniors. With their crisp white shirts and knives and forks in the proper hands, they were too superior for anything. It was not uncommon for a Middle House boy to declare, with blithe insouciance, that as he had swum three or four days before, there was no need to take a shower at all that week. So we found their fastidiousness about hygiene irritating. They did utterly pretentious things like splash eau du cologne on letters to girls. The school letter bag reeked of Drakkar Noir and Insignia and Old Spice.

And we envied their easy access to the Merrywards. In the year that Zaka was head prefect, relations were particularly strained. A top Razor called Innocent Zvarevashe, whom we called Zed, had made history by becoming the first boy ever from Middle House to be the boyfriend of a Merryward. The Merryward in question was called Hester and she was just brilliant. Not only was she the first girl to join the Maths Olympiad, she also beat all the boys that year, and took her A levels a year early. She was far from being the best of them, but she was a Merryward all the same, even though she had stick-thin legs, large round glasses and hair worn permanently in what were then called standing buns, pointy antennae that made her look like she was on permanent stand-by to receive alien signals.

Because of her hair, the Juniors called her Ripley, after the main character in the film *Alien*.

On the bus to and from that year's Maths Olympiad, Zed and Ripley had bonded over a shared passion for polynomial equations and the Fantastic X-Men. Before long, Zed found himself the only khaki-clad boy in the sea of white shirts at See Me time. He began to develop annoying Senior habits like washing daily. We had to stage an intervention when we caught him about to wear his Sunday best to attend Benediction on Thursday.

For the most part, we encouraged him in his conquest because it made the Seniors feel aggrieved. They saw the Merrywards as their rightful property and resented this Middle House usurpation. Under these circumstances, a Middle and Senior boy were as likely to embrace in friendship as Dingane's regiments and the Boers were to have a dinner party on the banks of Blood River. We may not have screamed '*bulalani bathakati*' every time we passed a Senior, but it was a sentiment close to our hearts.

The friendship between Zaka and Nicodemus started on Division Night. Perhaps the friendship had begun before, but that night was the first that we had any inkling of it. To try and overcome the age allegiances that the Houses created, Loyola was divided into four Divisions of a hundred boys and ten Marys in each. In these Divisions, we competed for the Division Cup. The Divisions were named after four of the Ugandan martyrs: Kaggwa, Kizito, Lwanga and M'kasa. Only the Juniors, Seniors and Marys really ever took this competition seriously: in Middle House, all the Divisions earned so many demerits that any points we earned practically cancelled each other out.

Zaka's Division, M'kasa, had won the Division Cup and thus the right to the best food. In addition to *sadza* and beans and rice and chicken, there were pork pies and corned beef, cake, jelly and custard. It was every schoolboy's idea of a feast. Zaka ate none of it.

Instead, he piled up all of his food on two plates, scraped back his chair and marched to Nicodemus who sat with the Kaggwa table.

'Here,' he said, and held out the food.

Nicodemus took the overflowing plates, grinned and said, 'Thanks, Zaka.'

There was a collective gasp.

Zaka knew that all the Junior and Middle boys called him by this name, but we never used it to his face. It was not uncommon, when he passed whole groups of us in the corridor, for us to mutter a sibilant chorus of 'ZakaZuluZakaZuluZakaZakaZaka-ZakaZulu' that died down the minute he whipped around to find us wearing innocent faces. In the ordinary case of a boy who had been as disrespectful as Nicodemus had been, any Senior boy, even one who was not head prefect like Zaka, would have been well within his rights to issue a demerit on the spot or order some other punishment.

The boys at Kagwa, and across at Lwanga and Kizito looked to see what Zaka would do. He looked down at Nicodemus as though to say something. Then he nodded, turned his back on the Kaggwa table and walked back to M'kasa. He blew the whistle for the prayer, the chatter died down and he remained seated at the table after we had all left.

Later that night, some boys who had snuck out to smoke behind the library said they heard him sobbing from inside the Prefects' Room. No one could quite believe it because, whichever way you looked at it, sobbing and Zaka the Zulu did not belong in the same thought. In any event, that moment on Division Night, when Nicodemus called Zaka by his nickname, was the beginning of their friendship. After that, when they were not in their lessons or at sport, they were almost always seen together.

✲

They were an unlikely pair. Nicodemus was not the kind of fellow who inspired intimacy. Without quite knowing why, we kept him at arm's length. He was one of the few boys that we called by his Christian name. We had a chap we admiringly called The Tsar Liberator, because, not only was he the most well-endowed of the boys in Middle House, he could also ejaculate the furthest in any ejaculation competition. Nicodemus claimed that he was just as endowed and wanted to be called Mamba.

Every school has its protocol when it comes to nicknames. Ours was that you did not choose your own: you waited to be given one. Nicodemus put our backs up by suggesting his own. Nor did we ever josh him about by his surname like we did each other. He was just Nicodemus.

He had had a brief notoriety earlier that year because the only other boy he had been close to, a volleyball setter called Takunda Gumbo, and who had also been in Middle House, had killed himself. Gumbo had been at the school for only half a term before he was withdrawn. The suicide had happened away from the school. We had subjected Nicodemus to some questioning and curiosity at the time, but we soon discovered that the reason for it was entirely unconnected to the school. Gumbo had tried to forge his stepmother's signature on a cheque. When she threatened the police, he had killed himself.

Nicodemus was one of the Razors in the middle school, always near the top of his form. He was at Loyola on a scholarship. He came from a family with many other children but only one income. On Visiting Sundays, Zaka's family brought groceries for Nicodemus too. Without Zaka's Visiting Sunday food, Nicodemus would have had only the food that the school provided and Loyola was given to what you might call Spartan conditions. We muttered to ourselves that he was taking things a bit far when he joined Zaka's mother and sisters as they leapt, ululated and danced around Zaka when he won the Maths Award and the St Loyola Award for Services to St Ignatius.

What surprised us the most about this friendship was that only Nicodemus seemed happy in it. Zaka seemed to shrink into himself whenever they were together. As the boys got closer, the other Middle House boys began to grumble that Zaka gave Nicodemus privileges that were denied them. On at least three occasions, Nicodemus was seen watching the Merrywards swimming from the Prefects' Room. He was even seen smoking in there. When another prefect reported the matter to Zaka, the head did nothing about it. Every time that Zaka had to clean up the San, Nicodemus was there with him.

We began to see that his friendship with Zaka gave Nicodemus a talismanic sort of power. We began to include him in our planning for that year's big mission, Operation Cashel Valley, a raid on the orchard kept by the Loreto sisters. The previous year had seen the successful completion of Operation Zinjanthropus, in which we had lifted Bibiana, the school's pet chimpanzee, out of her cage and left her to spend an afternoon making merry hell in the Prefects' Room.

On the night of Operation Cashel Valley, we snuck in through the wild area the Marys called kumapori. It was bad luck that Sister Hedwig came out early, shouted that she could see us, and when we tried to scramble over the fence, the more clumsy of us got stuck on the barbed wire.

When we refused to say who had been part of the Operation, Father Rector ordered that Zaka do a search of Middle House. We had taken the precaution of hiding the fruit in Nicodemus's locker, and, sure enough when he reached it, Zaka simply moved to the next without even opening it. That Sunday, he was in the confessional longer than usual.

°

By the time that Zaka had left and gone up to university, we had ourselves gone up from Middle to Senior House. We were now the white-shirted. We had our very own Marys, and found ourselves as protective of them as the Seniors before us had been of theirs. We sent them letters drenched in cologne.

Nicodemus did not go up with us. We heard in the first week of the new year that he had transferred to a government day school in Mount Pleasant. As the university was also in Mount Pleasant, someone joked about him following Zaka who was now doing Engines, but we thought nothing of it then. In any event, even if they did chance to meet in Mount Pleasant, they would not have seen each other for long. Before the end of the year came the news that Zaka had been asked to retake all his subjects. It surprised us that university gave this sort of second chance. It surprised us even more that Zaka would need it.

The next thing we heard, he was teaching maths in the valley, at St Peter Claver. We saw him during exam week, when we took a break from the stress of it all with a beer or two at Donhodzo.

Zaka was with a group of village men who were drinking from a shared calabash of beer as they played draughts. When he saw us, Zaka shot up. It seemed to us that he looked pleased and mortified at the same time.

He was in his old uniform. There is only one word to describe its state, well, maybe three: kutindivara, kusauka, faded. The white shirt looked as though it had been washed many times over in dirty water and had been dried in the dust. The black trousers were shiny from over-ironing. His shrivelled tie hung from his neck like a curse. He licked his lips and not meeting our eyes, said, 'Yes, yes, I am here now. How is everything at the school?'

Our eyes followed his to the neighbouring hill, to the rooftops of St Ignatius, red against the November sky. After we answered him, someone asked after Nicodemus.

Zaka said, 'Oh, Nicodemus. Fine, fine. Yes, yes.'

An awkward silence followed.

Then Zaka burst into speech.

How was Father Rector? Was he still studying the organisms that lived inside figs? Had he managed to beat Kasparov yet? How was Bibiana? Who had won the Ignatius Award? Had we defended the school's National High School Quiz title? How had we done at the Maths Olympiad? Who was head prefect?

We told him what we could: that the Entomological Society of Southern Africa had named some new organisms in Father Rector's honour, that Bibiana had escaped and been found outside Blessed Mary House, and that we had won the Olympiad but lost the Quiz. When we told him who the head prefect was, he made a moue of disapproval.

The conversation trailed off.

He sat back down with his companions. We moved away. It was strange to be drinking a few metres from him, and to recognise in this diminished Zaka our old head prefect. Though he kept glancing our way, he did not join us again.

The whole school saw him again a few weeks after that. We were at Mass when he walked in during the Profession of Faith. He left before the Recessional. We saw him as we emptied out of the chapel, a small figure in his faded uniform, walking down the hill to the valley below, his shadow long behind him. That was the last time that any of us saw him. He remained at Peter Claver for only one more year. After that he vanished. Then he appeared in the newspapers, accused of murder and looking as guilty as anyone would do in a mug-shot.

○

Over the years, Zaka's many irritations softened as they acquired the out-of-focus fondness of remembrance. First on the Alumni Forum of the school website, then, as technology advanced, on the Loyola page on first Myspace, then on Facebook, shared recollections of the time that Zaka had banned one thing or the other would be followed by a flood of more 'remember when's.

We were everywhere, home and abroad, displaced by ambition, and by the shrinking hopes of our own nation, but on the Internet, we gathered to live again the dappled, sunlit days of our boyhoods. Zaka himself never popped up in these discussions. There were occasional Zaka sightings both at home and out in the diaspora where Old Ignatians had spread out. An old boy based in London said he saw someone who looked like Zaka ducking into a train at Paddington station. There was a Zaka sighting in Dallas, and another in Auckland.

The most likely seemed to be one closer to home, in Zaka's original village. An old boy who was a doctor at Gutu District Hospital said he saw a Zaka-like figure waiting to receive treatment. When the old boy approached to confirm his name, the Zaka figure walked away. The old boy could not be sure that it had really been him.

By the time that we all met again for the College Diamond Jubilee, Nicodemus was dead and Zaka was awaiting death by hanging in prison. He escaped only because there was no hangman. Under the marquee that had been set up in the second sports field, old boy after old boy came forward to shake hands with Father Rector and slap each others' backs in fat-handed congratulation. We had reason to be pleased with ourselves. Our families had given us to the Jesuits as boys, and now, as men in the world, we had achieved what the motto of our Founding Saint had commanded. We had set the world on fire. We had not done it in the sense that he had meant, that soldier philosopher, we were not soldiers of God beneath the banner of Christ, but we had, all the same, placed our school at the heart of national life.

Among us were six members of parliament, ten judges, including the Chief Justice, enough lawyers to start a hundred class actions, enough doctors to staff ten district hospitals and enough engineers, architects and quantity surveyors to transform one of our many growth points into a small city. Almost every boy had slotted perfectly into his predestined hole.

Not Zaka and Nicodemus. We talked about them as the afternoon crept over Loyola. We asked the same question that had been asked in court: why did Zaka do it? An old boy who was a judge told us that he had followed the trial when it came before his colleague, an old Merryward called Justice Dendere. She had had no option but to find him guilty, the old boy said.

Zaka had refused to speak or offer any justification or defence. He had said nothing, and it was that silence that finally condemned him. There were no extenuating circumstances. It was a killing without a purpose, the judge said, without mercy or remorse. There was only one sentence possible: death by hanging.

We finally got the truth, or a glimpse of it, from Kasparov. The timid little chap who had shadowed Zaka was now the expansive and voluble owner of an employment agency that recruited care-workers for hospitals in Luton. In the heat of that August day, he had us hanging from his every word.

Just before the Division Night on which Zaka and Nicodemus had become friends, Kasparov had gone to play a game with Zaka in the Prefects' Room. As he hunched over the chessboard, Zaka had not appeared himself. He had lost three games in a row, but still insisted that Kasparov stay long past the Junior House bedtime.

Then he had burst into garbled speech about being caught by Nicodemus as he lay in the empty sanatorium with Gumbo, the boy who had died after forging his stepmother's signature. From that moment, Nicodemus had begun to bleed both boys of money. Gumbo tried to pay him by getting a big sum all at once. When he was caught, he killed himself. Nicodemus changed his tactics. It was attention he wanted now, attention and friendship. Zaka's friendship.

As Zaka spoke, Kasparov received the tale with mingled horror and panic. He did not want to be the recipient of these dreadful confidences. Foremost in his mind was the thought of the demerit he would get if Brother Peter caught him out of bed. When Zaka released him, with a forceful declaration that he would get it if he told anyone, Kasparov crept away. He was relieved to find that he had not been missed.

The next day, Zaka acted as though nothing of import had happened between them. By the time half-term came, Kasparov had almost forgotten about it. He did not tell anyone. He and Zaka were bound by the old College code of honour: come what may, you did not tell on another boy.

They never played chess again.

We heard all this with shock and horror. And though we exclaimed over the waste and pity, we could not blame him for doing nothing. When we looked at the faces of the boys around us, shining with hope in their uniforms, some of them our own children, it came to us just how young we had all been then. Kasparov had been only twelve years of age, turning thirteen that year. We had all of us been boys, even the oldest of us had been no more than seventeen. How could any of us have imagined, in the innocence of those days, of watching the Merrywards and smoking behind the library, in the laughter and japes of our annual raids and operations, that there had been this occluding darkness that cast such a long and pitiless shadow? That had led to two boys' deaths and would now, all these years later, lead to Zaka's own?

We did not linger long on Zaka. We immersed our unease in other, happier, memories. We hid our discomfort in talk of the economy and politics. During the special Celebration Mass, the choral voices soared as they sang the same hymns we had sung all those years ago. The drummers thudded out the *fata murungu fata murungu fata murungumurungumurungu* drumbeat that had been the soundtrack to our every Sunday. At the close of the service, we said goodbye to Father Rector and to our old teachers. The sun came down as we prepared to leave. As our long line of cars snaked down into the valley, the sun came down behind the red roofs of St Ignatius. In the distance we heard the high shrill of the siren that had punctuated our days, sounding now to signal to the children we left behind that the day had ended and it was time to rest.

The White Orphan

For they bind heavy burdens and grievous to
be borne, and lay them on men's shoulders; but
they themselves will not move them with one of
their fingers.

– The Gospel According to Saint Matthew –

*Vanosunga mitoro inorema, inotambudza kutakura,
vaciiisa pamafudzi avanhu, asi ivo vamene havadi
kuibata nemunwe wavo.*

– Evangeri yakanyorwa naMateo –

John Peters always insisted that he and Anatolia, his wife of six years take separate flights whenever they had to leave the country. They flew infrequently, but often enough for John to worry. He imagined himself and Anatolia as statistics in a three-day news story featuring a missing black box and a voice recorder and inclement weather conditions. Every year or so, they flew from Harare to London where Anatolia's best friend lived in an old council house in Luton. John was English but had no family there. Had it been entirely up to him, John would never again have set foot on English soil.

They died on the same day, not in an air crash, but in a car accident on the way to the Kamfinsa shops and rumours of bread. They were both thirty-five. From the town end of Enterprise Road came Anatolia and John, in their ten-year-old Toyota Hilux. From the Chisipite end, in a six-month-old Range Rover Sport, came the Chief Executive Officer of a blue chip Major Listed Company. Not only was the CEO speeding, he had also been drinking. He chose that minute to check his phone for a response to a message he had sent that morning. He hit a pothole, lost control of his car and left his lane. John swerved to avoid him, but too late. The cars hit each other with a crunch of metal. His driver-side airbag immediately cushioned the CEO. The impact threw Anatolia against the windscreen. They had to cut the steering wheel out of John's chest.

At Rotten Row, the CEO paid a five-hundred-dollar bribe to

the magistrate who presided over his culpable homicide trial and three hundred to the man prosecuting him. After his half-hearted prosecution, the magistrate fined him two hundred dollars and gave him a suspended sentence. There was no need, she said, to withdraw his licence: his remorse was sincere. Relieved, he took his family for a celebratory holiday in Mauritius. Six months after his return, he had another car accident. He killed another person, this time, a schoolboy who was the only child left in a family that had recently lost two other children. He paid another bribe. His remorse was, again, sincere. His company posted excellent results in the first quarter. His life went on.

✿

Life went on too, for the children that Anatolia and John left behind, his son, Jack and her daughter, Manatsa. For these two, John and Anatolia had arranged and changed many things in their lives. The move to their big four-bedroom house in tree-lined avenues of Greendale, far from the untarred streets of Zengeza in Chitungwiza where Anatolia had grown up; Anatolia's insistence that their children have all that she could not have, including a private education, Hartmann House for Jack, the Dominican Convent for Manatsa.

John was an economic researcher at the unfortunately named International Institute for International Development, whose acronym sounded like a bad stutter. A colleague had said to him, when he first arrived, 'There are a handful of schools that have retained the highest standards,' the highest standards being code for schools in which there was a reassuringly large number of white children and teachers.

Then came the changes: fast and sudden in some cases, slow and gradual in others. The chaos of the land invasions. The murdered white farmers, their battered bodies beamed around the world with their dogs whimpering about their corpses. Then international sanctions and exclusion, followed by double-digit inflation that became quadruple-digit inflation.

John did not flee to Perth or Auckland or Dallas, he did not go to London or Cape Town. 'We are scaling down our Harare Operations,' the IIID announced. John became the entirety of the Harare Operations. John had come to Harare to settle. Not even quadruple-digit inflation would sway him. 'I had a farm in Africa at the foot of the Ngong Hills.' John had read those words as a boy and had been seized by a violent longing for this place, Africa, where the Equator ran along the highlands and everything for miles around made for greatness and freedom and unequalled nobility.

He had grown up in the care system, without any written down, traceable roots. His parents were just names on a birth certificate. They were not even a key that could have opened up his past; the names of his parents were both so common that they may as well have had no names at all. He struggled to find an identity.

Until, at age thirteen, in a book whose title, plot or even author he could no longer remember, he read the words that would be his motto. 'What matters it what came before? Now with myself I will begin and end.' He wrote those words down and sometimes, when the yearning for a personal history traced onto a family tree lush with abundant branches got the better of him, he wrote the words in his sloping hand and the compulsion disappeared.

So that mystical place Africa became his escape from the grey drizzle of the drab streets of Manchester. It was his Secret Garden and his Enchanted Forest, his Narnia and his Middle Earth. In the public library near his school, he pored over maps of the continent, memorising and practising the names of the places, Ouagadougou and Timbuktu, Umdurman and Bulawayo, Krugersdorp and Antananarivo.

He imagined himself as Stanley doffing his peaked cap as he declared, 'Dr Livingstone, I presume.' He was with Gordon in Sudan, relieving the Emin Pasha. He was at the battle of Blood River, and with Baden-Powell at the Relief of Mafeking. He was Allan Quartermain too, handsome and rugged and, in this version, it was him and not Captain Good that the beautiful Foulata loved, and it was Gagool alone, and not Foulata too, who died. The biggest disappointment of his childhood was to find that the source of the Nile had been located, not in the Bangweolo swamps where Livingstone had died searching for it, but further away in the mountains of East Africa.

Then he grew up to discover that the mythical place Africa was but a British Airways flight away. By that point, life had gotten in the way of Africa, the dreams receded when he married, but they returned when his wife died, leaving him with a two-year-old son and an opportunity to start over, to find out where it was that he ought to be. Thus came John to Africa, staying first for work, and then for love. He found he loved his job; he found he loved his second wife.

This is what he loved about his Africa. He felt he could find himself in a place that did not stress personal histories. He was where he longed to be, where he could be just himself, John, married to Anatolia, stepfather of Manatsa, and father of Jack. So he found himself not in his past but in his present, and in Africa, his Africa, Africa, not of proud warriors in ancestral savannah, but an Africa of permanently low rankings on the human development indices, an Africa that valued economists, development and aid experts, like John with their degrees in Development Studies from the University of Sussex, the new type of missionaries and explorers.

He was a romantic, John, how else to explain the heedless, thoughtless, even careless manner in which he embraced his new country. When the Registrar-General demanded an end to double allegiances in the form of dual citizenship, he found himself at the British High Commission, seeking to renounce Her Majesty's dominion over him so that he was no longer her subject.

The official who served him at the British Embassy explained to John that the embassy's position was that people were renouncing citizenship under duress. Even if he renounced it, he could apply to get it back. John waved this possibility away. There was no need to issue a letter concerning his son, the official said, because the law allowed children to have dual citizenship.

This renunciation had not been welcome to Anatolia. 'Everyone wants UK citizenship', she sighed, 'and you go and try to give up yours. Why don't you think of the children?' He tried again to tell her of the life they would live there. No private school for the children. No pool parties, or bowling parties, no horse riding, no Kariba, no Singita Pamushana, no Mana Pools.

Of his son's mother, he said very little. 'She was an orphan,' he explained to his son, 'an orphan like me.' They had met in the system, clung to each other when they left it, gone on to the same Red-brick University, had a short and disastrous marriage that ended in her death by suicide at twenty-six, two years after Jack was born.

Anatolia was the jealous type, and was often offended when he spoke of any woman other than her. She did not believe in platonic friendships between work colleagues, and she most certainly did not believe in fond rememberances of even dead wives. John, never one for the path of most resistance when that of least resistance would do, had said as little as possible about what, in truth, had been a painful interlude in his life. To Jack, therefore, his mother was nothing more than a memory brought into shape by a picture of a woman with a soft face smiling from a photograph that his father had shown him.

So when John and Anatolia died, and both children were left orphans, the children had no closer relatives than Anatolia's mother who moved in from Chitungwiza for the duration of the funeral wake. The relatives came and after concerning themselves in the matter of who would get which clothes that had belonged to both the deceased, turned their thoughts to the matter of the children.

Her grandmother's house was the only place for Manatsa: thus the edict of Anatolia's brother, the head of the family. He and his family would move into the house, naturally, they would take care of the Greendale house until the time came when the children could take care of it themselves, he said. He caught his reflection in the mirror in front of him, and paused to admire the dark blue blazer he wore and that had once belonged to John. A little long in the sleeve, he thought, but nothing that his wife could not fix with scissors and her sewing machine. At the same time, his wife was thinking that as soon as they moved in, she would take out that bed of herbs and grow real vegetables, maybe even maize. And that cottage at the end of the property would come in handy, they would put in lodgers, extra income was always welcome.

Then came the catastrophic discoveries.

The house was rented, the car had to be written off. An examination of the bank accounts revealed that inflation had eaten what money had not been spent on private education and trips to London. The IIID had cancelled John's contract just two months before he died. There was now no Harare operation at all. The life insurance policies were as good as none.

Anatolia's brother could not believe that any white man could be this impecunious. It seemed almost a deception; worse, downright fraudulent, that John should have left nothing behind but his child. 'I should have charged that white man more for Anatolia's bride wealth,' he fumed to his wife.

'But what shall we do with the boy?' his wife asked.

It was all right for Manatsa to live in Chitungwiza, her mother had lived there after all, and she could live there too. For the boy to be moved to Chitungwiza seemed fundamentally wrong. 'Almost as though he were one of us,' said Anatolia's mother's neighbour.

Yet it seemed more wrong to leave him to the vagaries of social services who would place him, they were sure, in Chinyaradzo, or Vimbainesu or some other orphanage. Anatolia's mother, Jack's sister's grandmother, would not hear of his going to such an orphanage. 'You remember that child, *aka kasikana kakasiiwa na*Ndomudini?' she said. 'You know the one, the grandchild of the eledest daughter of that market woman from 59 Crescent? That child went to Chinyaradzo when first her parents, and then her grandmother died, and then what happened? The child died, that is what happened.'

Her son tried to convince his mother that the child was probably sick when she went to the orphanage, but the old woman was insistent: orphanages were no place for children. If it came to it, Jack would come home with her and Manatsa.

When no one came to claim the boy, the old woman had her way, and Jack and Manatsa moved into the house in which Anatolia had grown up. There was nothing left for Anatolia's brother to do but to throw up his hands and mutter dark predictions about the portentous things that were bound to happen when people tried to raise children whose family totems they did not know. That is how Jack moved from Greendale to Zengeza.

By the time that Shona fell fluent from his tongue, Jack had become so accustomed to silence that he remained encased within its walls. He looked at them with same colourless eyes that his father had, shaping his *sadza* into neat little balls and dipping it into his sauce. 'Is it good?' they asked, loudly, as if he were deaf. They commented on everything he did as though he were not there. '*Kanoringinyura sadza wena! Mukonde wese uyu!*' In the early days, his sister's grandmother struggled to talk to her new ward. With no English beyond 'yes', 'nice', and 'very good', she made do with these few words, and by dint of moving her face and hands, and asking Manatsa to interpret, managed well enough.

'Yes, nice, yes, yes?' she said. 'Very good, yes? Nice, yes? Very good.' With time, his Shona improved enough to release his sister's grandmother from the constrictions imposed by English.

He learned to make playthings of discarded objects, bottle caps polished smooth, old fabrics and plastics bundled together with string to make misshapen footballs. He had been an oddity at first, and the children cried *murungu, murungu* when he came out to play. He had sat silent watching the games, until tentatively he joined in. In the end, the only people who stood to watch curiously were the adults who marvelled at his skilled hands making delicate cars out of wire, his floppy hair in his eyes as he concentrated. '*Inga kamurungu aka karikutobvumwa nerukesheni,*' the neighbours said, and thus the consensus was that living in the township seemed to agree with the boy.

With time, Jack became immunised to Chitungwiza. The soles of his feet became hard and callused from their exposure. The clothes that he wore became as threadbare as those of his companions. He piled up car after car, until his sister's grandmother thought of selling off some of them at her fruit and vegetable stall at the market.

They fed and clothed him, and tended to his injuries when it was not enough to trust nature to heal. When he developed an abscess beneath one of his upper molars and he woke crying in the night, his sister's grandmother woke and made him drink hot water and told him stories and sang songs until fatigue made him drift off to sleep. In Zengeza Number Five Primary, he was the best student in English, his maths was barely acceptable, and after only two terms, he was getting sixty per cent for his Shona compositions.

Every time his headmaster saw him, he said to himself that something had to be done about that white child. He raised Jack's presence at the school a few times in the staff room and the teachers agreed that, indeed, something had to be done about the white child. One of the teachers went as far as to suggest social services, but life was difficult, everyone spent time queuing for bread, and nothing happened. So Jack stayed, no one came for him. He was settling, settling very well, his sister's grandmother reflected. Her only regret was that she had still not managed to find a way of cutting his hair so that it fell evenly about his head.

He settled outwardly, but there was a dissonance, a discord, an unease in his mind. It was not so much that he was among people who did not look like him, he got used to that in time; it was more that sometimes, he longed to see people, even just one, who looked like him. Then he heard that there was another *murungu*, a man who spoke fluent Shona and had lived in the township so long that he had earned the *nemererwa* name of Madzibaba Bob or Apostolic Bob, a name given to him because he wore a full beard of the kind normally associated with adherents of the Apostolic faith.

When Jack learned that this Madzibaba Bob lived a short distance away in Zengeza 4, he decided to find him. On a Wednesday afternoon when he did not have to stay behind for sports, he wandered in the direction of Zengeza 4. If you lingered long enough in the streets, he knew, you could see just about anyone you wanted to. He walked along, keeping an eye out while kicking an empty canned ham tin aimlessly in front of him and eating a mango that dribbled its yellowness onto the slinty red eyes of the Spider-Man shirt that his stepmother Anatolia had bought him from H&M in London the Christmas before she died.

Sure enough, there before him appeared a pale rider on a Black Beauty bicycle. Jack followed him until he turned into a matchbox house with bright flowers around the veranda. As the man dismounted, his eyes met Jack's. Man and boy stared at each other, Jack taking in the blue-grey eyes, the face hidden by long hair and beard, the lean body in the blue shorts, a bright green T-shirt, long brown socks pulled up to the knees and folded down neatly, like a policeman's, with the socked legs disappearing into thick canvas shoes. Madzibaba Bob took in Jack's worn clothes, the mango-streaked face, the fading Spider-Man T-shirt, and the dust-covered legs. He beckoned him to come over.

'Where do you live?' Madzibaba Bob asked him without preamble.

Jack pointed in the direction of his home. He swallowed; the walk had made him thirsty. The man reached inside his house and brought out a Fanta. As Jack drank, Madzibaba Bob asked him questions, and haltingly, what Jack knew of his own family was gradually told. His dead mother. His father marrying his stepmother. His dead father. His dead stepmother. Her live relatives. He finished his drink and began to blow noises into the empty bottle.

He looked up only when Madzibaba Bob, after staring thoughtfully at him, said, 'You are British, you know. You have another home.'

'I have a home,' the boy said, and pointed in the direction of his sister's grandmother's house.

Jack came to see Madzibaba Bob a few times after that. On those visits, Madzibaba Bob told him that he came from America, from a place he called The South. His full name was Robert E. McConkey. His ancestors originally came from Scotland, he said, from Britain where Jack was from. He had joined the Peace Corps, travelled all over East Africa, and had ended up in the country because he had heard there were some McConkey family members here. He had met but not taken to them. He had then met his wife, had taken to and married her, and had never gone back to The South.

Sometimes, when he visited, they did not talk much. Jack sat on the veranda making his wire cars while Madzibaba Bob smoked a pipe and read his newspapers. It was during one of these silent sessions that Jack finally worked up the courage to ask the one question he had wanted to ask after the second and third time that he had seen Madzibaba Bob. 'Do you always wear the same clothes?' he asked. 'The blue shorts, the green shirt? Do you wash them every day, to wear the next day?'

'I have six shirts,' Madzibaba Bob said. 'And seven pairs of shorts. My wife makes them on her sewing machine. '

'I have different clothes,' Jack said. 'They are all sorts of colours. Don't you ever want different clothes?'

'These suit me just fine.'

It was these visits with Madzibaba Bob that made Jack begin to think for the first time of what it meant to be a white person. He knew there were different people in the world, people who looked like his sister and her grandmother, people who looked him, like his classmates at Hartmann House, his old school. Somewhere were whole countries like Britain, full of people who looked like him and Madzibaba Bob. He could go there, one day, to Britain, or he could stay in Chitungwiza, stay and become another Madzibaba Bob, with a wife who made him six green shirts and seven pairs of blue shorts with her sewing machine.

Something in him rebelled at that notion, at the idea of himself in twenty years' time, with blue shorts, and a green shirt, cycling his bicycle with Chitungwiza's children screaming *murungu, murungu* after him. He would always be a person apart, a *murungu* like Madzibaba Bob, different, always having to be called by what, and not who he was, always identified by the striking singularity of his difference, just like Jonas who sewed overalls at the shop, known only as *chirema*, the cripple, or Lameck, the old albino man who lived in Seke, who was only ever called *musope*.

That there were only two whites in this entire place of thousands meant that this was surely not his place. But where was his place? Greendale, Hartmann House; that was no longer his life. Where else was there, if not here? Where was it that he ought to be?

'You are British, you know,' Madzibaba Bob's voice said in his mind, but what did that mean? Britain, he knew, was the place people went to get money. They worked as nurses, and sometimes doctors, they went and sent money home, like the two aunts of his friend Kudzai, like the brother of his friend Tauya, like the sister of his teacher Mrs Marere. Like his father John and stepmother Anatolia who often went to Britain and came back laden with presents like his favourite Spider-Man T-shirt. Britain was the place people went to get things.

Then one day, Madzibaba Bob asked to go with him to his sister's grandmother's house. He sat on the veranda, and after meandering from the price of sugar, the scarcity of bread and the possibility of rains, said what he had come to say. Jack had come to know by now that his sister's grandmother disliked *vana vaka-ganhira*, children who, among other things, listened in to adult conversation, and so he listened without being seen to be listening as Madzibaba Bob said, 'The boy is a British citizen, it may well be that he is best among his own kind, they will advise you better at the British Embassy. I suggest that you go there with him, it is in town, at Corner House on Samora Machel.'

But Madzibaba Bob's visit was followed by a funeral whose wake was held at his sister's grandmother's house. Jack slept on the floor, listening to the wails of the newcomers over the coffin in the living room. He tried to keep his memory from remembering that these songs too, had been sung at the wake for his father, and Anatolia, his stepmother.

That funeral was followed by more illness, then his grand-mother went away to see her sick sister. When she came back, she brought two more children with her. The new children stared at Jack. They laughed and pointed at Jack. But worse was to come: the new additions put pressure on the household.

They went through a bad period of hunger in which his sister's grandmother was reduced to cooking some of the wares she sold on her stall. The food was well cooked, but there was so little of it that eating it made them hungrier still.

Jack went to Madzibaba Bob's house. He was dead, the neighbours said. He went suddenly in his sleep. Just like Jack's parents, he was there one day, then the next, not. That night, his sister Manatsa had cried that she was hungry and her grandmother had broken down in tears. Jack knew he had to do something.

A morning came on which he feigned illness, and did not go to school. As soon as his grandmother had gone to her market stall, he put his plan into action. He climbed a chair and took down the box from the top of the wardrobe where he knew his grandmother kept her important papers. Inside, he found his father's passport, his stepmother's passport, and his own. He saw his face, two years old in this passport, his hair like an upside-down bowl resting on his head. He read aloud the first words on the first page, tracing them with his finger. 'Her Britannic Majesty's Secretary of State requests and requires in the Name of Her Majesty . . .'

He turned his attention to the other papers in the box. His and his sister Manatsa's birth certificates. Some old photographs, including a series that made his heart stop; his father Jack and stepmother Anatolia, dead in their coffins, eyes closed as they rested on white shiny pillows. His hand shook as he put these back. He thought again and took out the photograph of his father. He placed it in the middle of the passport.

He took only the passport but there was this: how to carry it into town? Not in his jeans pocket, that was certain. 'Town is full of thieves and vagabonds,' his sister's grandmother always said.

She kept her money and national ID card in her bra when she had to go to town. He knew because when his aunt got mugged, his grandmother had yelled at her for not being careful.

'You walk around with your money in your bag, inviting thieves to mug you, and then what happens? You are mugged, that's what happens, all your money is stolen,' she had said. '*Mari ndeye-kuviga mubhodhi*, I have kept my money in my bra all these years and not once have I been mugged.'

'How can I keep money in my bra?' his sister's aunt had said. 'Don't you know there is inflation, you need at least twenty notes just to buy a loaf of bread, how can I put it all in my bra? And you know how that money smells, all those thin notes, all that sweat.'

He had no bra, but he had Sellotape for sticking on the covers of his exercise books. Carefully, he held the passport to his chest, with his father's photograph in the middle, and wound the roll of Sellotape round and round his body until the passport was stuck to his skin. He looked under the bed and extracted some notes from the thin wad he knew his sister's grandmother kept there for emergencies.

He sat down and wrote a note on a page torn from his English exercise book, tracing out the Shona words carefully in his round handwriting. 'Dear Gogo, I have gone to the British Embassy so that they take me to Britain to become a doctor. I have taken 20,000 dollars to go to town. I promise that I will send you lots of money when I get there. I will send money for everyone, but especially for you, Gogo, and for Manatsa. Don't worry about me. From Jack.'

He cancelled out 'From Jack', and wrote, 'Yours Jack.'

He put the note on the coffee table in the living room, put on his school shoes and went out to the main road to get a *kombi* to town. He sat in the corner, his bus fare tightly clenched in his hand. The *kombi* was not full, and apart from one or two people who turned to stare at him, he was completely undisturbed. When it came time to pay, he counted out his money carefully. In town, he walked from Fourth Street bus terminus, asking every few metres for the way to the British Embassy. The black people he asked seemed more interested in his life story than in showing him where Corner House lay, they tried to get him to say more things in Shona. A man ran after him, and, frightened, he ran across Jason Moyo Avenue, almost colliding with a blind beggar who was led by a small boy. On the other side of the street, he was grabbed by a burly white man who gripped him tight and would not let go. 'Where's the fire, my boy?' the man asked him.

'*Ndisiye*,' he responded in Shona and struggled to free himself.

'Where are you trying to get to?' the man asked.

Jack looked up.

The man looked rough, but his voice seemed kind.

'The British Embassy,' he said. 'Corner House.'

'Come on, I'll take you there,' the man said. Jack's need was greater than his caution. He got into the passenger seat of the car that was parked a short distance away. The man barked a few more questions, but soon gave up when Jack refused to talk. They drove in silence for about six minutes. The only landmark that Jack recognised was the Meikles Hotel. He had been there once with his father John and his stepmother, to attend a wedding. He and Manatsa had begged to ride on the backs of the lions outside the hotel. His father had said they could not but had taken them to Greenwood Park afterwards. A lump formed in Jack's throat. He swallowed and blinked hard to push back the hot tears that he could feel gathering. 'That's Corner House,' the man said and indicated the building with a stubby finger. Jack got out, and so concentrated was he on not wanting to cry that by the time he remembered his manners enough to say, 'Thank you,' the man had driven off, shaking his head.

There was a security guard at the desk in the reception of the building. His nametag said Boniface. Jack spoke, but the desk was high, Jack was small and the guard did not hear him. Jack raised his voice. The security guard came round the desk and loomed down at him. With all the authority that he could muster, Jack looked up at him and said, 'You have to take me home.' He lifted up his Spider-Man T-shirt to expose the passport taped to his midriff. Then he sat on the floor without waiting for a response and, to the astonishment of the security guard, he pulled up his knees to rest his head, put his arms around his face and cried.

A Kind of Justice

So shalt thou put away the guilt of innocent blood
from among you, when thou shalt do that which is
right in the sight of the Lord.

– The Book of Deuteronomy –

Saizozo unofanira kubvisa ropa risinemhosa
pakati pako, kana waita zakarurama
pamberi paJehova.

– Buku yecishanu yaMosesi inonzi Deuteronomio –

On the third of Pepukai's eight days in Freetown, the Land Cruiser in which she rode with her assistant Anton and their driver Johnny drove over and killed a local chicken. A scrawny bird both fleshless and featherless, the chicken's death was soundless. So quick was its passing that Anton sitting with Johnny in the front failed to see it, Johnny failed to see it and the car drove on in a whirl of red dust. Only Pepukai, who sat in the back, saw the gathering congregation of mourners around the flattened body.

'You killed a chicken back there, Johnny,' she said.

'Jah, Jah, Jah, bless sweet Salone,' Johnny sang along to the music.

'Johnny, we have to go back, we killed a chicken.'

Above the volume, Johnny shouted, 'Are you sure?'

'Yes, I am. We should go back.'

'I saw nothing.'

Pepukai fought her mounting irritation. It was only three days since she had met Johnny but she was already beginning to tire of him. The terrifying helicopter ride across the estuary from the airport at Lungi to Freetown had not put her at ease, nor had the lengthy process of being harangued over every item in her bag at Customs. So she had been singularly unamused when Johnny, who held up the name of their organisation, had reached for Anton's bags ahead of hers and fawned over him while giving her a look that suggested he was appraising her only to assess her desirability. He had then spent the journey to the Mamba Point Hotel refusing to believe what Anton told him, that Pepukai was not his secretary but in fact, was, in Johnny's own words, Anton's 'Big Bussman'.

'Pretty girl like you can't be Big Bussman, no, no, that is not possible.' Then had come the personal questions, was she married, and why not, what was she waiting for, all women should have baby, many baby, but maybe she was too big, too important to have baby. And now this. Did he think she had flown all the way from London to Freetown to make up stories about squashed chickens?

Anton said, 'Perhaps we should drive back, Johnny. Just to check.' As Johnny turned the car around with no further protest, Pepukai thought wryly that, here in the continent of her birth, where a black woman could only suggest, coax, hint, cajole and hope to persuade, a white man could command and expect obedience.

They found a family group gathered around the body of the chicken, its blood vivid against the red dust of the road. It had clearly come from a house with a short driveway that led into the road. A man and a woman spoke to each other in furious Krio as they looked at the dead chicken. Two children, about six and eight, danced at the side of the road, next to them stood a bare-chested prepubescent girl who held a naked baby. They all looked as Johnny, Pepukai and Anton left the car. Johnny approached them with a greeting.

On hearing Krio, the woman broke into a mix of English and Krio and said, *'Wetin mek yu kill mi fol?'*

'Ah-ah! Mttsshw!' Johnny said as he screwed his mouth into a hissing moue. *'Udat kill yu fol? Nor to di fol run kam na di road?'*

His voice was rough, his manner insolent.

The man immediately said, *'Padi man, nor ala pan mi uman so. Nor tok to am so.'*

'Eh! Wetin mek yu uman in sef for tok to me so?' Johnny said. *'If ee respect me, ar dey respect am but if ee hala pan me, misef dey hala pan am also.'*

The woman immediately shouted, *'Haaay! Hot sun today o! Wey you don kill me fol don you dey kam opin you ass tok bout*

respect o? You wan tif me fol den yu dey can tok to me anyow?
Nor tok to me so o. Me no to yu uman o!'

In high dudgeon, Johnny said, *'You krase ehn? You dey mek lek*
say na by wilful I kill di fol!'

He turned to Anton and said, 'This crazy woman talk like I murder the chicken, like I kill it wilful.' He turned back to the conversation as he and the couple talked over each other. Pepukai was
about to remonstrate with Johnny when Anton put his hand into
his pocket to produce a five-thousand Leone note. He offered it to
the woman and said, 'Take this. It's for your chicken.' At the sight
of the coloured note, the woman looked even more offended.

'Mttssssshhw,' she said, and she made an even louder hissing
moue with her mouth than Johnny had. She spat on the ground
and curled her mouth in contempt. Anton took out another
ten-thousand Leone note, and pressed the money on to Johnny,
who tried to press it into the man's hands. The man did not grasp
his fingers around the notes and they fluttered unclaimed onto the
ground next to the chicken. One of the dancing children made as
though to reach for the money before receiving a sharp slap on the
shoulder from the woman.

'We nor want yu moni, yeri?! Na for ol am,' she shouted.

People from neighbouring houses began to gather, and sensing
that the atmosphere might get mutinous, Anton asked Johnny to
drive on. Johnny moved to the car, Pepukai and Anton following,
while the woman continued to gesticulate after them.

'God bless you una,' she shouted as they drove off.

These words seemed a strange benediction under the circumstances but they were familiar to Pepukai. Words such as
these were used seven thousand kilometres away, further south
in her part of Africa, where *Mwari ngaave nemi*, God be with
you, was said when the speaker was so consumed with helpless
anger and rage that the most that could be done was to leave

any vengeance in the hands of the Almighty.

'These people are a problem,' Johnny said as they drove on. 'Refugees from the war who came here with their chickens and rural habits and who never went back.' He paused in his speech to send a gob of spit through the window before continuing, 'This is Freetown; it is not Bo or Makeni.'

The incident had made him loquacious, and instead of singing to his music, he lowered the volume. 'This very nice part of Freetown,' he said as he avoided a pothole in the road. 'Up there is home of Chinese ambassador, Guinea ambassador, all the Big People.' He pointed in the direction of a dust road that seemed littered with shacks more suited to little people. Then beyond the shacks and through the trees, Pepukai saw them, the houses of the big people, shapeless, newly built constructions, box-shaped concrete promontories over the ocean.

'So you here to make a film,' Johnny said.

'Yes,' Anton said. 'We work for an organisation that works on transitional justice. We are doing a documentary on three countries.'

'We are *thinking* of making a documentary,' Pepukai corrected.

Johnny ignored this and directed his talk to Anton. 'You make film about the war? Like *Blood Diamond*. That is good film, very good film. Very, very good film. It was very bad war, long war, very, very bad war.'

'Well,' said Anton, 'it is not quite like *Blood Diamond*, and it is not about the war, it is about what happens now that the war is over, with the main guys being tried by the Special Court and everything.'

'Ah, Special Court,' said Johnny. 'Very good news for us, very good, Special Court from United Nations. It create many, many jobs. Like mine. The United Nations is very good, many jobs.'

He laughed as he swerved to avoid another pothole.

'But they don't get everyone,' he said. 'Special Court don't get everybody. Foday Sankoh, he die. Johnny Koroma, he escape, run away to Guinea, maybe he dead.'

They drove on in silence until Johnny said, 'We have same name, I am also Johnny Koroma, but not Johnny Paul Koroma. Maybe I am real Johnny Koroma, maybe you make film about me, and you pay me for interview. You pay US dollar.'

He laughed again. 'But better to forget the war. Too much talk talk about war is no good.'

At the intersection, a car beeped at them, and Johnny beeped back, and shouted '*How di bodi!*' and laughed loudly as he waved at the driver.

Pepukai tried to tune out Johnny as she looked at the passing billboards, one after the other, advertising mobile telephone service providers and cigarette brands. One billboard dominated with its picture of smiling Saloneans, enjoying the blessings requested in Johnny's song as they played pool with an enjoyment, the advert suggested, that was exclusive only to the smokers of its cigarettes. A token white man presumably included to give an international touch grinned inanely, while below were the words, doubtful, like the report of a rumour: 'The Director of Medical Services Has Said that Smoking May be Dangerous to Your Health'. Beyond the billboard, in the distance the Atlantic shone in the majesty of its vastness.

'The Court appears to be an oasis of efficiency in the middle of chaos,' Anton said as they entered the Special Court. Pepukai knew that Anton had ambitions beyond being a mere assistant producer, he wanted to write, and he was always making up and testing aloud the lines that he thought the narrators of their films would say. It had become a tic, and one, Pepukai thought, that made him sound like a single-voiced Greek chorus of singular unoriginality.

He was not entirely correct. In the Visitors' Room at least, the Court was unable entirely to shake off the poverty of the country outside. They sat on white chairs covered in grime on the backs of which the word SECURITY had been traced with an uneven hand. The air conditioner circulated only hot air while the 'Notice to the General Public' was peeling off with only the bottom legible.

Pepukai worried about their metal detector, and tried to remove her fifteen thousand bracelets, which normally set off the alarms at airports. She passed through with no sound. She surrendered to a search by the guard who did not rise from her chair for the search. She sat with her legs splayed as Pepukai stood between them, and ran her hands over her legs and bottom. With a wide smile, she gave Pepukai a friendly slap on the bottom as she finished searching her, and said, 'I finish.' Pepukai was too amused to protest.

'Is the court in session?' Pepukai asked her.

'Trial Chamber I is sitting in the matter of the AFRC accused and Trial Chamber II is sitting in the matter of the RUF accused,' the guard said without drawing breath. She spoke like an air hostess whose uncertain English was confident only in making stock announcements.

'And will the prisoners be in court?' Pepukai asked her.

'Detainees,' said the male guard who had been silent up to that point.

'Excuse me?' Pepukai said, confused.

'No prisoners, they are detainees,' he said.

Now Pepukai could truly believe that she was in a place run by the United Nations. No doubt, after endless debates at endless meetings, circulars had been sent in every official language to instruct the employees how to address the men accused of bearing the greatest responsibility for the killing of tens and tens of thousands.

A tall fair man strode towards them with a loping grace. He had the tensile strength of a man who spent half his life on a bicycle. 'I'm Patrick O'Connor,' he said. 'We have emailed. I am the Special Assistant for Public Affairs in the Registrar's Office.'

His accent was Irish. Pepukai was amused to see that he was dressed in the way common to men from cold climes who found themselves in hotter ones for work and not leisure. Used to seeing the heat as an excuse to dress down, they were completely incapable of finding the happy medium between comfort and formality. He seemed dressed for the beach in flapping shorts, a short-sleeved shirt with the three top buttons undone and bare feet in brown moccasins.

He walked them out of the security centre. Outside, they passed smartly dressed Mongolian soldiers who stared ahead without moving. Pepukai resisted a childish impulse to wave in their faces to see if they would flinch. Patrick O'Connor pointed to a building on the right.

'Those are the detention cells.'

'They are not at Pademba prison then?' Pepukai asked. 'Isn't that the largest prison in the city?'

'Oh Christ, no,' said Patrick O'Connor. 'They would not last a day there. The agreement is that they are to be housed in their own complex. And, of course, if they are found guilty, they will be imprisoned in countries willing to take them. And they won't be sentenced to death, like the poor buggers in Pademba.'

'So that means that if you kill a person now, today, you could actually get the death penalty, but none of these guys who killed so many people will get it?' said Anton.

'Funny that, no,' Patrick O'Connor said cheerfully. 'Charles Taylor was imprisoned just two hundred metres from here. It is a pity you cannot see him because of his transfer.'

He spoke of the former Liberian President as a zookeeper might of the passing of his favourite exotic animal. His face brightened as he said, 'But maybe you can do a segment of the documentary in The Hague and you can see him there.'

As he spoke, Pepukai saw women exiting the detention compound, six moving pillars of elegance in the local costume. What must it be like, she wondered, what must it be like to go through that security office and announce that your lover, husband, father, brother and maybe son is one of those men in that complex?

They walked to the canteen. It was called the Special Fork. Almost all the white men were dressed like the Special Assistant; as if they were on holiday, in casual clothes and flip-flops, while the women wore stringy tank tops with khaki trousers or dresses that were either diaphanous or very short. Only the locals, in their neat-ironed skirts and blouses, shirts and ties and flowing local clothing looked like their clothes had any sort of acquaintance with laundry soap and an iron. Pepukai shivered from the air conditioning. Here the notices were legible including one that instructed people to raise the alarm in the case of fire by shouting 'Fire, Fire, Fire'.

'The Special Court for Sierra Leone is unique,' the Special Assistant for Public Affairs in the Registrar's Office said. 'It is a hybrid court, an international court in a domestic setting. That is the element you should focus on.'

He spoke to both of them but mainly to Anton. In their world of office memos and Monday morning staff meetings, Pepukai is Anton's boss with an office bigger than his, where he comes to see her with impractical ideas for documentary programmes. Pepukai had a horror of pettiness and small-mindedness, and thus did not push herself forward, she knew that she made the decisions how-ever much people like Patrick O'Connor and Johnny might assume otherwise, and that was enough for her, some of the time. Better this, she thought, than the nudge-nudge-wink-wink that Anton and Pepukai had been getting at the Mamba Point Guest House as the other guests assumed that they were having steamy interra-cial sex under the mosquito net. Mo Hassan, the proprietor, had positively leered when he came over to their table to welcome them to the guest house as they had a late dinner last night.

A penetrating laugh from the next table brought her back to the conversation. 'You should be able to film inside the detention centre when you come with the crew,' Patrick O'Connor said. 'It is really first class; air-conditioned, with the best medical facility in Sierra Leone. In fact, I'd say the guys there have a better deal than they would in Europe or the US.'

'What do they do, the prisoners, I mean, the detainees, what do they do all day? Do they do any work?' Pepukai asked.

'Well, they sure as hell watch a lot of movies. They are supposed to do a few cleaning jobs and are paid under a Detainee Earning Scheme. Between you and me and the lamp-post, they do nothing but cause a hell of a lot of trouble. Christ, was there ever a bigger bunch of pains in the arse?'

'And do they get on, I mean, there are like what, leaders of three warring sides in there, right? The AFRC, the RUC, the CDC?'

'Oh, they get along all right. Very friendly. The only arguments they have had recently were about the World Cup.'

✤

Later that night, in her hotel room, as a fan whirred overhead and she lay in bed under a mosquito net and leafed through the Report of the Truth and Reconciliation Commission, Pepukai decided that she did not care for Patrick O'Connor. It was not anything in particular that he said, it was just something in his manner, a certain 'I am here to do good' attitude that she found insufferable. It was an attitude that Pepukai had met before from arrogant officials in different foreign capitals as well as well-meaning Christian aid workers.

But once she had fulminated about the arrogance of these attitudes, once she had dissected the patronising racism of low expectations that underpinned them, there was still this fact: they were here for a reason. It was conditions on this ground that fed such attitudes. The blood shed on this soil, the innocent blood, the bodies buried in this soil, in piles of corpses. That blood mattered. And it was then that she felt the weight of pain, the stain of collective victimhood. She could not avoid the question that forced itself on her.

What is it about *us* that these are our lives?

On an intellectual, cognitive level, she understood where it had gone wrong. She understood how it had all begun. She knew all the critical theory, about the image of Africa in the West, that Africa is not a country, that the terms of global trade were inequitable. She understood slavery, and colonialism. She knew all about the might of Bismarck's Ruler – that at the Conference of Berlin, all that long time ago in 1888, nations and ethnicities, rivals and enemies had been corralled into unitary states, and that now, in those forced nations, old hatreds played out to the staccato sound of new weapons.

She understood that rebel secessionist movements were sometimes nothing but assertions of age-old loyalties. She understood too that other regions had had their own Dark Ages, darker, bloodier than her continent's current problems would ever be; she understood all this, the burning witches, the Crusades, the madness and mayhem that had accompanied plunder and conquest around the world. It had all happened elsewhere, in other places. What has been will be again, what has been done will be done again, and there is nothing new under the sun.

But still. But still, but still, but still.

In the Report of the Truth and Reconciliation Commission she read of the fighters from every side who forced villagers to play games of chance that determined if they lived, and if so, with how many limbs. Villagers picked out their fates on scribbled bits of paper. Between the extremes of life or death, holding on to limbs or parts of limbs was also a prize, because to pick out a paper with 'long-sleeve' on it meant the loss of a hand, 'short-sleeve' meant an arm was cut off from the elbow, 'sleeveless' meant that the entire arm was hacked off from the shoulder. It was calculated and deliberate. In the hand was the power to vote, the rebels said, so the hand and sometimes the whole arm had to go.

Soldiers from all sides raped women and girls who went on to give birth to the children of war. And they developed weeping fistulas. The rebels armed children, drugged them and trained them to kill. They gambled and laughed as they guessed the sex of the babies in their mothers' wombs. To prove who was right, they sliced the mothers open. And the men who are said to bear the greatest responsibility for these crimes earned money in an air-conditioned detention centre and argued over the World Cup.

A song comes to her memory from her childhood. *'They held a congregation, the Apostolic Faith of Marange, to find out who it was who had painted us black, with paint from the can labelled "suffering".'* This is at the core of the pain that she feels once she has stripped away the intellectual and analytical buffers. In her most despondent moments, there is only that pain, the pain of the lives lost and ruined.

The innocent blood.

As a law student who cared about lofty principles, she had believed that she had the power to influence what happened in the world, even in conflicts as old as those in the Middle East. She had armed herself with every international law degree she could get. She had had one life aim, and one alone, pure in its clarity, determined in its singlemindedness and arrogant in the stubborn certainty of its own righteousness. She had wanted to change the world. For what purpose was she on this earth if not to bring some justice to an unjust world?

She had then come to realise that actually, she had only the power of anger, of frustrated anger, that her agony for a just world was no more than the powerless cry of the child who first realises that the world is not good and loving at all, but that it is unjust, unequal, unfair and unkind. She had come to accept that the only power she had, if she had any at all, is that of witness.

She had also learned to accept that it is her part of the world in which injustice most frequently found its expression. And again, she was able to wrap her understanding of it all in the intellectual fabric of Walter Rodney, Frantz Fanon or Achille Mbembe. She could dress it in post-colonial studies and intersectionality, but there was no intellectual reasoning, no analysis that would help her get over the fact that the paint in which her people had been dipped came from a can labelled 'Suffering', nothing that could remove from the soil of this land the stain of that innocent blood.

Pepukai spent the next five days listening to accounts of the causes of the war. 'The West has a lot to answer for,' said an aid worker. 'The roots of the war stretch all the way to the founding of the country.' 'It is the usual resource curse,' said a political scientist. 'We should never have discovered those diamonds. Because mineral wealth combined with weak governance in a poor country is a recipe for wars over primitive accumulation.' 'It was endemic corruption that did it,' said an opposition politician. 'How can there not have been a war?' a taxi driver asked. 'The soldiers were getting bags of rice instead of a salary.' 'And even then, there was so much corruption that someone would siphon off half the bag, so that they only got half-bags,' said a parliamentarian. 'The reason there was a war in this country', said the Secretary-General of the local chapter of a global human rights organisation, 'is because there was no human rights culture in Sierra Leone.' There were many reasons, concluded the Report of the Reconciliation Commission, but it ultimately came down to this: the nation had lost its dignity.

Pepukai highlighted that word. Dignity. When that went, abominations came in which men faced the choice to die, or to live, but to live meant that they were forced to rape their own mothers, sisters or daughters. When that went, children still to turn ten years of age were fed on drugs and taught to kill.

Pepukai read of an old man who was stopped by a group of fighters on his way to hospital. 'Where are you going, Old Father?' they
asked. 'To the hospital, my children,' he answered. 'My leg has been
troubling me for some time, and I am going to have it seen to.'

'We will see to it for you, Old Father,' they said, as they hacked
it off. For good measure, they saw to both his arms as well.

Then there was the woman who was forced to eat a piece of the
heart of her son, the six-year-old forced to drink her sister's blood
and told to laugh and dance as she did so, the seven-year-old whose
arms were cut off, and the young girl raped by soldiers from all
sides, including the men from the West African rescue force. The
nation had lost its dignity. And all the men who had done all this,
if they were not dead, were now living in that society, presumed
rehabilitated, and only eleven were supposed to pay for it all.

Pepukai had not yet found a title for the documentary, but she
knew that it would open with the words of Von Logau, a German
poet she had read at university in Austria. '*Gottes Mühlen mahl-
en langsam, mahlen aber trefflich klein. Ob aus Langmut er sich
säumet, bringt mit Schärf er alles ein.*' She would use the English translation from Longfellow: 'Though the mills of God grind
slowly, yet they grind exceeding small; Though with patience He
stands waiting, with exactness grinds He all.'

Maybe it was the nature of justice that it was not blind at all.
Maybe justice, when it came, always came late. Maybe a justice
that came late and that came imperfectly was better than none
at all. It reminded her of a saying of her own ancestors. *Mhosva
haiori.* Every crime will find its recompense.

'Your brother's blood cries out to me from the ground. What
have you done, Cain? For the earth has opened up its mouth to
receive the innocent blood that has been shed by your hand.'

❖

The next day, Pepukai sat in the public gallery of the Special Court as judges delivered this late justice in air-conditioned courtrooms. This was the trial chamber sitting in the trial of the three AFRC Accused: Alex Tamba Brima, Santigie Borbor Kanu and Brima Bazzy Kamara.

Patrick O'Connor, slightly more formally attired in a blue shirt and khaki trousers, assured her that the transparent glass of the public gallery was bulletproof. The judge from Nigeria questioned the Prosecuting Counsel on a point of law. There followed a duel between the Prosecuting Counsel and Defending Counsel of the three men, none of whom was in the dock. The woman sitting next to Pepukai nodded in her sleep, and her head touched Pepukai's shoulder.

The woman was startled awake by the sudden burst of laughter as the judge from Mali said something apparently witty and the judges, Prosecuting and the Defending Counsel all laughed.

The court called Witness 232 for the prosecution. He was a small nervous man who rocked in the witness chair the minute he sat in it and licked his lips. 'He cannot give his name as he is under witness protection,' Patrick O'Connor said in a sibilant whisper. Witness 232 licked his lips and rocked as he began his testimony.

'I was walking along a road when the men came and . . .'

'Will Counsel please direct the witness not to fidget?' The judge from Nigeria spoke. He did not look at the Witness, but made notes on the pad before him.

'Please don't fidget,' the prosecutor said, through the interpreter, who left out the please and just gave the command.

The witness continued. 'They walked along the road led by Commander Five-Five and then . . .'

'Witness 232, this is a courtroom and you are asked to maintain the proper decorum. Please keep still while giving your testimony,' the judge interrupted again.

The command was again interpreted for him. The witness started again, stuttered, and was still. The court adjourned the trial presumably so that the witness could realise the importance of not shaking and fidgeting in court.

Maybe, Pepukai thought, this too was justice.

✿

There was no other court session while Pepukai was in Freetown. She and Anton were not to worry, Patrick O'Connor assured them, because when they came back with the crew, there would be a lot more of what he cheerfully termed 'the real action.' On the day they were to take the helicopter to Lungi for their flight back to Johannesburg, Johnny sped to beat another driver to the roundabout at the Cotton Tree. From the other side came another car. Johnny swerved to avoid it and hit a road sign. Pepukai and Anton were flung around like sacks. There was a pile-up of traffic as people gathered around. Johnny looked dazed. The Special Court sent another driver to replace Johnny. The new driver, Mustafa, was quiet and not given to talking. Anton slept, and for the first time in more than a week, Pepukai travelled in a car the way she preferred, in the silence of her own thoughts.

As she boarded the helicopter to Lungi, she clutched to her chest the Report that she had come to know so well. She had read every page in the last eight days, she had highlighted the passages that spoke the most to her. She had made notes in the margins. Pepukai distracted her thoughts from the whirring blades of the helicopter by turning over in her mind the names of the men who had caused the devastation recorded in the Report that she held.

Dead or presumed dead: Johnny Paul Koroma, Sam Bockarie, Samuel Hinga Norman, Foday Sankoh. Arrested, the men from all three sides in the war, the AFRC, RUC, and CDF: Alex Tamba

Brima, Santigie Borbor Kanu, Brima Bazzy Kamara, Issa Hassan Sesay, Morris Kallon, Augustine Gbao, Moinina Fofana and Allieu Kondewa.

Unlike the prisoners just down the road from Pepukai at Pademba prison, who killed out of wartime, the detainees were safe from retaliation. They would not face the ultimate sanction of their land. They were safe from the death penalty because that was the condition for the fancy court and the long trial supported by the United Nations. They would not die for their crimes.

They would serve out their sentences far from their homeland. Perhaps their wives and families would continue to see them. They would have other children too perhaps, conceived on conjugal visits, with the elegantly dressed women who came to see them. As prisoners over which all states had assumed responsibility, the might of the United Nations would ensure that their human rights were scrupulously observed. They would earn more money under the Detainee Earning Scheme. They would argue with each other over other World Cups. Perhaps in time, one or all of them would find religion and wash themselves free of their sins.

Maybe that, too, was a kind of justice.

Pepukai turned to the final section of the Report that listed the names of the displaced, the enslaved, the killed, the raped, the abducted, the amputated and the forcibly conscripted. The names rolled on from page 273 to page 503, 230 pages of names and non-names, the youngest a two-year-old, the oldest seventy-five. Gailu Baindu, Ayena Gaima, Fatoma Gassma, Keni Gbakina, Anne Jakamu, Hassan Kamara, Mohammed Zoker. Victim 1, Victim 2, Victim 75, Girl 5, Girl 74. Perhaps this recording, this recounting, perhaps this was enough. Maybe this too, was a kind of justice. As the helicopter began its lurching, choppy descent to Lungi, Pepukai closed the Report, shut her eyes as though in prayer and hoped that she was not going to be sick.

At Golden Quarry

That which is altogether just shalt thou follow, that
thou mayest live, and inherit the land which the
Lord thy God giveth thee.

– *The Book of Deuteronomy* –

Tevera zakarurama kwazo cete, kuti urarame,
ugare nhaka yenyika yaunopiwa naJehova
Mnari wako.

– *Buku yecishanu yaMosesi inonzi Deuteronomio* –

From the pile of rotted vegetables and soggy paper came a shimmering glint that sent a rush of hope coursing through Gracious Saungwe. She had found only a few things that day, six things to be precise, four empty bottles of beer, one chipped and useless, a child's scuffed purple and yellow rattle with no stone inside to make a rattling sound and a square coloured scarf gnarled in one corner.

She scrambled across the cans and the old shredded newspapers and flat cardboard boxes with her gaze fixed on the gleam that seemed to shine brighter as she got closer to it. She did not flinch at the smell of decay but focused with mounting excitement on the face of the watch, for it was a watch that glinted in the sunlight. Smiling, she reached for it. There she had been, about to go back along Bulawayo Road to Kuwadzana, about to give up on finding anything of worth.

She put her fingers amid the rotting vegetables and grabbed at the watch. And as she did so, there came the immediate and certain knowledge that there was something wrong. Why was the watch so heavy, so hard to lift, why, she thought, were the rot and vegetables rising with the watch as she pulled?

Disoriented, she let go, the watch fell back into the rubble. It was then that she saw that what held the watch back was the hand to which it was attached, and beyond that, an arm. Gracious gasped and let go and fell back into the dump in one awkward motion. Not taking her eye off the hand, she scrambled to a kneeling position, and as she tried to stand, staggered back and fell into the dump, her head hitting a rusting bucket.

She struggled to right herself; the blow to her head had told, and fighting dizziness, she lost her balance, thrust her hands backwards to support herself, and cut her hand against a sharp tin. The piercing shock of the pain cut through the numbness in her brain and at last she screamed. The sound of her cries attracted two men who had been working several metres ahead of her. They were not who she would have wished to come to her aid; she had fallen out with Richard and Job before, they did not scruple to take what others had found, and Job did not hesitate to use his bulk to intimidate even the smallest children. But she forgot the past now in her fear and desperate need to share what she had seen.

'Pane chi-chitunha,' Gracious said without prompting and pointed at the arm that she had pulled up with the watch digging into the wrist. The two men looked to where she pointed. They removed the surrounding rubbish to reveal the body of a young man in a dark suit, his eyes glassy in death. He had not been there long, the only smell of contagion came from the waste around him. A swarm of blue-bottle flies rose from the small wound on his forehead. The three on the dump looked down at the body, the spell was broken only when Gracious screamed again.

A look from Job silenced her, and she stood to one side, sucking her cut finger, longing to move but rooted to the spot. She was fixated on the body, taking in the eyes, open, as though in mild surprise, the short neatly groomed hair that had evidently received the recent attentions of a barber.

As Gracious looked on, Richard bent down, removed the watch and held it up to his ear. In her head raged a battle between fear, caution, superstition and avidity mingled with the accumulated resentments from former battles with these men.

Bitterness and avidity won.

'*Ndipe heyo kuno*,' she said, and reached out her hand. '*Ndini ndaiwana*.'

When Job did not respond, she made a quick sudden move to snatch it. He was taller than she was, swifter too. He sidestepped her and made to walk away. She grabbed him at the elbow, her still bleeding hand leaving a trail on his skin. He turned and hit her full in the face with his fist.

Gracious felt her blood run down her nose. The choice was clear; she could accept defeat or risk further assault, and so, shouting, she walked away from them and the corpse. When she was a safe distance away, she hurled a fluent and practised curse at his mother's cunt. She walked off along Bulawayo Road, disregarding any thoughts of modesty, the hem of plastic carrier bag containing the little collection of gathered treasure.

She gave one last look at the men up on the dump, but they did not look up from their task. They were silent and efficient, and the corpse was pliant beneath them as they stripped it of its suit, shirt, shoes and belt. In the wallet, they found an Edgars discount card and ID in the name of Gabriel Makonyera and a staff card that said he was an employee of the Zimbabwe Broadcasting Corporation, ZBC. Richard pocketed the wallet. As Richard moved to take off the man's underwear, Job put his hand on the shoulder, and shook his head. Richard let go of the boxer briefs, and stood straight and looked down at the large yellow cartoon man with the letters *Who loves yah, d'uh* beneath his boxer-clad dancing self. There were red hearts surrounding the dancing figure. '*Ngati-baye*,' he said, and they moved off, down to Golden Quarry Road and turned right in the direction of Warren Park.

That afternoon came the rain for which farmers had looked out with anxious eyes, for which penitents in white garments in all the shaded places of the country had prayed in the heat of that baking December. It swept in from Chimanimani and Chipinge, delighting fleet-footed children who danced it a welcome and sang *mvura naya naya tidye mupunga* before the deluge got too much for them and they rushed laughing back to their mothers' huts.

The rain moved across the Eastern Highlands in a force of hail and winds that burst across the breadth of Mashonaland and reached Harare with a steady hardness that converted the city's gaping potholes and craters into smooth-surfaced ponds. At the corner of Park Lane and Julius Nyerere Street, just next to the National Art Gallery, the forty-one-year-old driver of a ten-year-old Nissan Hardbody truck drove into one such disguised crater and there met his death. And at Golden Quarry, the December rains beat down over the body of the man who had been Gabriel Makonyera in its Homer Simpson boxer shorts, lying among the discarded things of Harare, his eyes staring sightlessly at the pouring skies above. He would be missed and searched for, his name announced on all the radio stations, and his name in all the papers. For every day of her life until she died, his mother would say fifteen rosaries for his return. He would be found when the flesh had fallen from his bones, but not a single voice would mourn his passing, for in this state, he was just another of the nameless, faceless dead.

CRIMINAL

Religion is the sigh of the oppressed creature,
the heart of a heartless world, and the soul of
soulless conditions.

– Karl Marx –

'The President Always Dies in January'

Therefore is judgement far from us, neither doth justice overtake us: we wait for light, but behold obscurity; for brightness, but we walk in darkness.

– The Book of the Prophet Isaiah –

Naizozo kururamisirwa kuri kure nesu, nokururama hakusikiri kwatiri; tinotsaka ciedza, asi, tarirai, rima bedzi; tinotsaka kubginya, asi tinofamba pakasiba.

– Buku yaMuprofita Isaya –

Lying on a black leather couch in a small, overfurnished flat on Dunstable Road in Luton is a man called Fortune Mpande whose attention moves between four screens: an iPad, a 40-inch Philips TV screen playing a football match, a Sony Vimeo laptop and a Samsung Galaxy phone. The sound on the television is muted. The Mulemena Boys and Fortune's favourite band, Mokoomba, play in rotation from the iPad. It is Fortune's day off and this is his downtime. Fortune makes his living caring for Britain's ageing population.

Work in care homes is poorly paid but requires rich reserves of patience and unfailing good cheer, something that Fortune, the public Fortune anyway, possesses in abundance. At the care home, they consider him a quiet and useful member of staff. He volunteers for extra shifts; he has patience with the patients. They love his accent.

Like Mokoomba, Fortune is from the resort town of Victoria Falls, and that by the way, is how the resort town of Victoria Falls is always prefixed in news reports, by the words 'the resort town of', as though the whole town is on a permanent holiday. Though he is from the resort town of Victoria Falls, Fortune was taught in Bulawayo, which means that he says cattley for cattle, littley for little, wiggley for wiggle, brittley for brittle. Sometimes he exaggerates his accent for effect. They also love his name at work and they love punning on his name. We are fortunate to have Fortune, they say, what good fortune to have Fortune, such fortune!

Away from the care home is this private Fortune who lies prone on his black leather couch in a studio flat in the least salubrious part of Luton. His entire life is in this one room. He lives out his life before the screen. He bought all his top-end gadgets on credit. His successful asylum application means that he is now a refugee.

He is aware of the public view of asylum seekers and refugees. They are a burden on the state, they come to get our jobs. But in the ten years that Fortune has been in Britain, he has not met one single British care-worker, not one native, and what the natives will never know is that asylum, this safe harbour is, in effect, a prison.

He longs to travel to the United States or Europe, but his passport marks him because its cover states that it is a Travel Document (Convention of 28 July 1951). The document does not say refugee but it is clear enough what he is, and because it is not machine-readable, he has had to wait sometimes for as long as six hours while they checked him over.

He cannot go back home. If he does go back home, it will automatically disqualify his status because it will be a clear demonstration that he no longer needs asylum. So he leaves the country once a year, each time being stopped for six hours on leaving and re-entering the United Kingdom. He leaves only because he wants to see his mother and three sisters, and so he takes a plane to Livingstone, on the Zambian side of the thundering waters of the Zambezi and they come over to him from the resort town of Victoria Falls.

He had tried to invite them to see him once, but they had been thwarted by an official at the UK embassy in Pretoria who had turned down the application with the terse statement: 'I am not convinced that you will return if you are granted the right to enter the United Kingdom.' The official had misspelled his mother and sisters' names on the form.

Thus it was that Fortune was not able to leave the United Kingdom to go home to bury his father. Nor did he have the heart to fly down to Livingstone just to sit while on the other side, in the resort town of Victoria Falls, they were burying his father without him. He had sent money for his father's coffin, mourned his father on Facebook and consoled his mother over the telephone.

His sedentary lifestyle means that Fortune is well on the way to being overweight. He lives on processed food from Aldi and on social media. His favourite forum to troll is GreatZim.Com, where he is an active and permanent member of the Political Commentariat.

On that website, he has three alter egos that he uses as sock puppets. First, there is Nyamaende Mhande, a name taken from one of the Mutapa emperors, whose avatar consists of a picture of the Zimbawe Ruins superimposed on the flag of Zimbabwe. As Nyamaende Mhande, Fortune campaigns for the restoration of the Mutapa Empire. Because Nyamaende Mhande is Conscious with a capital C, Fortune spells Africa, not with a C but with a K.

Then there is Rhodesian Brigadier. His avatar is the Birchenough Bridge; a bridge over the River Save that when built was hailed as a spectacular feat of Rhodesian engineering. Across the bridge are the first words of the old anthem, 'Rise O Voices of Rhodesia'. It is Rhodesian Brigadier who riles people the most because Rhodesan Brigadier does not hesitate to remind people of the glories of Rhodesia and the failures of Zimbabwe. When Fotune is in a more playful mood, Rhodesian Brigadier will light up the Forum with one joke after the other.

Fortune also occasionally uses both avatars to fan divisions on ethnic lines. 'Ah, these murderous Shona, these mice-eating, ignorant fools,' Rhodesia Brigadier will write beneath a story about a man called Wonder who is said to be haunting Gokwe until his killers are caught. 'Look at them with their nonsense and goblins, the murdering bastards. They should just shut up and eat mice.' On a story about a *hwindi* from Bulawayo, who was subjected to mob justice after being accused of stealing a phone, as Nyamaende Mhande, he writes: 'Serves him right. These fellows always travel with knives. A knife for a knife, I say.' Fortune prides himself on being an equal opportunity offender.

His ventriloquism extends to female impersonation: he is also a commentator called Amai Bhoyi and here his avatar is a woman on her hands and knees with a large bottom invitingly offered to the viewer while she gives a knowing sideways wink. As Amai Bhoyi, he uses a caustic female voice to insult any woman who makes the news for any reason. Her most frequent comment for any woman in the news, whether for good or bad things, is always the same: '*Haiwawo, kushaya anokwira uku*, she just needs a good screw.' Amai Bhoyi's comments receive many more upward ticks of approval on the site than the other two avatars combined.

So popular has Amai Bhoyi become that Fortune has parlayed the character into her own blog, www.zvekwaamaibhoyi.com, where he writes long and inventive stories in Tonga, Ndebele and Shona about her sexual exploits. Here his degree in African Languages from the University of Zimbabwe really comes into its own.

In this iteration, Amai Bhoyi is a sexually rapacious, permanently available and ravenous woman who has sex with just about every man she meets. There is Amai Bhoyi, in her church uniform, pleasuring the Deacon. There she is, polishing the floor on her hands and knees when she is surprised by her gardener; there she is in the backseat of her car, paying her way out of a spot fine with the aid of an able constable; there she is, demanding payment in kind from her lodger and there she is, cross-border trading at the Beitbridge border post, subjecting willingly slash unwillingly to an intimate body search from two customs officials. '*Ah nhai vakuwasha, mungabva mabata ipapo!*' she faux protests.

There is something particularly raw, he finds, about writing sex scenes and fantasies in languages other than English. The words he uses are words that are never written down, they are words spoken in raucous laughter in pubs where the only women in attendance are hookers, so every time that Fortune writes them, he gets a thrill, almost like he expects his mother to reach out from the resort town of Victoria Falls to whack him across the head for even thinking such words. So popular is the website that he has half a mind to find online collaborators to help him expand Amai Bhoyi's exploits to the fifteen written languages in the country's constitution. He will of course, have to exclude the sixteenth, Sign Language.

Or perhaps not.

Of all the things that Fortune thought he would do with his degree, this is the last thing he imagined. In a previous, and better, life, he had been a popular radio personality on his way to becoming a national legend. He had worked at the Zimbabwe Broadcasting Corporation studio at Pockets Hill in Highlands where he was one of the most popular newscasters on Radio Zimbabwe. His nickname was Zikomo, taken from his signature ending, in Nyanja, 'Zikomo, zikomo kwambili,' thank you so much. He was also well known for the seven languages in which he greeted listeners: Ndebele, English, Kalanga, Bemba, Nyanja, and Shona ending in his native Tonga: 'Salibonani mahlabezulu, good morning listeners, mamuka sei vateereri, momuka tjini bawilili, muli bwanji, muli bwino, mwapona!'

The national broadcaster had been his dream since childhood. In his childhood home in the resort town of Victoria Falls, he had grown up to the sound of the radio. He could tell the name of a song just from its first bars. The people he admired were the radio personalities, Kudzi Marudza and John Matinde, Peter Johns and Noreen Welch, Colin Harvey and Tsitsi Vera, Barney Mpariwa and Simon Parkinson. He could imagine no greater joy than to go to work to talk about music in all the languages that he spoke.

That is what he did. After he specialised in African languages at the UZ, he had gone straight to work for the Voice of Zimbabwe. He woke up every morning to go to work and talk about Lovemore Majaivana, and James Chimombe and George Pada. Then before going home, he stopped at his local, the Oasis, the bar that was a small patch of Bulawayo in the Bambazonke land called Harare.

Fortune turns his thoughts from the past back to GreatZim. com where he reads that in Harare, the weekly Politburo meeting of the ruling party has been postponed. Of course it has been postponed, he comments on the forum as Rhodesian Brigadier, the news from Asia is that the president delayed his flight home because of a medical emergency. Only he does not use the term president, he uses a term of insult so grossly offensive that if he used it on his home soil it would have made him guilty beyond a reasonable doubt of the crime of 'Undermining the Authority of or Insulting the President' and thus liable to a fine not exceeding Level Six or imprisonment for a period not exceeding one year or both, as stipulated in Section 33 of the Criminal Law (Codification and Reform) Act, Chapter 9:23.

'Nasala neka ine mama, nasala neka ine mama. Nichite bwanji ine mama, nichite bwanji ine mama.' Mokoomba's beautiful wail makes him turn up the music. 'Insulting the president' is a specialisation of all of Fortune's three avatars. He has not forgiven the president and his government for starving ZBC of funding while they insisted that journalists spread ruling party propaganda.

Before he left, Fortune had been moved from music to news on the Voice of Zimbabwe, where he had worked for a full year without being paid. Working in news meant reading no news at all, but pure propaganda, all to elevate the man they were forced to call, not just the president, but the President and Head of State and Government and Commander-in-Chief of the Armed Forces.

After a particularly ambitious parliamentarian had said the president could not be compared to a mere mortal but was 'God's Other Son', Fortune and his best friend Gabriel Makonyera had combined his official title with this new one and added the self-bestowed titles of Idi Amin and Emperor Bokassa to style him: 'President and Head of State and Government and Commander-in-Chief of the Armed Forces, Lord of All the Beasts of the Earth and Fishes of the Seas, the Thirteenth Apostle of Jesus Christ and God's Other Son.'

It outraged Fortune that they used him and his colleagues in this way but were so contemptuous of them that they did not bother to pay them. In a calculated act, he had read an unedited version of the news, had made headlines for being fired, had spent two nights in the cells, and on his release, borrowed money and, with the news reports of his dismissal and arrest safely in his suitcase, had headed straight to the United Kingdom to the safe harbour of asylum.

Gabriel Makonyera had also done the same thing, but on television. Gabriel had also left, but no one seemed to know where. Fortune had come to suspect that Gabriel Makonyera had simply become one of the Disappeared. The responsibility bore heavily on him, because the idea to read the undoctored news had been his. When thoughts of Gabriel came to his mind he dealt with them by simply putting them out of his mind.

Fortune had hoped for greater things on his move to London, like working for the African Service of the BBC. But the closest he had come to that dream was to get a job with a company that cleaned offices at Bush House. He then waited on tables here and there, cleaned this and that office, all while living in a two-bedroom flat shared by eight other Zimbo men in Woolwich. They quarrelled over cleaning the kitchen; they stole his food. They brought in their girlfriends and relatives without asking. At one time, the flat had been so full that Fortune had spent a week sleeping in the bathtub while listening to the sounds of furtive copulation from the next room. In Woolwich, he had lived worse than he would have in any township in Harare.

The only secure work he could find was care work, and that is what he did now. To add insult to Fortune's injury, the president had made caustic comments about how all people who had fled Zimbabwe were nothing but British Bottom Cleaners, only good for wiping the bottoms of white people. Until that comment, Fortune had been willing to live and let live. He had left the country after all, he was making a living, such as it was. He was able to pay his mother's living expenses and for the education of his sisters.

Whatever happened out there was not his problem any more. To use an expression he first heard from a chap called Dave pronounced Dive, who had waited tables with him and had surprised him by not only by being gay but also normal and actually funny: 'It's not my circus, mate, not my circus, you know wha'I'mean? Not my circus, not my monkeys, mate.' That had been his attitude, live and let live, not his circus, not his monkeys, but that statement about British Bottom Cleaners had been to him an outright declaration of war.

It seemed to him that the president had come to his house, ordered its destruction then pissed all over the shattered bricks and glass before laughing at his wailing grief. As though anyone would leave Zim willingly to do this work. As though anyone would voluntarily leave the job for which they had been trained, never seeing their families and sleeping in a bathtub. As though anyone would want to move from Harare or the resort town of Victoria Falls to live in Luton, a town described in a survey he had read as the bit of Syria that Assad does not want to control, the town at the end of humanity whose only redeeming feature was that its one motorway, three railway stations and airport allowed escape. As though anyone actually aspired to be paid next to nothing to be a British Bottom Cleaner. It had been a cruel jibe that had exposed the heartlessness of the inner man. The insult had cut deeply.

Fortune entered the fray. He became a warrior using the only weapons he had at his disposal. The rallying cry of the Second Chimurenga, the war against the settler regime had been: *Tora gidi uzvitonge*: Pick up the gun and determine your own fate. Fortune's rallying cry along with his rowdy comrades in the new Chimurenga, which, on Twitter they call the Twimurenga, was *tora* keyboard *uzvitonge*, *tora* unlimited broadband *uzvitonge*, *tora* Photoshop *uzvitonge*. With these three weapons, Fortune became an Avenging Crusader and Keyboard Warrior.

The Dare reTwimurenga believed the Revolution would be tweeted, Facebooked and social forumed. They took it in turns to man the Twitter feed of the country's cantankerous Information Minister. They are on the clock for every hour of every day, working in shifts to mock and pour scorn on his facile attempts to defend the increasingly hapless president: he did not read the same speech twice, he merely emphasised it. He was not sleeping in public, he was merely nodding in agreement. He did not actually fall, he attempted to break his fall.

Fortune and the Keyboard Warriors had drawn blood when the president suffered a humiliating fall on the carpet at the airport. They Photoshopped him into patently ridiculous situations. There was the president doing the Pasodoble on *Strictly Come Dancing;* there he was, running from the truncheons of his own riot police, there he was, high on a broom in mid-air, facing Gryffindor in a Quidditch match; there was the president on a surfboard, California dreaming while hanging ten, surfing USA, and there he was on the moon's surface, arm-in-arm with Neil Armstrong, one small step for man, one giant leap for mankind. Revenge, Fortune believes, is a dish best Photoshopped.

Rhodesian Brigadier and Amai Bhoyi chime in to agree with Nyamaende Mhande. They have heard the same thing. The president collapsed. Other posters chime in so that by the time three hours have passed, Fortune does not need to support the rumour with his own sock puppets. The story is now feeding on itself, and growing as it feeds.

Fortune sings along to the Mulemena Boys as he types. *Ina'nga yati ye, umuti wafyashi, in'anga yatimishila yamukowe in'anga yeti le, imishilo yamikole ati tiye kuchipatala, umuti wabu fyashi, ati mai vali bwino.* Turning away from the forum, Fortune entertains himself by typing a new Amai Bhoyi story. There she is, Amai Bhoyi, pleading with the man about to cut off her electricity and offering herself as a bribe. By the time Amai Bhoyi has her electricity reconnected, the news is now the top thread on the column: LATEST FROM ZIM, PRESIDENT COLLAPSES!!

Fortune looks at the time. It is 6 p.m., and it is time to begin his evening shift. He whistles as he showers and dresses. In his neat ironed care work uniform, he is again the Public Fortune, the one who has patience with the patients. What good fortune to have Fortune!

As Fortune puts in his hours, all around the world, in every city where Zimbos have taken refuge, in every city on every continent, there is an ecstasy of typing on Twitter and Facebook and WhatsApp, in Washington and London, in Helsinki and Geneva, in Johannesburg and Gaborone, in Dallas and back in Luton, as his countrymen and women across the world join to discuss the horizons that are revealed by this news. Text messages flash from Johannesburg, and Leicester, Slough and Scotland. The news is debated in forums on every website: on ZimOnline, ZimDaily, ZimUpdate, ZimNews,

ZimSituation, ZimPanorama, ZimObserver, ZimTimes, ZimNow, ZimThen, ZimForever, RememberRhodesia.com.

The president gets progressively worse with each report. By the time that Fortune goes home to collapse in exhaustion at the end of his shift, the president is dead. In Manchester, a man called Tryson, who is of an entrepreneurial turn of mind, has to be convinced by his wife MaiKuku, that, money or no money, it would be in the worst taste possible to throw the party he is planning, a presidential death party with a cover charge of thirty pounds.

The news soon makes its way to international news channels, to Al Jazeera, BBC and CNN, only there the news is reported as what it is, not as a verified fact but a rumour of the president's passing, but it is precisely this international imprimatur that gives the news wings so that in Zimbabwe itself, the words 'BBC Reports President's Death' flash on Gift Chauke's mobile telephone at eight in the morning.

Gift Chauke is selling newspapers and airtime at Newlands shops, a few steps from Barclays Bank. He shows the message to his friends Biggie and Nicholas, whose business models see them as vendors and walking purveyors of everything possible. 'This cannot be true,' Gift Chauke says. 'Otherwise it would be in the newspapers.'

They turn to look at the headlines of the newspapers piled up next to Gift. Half the page of the *Herald* is given over to the headline that their already over-indebted country has secured yet another loan from China. 'More Mega Deals and Mega Loans on the Way.' As Fortune would say as Rhodesian Brigadier, has there ever been a country that has made so much of so little, trumpeting every loan as though it is a victory?

Nicholas fishes a cigarette from the upturned crate before him. On the box is a medley of his wares, cigarettes, plastic combs, and top-up cards that he sells to passing customers. Gift is about to say more when they see a man, portly and round-faced, approaching to buy a paper. For all they know, he could be a See-Ten. They are everywhere, the See-Ten, arresting people on public transport and in bars, listening on the street to punish those who would dare give their economic malaise a name, and that name, that of the president. They are often easy to pick out because they are usually the angriest-looking people in any crowd, ready, at any time and in any place, to get offended on behalf of the president.

They need not fear, for the man before them, who is called by his wife's sister Ba'mkuru'Ba'Selina, is not a See-Ten. He bears another kind of guilt. Six months ago, he forgot his phone at home, forgot that he had forgotten it, accused a *hwindi* in a *kombi* of stealing it, and the *hwindi* had been beaten to death at Copacabana.

The three talk over each other as they approach him. Biggie thrusts his wares at him and says, '*Ma*Chinese herbs *ese ari panoka m'dhara, ma*Tiens *zvese ne*fish.'

'Mapple *aya m'dhara*,' Nicholas says. '*Nema*grapes, *ma*pears *tinawo, pamwe nema*Afro combs, *ma*belts.'

'*Toita here* airtime *baba*,' Gift says. '*Kana muchida tinayo*.'

'No thanks,' the man says.

The three are not put off. They *nyin'inyira* around him, aggressively begging him to buy from them, all while making exaggerated claims about how bad things are for them.

'Just five dollars,' Biggie says, '*Kana yakawanda tinotaurirana*.'

'I said no thanks.'

'*Mhuri yafa nenzara*, please buy just one packet; it will help me feed my starving family,' says Nicholas. 'They have not eaten in days and days.'

'My mother is in hospital as we speak, please just buy something,' says Gift. 'If you don't want airtime, I have these windscreen wipers.'

It is a strategy that usually works because their aim is to irritate potential customers so much that they become actual customers and give in just to be shot of them. It does not work today. The man who is called Ba'm'kuruBa'Selina by his *muramu* ignores them, buys the *Daily News* from Gift Chauke and moves to the ATM at Barclays Bank where he joins a queue of seven people waiting to withdraw money.

Left to themselves, Gift, Nicholas and Biggie abandon their aggressive pleading and pass on the news of the president's demise to their WhatsApp groups, who in turn pass it on to theirs. Biggie catches a *kombi* to town and on to Highfield, where he delivers the news to Zodwa, Judith, Matilda, Ma'Shero and Shylet at Snow White Hairdressing at Machipisa. Amid talk of the death of Kindness, among the boy-cuts, and Rihanna weaves, the story of the president's death is fleshed out.

'He died, collapsed in the shower.'

'It was the first lady who called an ambulance.'

'But you know ambulances don't carry dead people.'

'It is true that he was ill.'

'He has been ill for months.'

'My son-in-law's aunt works at State House confirmed it. '

'My cousin sister's *muramu* saw him at that clinic in Johannesburg.'

'He had a coronary.'

'He had a wasting disease.'

'And it was prophesied by that man in Nigeria, that prophet *wezi*Afro, that this would be the year that it happens.'

And on they talk in Snow White Hairdressing, among the blow-dryers, the tins of hair gel, the containers of Dark and Lovely, the hundred per cent Peruvian hair made in Brazil.

While Biggie goes to Machipisa, Gift Chauke goes on to Mbare, where the news has already reached a group of unemployed youths listening to a new dancehall song: 'We see them through the eyes of Bob Marley, building mansions while we die of hunger. We see them through the eyes of Bob Marley, driving fancy cars while we push wheelbarrows. Only eleven per cent employed, with the eighty-nine of us just whiling away time.'

The news flashes on phones as the eighty-nine per cent huddle to discuss it. A youth nicknamed Chopper, a stalwart of the Grassroots Empowerment Flea Markets and Vendors' Trust Association, who is given that name not because of any violent tendencies, though he has these in spades, but because he loves the music of Simon 'Chopper' Chimbetu, overhears two of the eighty-nine per cent talk of the news of the death.

Chopper recently chased a woman called Anna out of the Mbare market, and he feels flushed with the success of his power. The two youths that have roused his wrath have put the small amount they have between them to buy one Scud of thick beer. They pass it to each other as they discuss the news.

'If he is really dead, then tight,' says the first.

'He was too old,' the second says. 'Really he was old.'

Nodding in agreement, his friend says indeed, he is just about the oldest person in the country. In anger at what he sees as their naked celebration, Chopper grabs their Scud and pours it to the ground. The youths retaliate with their fists. A fight breaks out as more of the eighty-nine per cent join in to attack Chopper who is soon joined by his comrades from the Grassroots Empowerment Flea Markets and Vendors' Trust Association, jobless youths whose main occupation, when they are not being empowered by empty promises, is to defend the president's honour by any means necessary. Policemen from Matapi police station drive up in a truck and round up seven youths including the two Scud drinkers.

'Arrest them, arrest them,' Chopper says. 'They were insulting the president. They said he is old.'

'But he is old,' says an officer. 'What is ninety-two years of age if not old? Do we not all wish we could be as old one day?'

Chopper says, 'They also said he was dead.'

'How is it an insult to say that someone is dead if he is indeed dead? Or is he never to die at all?' quips the same officer. 'Is he Jesus of Nazareth or is he just a mere mortal like you or me?'

'You are insulting the president,' Chopper screams. 'You said he is like you or me! You are insulting the president. You said he is a mere mortal.'

Chopper is locked up with the rest.

During the night in the police cells, Chopper and the other youths argue over Arsenal and Liverpool and in the process find they have a mutual antipathy for both Manchester United and Chelsea. By the end of their raucous night together, peaceful relations are restored to such a degree that the morning finds Chopper snoring in the dirty cell with his head resting on the shoulder of one of the Scud youths.

Constable Mafa, the joking policeman, wakes them by the simple expedient of throwing a bucket of cold water over their sleeping forms. 'Stupid fools, the lot of you. Go home and bathe, you are stinking the place out. Have you no girlfriends or something better to fight over? And don't you know that the president always dies in January? Then he rises to life again a week later in February. And have you forgotten about the president's testicles?'

The dripping youths look at him blankly. They are too young to remember that for years, it had been rumoured that the president's ability to father children had been a casualty of the armed struggle for their independence. This was definitively and resoundingly contradicted when he subsequently had children with the mistress who later became the Second First Lady, leaving them stumped, until the circulation of yet another rumour, that their Medical Marvel of a president had had his life-giving force returned to him through special surgery in China.

A few rational minds noted the absurdity of this; if indeed

the testicles had been reattached, they were surely not his own. Unless of course, said a caustic wit, Ian Smith had very kindly and thoughtfully kept the originals cryogenically frozen next to his peas and carrots, just for the eventuality that they would be needed for that special surgery in China.

In the evening of the second day after the nation's frenzied whispers of the news of the president's death, the news is denied by his combative spokesperson. Fifteen minutes of the nightly hour-long bulletin is devoted to shooting down the latest rumours, or contradicting the news in the remaining private newspapers. Those who cannot afford the private papers are left baffled by the rabid denials of stories whose genesis is not explained. On this night, the vitriol of the spokesman's invective is matched only by his inattention to grammar.

'The rumours of the president's passing and/or demise is nothing more than merely gossip circulated by those seeking to reverse the gains of our liberation struggle,' he says. 'One could doubt that there was a New Year recently, but you cannot doubt that there will be rumours of the president's death in January. Such malcontentious talk is the work of those detractors, sell-outs, malcontents and renegades who do not believe that the country shall ever be a colon again. The rumours have been engineered, disseminated, manufactured and/or otherwise concocted by imperialist forces and/or their puppets controlled from Downing Street.'

The denial has the unintended effect of confirming the news. Such is the national broadcaster's reputation that if it is to say that the sky is blue, people will look up to confirm that fact for themselves. But just three days later, Constable Mafa is proved correct.

The president is reborn.

His sixteen-vehicle motorcade is seen speeding into town from the airport, rushing past the rubble of houses destroyed by bulldozers in the last week. At the head are four outriders on motorcycles, wailing their bikes to clear the way. Then come two Mercedes sedans, a police car with flashing lights, four more Mercedes sedans, then the long black limousine labelled ZIM1 – with the windows darkened so that the Ozymandias within does not have to look upon his own works, this Mighty One, and despair – then two more motorbikes, followed by another Mercedes sedan, a small army truck filled with soldiers in camouflage carrying loaded rifles, and, finally bringing up the rear, an ambulance, the only one in the entire country that is guaranteed to be fully equipped.

Two nights later, the president appears on television, his wife beside him, a pillar of toxic elegance. In a voiceover, a reporter breathes that 'the president said he had the bones of a thirty-year-old'. Then another rumour starts, again, spread over internet fire and text messages and in whispers at the nation's street corners. The president is not, after all, ninety-two. He is, in fact, only seventy.

Washington's Wife Decides Enough Is Enough

Then Samuel took a stone, and set it between
Mizpeh and Shen, and called the name of it
Ebenezer, saying, 'Hitherto hath the Lord helped us.'

– The First Book of Samuel –

Zino Samueri akatora ibge, akarimisa pakati peMzpa
neSheni, akaritumidza zita raro Ebeni-ezeri, aciti:'
Jehova wakatibatsira kusikira pano.'

– Buku yokutanga yaSamueri –

The strained armistice in the fractious relations between Washington's wife and his mother was openly breached on the morning of the wedding of Washington's mother's brother's daughter Melody. The straw that broke the donkey's back was the contentious question of which of the women was to sit in the passenger seat of Washington's car on the drive from the house in Ballantyne Park to the wedding ceremony at the African Reformed Church on Samora Machel Avenue.

The battle lines were drawn just after the bride's departure for the church, which had been delayed because, in her ululating eagerness to celebrate the bride, an overenthusiastic rural aunt called VateteMa'Kere had stepped on the bridal veil, yanked it off Melody's head and dismantled the carefully piled up combination of real and artificial hair. The consternation that followed was soon over, VateteMa'Kere suitably chastened and – recoiffured, rearranged and consoled – Melody and her bridesmaids, who were resplendent in shimmering satin dresses of a particularly violent shade of orange, had left for the church in a flurry of perfume and powder.

The houseguests, all relatives close enough to the family to spend the night before the wedding at the bride's father's house, were to follow the bridal party. The cars for the bridal party – the parents of both bride and groom, and the ushers, in short, for everyone at the Top Table – was a fleet of Range Rover Sports hired for the occasion.

It had been arranged at the preparation meetings held by the family in the run-up to the wedding that the cars to ferry the rest of the guests would come from a common pool. The Transport Committee, headed by Melody's sister and Best Girl, Precious, had allocated the cars on the basis that the most senior relatives would get the most expensive or presentable-looking cars. Thus the five Mercedes Benzes available, the three Toyota Prados, four Nissan X-Trails and two Honda Civics, one of which was Washington's, were to take the most important family members from the house to the African Reformed Church on Samora Machel Avenue, then on to Pabani in Umwinsidale for the reception.

The second rank was to depart in seven inferior models belonging to the poorer sons-in-law. There was also M'zukuruTryson's Mitsubishi Pajero. The Pajero had initially been allocated to the first rank, but was subsequently demoted at the insistence of Precious. A week before the wedding, from her first-floor office at the Zimbabwe Tourism Authority in Karigamombe Building at the corner of Samora Machel Avenue and Julius Nyerere Way, Precious had heard a commotion of horns blaring from the street below. She had looked out of her window to see M'zukuruTryson's wife, MaiKuku, bottom straining against the red fabric of her skirt, pushing the Pajero up from Samora Machel in the direction of Julius Nyerere while M'zukuruTryson tried to jump-start it.

The family members who were unfortunate enough not to have their own cars and to live in the townships were to assemble at Market Square and crowd into five *kombis* that had abandoned their usual *Copacabana–Hatcliffe* and *Copacabana–Epworth* routes for the day.

The even more inferior branches of the family, or, in a word, the rural off-shoots, were to travel to Harare in a Hungwe Dzapasi bus that had been specially commissioned to ferry them to Harare. They had been ordered to assemble at dawn and wait for that bus at the Why Leave Guest House and Disco Bar, the bar at

Gutu Mupandawana Growth Point that was by owned Felicitas, the second oldest daughter of Melody's father's brother Vurayayi who was also the acknowledged Small House of the Member of Parliament for Gutu Mupandawana constituency.

There were some, like Melody's mother, who muttered that VateteMa'Kere, the ululating, veil-stepping aunt, should have waited for that Hungwe Dzapasi bus instead of hotfooting it on a Mhungu bus to Harare together with Keresenzia, her eldest daughter, and her two grandchildren four days before the wedding, but Melody's mother knew that this was wishful thinking. VateteMa'Kere may have been poor, she may have been rural, and she may have turned up announced with an oversupply of accompanying relatives, but now that she *had* turned up, they had to give her her due place as the most senior of the consanguineous aunts in the patriarchal line at the grandfathers' level.

She told long and detailed histories of every item of clothing she wore: who had given what to her when, what the giver had said to her on giving it to her and what she had said in turn. These histories sometimes segued into nostalgic reminiscences of what she called '*mazuva a*Smith', the time of Smith, where life was hard, she said, because Smith had a bad heart, such an evil heart and life was unjust but at least the bread was cheap.

She ended every sentence by exclaiming her daughter's name. It was her abbreviated way of saying 'I swear on my daughter Keresenzia' as an averment of the truth of her words.

'This jersey that I am wearing', she would say, 'was from the clothes that were part of VateteNyengeterayi's estate. She died just after independence, just imagine, so all she knew were the days of Smith. *Hoodenga Smith waiva nomwoyo wakashata. Takambogozhegwa novupenyu asi zvokwadi mazuva a*Smith *zvokurya zvaiwanikwa. Kana mabhotoro chaiwo aitengeka.* Keresenzia!'

'This *dhuku* that you see on my head is one I got from a white woman who came to give out donations when I went to Gutu Mission Hospital, *kwaMuneri kunopagwa meso*. She was wearing it around her neck and I said but it should be on your head and she said show me how to do it, and I did and she said you can keep it. Her eyes, do you know, they had no colour, no colour at all, Keresenzia!'

'*Aya matenesi aya*, these shoes on my feet are the shoes I got from Felicitas, do you know she is still with that MP but he will never marry her. *Achagarira guyo sembga* Felicitas, Keresenzia! I was wearing them the night that man died right in front of us. *Harahwa iya yokuveza mabhokisi, iya yokudzana yainz'aniko?* *Yekera*, Vitalis Mukaro. He was actually dancing with Keresenzia, they were the best two, Keresenzia was here, and he was there. Keresenzia was there, and he was here. Then he collapsed just like that, while he was dancing. *Hoodenga harahwa yaidzana iya*, that man could dance, *zvokugagwa zviya*, Keresenzia!'

'As for this *bheke* I am carrying, this was bought for me by Whiriyamu with his first pay, you know Whiriyamu, my middle son, *uyu wemagirazi*. He works in Bulawayo now, *ndookwato-tamira* Masvingo *yose. Hoodenga wavakutochisvisvina chiNde-vere ungatoti muNdevere wakazvagwako*, Keresenzia!'

Melody, Precious and their mother were particularly irritated because both VateteMa'Kere and Keresenzia had a seemingly insatiable appetite for fried eggs, sausages and gossip.

Particularly when they got on to the subject of MaiguruMai-Pedzisayi, there was no stopping them. MaiguruMaiPedzisayi had not only been VateteMa'Kere's detested senior co-wife to the same husband, but also, to hear them talk, a practised mistress of sorcery and witchcraft. She had been in her grave since Ker-esenzia was six, leaving VateteMa'Kere in sole possession of Ker-esenzia's father, but to hear VateteMa'Kere and Keresenzia talk of her, all the grievances might have arisen yesterday. *'Vairoya MaiguruMaiPedzisayi, vairoya.'*

And when MaiM'fundisiMukaro arrived the day before the wedding to make final arrangements about the placement of the flowers at the church with Melody, Precious and their mother, they had been interrupted by VateteMa'Kere's loud and firm attempts to toilet train her youngest grandchild. *'Dhota* Tapera. *Ndati dhota. Chitodhota izvozvi.'*

Keresenzia, who taught Fashion and Fabrics at Alheit Chin'ombe Secondary School, and thus considered herself an expert on matters sartorial, annoyed Melody by doling out unwanted fashion advice. 'It's all about matching, that is what I tell my girls, *zvokwadi mainin', mucheno kumecha.'*

She pestered Melody, Precious and the bridesmaids to buy the dresses made by her rural pupils. She had brought to Ballantyne Park an entire suitcase full of them. They smelled faintly of smoke and oil from old sewing machines and had high collars and long sleeves that would have delighted the heart of a governess in Victorian England.

'Hon'o, mugubvururu,' Keresenzia beamed as she held up a pleated and full-skirted voluminous horror in houndstooth fabric, 'but you can cut it short. I will cut it right here for you, *munongogurazve mainin', mogotoita dhuku nebhande. Munenge makamecha!'*

She used their things without asking. When it was pointed out to her that she had washed her children's sun-baked napkins using the bubble bath that Precious had bought on her last trip to Dubai, Keresenzia had replied, with cheerful wonder: *'Heya mainin'? Mati is'po yeDubai shuwa? Hes' mhani! Hamunzwi kunhuwirira kudai? Ndati haingava yomuno! Bva vachatihwa k'm'sha!* We will have to take it back with us so that others smell it too. *Zvokwadi gore rino vachamira ho-o!'*

The unexpected arrival of VateteMa'Kere was the reason for the altercation between Washington's wife and his mother. As no one had expected that VateteMa'Kere would come to the house, no seat had been set aside for her in the priority cars. In the original planning, Washington was to have driven his mother, her two sisters and another paternal aunt as well as his own wife to the wedding in his Honda Civic. That plan now had to change.

Of the four women to have been in the car, Washington's wife, who was a *muroora* and *mutorwa* and thus not an agnatic or consanguineous relative, was the most inferior of the four. Protocol demanded that she give way to VateteMa'Kere. It was particularly urged by Washington's mother that the troublesome aunt would sit in the back of Washington's car with the other women. This arrangement meant that, naturally, Washington's mother would sit where Washington's wife usually sat, in the passenger seat next to Washington.

It took moments to decide this without consulting either Washington, who was upstairs taking a shower, or his wife, that VateteMa'Kere and not Washington's wife, would go in Washington's car. And this was the core of the problem.

In the eyes of his mother and the family at large, the car belonged to Washington. But as far as Washington's wife was concerned, it was merely a matter of paperwork that labelled the car Washington's: it was his only because of the bureaucratic exigencies of the Vehicle Inspection Department. Only the issue of registration made the car his: that, and her inability to drive. As she saw it, it may have been a loan from Washington's company that allowed him to buy it but it was entirely her efforts that had procured it.

She had prayed night and day, loud and long at sessions with the Prophet Evangelist, a man of dapper appearance who promised prosperity with every tithe made by the members of his Celestial Church of the Power in the Blood International, Established 2012, and with the purchase of every pamphlet, DVD, CD, T-shirt and scarf.

'All you have to do,' the Prophet Evangelist had said to his congregation as he held up the scarves, 'is to buy one of these cloths with my name and face on them. I have prayed over each one. I have blessed them all. You buy one of these cloths for ten dollars each, you see a car that you want, and you rub its windscreen. Then you come back and you pray, always keeping this cloth with you.'

Washington's wife had bought a scarf and rubbed it on several cars. She had taken two *kombis* from their house in Ruwa to get to Sam Levy's Village to be sure to find the right kind of car. Then she had attended prayer sessions with both the Prophet Evangelist and his wife, the Prophetess. She had wheedled and needled at Washington to buy a car and prayed that the wheedling and needling would work. Sure enough there it was, a Honda Civic. It was not one of the cars whose windscreens she had rubbed with the Power in the Blood cloth. It was not a Mercedes or a Range Rover Sport, it was not even a Pajero like M'zukuruTryson's, but it was, incontrovertibly, a car.

To crown her joy, the Prophetess had touched her hands to her after her Testimony of Gratitude for the car she had received through the grace of God, had touched her with soft, gentle hands that knew only prayer, and given her the gift of a bumper sticker that said 'This Car Is a Result of Prayer: 2016 Is the Year of Results.'

The Prophetess had quoted from the First Book of Samuel and said, 'Shout "Ebenezer", for it is His grace that has brought you this far.'

Her eyes closed and body shaking in ecstasy, Washington's wife had shouted, 'Ebenezer!'

'For your God is a God of silver and gold,' the Prophet had thundered. 'Your God is a God of silver and gold. Of silver and gold, silver and gold, you worship a God of Silver and Gold.'

The Honda was silver.

On being told that she was to be in this car of prayer, Vatete-Ma'Kere gave a peal of ululation that landed in Washington's wife's ear with such a clanging clarity that it stunned her for a moment. She did not say a word, but simply turned and walked to the second lounge, where the bridal party had dressed. She picked up a discarded mirror and cotton wool ball and began, with deliberate slowness, to burst the pimples on her forehead.

Apart from VateteMa'Kere and her daughter Keresenzia, no one else thought anything of it. This was her usual way. In the middle of any gathering, particularly those where her mother-in-law held court, Washington's wife was known to pick up a novel and go off to read on her own whenever she felt slighted.

The younger relatives, particularly Melody, Precious and the other nieces, began to call her 'Miss Manchester' because M'zukuruTryson, who had been deported from England but lied to everyone that he was back because he was tired of the British way of life, had told them that the weather in Manchester, which he and his wife MaiKuku pronounced 'Men Chester', was more predictable than Washington's wife. Less charitably, Washington's mother called her MaininiKwindi or VaMasvanhikongonya, nicknames that mocked the way her mood just changed without notice. '*Kumudhura kani, MaininiKwindi vedu, kumudhura VaMasvanhikongonya,*' said Washington's mother.

It had been so from the moment she arrived at Washington's mother's house in the Chicago suburb of Kwekwe. As Washington's mother told the story, 'She came, just like that, very suddenly without warning in the middle of the night . . .'

'It was actually around eight, mhamha,' corrected her daughter, Washington's sister Winnet.

'Midnight, after eight, what does it matter. The news on ZBC was over, wasn't it? The news was over and I was sitting there with

Winnet going through my Planning Book, this year I am teaching dunderheads like you won't believe, *vanongoimba chinamira disappear vakamirira kukohwa ma*U. So different from Washy who passed just one time, with six As and two Bs, one for Shona, one for English. And I was sitting there just thinking *baba'ngu* Madyira *imi*, very soon the power will go out, and sure enough, just as I had said that very word, the power went out because it always goes after the news, it is the same all over Kwekwe even for us here in Chicago who are well up and there was a loud banging at the gate, and I said to Winnet, *nhai* Winnet, *zvatichapindirwa nembavha takam'ka*, and there was more banging. Winnet looked for the torch but it had no batteries, *ari mabasa a*Caritas it was all thanks to that foolish maid of mine because she forgot to get them. *Mazuvano vasikana havashandiki navo*, so she went out in the dark to see who was at the gate and there she was, all on her own, with just one bag and she said, I am pregnant, and it is Washington's, just like that, no how are you, no whose daughter am I, no nothing, she did not even sit down. *Ko, iko kungotushura-tushura mapundu pane vanhu?*'

As she had come to know her daughter-in-law's ways, Washington's mother found there were many things wrong with Washington's wife. Of course, no one could ever have been good enough for her First Born and One and Only Son Washy, the first person in his family on his father's side to go to university, but such a daughter-in-law was not the wife she had hoped for for her son.

First, there were the O levels, or rather, the lack of O levels. Washington's mother was a teacher of the Old School. She had been trained and taught in the time that VateteMa'Kere referred to as *mazuva a*Smith. Washington's mother would certainly have agreed with VateteMa'Kere's often-repeated statement that 'Hoodenga Smith *waiva nomwoyo wakashata, asi mazuva a*Smith *vana vaitsvunha*, Keresenzia!' For more than thirty years, Washington's mother had known the power of walking into a class to have the entire body of children stand up and chant 'Good Morning Mistress', before she waved them to sit with their backs straight, and, for the girls, their legs closed.

Washington's mother had firm and uncompromising views on a number of things, like fancy hairstyles on schoolgirls and haircuts with lines and patterns in them on schoolboys. She believed these hairstyles, together with Zimdancehall music, the introduction of the bottom-focused *kongonya* dance in Traditional Dance competitions at schools and the fact that children now started school at Grade Zero, without first showing whether they could put their right arms above their heads to touch their left ears, had a pernicious influence on standards. Taken together with the government's increasing censure of teachers who used corporal punishment, it was no wonder that the national O level pass rate had not reached thirty per cent in the last ten years. So Washington's mother disapproved of Washington's wife because she belonged to the failing seventy per cent: she had attained *nekunongera* just four Cs, two Ds and an E achieved over three sittings in two years. 'Can you believe she got two Us for maths in every exam?' Washington's mother said. '*Kutokundwa nesu ma*mistress *emazuva a*Smith?'

Being an unschooled girl, Washington's mother had expected her to at least make a greater effort in the housekeeping department. But though she was neat and tidy enough, and seemed to have an eye for order and organisation, Washington's mother considered Washington's wife's cooking abysmal.

To be fair, it was not that Washington's wife's cooking was bad in itself; it was mainly that she was unable to cook *sadza* to the exacting standard imposed by Washington's mother. The ability to cook the staple maize meal so that it was not too hard, too soft or too sticky was such a crucial test of womanhood that a woman who cooked all other dishes like a Michelin-starred chef but cooked *sadzambodza* would be considered not just a bad cook but no woman at all.

Washington's mother also took exception to the fact that Washy often cooked together with his wife, husband and wife slicing onions, tomatoes and chicken as they listened to Fungisai Zvaka-vapano, Shingisai Suluma, or Delta Chadoka and the Voice of God. '*Gore richitanga, richipera, tinoda makomborero! Anouya makomborero*,' they sang as they cooked. '*Inga Jobhu muranda, muranda waBaba!*'

Though the Catholicism she had taken on when she married her husband discounted Chivanhu, Washington's mother began to fear that his wife might have fed Washy an aphrodisiac that made him docile. And Washington's wife's languor sorely tested the energetic zeal with which his mother took on every task. Washington's mother believed firmly that any woman who was still in bed after six in the morning was lazy beyond redemption.

To the laudable qualities of the Virtuous Woman of the Book of Proverbs who rose before dawn, prepared the meal for the household, and who, like a merchant ship, brought food to her family, who girded her loins, strengthened her arms, planted a vineyard with the fruit of her hands, and whose candle goeth not out by night and was thus held as the model for the nation's daughters-in-law, Washington's mother added an extra quality: '*Mukadzi wemunhu ndiye anotomutsa jongwe.* A good wife is one who rouses the rooster so that it can rouse the household.'

Then there were the novels. Washington's mother simply could not understand how a woman who did not work had any business spending so much time reading. Perhaps if Washington's wife had loved her books enough at the appropriate time, which was when she had been at school, she would have hit them hard enough that she passed her O levels.

Washington's wife bought the novels from the boys who sold

them second-hand from the roadside pavements. They cluttered up the Chicago bedroom she shared with Washington, the Barbara Taylor Bradfords, Victoria Holts and Catherine Cooksons, the Irving Wallaces, Herman Wouks, Louis L'Amours and Harold Robbinses, cheap out-of-print paperbacks reclaimed from the detritus of dispossessed commercial farmers and the pitiful leavings of the estates of the white poor.

Then there were the allergies. Washington's mother did not believe in her daughter-in-law's allergies. She simply could not fathom how anyone raised in the township of Mbizo Section One could afford to have the kind of allergies that Washington's wife claimed debilitated her so severely. 'For heaven's sake,' Washington's mother said, 'her father was a miner who worked for Lancashire Steel. Where would the allergies come from?'

Rather suspiciously, the allergies seemed to operate in a manner that meant that Washington's wife could not use those things that her mother-in-law preferred. Thus Washington's wife was allergic to Washington's mother's favourite detergent, Cold Power. She preferred Surf or Omo. Washington's wife sneezed like fifty ancestral spirits were about to descend upon her when Washington's mother sprayed the air with her favourite Air Glade Pine Fresh air freshener. She preferred the Lavender spray. Washington's wife was not able to use a *mutsvairo* hand broom to sweep the house like a normal daughter-in-law because she was allergic to dust. Washington bought her a vacuum cleaner.

This was yet another black mark against Washington's wife. Washington's mother distrusted washing machines, vacuum cleaners and all labour-saving devices on the principle that any machine that worked that quickly could never do as thorough a job as the human hand, particularly, and preferably, if that human hand was female, and that female was Washington's wife. 'Allergic to dust, allergic to dust,' Washington's mother muttered

whenever she heard the sound of the vacuum cleaner. 'Pwallergic, pwallergic. Funny how she is never sneezing when she reads
all those Pavement Books of hers. She may as well say she is allergic to work.'

Finally, there was what Washington's mother referred to as
'This Church Church Business.' Washington's wife had managed
to persuade her husband to leave the Catholic faith in which he
had been raised and join her at the Celestial Church of the Power
in the Blood International, Established 2012. When she raised
This Church Church Business with him, Washington only said to
her, 'Mhamha, we don't want to worship idols,' and indicated the
Virgin Mary who sat serene in white and blue Dresden porcel-
ain, arms out in benediction, in the place of honour next to the
enlarged portrait of Washington's deceased father.

This Church Church Business meant that Washington and
his wife did not just go to Mass on Sundays like normal people
and confess sins that they sometimes had to rack their heads to
remember. They seemed to actually live in church. Night and
day they went to prayers. Unless they had to go to visit or bury
relatives, This Church Church Business meant that they associated only with their church people. It was one church wedding
and one church funeral after the other. It seemed to Washington's mother that Washington's wife had greater zeal in helping
out when it came to people associated with This Church Church
Business than she did in helping her out at home.

'This Church Church Business is enough to make you think',
Washington's mother said in the staff room, as she dunked pieces of bun into her chicory instant coffee, 'that they are the very
ones who raised Jesus from the dead while the rest of us were
busy manufacturing the nails and the cross that killed Him. *Shuwa vanoita sekuti isu vamwe tisu takatomurovera pamuchinjikwa!*
And since when has Maria Musande been an idol? Aren't idols

those golden calfs they had in those days, *zvaana* Baal Baal *zviya*? *Saka nhasi* Maria Musande *ndiye ava* golden calf? *Ngavatibvire.*'

The situation might have been saved with the arrival of the first grandchild, Tinomunamataisuwenyasha, which meant 'We alone worship a God of grace', a mouthful that just about managed to fit the First Name space on the birth certificate without leaving room for a middle name before being mercifully shortened to Tino. Washington's wife proved to be a competent and doting mother with a happy and suitably fat baby that gurgled its joy to every face, but even here, Washington's mother found something to criticise. Mother, it seemed, had passed on her famous allergies, and, horror of horrors, Baby Tino was not allowed to eat peanut butter.

This meant that peanut butter porridge, which, according to Washington's mother, was the only healthy breakfast for every child born on this soil, and many an adult too, was never to pass the child's lips. Washington's mother did not hesitate to express her deepest shock. 'Everyone knows that an early bowl of por- ridge is just what a child needs to settle the stomach in the morn- ing,' Washington's mother said. 'Especially if it has peanut butter. *Chirumbi chenyu ichi. Mwana wepi asingadyi dovi*?'

She considered it a personal slight to her own cooking; she particularly loved peanut butter. As a girl pupil boarder at Gutu Mission School, she and her classmates had invented a treat they called *chidoko*, peanut butter mixed with sugar. Her *mashakada* peanut butter rice was famous in the family, as was her *chim'kuyu chine dovi*, dried meat soaked in water to soften it then cooked in peanut butter sauce. Legend had it that Washington's Zezuru father had at first been disconsolate by the amount of bride wealth demanded for his Karanga wife, but having tasted these dishes, as well as Washington's mother's *mutsine* vegetable leaves with peanut butter and her mashed pumpkin *nhopi* with peanut butter, he had come to see that he had, in the end, not been unduly overcharged. 'If mhamha would have her way,' Washy and his sister Winnet often teased her, 'she would cook just peanut butter on its own but with additional peanut butter.'

The implacability of Washington's mother's resentfulness towards Washington's wife was matched only by that felt towards her by her daughter-in-law. Each woman was equally convinced that her place in Washington's life was more important than that of the other. Who was it who had birthed him, nursed him and educated him on her own after Washington's father died and left her with nothing but debt; who was it who had made him the man that he was today if not his own mother? But who, if not his own wife, had given him his first son, with many more to follow, who was it who knew him in a way that no mother ever could; who was it who had a present and a future with him that eclipsed everything in his past?

Things could have exploded quite spectacularly had Washington not moved from Kwekwe to Harare with his wife and child. Now, when they met, although they struggled to hide their mutual antipathy beneath a cold veneer of civility, enough had happened between the two women to give a frosty edge to every meeting, a barb to every compliment.

To Washington's mother's combativeness, Washington's wife responded with brittle defensiveness. She was practised in the passive aggressive way of talking called *kuruma nekufuridzira* where words of honey are dropped with just the right amount of poison. 'That is a nice new dress: it is so much better than what you usually wear.' 'Oh look at you, cooking such a nice meal. It must be nice to have some money for once.' And in response, Washington's mother would apologise for the definciencies of her house in tones of sarcastic humility: 'Such a pity I have so much dust and not enough novels. Or satellite dishes and DStv. *Ndimika vekuturika tumasamburera-samburera pamba.*'

Thus it continued, an uneasy ceasefire that did not acknowledge the war, a détente achieved without acknowledging that there had ever been any hostilities.

On the morning of Melody's wedding, when Washington's wife heard that his mother had volunteered Washington's car without first consulting its owners, and that she was to be replaced by Washington's mother in the passenger seat, she did not say a word. After she finished picking at her pimples in the second lounge, she walked to the upstairs guest bedroom where she and Washington slept, picked up *Hold the Dream*, the Barbara Taylor Bradford novel she was reading, collected the keys to the Honda, went out to the car, opened the door, sat in the front passenger seat, and read her novel. She would not let her mother-in-law get away with such a public humiliation. She would not budge, and was not budging for anyone on earth, not for fifty thousand rural aunts.

When she realised what had happened, Melody's mother went out to the car. From the locked interior of the car, Washington's wife looked up from her novel and glared out at her through the window. 'Did you not understand the arrangements?' Melody's mother said, as she knocked at the window. 'VateteMa'Kere and the others will travel with Washy. You can follow on later.'

'I understood them perfectly,' Washington's wife said through the open window, her eyes on her novel, 'but I am not moving.'

'But Washington's mother said VateteMa'Kere . . .' said Melody's mother.

'If there are those who want VateteMaiKere to go to Melody's wedding in a car,' Washington's wife said as she turned a page in her novel, 'then it would be a very good idea for those ones to buy their own car and not use other people's cars without their permission.'

She turned away from Melody's mother and focused her attention on *Hold the Dream*. Melody's mother threw her hands to the skies in defeat and walked back into the house. After a short consultation, a deputation of *vanyarikani*, the small group of the senior relatives before whom Washington's wife could not afford to be seen losing face was sent out. In their wedding finery, they knocked at all the windows and asked her to leave the car.

Washington's wife responded by raising *Hold the Dream* from her lap to face level in an ostentatious show of reading. To drown out the voices, she put the keys in the ignition and turned on the radio. It was pre-set to play Oliver Mtukudzi's 'Totutuma'. The celebratory song, a staple at all weddings, graduations and other occasions celebrating achievement, was to have accompanied the beeping horns and ululating women as Washington's balloon-festooned car moved in the long triumphal procession from the house to the church.

'*Rwendo runo wadadisa, inga watipembedza. Kupembedza dzinza rese. Dzinza rese rotutuma,*' Oliver sang as Washington's wife glared at the *vanyarikani* above her novel.

The *vanyarikani* surrounded the car and knocked at the windows.

'*Nhasi ndezvedu,*' sang Oliver's back-up singers. '*Itai makorokoto korokoto kwatiri. Wedu wadadisa.*'

'Open the door at once,' an impatient *munyarikani* commanded.

'*Haa, wandinzvaka,*' Oliver sang.

'*Wazvinzvaka iwe!*' agreed his back-up singers.

Washington's wife turned in her seat and completely hid her face behind *Hold the Dream*. It was at this point that a *munyari-kani* asked that Washington, who had been upstairs showering, should be called to come out to talk to his wife. On hearing what was happening below, Washington rushed to the car, he had had only time to put on a pair of trousers and receive a loud and heated explanation from his mother. With his hair still wet and trickles of water going down his back, he addressed his wife by her formal title, as the mother of his son. 'MaiTino, please open the door. This is embarrassing for all of us. Please, MaiTino.'

'*Hona muzukuru Kandondo, hona sahwira wotamba bopa!*' Oliver sang.

Washington decided to appeal to her not just as the mother of his child, but also as his best beloved. '*Bhebhi, sha,*' he said. 'Please *bhebhi*. Please, sweetheart. *Vhura* door *sha.*'

This appeal might have worked and the coming implosion been avoided had Washington's mother, who had followed Washington, not chosen that moment to say loudly, '*Bhebhi bhebhi chinyikovo iwe! Kujaidza makudo neanokamhina.* What sort of nonsense is this? What sort of daughter-in-law behaves in this manner? You would think she made that car with her own two hands, the way she goes on about it. *Kushaya anorova uku!*'

Washington's wife put down her book, lowered the car window, and said, '*Mati chii? Mati chii?* What did you say? *Kushaya anodini?* What do you know about whose car it is? *Mbuya yepi inotongera mwana imba?*'

So incensed was she that she opened the car door roughly, in the process almost hitting VateteMa'Kere who had come out to enjoy the spectacle. '*Washy, kana uchiri kuda nezvangu,* tell that woman not to address me ever again,' Washington's wife said to Washington as she left the car.

'That woman? That woman? Who is she calling that woman? Is it myself, the granddaughter of Bambo Mutimhoryo, Madyirapazhe? Is it me she is talking to? *Ini chaiye chidinhamukaka mhuru inobva muGona?* Myself, being called that woman by this woman? If I am your mother, Washington, you must tell your wife to watch her mouth or else she shall know straight from my mouth what it is that prevents the dog from laughing even though it can show its teeth,' Washington's mother said to Washington. 'She will know straight!'

'You can tell your mother that today, this very day, I spit on this ground in front of her and say enough is enough. *Pthu. Oh. Ndatopfira,*' Washington's wife said to Washington. 'Nonsense

mhani! *Handilikiliki munhu inini. Mbuya yepi inongoda kungo-
likwalikwa pese pese.* I suck up to no one. And you can also tell
your mother right now that I know what she did. I know. I know
that she tried to give peanut butter porridge to Tino. She thinks
I don't know but I know what she tried to do to my child. *Hee
dovi rinokudza, hee dovi, hee dovi kuri kuda kundidyira mwana.*
Enough is enough. *Handilikiliki munhu.*'

Washington's mother responded: 'Surrender, *bhazi rekwa*Mu-
sanhi! This is why I said my son is too good for the likes of you.
*Hee, ndini mukadzi waWashy. Hee ndine ma*allergy, *handigoni
kutsvaira nomutsvairo. Hee ini mukadzi waWashy ndine ma*allergy *saka ndinovata zuva rose.* Allergy pwallergy *iwe wakafuratidza
mwoyo wemwana wangu.* What did you give to my son that makes
him so docile, so stupid that he cannot see you for what you are?
Where have you heard of a graduate from university marrying
a woman who is not even good enough to be a housegirl, to be
someone's maid? *Seka zvako mwana wa*Denford!'

As she spoke, Washington's wife moved towards her mother-in-
law and gave her a ringing slap that knocked her bright orange
wedding hat from her head to the ground. Washington's mother
reacted with a thump to Washington's wife's chest. The two women
grappled with each other.

'*Kamani, kamani!*' said Washington's mother. '*Kamani!*'

'*Handilikiliki munhu ini,*' said his wife.

The *vanyarikani* found themselves in a position of the greatest
difficulty. The only way to stop the fight was to separate the wom-
en, but there was the risk of touching one of the women on a body
part or in a manner that was culturally inappropriate for a *munyarikani* to touch. They stood stupefied until Washington, praying
in his heart that he would not have to touch his mother inappropriately, seized his wife by the waist. As he grabbed her, his wife
kicked out and struck her mother-in-law in the face with her foot.

'*Kundikava ini*? Did you just kick me?' she shouted as she held her hand to her face. She made for Washington's wife but was restrained by a wall of pleading *vanyarikani*. Unable to reach her daughter-in-law, Washington's mother resorted to the only weapon she had in her arsenal. '*Ndinobvisa nguvo*,' she shouted. 'I will strip naked here in front of my son, in front of *vanyarikani*. How can you disrespect me so in front of my own son? I will strip naked.'

As the prospect of seeing his naked mother was even more horrifying than that of accidently touching her inappropriately, Washington, his arms still around his struggling wife, joined the *vanyarikani* as they pleaded for forgiveness. No, no, they said. *Pakonekwa, mhai, pakonekwa. Zvokwadi vatete mwana wakonewa.* So much wrong had been done, such terrible things said, there would be time for those who said what they said to redress it. *Nguva yokuripa ichavuya, vanoripa vacharipa, pashata pachagadziriswa, zvokwadi pakonekwa.* But whatever the wrong, the *vanyarikani* said, it was not right that a mother strip naked in front of her own son.

Not pleading with the *vanyarikani* was Melody's mother, whose chief characteristic was to take every single thing that happened to anyone and make it all about her and the success of her family. She raised her face skywards and wept loud sobs. 'What wrong have I done to anyone that I should deserve this? Is it my fault that we are a family that others look up to? *Nhai zvondoshinhirwa pamuchato womwana wangu* Melody! *Chava chitadzo here kuti ndine vana vangu vose vanongochatawo zvakangonaka*?'

Also not pleading was VateteMa'Kere, who had been enjoying the spectacle as closely as she could get without being in the path of attack. She shouted to her daughter, 'Get a blanket to cover her. *Tora jira mumba iwe! Kana zambiya rangu riya rekwa*Whiri-yamu! *Zvokwadi vachafukura.* Keresenzia!'

Her daughter ran to the fence that enclosed the swimming pool, and on which she had, just that morning, hung out to dry the blankets and sheets on which her son Tapera had urinated the night before.

'*Ndinomubvisira nguvo!*' Washington's mother shouted again. From inside the house came the shrill peal of the telephone. Sisi-Maidei, Melody's mother's maid came out and touched Melody's mother on the shoulder. 'Mhamha, it is the next-door neighbours. They said they have called the police.'

Furthermore, she said, a hysterical Precious has been calling for the last forty minutes to say the church was filling up and where was everyone. Melody was crying that she could not possibly get married without her mother there, it was all too much and they have been circling the church waiting for the rest of the cars.

'Now listen to that. The police are coming. You can't strip in front of me, Mhamha,' Washington pleaded. He tried to leave the scene dragging his wife with him. She chafed her resistance and shouted, '*Handiliki munhu ini! Ngadzibve tione hembe dzacho.*'

Close to a cluster of Elephant's Ear plants next to where the Honda Civic was parked stood VateteMa'Kere, clutching the urinated-on blanket and ready, at any time, to pounce and cover Washington's mother should she expose herself. Already, she was rehearsing in her mind just how she would tell this story when she got back to Bhasera.

Melody's mother gave up on the matter, brushed the tears from her face, picked up her hat and matching handbag, and, with her two sisters, headed to the Range Rover that was to have taken the Mother and Aunts of the Bride to the church before Washington's wife had decided that enough was enough. As they drove out, they passed a police car, blue lights on, heading in the direction of their house. Melody's mother closed her eyes and insisted that they drive on.

The police found Washington's wife still daring his mother to remove her clothes while Washington's mother still threatened to strip naked and the *vanyarikani* still pleaded with her not to dis-robe. It was left to Sergeant Mafa of Borrowdale Police Station to have the last word. Formerly stationed at Matapi, he made every house call he could in the Borrowdale area, and afterwards sent to the *Metropolitan* exclusive inside scoops on the scuffles of the well-to-do, for which he was handsomely rewarded. When the news of the scuffle made its way to the *Metropolitan* under the headline: 'WEDDING PARTY STUNNED BY STRIPPER GRAN', Sergeant Mafa was quoted as stating that members of the public are urged to refrain from using violence to resolve family disputes. Public nudity, he added, is encouraged under no circumstances.

Miss McConkey of Bridgewater Close

But he saveth the poor from the sword,
from their mouth, and from the hand of the mighty.

– The Book of Job –

Asi iye unorwira paminondo yemiromo yavo,
unorwira unoshaiwa pamavoko avanesimba. Saka
murombo unetaririro, kuipa kunozifumbira muromo.

– Buku yaJobo –

When I saw her yesterday, Miss McConkey looked vital and frail at the same time, like a cross between Doris Lessing and poor, murdered Cora Lansquenet in that Agatha Christie novel. She stood in the queue for the only cashier inside the Bon Marché supermarket that replaced the OK at Mabelreign Shopping Centre. I immediately thought of cake and porterhouse steak.

As often happens with sudden flashes of memory, the association made sense just half a minute later. 'You can bring Pearl she is a dem nice girl but don't bring Lulu. You can bring cake and porterhouse steak but don't bring Lulu.' In my mind, I was a child again and in the school music room, Miss McConkey's fingers were flying over the piano keys and we were singing that song. Miss McConkey was at the piano and a knight won his spurs in the stories of old. Morning was breaking, like the first morning, blackbird was singing and I was a child again and it was the Allied Arts competition and I sprang to the stirrup and Joris and he, I galloped Dirk galloped, we galloped all three and there was a whisper down the line at eleven thirty-nine and the night train was ready to depart.

She carried her head as she always had done, slightly tilted to the left, and her hair, all white now, was pinned into a large bun at the top of her head. When I was a little girl, her hair reminded me of Mam'zelle's at Malory Towers. Not Mam'zelle Rougier, who was thin and sour and never any fun, but Mam'zelle Dupont, who was plump and jolly. Her eyes, unlike Mam'zelle Dupont's, which were never still and sparkled and gleamed behind her lorgnettes, did not twinkle behind her round glasses. For all the time that had passed, I would have known her anywhere, and besides, you can count on all eight fingers the number of white people left in the whole of Mabelreign, from Sentosa to Bluff Hill, from Meyrick Park to Cotswold Hills.

She took an inordinate amount of time to get her things onto the counter, sugar, and pasta, tomato purée, a packet of onions and two cans of condensed milk, Mazoe orange crush, a loaf of bread, a crate of eggs, seven packets of candles and three packets of Pedigree Pup pet food.

'That will be five billion three hundred million and six hundred thousand dollars,' the cashier said.

She took out four bricks of notes, unpeeled some from one and handed over the rest. The cashier took the bands off the bricks and put the money through a money counter. When the whirring sound stopped, and the red button blinked to indicate the amount, the cashier said, 'It's short by five hundred million.'

'That can't be,' Miss McConkey said. 'Your machine must be broken.'

The cashier counted out the money, spreading the notes in little heaps of billions and millions across the counter. By now the line of shoppers holding their shopping, mainly the packets of candles that had been rumoured to be available only at the Bon Marché in Mabelreign, were murmuring mutiny. The counting continued. The machine was not broken.

'Do you have enough?' asked the cashier.

'What?' said Miss McConkey.

The cashier scowled and sighed and said, 'Money. Do you have enough money?'

'More money,' Miss McConkey said.

'Par*don*?' said the cashier.

'More, not enough. Have you more money is what you should say.'

'Have you more enough money?' the cashier said loudly.

'There is no need to shout like that,' Miss McConkey said. 'Wait.'

She rummaged in her bag to find the notes she had unpeeled. As she fumbled with it, the bag fell from her hands, spilling its contents to the floor, keys, dirty handkerchiefs, old dog biscuits, two more packets of candles, biltong dog treats and two boxes of matches. The security guard who had been watching from the door moved over to the cash register. On his nametag was the name Boniface.

He picked up the candles, matches and the dog treats and shoved them in Miss McConkey's face.

'What is this, Medhemu?' he demanded.

Miss McConkey looked at him and blinked.

Behind her the muttering rose.

'You come with me, Medhemu,' he said. 'You come with me right now. Come, Medhemu, come.' His manner and voice were a mix of obsequiousness and officiousness.

'*Kanotofidha imbwa mari kasina*,' said a voice behind me.

When Miss McConkey did not move, he grabbed her arm as though to drag her off. I moved forward to the security guard. 'I know her,' I said to him in Shona. 'She is very confused, she does not know what she is doing half the time.'

The security guard looked doubtful. I repeated myself, and added that she was always doing this, but not to worry, I would pay for everything. His anger melted before my authority. He gathered up the rest of her things, even the dog biscuits, put the pilfered items before the cashier, and said to Miss McConkey, 'Have a nice day, Medhemu, thank you for shopping at Bon Marché.'

If she was confused by this turn of events, Miss McConkey did not show it. In English, I said to her, 'I would be very happy to help you pay for your groceries.'

'No, thank you,' Miss McConkey said without looking at me.

'Miss McConkey,' I said.

She looked at me then.

'You live on Bridgewater Close,' I said. 'At number seventeen. I know your house, and I can always get the money later.'

I ignored the mutters coming from behind me and continued, 'You were my headmistress at HMS Junior.' Then I told her my name. She looked blank. When I realised that I had given her my real name, I told her my school name, the name that she had insisted I should use to make it easier for my white teachers and schoolmates to call me, creating for me two identities, one for home, and another for school.

'Of course,' she said. 'You were in Kudu.' She repeated the names of my brother and sister who followed me.

'You have a good memory,' I said.

I gave the cashier the money for the groceries and paid for mine. After a tussle, Miss McConkey agreed that I could carry her bags to her car. Her car was parked on the other side of Stortford Parade, facing the market and the church. It was the yellow Datsun 120Y that I remembered, the car that made my heart beat as I saw it drive past.

'I was not headmistress for long after you got there, was I?'

She looked straight into me, and I was a child again, but gone was the old fear that used to grip me when I thought that she must know that it was because of me that she no longer stood on the stage of the school hall, flanked by the Merit and the Dux boards, as all of HMS Junior, from KG1 to Grade 7Blue sat cross-legged on the floor and with one voice said, 'Good morning, Miss McConkey.'

✿

We were always the first at the things that mattered to my parents. So it was no surprise to anyone when my parents moved to Cotswold Hills, when I was seven, the year that Rhodesia opened up the residential areas that they had closed to black people.

My father worked for Barclays Bank in town. Our family was the first in the street to own a car, a yellow Citroën called *bambadatya* in the township because of its crouching frog shape. I was the first child I ever knew to get on an aeroplane, to the resort town of Victoria Falls, to see the waterfall and my father, who worked there briefly for six months.

For years after that, my mother kept the tickets stuck prominently in the photo album, next to a picture of us standing by the Air Rhodesia plane. When visitors asked to see the photo album, and they asked what the tickets were, my mother, in a voice that worked too hard to be casual, said, 'Oh, these are just plane tickets from the time we went to Vic Falls.' She made sure to call it Vic Falls because that is what the captain had said when we landed, 'Welcome to Vic Falls,' he said, 'on this bright and sunny day,' and she never called it anything else after that.

Shortly after the plane ride, but long after he bought the car, we moved out of Specimen and into Glen Norah B, to one of the smart flats that were a street from the township, where we were not the first to have a car, but we were the first to have both a telephone and a television. My father was not content to live in the African townships, in Mbare and Highfield, Mabvuku and Glen Norah; nor for him the African suburbs of Westwood, just one road from Kambuzuma, or Marimba Park, ten steps removed from Mufakose. On Sundays after church, he took us for long drives along Salisbury Drive and pointed out Borrowdale, Ballantyne Park, Cotswold Hills, Marlborough and Mount Pleasant, Highlands and Avondale, Bluff Hill and Greystone Park, places whose very names evoked wonderful lives that were closed to us because the Prime Minister had decreed that not in a thousand years would black people ever rule Rhodesia.

We moved in the year of the internal settlement. The houses were quiet on undusty streets. There were trees, flowers and lawns everywhere. There were green hedges, and low gates with signs on which a silhouetted dog snarled at a man with the words 'Beware of the dog, *bassopo la inja*'. Milkmen deposited bottles of milk with gold and silver tops outside, and no one stole them.

We no longer sat around the radio listening to our favourite show, *The Surf Show Pick-A-Box* where the announcer shouted, 'Fifteen dollars, money-or-box,' and the player responded, 'Box,' then the announcer said, 'Twenty dollars, money-or-box', and the player insisted, 'Box,' before finding that the box contained something disappointing like coackroach powder or shoe polish. Instead, in our living room with a fireplace and a maroon fitted carpet, we watched television adverts for Solo, the margarine for families with an appetite for life, for Pro-Nutro, the balance of nature, and Sunlight, for that fresh, sharp clean.

That Christmas, my parents had a party for all our relatives. My father danced my mother around and around while David Scobie sang 'Gypsy Girl'. All the guests cried *enko enko enko* so that by the time I went to sleep that night, I knew all the words to the song and the *tanatana tanatana tanatana* of the chorus wove its way into my dreams.

✿

In January I started at my new school, Henry Morton Stanley Junior School. Everyone called it HMS Junior. On the morning of my first day, I met Miss McConkey. 'I can't pronounce Zvamaida,' she said, as she wrote my name down. 'Has she no other name?'

As it happened I did have another name, my second name,

Hester, a duty name, named for my father's second oldest sister, my Vatete Hester Muponda who was to die of grief while I was in Australia many years later, just one of the many funerals I would miss. It was a name I hated. I was lucky, I suppose. Emily in Grade 3Red did not have any name other than Pepukai, so her mother plucked Emily out of the air of Miss McConkey's office. She sometimes forgot her new name and got into trouble.

I left Zvamaida behind in Glen Norah, and Hester took her place, a Hester who missed the old school, where the voices of children in unison could be heard chanting the twelve times table, or 'Sleep baby mine, the jackals by the river are calling soft across the dim lagoon where tufted rows of mealies stand aquiver under a silver moon.' I missed the noise and clamour of the township, and the made-up skipping games, with their invocations of 'Vasco da Gama, Vasco da Gama, Vasco da Gama Gama, Prince Henuri!', references that incorporated into our narrow lives the incomplete knowledge we gained of a wider world.

In March, all the five black children who had started school on the same day were called to Miss McConkey's office. A missing book had been found in the bag of Gary in Grade 5Red who was Garikai at home. One of us had been found to be a thief and a liar, she told us. She gave a long talk about standards, and when we looked down at our feet, in the manner of respectful African children trained not to look adults in the eye, she talked about the importance of not being shifty.

Gary's theft came to define our relationship to one another. Until more black children joined the school much later, among them my cousin Melody and her sister Precious, the five of us were linked by the hard fact of our colour, but separated by the greater gulfs of sex and age, and above all, by an urgent need to show that we were not all like each other. We wanted white friends because they had all the nice things we did not.

Their mothers knew to put different things on their sandwiches, like Marmite and polony and cheese, not just eggs, eggs and eggs. They went to South Africa on holidays, and brought back Smarties. They knew all the Van jokes and what you got when you crossed a kangaroo with a ball of string, what was black and white and red all over, what the biscuit said after it got run over and why the one-handed man crossed the road. For Christmas, they didn't get clothes from the Edgars Red Hanger sale that they wore to school on Civvies day, they got annuals, like *Misty* and *Jackie*, and the *Beano* and *Whizzer and Chips*. They got Rubik's cubes, and yo-yos, and Monopoly and Ludo.

They could hold their breaths for two widths underwater, and sometimes, like Evan Smith who later swam for Zim at the Commonwealth Games, for two lengths. They had their own hockey sticks, tennis rackets, and cricket bats, and did not use the old worn ones belonging to the school. Their mothers got their nametags from Barbours' Department Store; they did not sew them on with uneven hands. And their fathers' radios did not say, '*Ndikati nzvee kwaAmato wandiona*', or have the Jarzin Man's exhortations to shop at Jarzin '*kune zvekudya zvine mitengo yakaderera.*'

The only white children who befriended us, at least in that first lonely year, were the misfits and outcasts. Gary took up with Keith Culverton whose family was large enough to be African, whose two dogs were said to have rabies, and who often came to school dressed in the big shorts of his older brother. After Ian Moffat's mother came to the school and threw her shoes at the blackboard because her husband ran off to live with Miss Adamson, who taught Grade 5Red, Ian Moffat turned from the humiliation his mother's scene had caused him and became friends with Vusani. When Antonia de Souza dropped the baton and made Kudu come last at the inter-house race, no one would play with her because, said Tracey Collins, she smelled like a *munt*, ran like a spastic and besides, she was not really European, just Portu*guese*, so she talked mainly to Emily who had made Eland come first in the same race but was only given the shared cup long after we had forgotten that it was she who had led Eland to victory.

I had Lara, Lara van Tonder, the only 'Van' in a class addicted to 'Van' jokes, Lara whom everyone began to call Blubber after Mrs Crowther taught us about whales. She was too fat to run or swim and when she walked fast her breath came quickly in little hisses. Lara had mud brown hair. She wanted it to turn gold, like her mother's. Her mother was so thin you could see her veins under her skin. She smoked Madison Blue cigarettes and told me to call her Stacey and not Mrs van Tonder. She was a famous person, she said, she had been Miss Gatooma before Lara was born.

Lara liked me to brush her hair a hundred strokes in the school playground, and she made me count each one. 'If you brush it enough, at least three times a day,' she said, 'it will become gold-en, like Pauline Fossil's in *Ballet Shoes*.'

I did not believe this really, but I did it anyway, because Lara had a pool at home that she could not swim in, so she sat with her legs dangling in the pool. I loved the water, and it was like having my own pool. I dived in and out of the water, picking up five-cent coins from the bottom of the pool and I was happy because Lara and I were just like Darrell and Mary-Lou in Malory Towers.

✿

Miss McConkey lived two streets away from our house, in Bridge-water Close, and she often passed me in her Datsun 120Y. I made sure to straighten my shoulders when I saw her car, or when I walked past her house to take the short-cut home. One time, as I walked down Pat Palmer Owen Drive with no shoes on, enjoying the hard heat of the road under my feet and pretending that it was the desert at Omdurman and I was Gordon, I saw her car and hid in the ditch until she passed.

At school, I saw her every day at assembly, and in the corridors when she saw us walking in clusters she said, 'Single file, children.' Only in the third term, as Prize Giving Night approached, did I see her frequently. It was the school tradition, we were told, for HMS Junior to celebrate on that night the discovery of David Livingstone by Henry Morton Stanley. There was a poem that the school recited, a long and active poem in which there was a Livingstone and a Stanley, lots of concerned people in England wondering what had happened to Livingstone and lots of natives doing dances and naming all the places Livingstone had discovered.

The star was Keith Timmons, the captain of Roan. He was Stanley in an explorer's hat and declaimed, in a voice loud with concern: 'Oh, where is Dr Livingstone, Dr David Livingstone, who went away to darkest Africa to tread the track unbeaten?' Then twenty children, who were supposed to be the people in England said: 'We haven't had a letter for so long, perhaps we'd better send Mr HM Stanley, just to see if he's been eaten.'

'And sing with me in chorus,' said Stanley, 'while the natives do a romp-o.' The five of us, the five black children, were to be the chorus. In loud voices, we chanted, 'Nyasa and Zambezi and Cabango and Kabompo, Chambese and Ujiji and Ilala and Dilolo, Shapanga and Katanga, not forgetting Bangweolo!' We danced and stomped and beat our drums like our lives depended on it. Emily and I added a little flourish by trying to ululate like we had seen our mothers do.

'Well done, my girls, well done, my boys,' Miss McConkey said. We were the finest natives that the school had ever seen, she said.

✿

It was my uncle Gift who changed everything. He had fought in the war as Comrade White Destroyer, and returned with little patience for what he called diehard renegade elements. He worked in the Department of Youth Affairs and Employment Creation, and he told his boss about our poem and his boss called someone at the *Herald*, and Miss McConkey was in the news and then she was not the headmistress any more. There was another headmaster, a Coloured man called Mr Marchand and the teachers, said my parents, would not work under him so they would all go to the private schools like Cisi and Hartmann House or go all the way to South Africa. Uncle Gift said there was no place for people like that in the country, but my mother was worried about the white teachers leaving because she wanted me to have a good accent.

I was never called to Miss McConkey's office again. She was no longer headmistress but she stayed on, teaching the remedial class for the slow learners, playing the piano during music lessons, she stayed on until there were no white teachers left at the school and only a sprinkling of white children. I became so afraid of Miss McConkey that I took to going the long way home, down Pat Palmer Owen Drive and into Cotswold Way, and thus managed to avoid Bridgewater for the rest of my life at HMS Junior.

When I left to go to secondary school, she was still teaching the remedial class, never knowing that it was I who had changed her life forever. I did not see her again until yesterday, when I saw her looking small, frail and utterly defeated as she tried to steal two packets of candles and dog treats at Bon Marché.

*

I carried her bag of groceries for her and walked her to her car.

'Out there then, are you?' she said.

'I live in Australia now, Miss McConkey,' I said. 'I am a paediatrician in Melbourne.'

'How long are you here?'

'Two weeks, Miss McConkey,' I said. 'Actually, I am here for my cousin's wedding. She was also at HMS. Do you remember her?' I told her my cousin's full name.

'Melody, with a sister called Precious?' Miss McConkey said.

'That's right,' I said. 'You do remember everyone.'

'That's a name I would much rather forget, thank you very much,' Miss McConkey said. 'Precious. Silly name. I always thought it a silly name. A child is not a poodle.'

I thought she would say something more and waited, but she she got into her car.

'Silly name,' she said again.

She closed the door and said, 'You make sure you come and get your money.'

'Yes, Miss McConkey,' I said.

'Run along now, my girl,' she said.

'Yes, Miss McConkey. Goodbye, Miss McConkey.'

She started her car without another word, drove into Stortford Parade, past the Polyclinic that used to be the veterinary surgery, and past Wessex Drive. I watched her until her car, the same Datsun she used to drive, turned left into Harare Drive, the old Salisbury Drive along which my father had driven us a lifetime ago. I watched her until she disappeared from my view.

Anna, Boniface, Cecelia, Dickson

For I know your manifold transgressions and
your mighty sins: they afflict the just, they take a
bribe, and they turn aside the poor in the gate from
their right.

– The Book of Amos –

Nokuti ndinoziva kuti kudarika kwenyu kuzinji, vuye
kuti zivi zenyu zikuru, kwazo, iyemi, munomanikidza
vakarurama, munogamucira fufuro, muciramba
unoshaiwa pasuvo.

– Buku yaMuprofita Amosi –

If you come with me this way, east of Rotten Row, walk straight past Town House on Speke Avenue, cross the flyover into Julius Nyerere Way, walk past Robert Mugabe Road and stop before we get to Kenneth Kaunda Avenue, we will find ourselves outside the downtown supermarket that used to be called Amato. '*Ndikati nzvee, kwaAmato, wandiona!*'

They are long gone, the Brothers Amato, as are many of their brethren and indeed, there has not been a Bar Mitzvah here for more than ten years but that is all by the way. Nor does it matter what the supermarket is called now because we won't stay here long. Inside, we will see a young woman walking down the third aisle from the cashiers' bank, between the jars of baby food on the right and the plastic hair weaves on the left.

Her name is Anna.

No, she is not the tall woman pushing a shopping trolley. Nor is she the scowling beauty in the skinny jeans who is examining the hair weaves. That one is not Anna, her name is Deliwe, and we may return to her later. Look behind her. Yes. That's her, the small slight woman, not a full woman really, a newly made woman, just out of girlhood, with a brown cardboard box in her hands and a shifty look on her face.

Well, shifty in the eyes of the security guard, whose name is Boniface, and he should know. To his wife in their village in rural Gutu, on the dry, parched banks of the Nyazvidzi River, Boniface is the Manager of a Shop in Town, but to the Manager of the

Shop in Town, Boniface is just the Shop in Town's security guard.

If Boniface is to tell the truth, he will admit that there is not much training to be a security guard. There was a lot of marching though. As a trainee, he marched and marched around the security company's complex at the corner of Livingstone and Selous Avenue. He marched and shouted war chants and marched and did press-ups and marched some more.

Chengeta chikwama chababa chine madhora, he sang as he marched with the others. Boniface could march for Zimbabwe if he had to, yes he could. *Sabhuku marasika man'a haasonwiba!* Marching and marching with his head shaved bald. *Chenjera kunyengwa nerovha murima*! There was no correlation that he could see between his shaven head and his training, no reason why one was a precondition for the other, no reason why one could not exist without the other, but it was not his to reason why. *Marovha tawanda mbeva dzichapera*!

Before Anna entered the shop, Boniface's phone had pinged a message from his WhatsApp Church Group. It was the Bible verse of the day, Romans 1, verse 28: 'And just as they did not see fit to acknowledge God any longer, God gave them over to a depraved mind, to do those things which are not proper, being filled with all unrighteousness, wickedness, greed, evil; full of envy, murder, strife, deceit, malice; they are gossips, slanderers, haters of God, insolent, arrogant, boastful, inventors of evil, disobedient to parents.'

He has yet to encounter this catalogue of sin in any one person, Boniface, but what he knows without a doubt and this he knows without question, what he knows and knows full well is that he knows a shifty look when he sees one. As far as Boniface can see, Anna has just about the shiftiest look he has seen in his seven-year career as a post-marching security guard.

Boniface is particularly eager to prove himself in this job

because he was lucky to get it at all. He was recommended to the shop manager by a fellow guard who has risen up a little in the world. Until two months ago, Boniface had been the guard at Corner House, a building at the corner of Samora Machel and Kwame Nkrumah Avenue, where his job had been to man the desk and write down the names of people who came in and out, along with their ID numbers. So his job had been to control access to this Very Important Building, a job he took Very Seriously Indeed, particularly as A Very Important Embassy was in that building.

So seriously, in fact, that one Friday morning, at about nine, when a visitor to the building had come to him and asked, '*Shasha*, where can I find a toilet on this floor?' Boniface had looked at the visitor's dreadlocks and had smelled the stale smoke on his shabby clothing and shouted, 'So you came all this way from wherever it is you came from just to shit here in town? *Kutobva kwawabva zvako uchitosiya ma*toilet *eko kuti uzomamira muno mu*town?'

Alas, the man he had upbraided in such vulgar terms may have looked unkempt, but he had been a Very Important Person. The Very Important Person had made a complaint to the Very Important Embassy and it had made a damning complaint to the company that employed Boniface, and within a day, Boniface had been asked to hand in his uniform and the embassy cap. Here, in the Land of the Unemployed where security guards are two a Bond Coin, another had stepped gratefully into his old place. So Boniface is keen to keep this job, and keeping this job means Utmost Vigilance, and Utmost Vigilance means that he has to watch out for people with shifty looks on their faces.

Poor Anna does indeed look shifty, as you see, but that does not have anything to do with being in this shop over which Boniface has absolute dominion. She has no ill intentions at all towards the jars of baby food in this aisle, or the 100 per cent human hair made in Brazil, from Peruvian hair no less, opposite. She is only in this supermarket because she saw her greatest enemy walking towards her from the Mbare end of Julius Nyerere. So she had ducked into the shop to avoid coming face to face with the woman called Cecelia.

You may not know what it is to be hated, or loathed, to be disliked with passion or to have someone wish you gone from this earth in the most horrible way possible, and if that is so, kiss your beloveds and bless your good fortune that you are not like Anna. For she knows what it is like to be the object of the kind of hatred that comes from that corrosive combination of *godo* and *shaisano*, the poisoned mixing of envy and spite.

Anna is a Dollar-for-Two vendor. You may have walked past her before without really seeing her, and who can blame you, the City Centre being what it is. She sold traditional medicinal herbs for a dollar for two from the Robert Mugabe end of First Street. She sells *mushonga wemangoromera*, powder that you mix into a potion that will give you strength like the Terminator crossed with the Wolverine, and *vhukavhuka*, a male aphrodisiac that reputedly has Viagra-like properties and that translates as 'rise, rise'. It is so good you have to say it twice. Her most popular herb, though, is an aphrodisiac called *Weti yeGudo*, which means 'baboon's piss'.

You need not shudder in that dramatic way. If there is indeed baboon's piss in Anna's concoctions, it is in such diluted quantities that you would not taste it if you were to drink it. Even here, in the Land of Miracles, where Pentecostal prophets offer instant weight loss, and can add extra height to a person with just one prayer, where magical snakes spit out United States dollars complete with serial numbers that follow the sequence established by the Federal Reserve in Washington DC, and where haunted lorries sigh out loud, 'Oh I am so very tired' at the end of long journeys, baboons are not exactly known for even-temperedly pissing nicely into containers upon request.

Anna buys her baboon's piss from a man who claims to make it from the soil on which a baboon has actually pissed. The idea behind it is that a woman who uses the powder on her man will find that there will be no more cheating or skirt-chasing from him, no more giving other women lascivious looks, no more spending all his wages on the temptations of hookers and other good-time girls. Instead, he will piss only on her. Well, obviously we are not talking about actually pissing, but there is no need to draw a picture.

The Cecelia that Anna is escaping is also a vendor. Her stock in trade is pirate DVDs and CDs. When the municipal police did their raids just four months ago and moved the vendors out of First Street into Mbare Musika, Cecelia's wares had been smashed by municipal truncheons. The vendors have now been corralled into Mbare Musika where they are to pay a dollar a day to the Council, but in addition, they had to buy a ruling party card, as well as join the Grassroots Empowerment Flea Markets and Vendors' Trust Association, paying ten dollars a month for the privilege of being empowered.

Anna is able to meet her target, and actually exceed it, but on most days, Cecelia comes to the market just to stand. People just do not seem to want her pirated wares as much as they want Anna's baboon's piss. And no, they do not also sell, who only stand and wait. So Cecelia has seen Anna collect dollar after dollar for packets of baboon's piss. It does not help that Anna likes to remind herself how much she has earned by occasionally fishing out her takings from her bra and counting them over and over again, counting and recounting, licking her finger to the dirty notes to separate them while from the next stall, a dour Cecelia looks on with a sour face.

We will probably find many things on which we disagree as we go along, you and I, but we can probably agree that it is rather too much to expect the human spirit to rejoice without reserve at the success and good fortune of a neighbour, particularly when that neighbour has waxen fat, thick and sleek on baboon's piss.

Cecelia believes two things, firstly that Anna has a secret herb or something that gives her the power to make money. Maybe she even has something like a bushbaby limb. Cecelia has heard that the nocturnal and deceptively cute bushbabies are such powerful creatures that a person in possession of a bushbaby limb only has to declare what she wants and it will happen. Just like that. So Anna is probably using something like that, or a *divisi*, no, not a *divisi*, that is a lucky charm to make crops prosper without rain or fertiliser.

Cecelia also believes that she herself has a *munyama*, a bad luck that sticks heavily to her like a leaden smell. The combined effect of these two is to increase Anna's prosperity while decreasing Cecelia's own. Of course, you could look at it in economic terms and advise Cecelia that her *munyama* is nothing more than an unfortunate choice in the consumer product she has chosen to peddle in a saturated market.

Or you could look at it in psychological terms and advise Cecelia that if she laughs, the world will laugh with her. If she weeps, she weeps alone, because this sad old earth must borrow its mirth, but has troubles enough of its own. Sing, and the hills will answer! For the truth is that Cecelia's sharp tongue does not encourage people to linger over her wares, not to mention that Cecelia is unfortunately endowed with a cast of countenance that makes her look permanently bad-tempered, which, as it happens, she is, particularly when Anna is near.

Anna, on the other hand, is as effulgent as the lark on the wing in springtime, the only pretty ring time, when birds do sing, hey ding a ding ding. Sweet lovers love the spring! She is there first thing in morning, cleaning her stall and laying out her herbal remedies to look as attractive as possible. The minute she sees someone look her way, she is out there smiling and coaxing and singing the endless virtues of her products. She even has a loud recording that repeats on a loop the message dollar-for-two-dollar-for-two-

weti-yegudo-dollar-for-two, dollar-for-two-dollar-for-two-*weti-yegu-do*-dollar-for-two. But Cecelia believes it is just *munyama*.

The crisis had come a week ago. Cecelia had managed to sell a DVD that claimed to contain all of the *Twilight*, *Hunger Games* and *Fifty Shades* films on one disc, including two, *The Hunger Games: Doing Snow* and *Fifty Shades Raw*, whose existence would have come as something of a surprise to studio executives in Hollywood.

The DVD had cost four dollars and, in payment, the customer had given Cecelia a ten *yakabatana*. She had then asked Anna to split the ten-dollar note into smaller denominations so that she could give the customer his change. Anna had given her five notes, a five-dollar note, one two-dollar note and three one-dollar notes. Cecelia had then given back to the customer the five-dollar note and what she thought was a one-dollar note, but had in fact been a two-dollar note. So that by the time the customer had left and she had recounted her own money, Cecelia found that she was a dollar short.

'It is an easy mistake to make,' Anna said. 'The notes are so dirty that you gave away the two dollars in error.'

'The mistake is yours if you think I am a fool,' said Cecelia 'You think you are so superior, sitting there counting out your money then short-changing people when they ask for change.'

The ensuing quarrel had drawn a crowd of other vendors and onlookers. 'It was a mistake,' Anna said. 'Look, here is a two-dollar note, here is another one. Look, you can see on the front the president is different to the one dollar, and at the back there is a group of presidents. But if the note is very dirty you can hardly see them.'

A Form Two boy dressed in a George Stark High School uniform piped up to say, 'They are not presidents, actually, they are the men who signed the independence document in America. They are called the Founding Fathers.'

Cecelia had waved away the Founding Fathers as she insisted

that whoever they were, they were not on this note that Anna had given to her. The *povo* around her had various opinions. Some said yes, the money was so dirty that you can't see which one is which. Even where the money was washed, it was sometimes so frayed that you could barely make it out. For instance, this note was so caked in dirt it was hard to see which president it was, while others, led by a large-limbed tomato vendor called Ma'Nelly said, yes, that may well be but two dollars is two dollars and it is one more than one and if you have two dollars you will just know you have two dollars and you will not have the stupidity to confuse a one-dollar note for a two-dollar one. The general mood was summed up by a man who said, impatiently, 'Why do they even have the two-dollar note *mhani*, it causes nothing but confusion.'

A dreadlocked man called Jah T, who, in another life and another country, might have been a fiscal economist and not a roasted maize vendor said, 'Y'see, the problem is with the small denominations that circulate the most, y'see. They are the ones that cause confusion because they get dirty quickly. And of course, we can't recall the notes to destroy and reprint because it is not our money, y'see.'

Cecelia, mishearing, had flared up and said, 'What do you mean, it is not my money? Were you there when she gave it to me? What makes you so certain? Who are you, the school monitor *wepamusika*. Are you the market monitor?'

'*Une pamuromo iwe,*' said Jah T, 'I said it is not *our* money.'

Anna had attempted a pacific settlement to the dispute. 'Sorry *horaiti,*' she said in a conciliatory tone. 'If it was me, I am sorry. Here is your dollar.' But sensing the crowd was really on Anna's side had enraged Cecelia further.

'First you try to hoodwink me and rob me thinking I am a fool, then you show off and wave money in my face,' she said as she worked herself up into a passion. '*Musatanyoko. Handisi fuza ini. Kutopfuma nemaziweti egudo. Handibati zvemushonga.* I am a

Child of Christ. I was bathed in His blood. I am perfumed by his Grace. I am a Child of Christ.'

The Child of Christ had lunged at Anna. To the great delight of the crowd, Anna and Cecelia had managed to trade a few blows, scratches and ripped buttons before a passing constable had stopped them, broken up the fight and arrested them for causing a public nuisance. At Matapi Police Station, they had both been warned, cautioned and made to sign Admissions of Guilt for which they had to pay police fines of twenty dollars each.

Anna had fished out the money from her bra and paid it there and then. Cecelia had had to ask to call her brother, who had not come himself but had sent the money with his wife, Cecelia's sister- in-law, and their stepmother. The stepmother, the sister-in-law and Cecelia all disliked each other intensely, coming together only to form a triangulated circle of gossip about other family members. The two women had grudgingly paid the fine, but first, in front of the police and within earshot of everyone within hearing of Matapi Station, which meant a rather significant population of Mbare, they had upbraided Cecelia in the most unpleasant and scatological terms, so abusive in fact, that a policeman called Sergeant Mafa, who normally did not flinch at such language, being a master of it himself, had had to warn them that they too faced a fine for breaching the peace if they did not stop. Cecelia, unable for once to retaliate with equally stinging retorts because she needed the money they had brought, had smarted and burned under the humiliation of being addressed thus in public. This too, she had laid at Anna's door.

Thus, while Anna had thought the matter finished, Cecelia had borne a hatred that sometimes threatened to choke her. She nursed her dislike and envy of Anna into an obsession to destroy her. And so it was that Anna called in the Highest and Darkest Power she knew. This was Chipangano, the youth group that was the enforcer for the ruling party in Mbare. The weak often turn to a Higher Power, which is as it should be if such a Power is a Benevolent one, because those who are both weak and malevolent often turn to the less Benign.

Cecelia had gone to see Chopper, one of the leaders of the group. Anna was an opposition supporter, Cecelia said and should such people be allowed to prosper when they were against the ruling party. Chipangano had directed her back to the Grassroots Empowerment Flea Markets and Vendors' Trust Association, which had voted to throw Anna out of Mbare without hearing her side of things.

And so poor Anna, who had never before inked her pinky finger in a universal franchise to select the candidate of her choice in a free and fair election in ha ha ha Harare, Africa's fun capital, who had never ever voted, not once in her whole life, had been forced back into town, away from her secure spot. She had applied for a stall at the Fourth Street flea market, but they had not yet considered it, and so she was back in town, walking along Julius Nyerere and along First Street, trying to find a medium between calling so softly that potential customers would not hear her and calling so loudly that she risked attracting the police.

So it was here, on Julius Nyerere, just outside the supermarket that used to be owned by the Brothers Amato that she had seen Cecelia. And it was seeing Cecelia that caused her to duck into the supermarket, with the look on her face that Boniface considered so shifty. Boniface follows her and without warning grabs her shoulder.

'What are you doing? What is in that box? You are supposed to leave the parcels at the parcel counter. Where are you going? Come back here at once.'

Anna shakes him off and runs towards the door. Caught between the Scylla of Cecelia's wrath and the Charybdis of Boniface's suspicion, she hesitates. Boniface grabs at her again. But Cecelia is out of sight now and Anna takes her chance to run straight out of the supermarket and into the road where a car screeches to a halt as it swerves to avoid her. The car just misses Anna, swerves to the sidewalk where it hits a metal City bin. Horns blare as the cars behind screech to a sudden stop. Anna stumbles to safety but her box is not so lucky. It flies from Anna's hands and is flattened by a *kombi* speeding in the direction of Mbare Nash. Packets of baboon's piss and other herbs are scattered all over Julius Nyerere and run over by passing cars. Anna takes advantage of the commotion to disappear from Boniface's pursuit into Joina City where she melts into the crowd.

❖

The man who almost hit Anna with his car gives a fluent curse as he inspects the damage that has come from the collision of his silver Pajero with the City bin. His name is Dickson. His car has dented the smiling face of a man advertising Protector condoms. He should wait for the police, he knows it will help with the claim from his insurance, but he sees no point, and in fact, he would rather they did not know. Dickson has the distinction of being both a fine and upstanding member of the establishment *and* a criminal. Fear not, he is not your MP or other occupant of High Political office. Rather, Dickson is a junior doctor under contract to the Parirenyatwa Group of Hospitals, which is just a fancy way of saying that he is a poorly paid civil servant indentured to his government until he can achieve his manumission. Dickson, is, however, more special than other junior doctors. You could say in fact, that he is the only doctor who makes house calls, only he comes to kill and not to heal.

Dickson is aiming to do a Master's degree in neurosurgery in the United Kingdom or in Australia, and from there enter the exclusive club of neurosurgeons. But it takes a King's Ransom to educate a neurosurgeon, and Dickson is no king. As he can't make money as a junior doctor, he raises money to study the brain by extracting unborn foetuses from women who would rather not be pregnant.

Dickson is sick of being a doctor but not a healer. He is tired of daily death. It has even touched him, and not just in a professional capacity. A few months ago, a woman he was sort of sleeping with without sort of intending anything serious was murdered by one of her sort of boyfriends. The death of Kindness had been, you could say, his Wake-up Call. He is tired of dispensing palliative cures, of being surrounded by the Walking Dead.

In the Land of the Medically Uninsured, his kind of medicine is the last resort, precisely because his services will cost families everything. So firmly have ChiKristu and ChiVanhu gripped the country that his patients come to him only after the prayers of the Pentecostals and the traditional remedies of the *n'anga* have all failed. He sees patients when it is far too late to help them.

He is sick of sickness, of disease and contagion and sick of being sick of it. He reads the *Lancet* and other journals. They are filled with tales of medical developments so advanced they could be miracles. He finds himself in the grip of real envy. He wants to be a god among men. He wants to open up the brain, with all its synapses and neurons, to look upon the medulla oblongata and study it, repair it, to have the patient wake in the morning and say, 'Doctor, what power is in your hands' for what is it but Godlike to slice open a human head.

Vagoni zvavo, in the words of the Beatitudes that his grandmother, who raised him, loved so much. Only his Beatitudes are not about the Peaceful and the Lovers of God and the Meek. To own the truth, he is extremely impatient with the Meek, and thinks the Meek deserve everything they get. No, he has other Beatitudes, Dickson. *Vagoni zvavo* who have clean hospitals and drugs in them. *Vagoni zvavo* who do not have to kill to heal. *Vagoni zvavo* who can imagine any life they want, and take it. *Vagoni zvavo, vagoni zvavo, vagoni zvavo.*

Through his hands have passed at least twenty-three foetuses in the last seven months. Before twelve weeks, he uses dilation and curettage, an operation that he carries out in broad daylight in hospitals under cover of the need to scrape excess lining from women's wombs. The nurses nudge each other in knowledge but no one says a word. For the more advanced pregnancies, well, I do not want to cause you any distress, so let us stop there.

It is a thriving business, abortion. But that is too harsh a word for what it is. That is the word on the 'Abortion Kills' homemade signs that are posted on every third tree in the Avenues, the district of the City Centre where in the night, prostitutes stand and flash drivers as they crawl past, checking out the flesh.

He and those who perform these operations prefer the language of the law. What he does is not abortion, it is just an illegal operation, or, if you like, a termination, an unlawful termination of pregnancy in violation of Section 60 of the Criminal Law (Codification and Reform) Act as read together with the Termination of Pregnancy Act: 'Any person who unlawfully terminates a pregnancy or terminates a pregnancy by conduct which he or she realises involves a real risk or possibility of terminating the pregnancy shall be guilty of unlawful termination of pregnancy and liable to a fine not exceeding Level Ten or imprisonment for a period not exceeding five years or both.'

But you need not worry for Dickson.

There will be no Level Ten Fine for him, no Imprisonment For A Period Not Exceeding Five Years, no Both. Not for Dickson. It is not doctors like him who are caught. It is only those whose instruments are coat hangers and knitting needles, those who use traditional herbs such as the other herbs sold by Anna, the ones she does not advertise, it is those who use Norolon pills, the self-terminators and township women, and oh yes, they are only ever women, those are the ones who are caught and Imprisoned or Fined or Bothed. So don't eat your heart out for Dickson. And it won't be for long. He needs to perform just thirty or so more terminations before he has enough money to leave the country. He is almost there, Dickson, he is on his way.

✻

As, incidentally, are we, for the day is yet young and there is much more to see. Next, we cross Nelson Mandela Avenue, head to Angwa Street and on to Samora Machel, to Pegasus House, where triumphant Pegasus, wings aloft with no Bellerophon astride him, is looking down on a man called Edwell, Eddie to you and me, who is about to be beaten up by an angry crowd.

Just moments ago, as Anna dashed out of the supermarket, Boniface in pursuit, a brown house snake, the *Lamprophis Capensis* of the order *Squamata* and the family *Colubridae*, was seen making its way to the coolness of the shade under Eddie's car. Now, the instinct of a house snake under attack is to flee and not to bite, so the snake, lucky creature, managed to escape in the commotion, but Eddie may not be as lucky. The crowd thinks he owns the snake, you see, they are firm in their conviction that he is the owner and master of this evil creature.

A Good and Rational but Ultimately Foolish Samaritan who looks like he might be called Fungai will try to reason with the crowd, but it is not to be reasoned with. The crowd is relentless in its logic. If Eddie is not its master, why else would the snake have chosen this car, and only this car to rest under, it must mean the snake is his, and people like this fellow who seek to Defend the Indefensible must know something about it. The crowd plans to show Eddie, and his defender Fungai, just what they do with sorcerers who think they can just move around the city with their snakes in broad daylight. Come now, don't loiter, we don't have all day.

From a Town Called Enkeldoorn

Of the increase of his government and peace
there shall be no end, upon the throne of David,
and upon his kingdom, to order it, and to establish
it with judgement and with justice from henceforth
even forever.

– The Book of the Prophet Isaiah –

Kukura kwovumambo bgake nokworugare
hazinamugumo, agere pacigaro covushe
caDavidi napavushe bgake, avusimbise avutsigire
nokururamisira nokururama kubva zino kusikira
panguva isingaperi. Kushingaira kwehondo
kwaJehova wehondo kucaziita.

– Buku yaMuprofita Isaya –

WWW.GREATZIM.COM

Zim's Biggest Home Online! We Put the Great in Zimbabwe!

HOME | NEWS |SPORTS | BUSINESS | OPINION
DAILY POLL | CARTOON | FORUM

FORUM TOPIC 6676: **LOOKING FOR MCCONKEY FAMILY FROM ENKELDOORN, ZIMBABWE**

WILL IN VANCOUVER : 1847 GMT+2

Hi there! I'm Will, from False Creek in Vancouver, Canada! That's the country in North America that's NOT the United States LOL! Greetings! I came to this forum hoping to track down anyone who knew my granddad and his sister and their kids! I am not looking to write a detailed family bio or anything like that ha ha ha!

My granddad was called Douglas James McConkey. He was born in Scotland, in Dunfermline parish in a place called County Fife. He emigrated to Rhodesia together with his sister Rosaleen. My granddad was from a town called Enkeldoorn in your country. That's where my mother Noelene (!!!) was born! She was born on Christmas Day! I know, right??? Her older sister was called Mary and she also had a brother, Fergus. I have not been able to trace Mary or Fergus or my granddad's sister, I guess that would make her my great-aunt Rosaleen. Any help would be appreciated! Thanks! Will in Vancouver, Canada.

TOBAIWA NEHASHA : 1850 GMT+2

Enkeldoorn what, you idiot fool. It is called Chivhu, not Enkeldoorn.

Sorry, what do you mean?

TOBAIWA NEHASHA : 1855 GMT+2

It is Chivhu you moron, not Enkel****ingdoorn.

WILL IN VANCOUVER : 1857 GMT+2

I don't understand, have I written it wrong? My spelling is not the best ha ha ha! It says Enkeldoorn, and not Enkelingdoorn, on mom's birth certificate. She said it like 'Angledon', but it has a K and two Os!! I know, right??

CLIFF DUPONT : 1905 GMT+2

**** off, Tobaiwa. You are always doing this on this forum. It is perfectly fine for Will in Vancouver to say Enkeldoorn if he means Chivhu. It's what the place was called when his mother was born for ****'s sake. It's what's on her birth certificate.

TOBAIWA NEHASHA : 1916 GMT+2

You **** off, you racist prick. We renamed those places, okay, we renamed the places that you took. Enkeldoorn my ****ing ****. It was never Enkeldoorn. Birth certificate or not, I refuse to accept that there was ever a place called ****ing Enkeldoorn because it was named that by a renegade racist regime of ****ing plundering thieves. It is our land and we took it back, and you have no ****ing right to call any of OUR places anything else.

RHODESIAN BRIGADIER : 1947 GMT+2

Before 1980, the Zimbabwe Ruins were a prehistoric monument in Masvingo. Now, 36 years later, the Zimbabwe Ruins cover the whole country. *Ki ki ki!*

BHOKI YABABA JUKWA : 1952 GMT+2

CLIFF DUPONT : 2000 GMT+2

Christ on a bike, you really do have shit for brains don't you Tobaiwa. The point is that it was not called Chivhu in 19whatever it was that the man is asking about. How about just trying to think from time to time? It's really not as hard as it seems, and you might even learn to enjoy it.

TOBAIWA NEHASHA : 2005 GMT+2

Don't tell me I don't know how to ****ing think you ****ing Pale Devil.

CLIFF DUPONT : 2007 GMT+2

Oh here we go with the Pale Devil stuff. You are certainly doing a good job of demonstrating you don't know how thinking works, Tobaiwa. Here's a hint: first engage brain, then write. Guess no one can teach you anything now. A case of old dog, new tricks?

TOBAIWA NEHASHA : 2011 GMT+2

Who are you calling a dog, you dog? Who are you calling a dog? Do you know who I am?

CLIFF DUPONT : 2013 GMT+2

No but I can bloody well guess. You are a bootlicker aren't you.
A Brown Noser.

RHODESIAN BRIGADIER : 2015 GMT+2

Where is the capital of Zimbabwe? It is in Switzerland! *Ki ki ki*!

BHOKI YABABA JUKWA : 2017 GMT+2

COMRADE MARLEY : 2021 GMT+2

Ha ha ha Cliff. Just come out with it. You mean Tobaiwa is a bumlicker
of epic proportions. As his record on the forum shows, he is the
Paramount Chief of Bumlickers. Likes to get his nose nice and brown!
A real bottom feeder, *ki ki ki*.

TOBAIWA NEHASHA : 2025 GMT+2

**** off Comrade Marley, you are nothing but a white man's condom. I
have read your posts on this forum. I know your type. You are one of
those Useful Blacks who defend the Pale Devils. You are the kind that
would have been against the Liberation Struggle. You would have
been on the side of Muzorewa and the whites, dancing and ululating
in favour of your own oppression. You are a ****ing Native Informant.

COMRADE MARLEY : 2031 GMT+2

Who's dancing in favour of his own oppression if not you Tobaiwa?
You sit on your laptop in whatever Western city you live in to
ululate and celebrate the regime that chased you out to look for

opportunities you could not find at home. Sorry *maningi, shem'* *stereki. Kupembedza n'anga ichabata mai.* The only thing you are good for is breathing *mugotsi mavamwe varume.* Idiot fool.

TOBAIWA NEHASHA : 2039 GMT+2

Well you would know all about breathing into the backs of other men's necks wouldn't you, seeing that is what you specialise in? ****ing pervert. And I can live in any country I want to and support the government of my choice, okay? It is MY right, it is MY right that was gained for me through the sacrifice of the BLOOD that was shed in the Liberation Struggle!

CLIFF DUPONT : 2045 GMT+2

Well that's the whole point isn't it? It may be your choice but it is not the choice of the majority of people who have voted that government out three times already! You do not speak for the whole country, Tobaiwa. That this government is still in power is a shocking outrage against democracy.

TOBAIWA NEHASHA : 2047 GMT+2

You are the ****ing outrage Cliff Dupont. You are the outrage. I am not going to sit here and take lessons in democracy from Pale Devils, ****ing Rhodies and Useful Blacks. What did Rhodesia know about democracy exactly? Did Ian Smith and his government allow black people to vote in Rhodesia, yes or no?

And how many people, all of them BLACK, did Cecil John Rhodes kill to establish Rhodesia? Who voted for him to come to this country? Where was the democracy then? Who said he could just take other people's land, expropriating it and stealing it with no compensation? Who gave him permission to come into our country and just take all the land that he wanted and grow rich from looting minerals from our own soil?

If you expect me to be ****ing grateful for being ****ing colonised like some Pale Devil loving Uncle Tom you can ****ing piss off. Don't ****ing talk to me about ****ing democracy as though it was you Rhodies who invented democracy. We got our democracy through the barrel of the gun, okay? We got it though your surrender. It was not ****ing donated to us by the likes of you.

RHODESIAN BRIGADIER : 2100 GMT+2

What did Zimbos use for light before they started using candles? They used electricity! *Ki ki ki.*

BHOKI YABABA JUKWA : 2106 GMT+2

GREATZIM FORUM MODERATOR : 2115 GMT+2

As you can see from the active moderation, we have been getting a few complaints about this thread. So just to remind you again of the terms of our forum which you can view at the bottom of this page by clicking Forum Guidelines. We welcome robust debate on all issues but not personal insults. Thanks.

CLIFF DUPONT : 2121 GMT+2

Well, some people's very existence is a personal insult. Like monkey brain over there.

TOBAIWA NEHASHA : 2125 GMT+2

Who you calling a monkey you Rhodesian ****wit? Who you calling a ****ing monkey?

Hello GreatZim Moderator, I am not from your country, and I do not speak any of your languages but I thought I should sign up just to say GreatZim is the best forum on the Internet. You guys rock. Keep it up! *Mutakunanzva chaiwo. Dapitapi. Matindimutibvu nhopi inopisa!*

COMRADE MARLEY : 2140 GMT+2

Ki ki ki, Bhoki yaBaba Jukwa. You are too funny. *Ndiwe une yese.* Ko, Tenzi *varipi mazuvano*?

JONONO : 2140 GMT+2

£££ £££ £££! Pounds pounds pounds! Make money from home. I get paid £85 every hour from online jobs. I never thought I'd be able to do it but my best friend is earning £8k monthly by doing this job and she showed me how to do it. To find out more, just click on this link.

NYAMAENDE MHANDE : 2141 GMT+2

It is an OUTRIGHT LIE to say the White Man first arrived on our AFRIKAN soil in 1890. He arrived long before that, in the shape of the Portuguese Marauders who invaded the Mutapa Empire. By 1629, they had forced Mavura Mhande to convert to their religion and installed him as their Vassal, as the Puppet Mutapa they called Felipe. Since that moment, the AFRIKAN has known no peace. Only if the Mwenemutapa who is the true OVERLORD of this land is restored to His Rightful Place and only if AFRIKANS have taken back our LAND and given the White Man back his BIBLE and restore AFRIKAN Ancestors to their Rightful Place of

REVERENCE will this country know PEACE and PROSPERITY. Bring back the Mutapa Empire. Today!

RHODESIAN BRIGADIER : 2144 GMT+2

So the headmaster at the school where Comrade Zuze has his child enrolled calls Comrade Zuze to the office to tell him that unfortunately, his son is as dumb as he is and if things don't get any better they will have to expel him because *idofo ramakoko*. Comrade Zuze says no, that can't be, his son is a very clever boy, just like his father. So the headmaster calls the son into the office and in front of his father, asks him: Son, who signed the Rudd Concession?

Comrade Zuze's son just blinks and is quiet. Who signed the Rudd Concession, the headmaster asks again. The son obviously has no idea that it was Lobengula back in 1890, so he just blinks again and remains quiet. Comrade Zuze gets really angry at his son's unresponsiveness, and shouts angrily: Look, son, if it was you who signed this Rudd Concession, just admit it right now! *Bvuma zvipere!* Just admit! *Ki ki ki.*

BHOKI YABABA JUKWA : 2146 GMT+2

WILL IN VANCOUVER : 2200 GMT+2

Hi there! I'm Will, from False Creek in Vancouver, Canada! That's the country in North America that's NOT the United States ha ha ha! Greetings! I came to this forum hoping to track down anyone who knew my granddad and his sister and their kids! I am not looking to write a detailed family bio or anything like that ha ha ha!

My granddad was called Douglas James McConkey. He was

born in Scotland, in Dunfermline parish in a place called County
Fife. He emigrated to Rhodesia together with his sister Rosaleen.
My granddad was from a town called Enkeldoorn in your country.
That's where my mother Noelene (!!!) was born! She was born on
Christmas Day! I know, right??? Her older sister was called Mary and
she also had a brother, Fergus. I have not been able to trace Mary
or Fergus or my granddad's sister, I guess that would make her my
great-aunt Rosaleen. Any help would be appreciated! Thanks! Will in
Vancouver, Canada.

AMAI BHOYI : 2215 GMT+2

You really want to find this grandfather of yours don't you, *dhali*?
Ende kulez vako wavalavha dhiya. Did he leave you an inheritance
or something?

COMRADE MARLEY : 2217 GMT+2

Well, if the inheritance was a farm in Zanuland, he can forget about
it. *ki ki ki.*

BHOKI YABABA JUKWA : 2219 GMT+2

And if the farm had oranges on it, they have all been turned to *zhingy
zhongy* lemons in Chinambabwe. *Ki ki ki.*

COMRADE MARLEY : 2221 GMT+2

Or they have been turned into Mazoe Orange Crush in Zvimbabwe!

BHOKI YABABA JUKWA : 2222 GMT+2

ROBERT THE BRUTE : 2247 GMT+2

Hello there, Will from Vancouver. I grew up on a farm near Enkeldoorn. Our family knew a Doug McConkey and his wife. They were friends of my parents. They had two kids, Mary and William, who were both much older than me, but were in the same school I was. They also had a baby girl. Only it was Doug's wife who was called Rosaleen. He had no sister.

WILL IN VANCOUVER : 2300 GMT+2

Hi there Robert! How you doing? I managed to get something called extracts from the parish register for both Douglas and Rosaleen McConkey. They say his sister was called Rosaleen. They had one other brother, William Henry, who died as a kid. They emigrated together, my granddad Douglas and his sister Rosaleen. Their parents' names are the same on the extracts from the parish register.

ROBERT THE BRUTE : 2304 GMT+2

I can assure you Will that I do not forget a name. I knew them well because they were close friends of my family. We called them Uncle Doug and Aunt Rosie. Your grandfather managed a farm down in Enkeldoorn. It was his wife who was called Rosaleen, not his sister. She was also born in Scotland, in the same village as your grandfather. They had known each other all their lives, they said.

Neither had family, they were both only children. They had a daughter Mary who became a teacher. Their son was called William. I think the baby was called Noleen or Noline – I am not sure how to spell it.

WILL IN VANCOUVER : 2306 GMT+2

My mom's name was Noelene because she was born on Christmas Day. She had a sister called Mary and a brother called William. I guess that's who I am named after, but she didn't talk about him much.

ROBERT THE BRUTE : 2310 GMT+2

To be honest with you, I don't know much about your mother because she was quite young when we knew the family. But I bumped into Mary McConkey much later and by then she was headmistress at a school in Mabelreign, David Livingstone Primary or something like that, and she said her little sister was living in South Africa. She didn't talk much about her brother William either, he was a bit of a no good sort of 'oke. He was supposed to get married to some woman from Gatooma but that didn't take off, then he went off to manage a farm up in the Eastern Highlands. Might still be there for all I know. There were all sorts of rumours about him, some people even said he was the country's hangman at one point, which is nonsense of course because a softer and more useless 'oke you never met.

CHAMU NEBETA : 2313 GMT+2

Is this Miss McConkey who lived in Cotswold Hills in Mabelreign? She was my headmistress! She used to make us do this annual play about Stanley finding Livingstone.

LADY SQUANDILO : 2315 GMT+2

Do you mean Miss McConkey from HMS Junior? From Henry

Morton Stanley? I remember her! She was STRICT!! She taught the Remedial Class. I can still feel her wooden ruler on my knuckles. *Ki ki ki*!

Yes that's her. I saw her last time I was in Zim, she is still driving that yellow Datsun 120Y *ki ki ki*. My sister says she still lives in Bridgewater in Cotswold.

Eish but she was strict! What was that song we used to sing? 'Thou who didst guide our Fathers' feet' or something like that.

Kambo kaikotsirisa ikako! That song used to send me straight to sleep, especially because we sang it first thing in the morning. What year where you there, Lady Squandilo? Was that before or after she got demoted?

The Mutapa Empire covered all of present-day Zimbabwe and much of Zambia and Mozambique. The first Mutapa, Nyatsimba Mutota was a Prince of Dzimbahwe. They are the only legitimate rulers of this land of the AFRIKAN. Only if the Mwenemutapa is restored to His Rightful Place and the bones of Cecil John Rhodes are cast into the Zambezi River will AFRIKANS experience PROGRESS! Until then, AFRIKANS are CURSED! Bring back the Mutapa Empire!

WILL IN VANCOUVER : 2325 GMT+2

Hi there Robert! My mother met my father in South Africa. They married and moved to Vancouver. But Rosaleen was the name of her aunt not her mother.

ROBERT THE BRUTE : 2327 GMT+2

I can assure you I am not mistaken, Will. Uncle Doug and Aunt Rosie were our neighbours and I knew them well.

WILL IN VANCOUVER : 2330 GMT+2

That can't be right. You are saying my granddad married his sister. That can't be right at all.

TOBAIWA NEHASHA : 2333 GMT+2

*Chabvondoka pa*Enkeldoorn! 😆 😆 😆 Now this is explosive stuff!

BHOKI YABABA JUKWA : 2335 GMT+2

I am getting the popcorn for this one. Just bring your own drinks! *Zvaatori madhambudhanana masokisi ejongwe!* 😝 😝 😝

AMAI BHOYI : 2338GMT+2

Huya zvako dhali timboti chachacha kuno. I tell you Will, Will, Willowvale *muzukuru wa*Dougie, in my arms all your sorrows will disappear. You will forget that you ever had a grandfather. In fact, by the time I am done with you, I will have taught you how to say 'Grandfather' in Yoruba – and I don't even speak Yoruba!

BHOKI YABABA JUKWA : 2340 GMT+2

TOBAIWA NEHASHA : 2345 GMT+2

Ki ki ki

WILL IN VANCOUVER : 2351 GMT+2

That just can't be right. You must have the wrong people.

GREATZIM FORUM MODERATOR : 2355 GMT+2

Just to say we will shortly be closing this thread for the night.
Goodnight all and thanks as always for your contributions. It is you
who make this forum GREAT!

Comrade Piso's Justice

Put not your trust in princes, nor in the son of man,
in whom there is no help.

– The Book of Psalms –

Regai kuvimba namacinda, Kana nomwanakomana
womunhu, usingagoni kubatsira.

– Buku yaMapisarema –

When I heard his name called out three times in Courtroom B at Rotten Row, I did not immediately recognise it. It was only when I saw him mount the three steps to the dock from the door to the left, which led to the narrow corridor used by prisoners on remand that I realised it was Comrade Piso. The surprise was not seeing him there, because it is never a surprise to bump into a legal practitioner at Rotten Row, the surprise was seeing him in the khaki garb of a *bhanditi* in the dock. Although, come to think of it, even in his heyday as a solicitor, the criminal courts at Rotten Row were not where you would have expected to see Comrade Piso.

After we graduated and left college, Piso went on to one of those three-name white firms that specialised in corporate and commercial law and recruited only though selective headhunting. This was a stunning achievement for him. In our very first week at the law faculty, Kempton Makamure, the Dean of the Faculty, had divided us into two groups.

We were either members of the Nose Brigade, those educated at the former white schools who spoke English through the nose, he declared, or we were SRBs, those with Strong Rural Backgrounds with accents to match. As we SRBs made up the majority of the class, it was a joke we took in good spirit. A small-town boy from Chipinge, and not even Chipinge proper but one of its outlying villages, Comrade Piso came to the UZ from his mission school, St Augustines – '*Ndakafunde kwa*Tsambe', as he said in his Manyika accent – as a full-grown SRB. By the time he left to join his white firm, he had become a full-blown member of the Nose Brigade.

At the University of Zimbabwe, we had been part of a group of male students that called itself the Quorum. We formed the Quorum just after we had completed a first year course on Roman and Roman-Dutch Law, and though we sometimes called each other 'Paterfamilias', that title did not stick. Instead, we addressed each other as Comrade. The aim of the Comrades in the Quorum was primarily to gossip about fellow students – paying particular and speculative attention to the sex lives of the female students – and to pass exams without doing a jot of work. It was not as hard as it sounds.

Most of the lecturers were a lazy bunch: they had not adapted their notes from the country's Marxist heyday of the eighties. It was all Marx and Engels this and dialectical materialism that, with just enough law to keep the Law Society satisfied. They tended to set questions like, 'It is not the consciousness of man that determines his material being but his material being that determines his consciousness: Discuss.' You just had to put in enough guff about dialectical materialism and the withering away of the law, private property and the state and you would get through. And if you failed, you always had a second chance with a re-sit or *supp*, as we called it.

Our interest in our studies extended mainly to the use of stock phrases. We dismissed opinions as frivolous and vexatious, we said claims were vague and embarrassing. We talked about the man on the Clapham Omnibus; we made crude jokes about piercing the corporate veil; we described the law student who lost her head in an exam as an unfit and improper person. We showed off the new language we learned: *contra bonos mores* and *in flagrante delicto*, *mutatis mutandis*, and *mero motu*.

We laughed at Makamure's aphorism that if you want to hide something from an African, all you have to do is to put it in a book, but as far as we were concerned, the law was hidden from us because we opened no books. We gave the name Denning to the one Quorum member among us who had read just one entire case and not stopped at the headnote. That case was *R v George Joseph Smith* and we sometimes we made him recite our favourite part of the judgement: 'to lose one wife is careless, to lose two unfortunate but to lose three begins to look like murder.'

Indeed, we only took down any notes because we had to pass exams. We called it 'Defending our Pay Out'. The Pay Out was the stipend that each student received as part of the government grant that went to all students. If you did not pass your exams, you forfeited your right to the grant, and to the Pay Out. So that was the Quorum. We were not law students at all, just gossips and layabouts, and Pay Out Defenders.

For no reason at all that we could see, in third year, Piso started to take it all seriously, going to the library at night and at the weekend, studying for more than two weeks before the exams, and reading more than the headnote of each case. Then, one day during a tutorial in Company Law, he had a twenty-minute argument with Emily, an eager beaver Nose Brigade, over whether *Salomon v Salomon* had been properly decided. The argument turned into a quarrel that continued even after the tutorial. After that, he started to track down cases that were not on the reading list. He talked of doing case notes on *In Re Southern Rhodesia* and *Madzimbamuto v Lardner-Burke* for the *Law Review*. There were perspectives, he said, that had not been fully shared. He tried to convince us that there was more to *R v Bedingfield* than the statement: 'See what Bedingfield has done to me.' He talked of working at the Law Development Commission during the holidays.

The final nail was when he joined the Moot Court team and spent his weekends preparing to argue fictitious cases with his partner Emily, the eager beaver student he had argued with after the Company Law tutorial. That same year, she lost her head in an exam, and instead of making jokes about her with the Quorum, about how she was an unfit and improper person who qualified for coverage under the Mental Health Act, Piso bought her flowers from the Interflora shop at Bond Street and went to see her at the Annexe, where she had been locked up after her breakdown.

The Quorum began to worry for him.

Comrade Piso got that name from the Quorum because he is the one who told us one of our favourite stories in first year. As he told it, there are these three soldiers who lived in Roman times. One day, two of them go out of the camp together on leave, but only one returns. The governor of their province, who also controls the army, a particularly flinty-hearted fellow called Piso, tells the First Soldier that as he has returned alone without the Second Soldier, he must have killed his companion. So Piso orders a Third Soldier to take him out and kill him. Just before this soldier does so, the Second Soldier returns and claims that he has escaped from the enemy.

All three then appear before Piso to explain themselves. Piso starts to eat hot coals. He orders all three of them to be killed at once, the First Soldier because the sentence had already been passed and must be carried out, the Third Soldier because he had failed to obey a lawful command and the Second Soldier because he had caused the death of two innocent men. We laughed like hyenas when it came to that part.

I suppose we should have known from his reading of Seneca, the narrator of the original story, that our Comrade Piso had the potential and ambition to rise above the Quorum's ingrained laziness. It was an ambition that led him to modulate his vowels and shorten his consonants, thus beginning his ultimately successful conversion from an SRB to a Nose Brigade.

To cement his Nose Brigade status, he began to go after girls who studied things like French and Portuguese, who played tennis and squash and swam for leisure. He joined a French-named society for students that seemed to exist only to have picnics at Cleveland Dam. He even had a semester-long affair with a German exchange student. We mocked his sheepish grin as he walked with her around campus, his hand firmly clutched in hers. He knew as well as we did that no self-respecting member of the Quorum would demean himself so far as to hold hands with any girl in public.

And there was the matter of English. It was our official language, of course, and we spoke it when we had to in our lectures and tutorials. We wrote it when we were compelled to in our essays and exam scripts. But the idea that anyone would willingly and voluntarily subject himself to its constricting confines and give himself up to a life that required that he speak English even in his most intimate moments seemed something that only a Nose Brigade would willingly do. It was preposterous to us that anyone would choose to speak English when he did not have to. According to Bakunin, a stalwart of the Quorum who took his admiration of the Russian anarchist to a degree that in the end cost him his studies, Piso probably dreamt in English because evidently he screwed in English.

Even after his flirtation with the German student ended, he no longer attended the Quorum. When he drank at the Students' Union at all, it was not in the main Union bar, but in the smaller bar between the squash court and the swimming pool, the small bar with unbroken chairs and proper tables that we called October 4. We knew then that Comrade Piso was lost to us. He broke all ties with the Quorum after his falling out with Bakunin.

Bakunin was not only in the Quorum but also in the SRC, the Students' Representative Council that was supposed to represent the students in the meetings of the University Council, but instead spent student dues on parties and travel. On the SRC, Bakunin held the coveted Entertainment portfolio.

Bakunin was the first person we knew to rig an election. To support his challenge for the presidency, Bakunin gave out free beer, threw wild parties at the Students' Union and was rumoured to have secured the remaining Bhundu Boys to play at his victory party. He also manipulated the presidential debate by bribing a blind student called Kuda to ask a question to the leading candidate, an Economics student called Frederick Alumeda. Kuda raised his white stick, was given the floor in the Great Hall and said, 'I have a question for Alumeda, Arumedza, Tarumedza.'

The commotion that followed drowned out the rest of the question. Kuda's play on Alumeda's name was meant to appeal to the Shona chauvinists who made up the majority of students. By drawing attention to the L in Alumeda's name, Kuda meant to imply that he was a muBhurandaya or Nyasarandi from Malawi or else a Mosken from Mozambique, and not, therefore, a son of this soil. When the ensuing fall-out resulted in Alumeda losing the election, he gained the nickname Moshood, after Moshood Abiola, the politician who was in the news at that time as 'the man who is said to have won the presidential election in Nigeria'.

Though Bakunin toppled Moshood, he was still beaten and so he left the SRC to become Sub-warden in New Complex 5, the male hostel known as Baghdad. Sub-wardens were meant to keep the peace and ensure that students lived by the rules, but under Bakunin's subwardenship, Baghdad became positively ungovernable.

Girls were often spotted in the mornings, and not just *girls girls* but also prostitutes, scuttling from their companions' rooms, lost in the maze of Baghdad's corridors. When Piso complained that the Engines student next door to him was playing his CDs far too loudly and disturbing both his sleep and studies, Bakunin had come over for an inspection *in loco*. He took one listen to the Engines student's music and said, 'But this is not noise, Comrade. This is Gregory Isaacs. This is the author of "Night Nurse", Comrade. How is this noise? You must surely concur, Comrade, that he has no competition, the man has no equal.'

Over Piso's protests, he had turned up the volume even further and shouted, 'Listen to this. This is why he is the Ruler of them all, Comrade, the Cool Ruler. The only quarrel we might have is over whether "Cool Down the Pace" is greater than this one. Listen to this, listen to this. "Please give me a chance, so I can make my confession." Obviously, Comrade, if we can't agree on Gregory Isaacs then perhaps Baghdad is not the right place for you, Comrade.'

Piso exchanged rooms with a fellow who lived in Carr Saunders, the residence shared by mature-entry male and female students where all was much too clean and civilised for comfort. Piso thrived in his new halls of residence. He then went a step further and served as the researcher for both Pearson Nherere, the brilliant lecturer in the public law department who had been born blind and yet still managed to go to both Cambridge and Oxford, and Lawrence Tshuma who was the country's leading land law expert. That was the year of his biggest success, getting firsts in six subjects as well as the University Book Prize, an honour he shared with Emily who by then had recovered her wits, only she now insisted on being called by her second name of Pepukai.

Piso and Pepukai also went on to get first-class passes and receive the Law Society Prize for the top students of the last four years. They received their prize directly from Eddison Zvobgo, the Minister of Justice who was also the first black lawyer in our country to go to Harvard Law School, and to do so, too, in a Rhodesia when education had been constricted for those of our race. It may have been the gun that got Smith to the table, but it was

Zvobgo's legal skills that guided the Lancaster House talks that created the constitution. As we saw Zvobgo joking and laughing with Piso and Pepukai as he handed them their prizes, it was Bakunin who expressed the general view of the Quorum that maybe there were rewards in hard work after all.

By the time we left college, Piso had changed everything about himself. From his voice to his clothes, from his girlfriends to his work ethic, from his attitude to his books to where he drank and his sense of dress, the essence of Piso had changed so completely that you could have sworn he had been born a Nose Brigade.

The Quorum did not keep up with him after college. In only his second month of employment, he was heard to declare that he could not tolerate any other drink but whisky, and not just whisky, but Scotch, which he pronounced 'Scarch'. It was just as well that by then had he left the Quorum behind because with his Scarch this and Scarch that, he would have been much too expensive a drinking partner for our shallow pockets.

Over the years, we watched the rise and rise of Comrade Piso. We heard that he had left his white firm and moved to work as in-house counsel for a listed beverage company. Then he moved to a bank. Not a retail bank, but a merchant bank, a crucial difference because this was in the days when there were probably only two such banks in the whole country. From what we gathered, he left the bank under something of a cloud, though the details were never explained. There was a whiff of criminality about his departure, there was something about it that smelled of fraud, which we pronounced frowd, and those who whispered said he had tried to take a few short-cuts to riches, but as he was never prosecuted, nothing was ever proved and he remained on the Law Society's Roll of Legal Practitioners as a fit and proper person.

We then heard that he had set himself up as a tuckshop practitioner, a one-man band. I only knew about this because I had gone to see a client in Chipinge and found myself forced to spend an afternoon there to be followed by an overnight stay in Mutare. There is nothing more tedious than attending court in these little out-of-the-backwoods spots. They never have decent places to stay in so if your magistrate decides not to turn up two days in a row, well, too bad for you because that's your two days wasted driving between Harare and whatever backwater you are in.

There is only one high street in Chipinge with its sole doctor's surgery that is also used by the town dentist, it is a one-hotel and one-solicitor town and it seemed that solicitor was Piso. As I crossed the road to buy lunch from the supermarket, I saw him trying to hide behind the crumpled pinkness of a *Financial Gazette*. I gave him no choice as I grabbed him jovially by the elbow. He looked good, I will give him that, he looked quietly prosperous in his well-cut suit, a shirt that was just the right hue of blue, an impeccable tie, and shoes that shone without the slightest hint of patent leather.

I hailed him as Comrade, but he spoke to me in a most uncomradely manner. Indeed, he spoke to me like I was someone he had once known but long since forgotten. I must say that I pressed my claims on his notice so persistently that I left him with no option but to recognise me, or at least to pretend to, even if he did not actually remember the days of the Quorum. He was defending a man who had killed two people, he said, a drunk driver. It was a tough one, because the man had killed about three other people before. A real menace this one, Piso said as he laughed, the usual inducements are unlikely to work in this case. I was startled to hear him say this, we all know how the usual inducements work, but it was shocking to hear a fellow solicitor admit so breezily that he used such methods. Throughout our conversation, he kept laughing a shallow, hollow laugh whose mirth did not reach his eyes.

The next time I saw him, he was in the dock of Courtroom B. As I said, I did not pay attention at first. I was at Rotten Row in one of those instances where fortune smiles on a lucky lawyer and showers him with the lucrative coincidence of two matters being set down on the same morning. It meant that I could bill both clients for the same hours. The first client was a woman, some small house from Borrowdale Brooke who had had sex with a mad man for ritual purposes. I had rather hoped for a long trial, but halfway through, she suddenly found Jesus and decided to plead guilty.

The second was a client on a traffic charge. He was one of those principled fellas who refused to pay twenty-dollar spot fines for minor offences, arguing that it was the principle of the matter that he was defending. The policeman had to go the office, sit down and draw up a summons, he said, he was paying no spot fine. He normally got away with it, what policeman ever wants to do work behind a desk when he can get fines on the road, but on this one day, he had run into the one policeman in the city who was willing to issue court summons instead of a spot fine. So the client had come to me, insisting that I defend him because it was the principle of the matter. The police, he said, had a duty to have their speed trap machines recalibrated every six months and he wanted to see reports that the machine that tested him was up to code.

On and on he went, he was a tedious fellow, meticulous to the point of annoyance, but I was happy enough to represent him because it meant I charged him the highest tariff that the Law Society allowed me to charge. These are the clients that every lawyer dreams of, the ones that ask you to pursue cases that could be avoided with just a quick admission of guilt. My client's matter had been stood down to be heard after a series of bail applications. It was then that Piso's name was called out as one of the bail applicants.

As I said, I did not realise that it was Piso at first. It was only when he spoke, denying the charges and asking for bail that I realised that it was him. The charge was engaging in immoral conduct in contravention of Section 77 of the Criminal Code. According to the charge read by the prosecutor, on or around 18 April 2010, at or around 11 p.m., on or near Josiah Chinamano Avenue, Comrade Piso had caused a public nuisance after refusing to pay for a hotel. He had also refused to pay the services of a woman called Manyara who claimed they had agreed a fee. Piso had then been attacked by the woman, he had retaliated, a public affray had ensued, and Piso had been arrested. He was charged with immoral conduct, causing a public disturbance and assault. When the charge was read, a woman who had been sitting in the dock stood up and said yes, he can't get away with no paying, lock him up. She brandished a copy of *Metropolitan* newspaper in which Piso's face was photographed in blurry tones and under the headline LAWYER FIGHTS HOOKER AFTER REFUSING TO PAY.

Without looking up from his papers, the magistrate directed that he apply for bail to the High Court. Still reeling from this unexpected turn in the life of Comrade Piso, I did not immediately hear it when my client's case was called. I was not at Rotten Row on the day that Piso was sentenced to a year and a half, with six months suspended on condition that he did not commit the same crime for two years.

Apart from ending up in prison, the most serious consequence for him was that he was disbarred. Whatever whiff of suspicion had followed him after his previous scandals, he could not explain away his conviction for procuring the services of a prostitute, public affray and disorderly conduct. This was a far greater punishment than prison. Once the Law Society strikes you off, your life as a lawyer is finished. In the event, he served less than a year. The lucky beggar benefitted from the presidential amnesty after the election, an amnesty that cleared the prisons of all but the most hardened of the convicts.

Piso disappeared from Harare after that, and the next we heard, he had returned to live in Chipinge. Then he was in the headlines again, this time, for camping in a caravan on a tea estate that belonged to a white farming family. He paid a bunch of youths in Chipinge to terrorise and drive the farm manager out. It all worked out for him, the manager was found one day early in the morning, having hanged himself. Gwata, who I drank with from time to time, and who was the pathologist who examined the manager's body, said he had never seen such a professional knot on a suicide.

After that, it should have come as no surprise to see that Piso had joined the ruling party. He devoted himself so slavishly to its service that in a matter of just four years, he went from an ordinary party member to provincial governor.

I saw him next on television, no longer just a joke Comrade, but a proper Comrade. As a proper Comrade, he not only had the party regalia with the president's face on his shirt, he also had the requisite angry speech and the ruling party stomach to signal ruling party prosperity. As he delivered a speech denouncing the most recent 'defecations' from the ruling party and the 'Nicodemus machinations that were nicodemusly carried under cover of the darkness' and as he praised the president and his cabinet for 'dying for this country' which he declared would never be a 'colon' again, I realised that not only had Piso claimed his original voice, he was now speaking in an exaggerated parody of it.

Comrade Piso had come full circle.

In the Matter Between Goto and Goto

If there be a controversy between men, and they
come unto judgement, that the judges may judge
them; then they shall justify the righteous, and
condemn the wicked.

– The Book of Deuteronomy –

Kana vanhu vakaita nharo, vakavuya kutongerwa,
vatongi vakavatongera, vanofanira kururamisira
wakarurama, nokupa mhosa munhu wakatadza

– Buku yecishanu yaMosesi inonzi Deuteronomio –

In the High Court of Zimbabwe
Reportable
Case No 667/2016

IN THE MATTER BETWEEN:

Naboth Tapfumaneyi Goto   PLAINTIFF

and

Immaculate Avila Goto   DEFENDANT

S Bwanya, for the Petitioner
T Mafukidze, for the Respondent

JUDGEMENT

[1]   It is no exaggeration to say that the two parties to these proceedings are living in what can only be called a state of competitive unhappiness. The Plaintiff, Mr Naboth Tapfumaneyi Goto, is an unhappy man. The Defendant, Mrs Immaculate Avila Goto, his wife, is an equally unhappy woman. Each party claims to be more miserable than the other, and each accuses the other of being the source of that misery.

[2]   My ruling will satisfy neither completely. It will certainly not accord them the essential happiness that they seek. The most that this court can do is to give each party, according to the merits of each party's case, succour of a legal nature.

[3]   On 15 January 2016, the Plaintiff, Naboth Goto, issued a summons in which he seeks a divorce from his wife, Immaculate Goto, on the grounds that his marriage has broken down irretrievably because of his wife's unreasonable behaviour.

[4]   In response to that summons, the Defendant, in Heads of Argument filed on 29 January 2016, refuses to grant the divorce and instead brings her own summons to compel her husband to uphold, in her words, 'the sacred vows that he undertook by entering into the sacrament of marriage in accordance with the tenets of the Roman Catholic Church.'

[5]   Immaculate Goto also seeks an order to compel the removal from the matrimonial home of a Miss Benevolence Mhlanga, whom she describes in her sworn affidavit as the 'concubine' or 'small house' of her husband, and as a 'loose harlot' and 'painted Jezebel.' Moreover, Immaculate Goto makes a claim of adultery damages against Miss Mhlanga in the amount of $50,000 broken down into $30,000 for loss of consortium and $20,000 for *contumelia*.

[6]   The facts of the matter are simple enough.

[7]   In May 2005, Immaculate Avila Chatidonhe, a spinster of Kwekwe, aged 24 years of age, was married to Naboth Tapfumaneyi Goto, a bachelor of Gweru, aged 34. Miss Chatidonhe, as she then was, was studying articles with an international accounting firm. Naboth Goto did not then have fixed employment, and describes himself now as he did then as a 'commodity broker'. His wife dismisses this description and states that it is a more sophisticated way of saying that her husband is, was, and has always been, a 'wastrel' and a 'dealer'.

[8] They married again six months later, on 10 December 2005.

[9] The first marriage between the parties was a customary law union contracted under African customary law and registered in accordance with the then African Marriages Act, Chapter 238. The form of such marriages is well known. The bride receiving family, through an emissary called a *munyai*, approaches the bride giving family to enter into negotiations on the amount of the bride wealth, variously called *fuma*, *roora* or *lobola*.

[10] Negotiations are then concluded to the satisfaction of the bride giving family, and, with no further ado, the couple is considered married by their families, the wider community, and under the law of Zimbabwe.

[11] There is a long line of cases stretching as far back as *Chiutsu v Garira* [1969] and *Jirira v Jirira* [1976] that have upheld the legal validity of marriages contracted in accordance with African customary law.

[12] According to Naboth Goto, he had only given in to the second marriage, contracted under civil law, because his wife refused to live with him after the first marriage as she was willing to do so only after a marriage blessed in the Roman Catholic Church.

[13] Immaculate Goto has herself attested that she is a devout adherent of the Roman Catholic faith. It was a point of honour and faith for her that she and her husband consummate the marriage only after they had solemnised their marriage though an exchange of wedding vows in church. Indeed, so seriously did Immaculate Goto take her chastity that, after the consummation of that marriage, she insisted that a *chimandamanda*, or *mombe yechimanda*

be purchased by her husband's family to send as a gift to her own family. It is established under custom that the giving of this cow is an indication from the family of the groom that they are satisfied that the bride has known no man other than her new husband.

[14]   The second marriage between the parties was a more elaborate affair. It involved a white wedding dress, a marquee, a towering cake, and expensive catering for four hundred guests. Both parties have shown this court a video of the wedding. From the speeches and dances and the smiling approbation of both families, it was a happy occasion. Both parties signed the marriage register in accordance with the then Civil Marriages Act, Chapter 37.

[15]   The marriage produced no issue, that is, there are no children born to the couple.

[16]   Some ten years after the second marriage, Immaculate Goto was summarily informed by her husband that as she had provided him with no children, he had chosen to take another woman as a wife. He informed her that he had, in fact, fathered a child with the aforementioned woman.

[17]   The mother of the child that Naboth Goto says is his is the Miss Benevolence Mhlanga, aged 28, who has been described by Immaculate Goto in the colourful terms above. On the same occasion, Naboth Goto also informed his wife that Miss Mhlanga was presently expecting his second child and that he wished to live with her as man and wife. Indeed, Naboth Goto declared, he had already taken her as a wife as he had negotiated bride wealth with her family and had thus contracted a second customary law union of marriage.

[18]   In accordance with the Rules of Procedure of the High Court of Zimbabwe, petitions for divorce are normally determined on the basis of the papers filed by the parties. The procedures do however allow the parties to appear in person before the court. Immaculate Goto asked to see me in person. I acceded to this request. I also reminded both parties that they also had the option to proceed by way of a court action, and could thus go to a pre-trial-conference followed by a full trial.

[19]   In this case, in a communication to the Court, Mrs Goto indicated that she did not want a full trial, but only wished to appear before me to reiterate certain points in her sworn affidavit.

[20]   The maxim *audi alteram partem,* which compels that both parties to a dispute be given an equal and fair hearing, is a core principle not only of our legal system but of natural justice generally. In fairness to all the parties, I also agreed to see Naboth Goto in my chambers, who came in the company of Miss Mhlanga.

[21]   Immaculate Goto struck me as a woman in the grip of an intense emotion. Whatever that emotion may be, it seems to me that it is not love. It seems clear to me that Mrs Goto has no affection at all for her husband. From her testimony, he has done everything possible to kill whatever affection she retained for him. Yet she still wishes to remain married to him.

[22]   I do not accept that Immaculate Goto's intransigence in this matter is motivated by religious scruples alone. I would recommend that she seek urgent counselling before it enters her mind to pursue other actions.

[23] Naboth Goto, for his part, struck me as a man impossible to love. His insistence on bringing Miss Mhlanga into these proceedings was an unnecessarily aggressive and provocative act. It is regrettable that I had to suspend proceedings while the High Court security officers separated the two women and rearranged the furniture in my chambers.

[24] According to his testimony in chambers, Naboth Goto considers himself to be the victim of a fraudulent transaction. In his view, his first marriage is void *ab initio* because it did not produce issue.

[25] The plaintiff submits that the *fuma* that he paid to the Chatidonhe family on marrying his wife was on the understanding that his wife would bear him children, and especially, sons to continue his name, and daughters who would in turn bring their own bride wealth into the family. As his wife has not borne him children, she has not honoured the contract between them. Mr Goto thus considers his first, customary law marriage to be more valid than the second, civil law marriage.

[26] Immaculate Goto responds that Naboth Goto has infected her with at least three different strains of venereal disease. It was after the third infection that she closed her bedroom door against him. Naboth Goto uses this as an example of her unreasonable behaviour.

[27] He also claims that she acted unreasonably when he told her that he had married another woman. Using the traditional mode of resolving disputes between married couples, Immaculate Goto consulted her family, who, in turn consulted his. There were attempts at family counselling. The families then both decided

that the only option available to preserve the marriage was for Immaculate Goto to accept the role of senior wife to her husband, while Miss Mhlanga would become her husband's second wife.

[28] Naboth Goto was prepared to accept this compromise, as long as Immaculate Goto was willing to live with Miss Mhlanga in the matrimonial home.

[29] Immaculate Goto testified that the information about the children came to her with considerable shock and distress. She wrestled with her conscience about the children and came to the conclusion that though they might be the children of God and were unable to help their birth, they were still, in her terms, 'my husband's bastards'.

[30] She also averred that in the last four years, she had undergone medical investigations to investigate the source of her infertility. None of the specialists that she consulted saw any reason she could not conceive a child.

[31] It was suggested to Mr Goto that he also undergo fertility testing. He declared this to be unnecessary, and used the children he authored with Miss Mhlanga as evidence of his own fertility. He suggested that his wife should stop consulting what he termed 'Western doctors' and, rather, focus her efforts on divining the reason for her infertility through traditional means.

[32] Immaculate Goto declared, however, that she was unwilling to compromise her faith as far as visiting traditional healers. She had even fewer kind words for such practices, calling them 'heathenish' and 'devilish'. She then pleaded with her husband to respect his marriage vows and abandon Miss Mhlanga. She

grudgingly conceded that he could continue to pay maintenance for the children, but he had sworn before a priest, she said, that he promised to be true to her in good times and in bad, in sickness and in health, to love her and honour her all the days of their lives.

[33]   Her husband was unmoved. He declared that she had forfeited her right to be his wife by reason of her infertilty.

[34]   When the parties reached a stalemate, Naboth Goto moved Miss Mhlanga and her minor child into the matrimonial home. Immaculate Goto refused to vacate the home. She put a lock on the fridge and turned off the electricity every time she left the house. Tensions escalated because Immaculate Goto stated that Miss Mhlanga would scream particularly loudly when she enjoyed the conjugal visits that she considered her lawful right.

[35]   Naboth Goto for his part states that he would have willingly satisfied both his wives conjugally but Immaculate had locked the bedroom door against him. Immaculate Goto responds that as he had given her venereal diseases on at least three occasions, she was unwilling to entertain his advances any further.

[36]   As I have already stated, Mr Goto uses that statement as evidence of his wife's unreasonable behaviour. He states further that on at least five occasions, he managed to force the door open and, as he says, 'take his due rights' over his 'own wife'.

[37]   The parties thus continued to live in this state of attrition.

[38]   These, then, are the facts that provide the background to this petition.

[39]   In giving judgement, this Court notes that it is trite law that persons subject to this jurisdiction who are of an African background have the unique privilege of choosing to be married under customary law and/or under civil law. Both these forms of marriage are equally valid legally. The choice of a civil law marriage is, not, however, without legal consequences.

[40]   As confirmed most recently in *Karimatsenga v Tsvangirai* [2012], a customary law union is open to polygamy, but a civil law marriage is not. Once the parties proceed with a marriage under civil law, they are compelled to respect all aspects of civil law marriage, including the fact that it forecloses all polygamous unions. Any further civil law marriages can only be sequential and not contemporaneous. A man who marries under civil law can only marry another woman upon his divorce from the first. To contract a union when one is already married is considered bigamy.

[41]   Indeed the Criminal Law (Codification and Reform) Act, in its Section 234, states that bigamy occurs when a man married under civil law to one woman contracts a customary union with another woman, or when a man married under customary law to one woman contracts a civil law union with another woman. The law is thus clear on the effects of a civil law marriage. By electing a civil law marriage, the parties opted to keep their marriage exclusive and monogamous.

[42]   The civil law marriage between the parties took place half a year after their customary law marriage. Naboth Goto states that he opted for this marriage under duress. I am not persuaded that is the case.

[43] I, therefore, find that the purported union with Miss Mhlanga has no legal validity, and is a bigamous marriage. It is void at law and leaves Naboth Goto vulnerable to criminal sanctions.

[44] I make no comment on whether his prosecution for bigamy would be in the public interest, and comment only that the Public Prosecutor may well decide to prosecute this matter as such conduct is dismayingly common among men who choose to enter illegally into second marriages even after contracting marriages under the civil law.

[45] With respect to the cross-application made by Immaculate Goto, I conclude that I have no powers to compel Naboth Goto to remain married to Immaculate Goto. As with labour disputes where our courts are reluctant to enforce demands for specific performance, in a marriage where one party alleges a breakdown of a marriage, it is not possible to order such a party to remain married. Marriage is a contract whose full perfomance requires both parties to be willing to remain in it. The bedrock of marriage is consent.

[46] There is no question that, unlike labour and other contracts, marriage is a contract of great peculiarity as it has both a private and public character. In the cases of *Wood and Another v Minister of Home Affairs and Others, Shalabi and Another v Minister of Home Affairs and Others, Thomas and Another v Minister of Home Affairs and Others* [2000] the Court underpinned the importance of marriage as an institution.

[47] In the words of O'REGAN CJ, 'Marriage and family are social institutions of vital importance. Entering into and sustaining a marriage is a matter of intense private significance to the parties. Such relationships are of profound significance to the individuals

concerned. But such relationships have more than personal significance, at least in part because human beings are social beings whose humanity is expressed through their relationships with others. Entering into marriage therefore is to enter into a relationship that has public significance.'

[48]   This decision was cited recently by this court in *Njodzi v Matione* [2016], where MWAYERA J stated that: 'Marriage and family remains the basic structure of our society, the preservation of which squarely lies on the couple and the nation as per our Constitution . . . The importance of the marriage and family social institutions cannot be underplayed, given that the relationship is not only significant to the individuals concerned but also for the public at large.'

[49]   While the public significance of marriage is unquestionable, it is at heart a private contract between two individuals. That only one party to that contract is willing to remain in the union is by itself a sign that the marriage has irrevocably broken down to such degree that the only fair option is to sunder all relations. The marriage between the parties is of such a nature.

[50]   I, therefore, grant the application for divorce on the grounds that the marriage between the Plaintiff and the Defendant has irretrievably broken down.

[51]   As the core principle of our divorce laws is the principle of 'no fault', I find it unnecessary to attribute the breakdown of that marriage to either the Plaintiff or the Defendant.

[52]   I find it unnecessary to consider the further contentions advanced by Immaculate Goto, namely, that no divorce petition

that I grant can dissolve or sunder the marriage ties between her and Naboth Goto. While Immaculate Goto may believe that she and Naboth Goto remain married under the law of God, the law of this country declares their marriage hereby sundered.

[53]   I also find it unnecessary to rule on the claim by Immaculate Goto that Miss Mhlanga should pay damages to her in the amount of $50,000 broken down into $30,000 for loss of consortium and $20,000 for *contumelia*.

[54]   It is true that the proper party from which to recover adultery damages is the paramour concerned, and not the cheating spouse of the aggrieved party. This is because the aggrieved party has two remedies with respect to the cheating spouse: either to condone the adultery and continue the marriage or seek to dissolve the marriage through divorce.

[55]   The basis for the application for adultery damages from the adultery paramour is the established principle that adultery occasions injury to the aggrieved spouse, who is entitled to recover damages. These damages are commonly understood to be damages for loss of a spouse's consortium as well as any patrimonial loss suffered, and personal injury or *contumelia* suffered by the aggrieved spouse, including loss of the adulterous spouse's comfort, society and services.

[56]   Thus, while Immaculate Goto does indeed have a cause of action in law, her claim for damages is not properly before this court. If she wishes to pursue her claim for damages, she is best advised to bring separate legal proceedings against Miss Mhlanga.

[57]   With respect to the distribution of the matrimonial assets,

I order that the parties enter mediation to discuss an equitable share of the property, taking into account that they were married in community, and not out of community of property.

[58]   I would also caution Naboth Goto that should Immaculate Goto seek to press charges against him, he is extremely vulnerable to a prosecution for rape. While he believes that the act of forcing himself on his wife was nothing more than taking what was his by conjugal right, the law of this land sees the matter entirely differently.

[59]   The presumption that a man cannot rape his wife, which was a part of Roman-Dutch common law for far too long in this jurisdiction, was overturned by Parliament in the Criminal Law (Codification and Reform) Act of 2004.

[60]   Section 68 of that Act removes from our law the presumption that a man cannot rape his wife. Section 68(a) makes it very clear that 'it shall not be a defence to a charge of rape, aggravated indecent assault or indecent assault . . . that the female person was the spouse of the accused person at the time of any sexual intercourse or other act that forms the subject of the charge.'

[61]   This court is not a criminal court however, and I will comment no further on this aspect of the case.

[62]   I also find it unnecessary to enter into the findings of a detective hired by Immaculate Goto who has concluded that Miss Mhlanga, the woman who claims to be the mother of Naboth Goto's child and pregnant with a second, is in receipt of maintenance from two different men in respect of the child that Mr Goto claims is his.

[63]   I have, however, conferred with the Registrar of the High Court and can confirm that this court made an order of maintenance in respect of a Mr Fortune Mpande, formerly an employee of the Zimbabwe Broadcasting Corporation, who has also been claimed as the father of Miss Mhlanga's first child, supported by proof of a paternity test. The order has not been served. Mr Mpande fled this court's jurisdiction and is reported to have sought political asylum in the United Kingdom.

[64]   While I can make no further comment on this matter, I would caution Mr Goto not to disturb his life unduly without absolute certainty that he is indeed, the father of the first child and the author of Miss Mhlanga's second pregnancy.

[65]   I appreciate that this information may come as a considerable shock to Mr Goto who appears to have been unaware of this state of affairs.

[66]   As to the legal costs of this matter, I order each party to pay their own costs. This may be somewhat new territory for Naboth Goto, who has never had to pay his own way, but when it comes to learning new skills, there is never a time like the present.

———————

ANTONIA D. DENDERE

JUDGE

The Lament of Hester Muponda

Doth God pervert judgement? Or doth the Almighty pervert justice?

– The Book of Job –

Ko Mnari ungakanganisa pakutonga here?
Wamasimba ose ungakanganisa zakarurama here?

– Buku yaJobo –

After Hester Muponda's first child died in a national bus disaster that made the front page of all four daily newspapers and the regional versions of the main Sunday paper, she turned her face to the heavens to pour out her grief, but her church people said to her, find your strength in God, they said. After the second child died with fifteen others on an overcrowded boat on a school trip to Darwendale Dam and the men responsible paid a three-hundred-dollar bribe to a prosecutor and another three to a magistrate, and thus escaped conviction and imprisonment, she wept deep sobs into the folds of her *zambiya* wrapping cloth. The Lord gives and He takes away, blessed be His name today, Hester Muponda's church women said.

Then her third child, her last child, was killed by the car of a man who had been drinking to celebrate the financial success of his public-listed company. On the night of that last child's wake, she lifted him from his coffin and laid him in the second bedroom, and would not let anyone in until they forced the door open. It took five men to prise her off him.

'He does not give us more than we can bear,' Hester Muponda's church people said to her. And her church woman Mai-Ngwerume whispered to her friend MaiMutero something about Hester Muponda's midnight ways and MaiMutero said to MaiNgwerume, 'A mad chicken eats its own eggs, but shush now, she might hear,' and MaiNgwerume said something about a payment in blood.

Hester Muponda stayed in her room for six nights and five days and when she opened the door again, she had the beginning of a beard on the chin of her disappearing face. Only women with evil tempers grow beards, her husband's paternal aunts said.

Her husband Peter Muponda woke up in the night and, reaching across the pillows, brushed his hand across her chin. He moved to the spare bedroom, and the day after the memorial service of their last child, he moved out of the house and Haig Park altogether and moved in with Gertrude Chinakira, his small house in Sunridge who had no beard or grief stench but smelt of Angel perfume and the Takatala sauce in which she marinated all their food.

Hester Muponda took up her large pots, her black pots she took up, the funeral pots in which had been cooked the meals that fed the mourners that cried her children away. She took up her pots and lit three three-stone fires, a fire for *sadza*, one for chicken and a third for vegetables, three fires she lit at the corner of Clavering and Cotswold Way next to Gift Chauke who sold individual cigarettes and Buddie airtime cards and the *Financial Gazette* on Thursdays, the *Independent* on Fridays, and the *Daily News*, *Newsday* and the *Herald* on every day but Sunday when he sold the *Standard* and the *Sunday Mail*.

In her pots she made *sadza*, thick and white, and chicken stew and vegetables that she sold to Gift Chauke and to the drivers and to the *hwindis* in the *kombis* that passed her every day. And even though her cooking smells reached into the neighbouring houses along with her pain, Edgar Jones, the only white person left in Haig Park, did not complain about property values as he had when his neighbours first started to grow maize in gardens meant for flowers and to park the heads of long-distance haulage trucks on the narrow strips of lawn outside their houses.

She is mad, Hester Muponda's church women and neighbours

said. They crossed the street when they saw her coming. Mad, mad, echoed the *kombi* drivers and the *hwindi* and Gift Chauke as their teeth tore into the chicken that she cooked in just a little oil, along with onions and tomatoes, and seasoned with just the right amount of salt. And when Hester Muponda was hit by a speeding *kombi* and she took up the blanket that covered her in the darkness that her children had found before her, the only people who felt her loss were those drivers and *hwindis* who missed the firm but soft *sadza* and the chicken and vegetables that she cooked at the corner of Clavering and Cotswold Way.

A Small House in Borrowdale Brooke

Now faith is the substance of things hoped for, the evidence of things not seen.

– The Epistle to the Hebrews –

Zino kutenda ndirwo rusimbiso rwezinhu zatinotarira, neciratidzo cezinhu zatisingavoni.

– Nwadi kuvaHeberu –.

Everything that happened to her, her trial and imprisonment, losing her man, her job and the sight in one eye, arose from her lack of curiosity about the nature of his psychosis. That term and all that was behind it did not come within her knowledge. This is not to say that she was a stupid woman. If anything, her tragedy was that she was both educated and ignorant.

Like many others before and after her, she had imbibed and absorbed into her core the simple message that the purpose of learning was to get to the next school grade or form terminating in passing exams. The point of passing exams was to get a good job, a good job was essential to getting a promotion, getting a promotion was necessary to getting an even better job. Education was not about knowledge or enhancing her understanding of the world and her place in it, or expanding the mind. It was primarily to enable the accumulation of material things.

Reading was what she did to pass the exams, it was what she did in her job, it was what she did to her beloved *True Love* and *Destiny* magazines, to *Home and Garden* and *African Interiors*. It was what she did to *Dish*, the magazine that came with her DStv subscription. It was what she did to the Bible, to the messages on her phone and occasionally, to the lifestyle sections of newspapers.

She believed in sorcery. She believed that herbs and animals had magical properties, and that these were not just psychedelic effects, but heart- and mind-altering properties. There were roots that made you fall in love, and out again. There were incantations that made you lucky, and unlucky again. Evil was all around: it lived in snakes, and in dark things. It lived in chameleons and bushbabies and owls.

The opening up of horizons offered by television, by films and other books beyond that one Book, all this was closed to her. Her favourite films were from Nigeria's Nollywood, two- or three-part films with linear stories and gratifying outcomes. Women with impossible hairstyles and facial skin lighter than the rest of their bodies battled evil and overcame it, men of poverty and ambition battled fate and conquered it. Any psychosis there was simply called madness. She watched pastors on television cast out, with spittle and verve, the demons of poverty and illness and want.

So there was nothing in her life, no foreknowledge that could have equipped her to appreciate that the damaged mind can be dangerous. The only thing she knew was that she needed a mad man, and when she found the right one, she saw only a man who was mad in circumstances where a mad man was what she needed.

She had watched to see which of them would do. For two weeks she had watched the homeless until she knew them well, the street children aged between four and seventeen, the blind women led by their children, the blind old man who was always led by a young boy who wore shirts and shorts belonging to two different school uniforms. The street kids, reed-thin saplings just sprouting into manhood, she dismissed almost at once. They looked after cars and begged for money. They drank broncho strong cough mixtures to get high and caused fights, all activities that required a degree of sentience, of awareness.

The prescription was clear: she needed the essence of someone who was out of his senses. In the semi-darkness of the half-lit room in Seke, children's laughing voices reaching in from outside, she had not questioned why it was necessary that it be such a person, what it was about the alchemy of this person's essence that made it a powerful restorative of the affections of her man. She knew only that it was vital. It was necessary. Without it, her man would cease to be her man.

She called him her husband but he was not that at all, he was not even fully hers. She might have been exclusively his, but he was not exclusively hers. She was a small house, meaning she was not a proper wife but an official mistress and more elevated than a girlfriend.

She was by nature an exhibitionist. She liked things, and she wanted to shout out her love, but the constrictions imposed by her secret life meant that she was reduced to writing cryptic posts on Facebook referring to first, second, third anniversaries without ever declaring who her man was. He had given her this house in Borrowdale Brooke, she could post about the house, but not how she got it. He had paid for their holidays to Mauritius and Dubai; she could post picture after picture as long as his face did not appear in them.

The most she could do was to post pictures of their feet next to each other on a beach in Mauritius, or black-and-white and sepia-toned photos of their intertwined hands. Luckily, her married man has no burns, scars or other distinguishing features on his hands and feet, he had nothing that marked him out; his were just the ordinary hands and feet of a common-or-garden variety cheating married man.

In contrast, deep in the heart of the golden triangle, his real wife posted picture after picture of her handsome and amazing husband, the award-winning human rights activist, declaring in each one what a gift God had given her, and the country, in him. His wife's claim on him and his position in society meant that theirs was a love that dared not speak its name.

There had been other small houses in her man's life, she had replaced one herself and, she feared, was on the verge of being replaced. The one thing she knew about other women was that they were the enemy, every single one of them. They would stop at nothing in the pursuit of her man.

Thus, she had moved around the townships, going from herbalist to herbalist as she sought the one substance, the one *mupfuhwira* that would cleave her man to her. A herbalist in Glen View had sold her *chipotanemadziro*, a potion that would make a straying husband stay at home. The herbalist claimed it was made using the dried and pounded tail of a lizard so that her man, like the lizard, would circulate only the walls of her home.

From a woman at the Robert Mugabe end of First Street, she had bought *Weti yeGudo*, a powder that was supposed to make her man behave like a baboon that wanted to urinate in only one place. From a woman in Mbare called Sekuru Muchabaya, she had brought home a needle dipped in a secret substance, and that she was supposed to encase in a yellow duster when her man was far from her. In desperation, on the advice of a woman in Mufakose, she had even cooked him chicken to which she had added her own menstrual blood.

None of this had worked, and so it was that she had eventually found herself in a hut in Seke, and there been told that as all other remedies had failed, there were just two left. The remedies had both terrified her, but the healer assured her that the fact that they were so terrifying was surely a sign of their power.

The first remedy was to prepare a bath for him to which she was to add water in which a dead body had been recently washed. This way, her man would become as malleable as a corpse. The second was this one, the one she had opted for. She was to find the essence of a mad man, and prepare her husband food in which she added that essence. That way, he would become as docile as the man from whom she had taken the essence.

She was perhaps too desperate to ask, why did this woman who promised so much, live in this township, where a burst sewer announced itself to all within it? Where, she could have asked, were these riches that she promised others, why did she grab, did they all grab, with such eagerness at the dirty dollar bills that they demanded? Why, if these treatments were so powerful, had no one thought to patent them, to sell them in bulk, to make them part of the balance of imports and exports and bring them firmly into the heart of globalisation? For markets were surely plentiful for powerful medicines against heartache and loss. Patents could be filed for curatives to infidelity and loneliness and rejection.

Why, she could have asked, was so much of this medicine based on imitation and the manipulation of nature? Why was it that a heart-shaped leaf was supposed to cure the heart simply because of its shape, why was it if you slapped a child with the lung of a sheep that child would be as tranquil as a sheep in the face of provocation? Why was it that if a man ate lizard tail, he behaved like a lizard; if a man was treated with baboon's piss, he behaved like a baboon; a man bathed in the water that had washed a corpse would become as malleable as that body; and a man fed the essence of a mad man would become biddable, unable to follow his own thoughts? She asked none of this, because she did not know the questions to ask. She had, and she saw, only her need.

She finally saw the one she needed outside the Chicken Inn on Inez Terrace, rummaging in the bins. She shuddered as she imagined what she had to do, imagined his hands, those hands in the bin, on her body, that black grease on his skin on hers. In the end, getting him into the car was easier than she had imagined. He came to the side of her car. He looked exactly how she imagined a mad person would look. He stared straight at her, and then suddenly he smiled.

'Let me take you home,' she said.

'I want to shoot some birds,' he said.

'That's right, let's go to shoot some birds.'

She opened the car for him. He got in. She clicked on the child lock. No one gave them a second look. It was a time of night at which the only motorists were men looking to buy lukewarm sex with cold cash. It was all darkness, the only light came from other cars. As she turned into Carreigh Cleagh, the driver of an oncoming vehicle neglected to dim his lights. The powerful beams shone so brightly that it was as though the momentary glare had exposed every dark thought in her mind.

By the time she got to the gates of the estate, he was asleep. The guard stood at attention when he recognised her car. 'My husband has gone on a trip, and I will be working at home for a week. Make sure no one disturbs me, please.'

'Yes, Madam.'

He saluted her as she drove on. It was an extra precaution, but one she was sure she did not need. This was the Brooke, after all, the fortress to which only the invited came through. No vendors, hawkers or jobseekers were allowed. No uninvited relatives dropped in, there were no unexpected callers. She had told the people at work that she had taken the whole week off to be in the Eastern Highlands with the man they thought of as her husband. And he was safely in Nairobi, and, she knew, would not even call her.

When she got into the house, she looked about, and tried to see the house with his eyes, if his eyes saw what she saw. The house had been paid for by her man, but she had furnished it herself on the many trips that she took outside the country. The view over the golf course. The sunken lounge with its lounge suite from Dubai. The plasma screen television, framed by the totem animals, a nice touch, she thought, and one much admired (and to her irritation, imitated by her friends), his the lion, menacing fierce, hers the monkey, defiant, cunning. She would need all her cunning now.

She gave him the only alcoholic drink that she could stomach: rum and Coca-Cola. It would make him more pliable, she thought, easier to manage. It proved more effective than she thought. It was easy to lift him, all those years of helping her mother bring home her drunken father from the township beer halls had trained her in the art of leading a drunken man from one place to another without letting him fall and drag her down with him.

She took off his clothes. His hands and feet were callused with dirt wedged in the cracks. The rest of him, while caked with dirt, could be managed. He fell asleep in the bath. The grease defeated her, but at least the smell was gone. After the second unyielding bath, she had the wild notion to use something tougher, Vim perhaps, or caustic soda, but that would sear the skin. It had happened to her last maid but one, who had needed a hospital visit. No, she had all the time in the world to get him clean. She went through two bottles of Dettol and a tub of camphor cream.

Every time he protested, she said, but you are home. The alcohol kept him peaceable and in between, he ate and watched television. It did not matter what she put on, sport on Supersport, *Big Brother Africa*, decoration programmes, he watched it all, lying on the bed in the guest bedroom, looking at the screen almost without blinking.

On the third night, after she had given him seven baths in two days, she decided the time had come. She gave him more rum and Coke. Her courage almost failed her. She had some herself. She could not bring herself to take him into the bedroom she shared with her man, so she led him into the room she had given him. She lay him back on the bed.

She had noticed when she bathed him that he had no problem getting hard. During the first bath, he had convulsed right there in the bath, and she had looked with dismay at the wasted essence that was washed down the drain with his grease and dirt. But at least she knew that he was capable.

Afterwards, she unpeeled the condom, careful not to spill any of its contents. Who would have thought he would have so much in him? She emptied the condom into the old can that the woman had given her for this purpose. From its label, it had once contained condensed milk.

'*Ane madzihwa ane kondenzi,*' she sang.

She burst into hysterical laughter, which became a sob, then laughter again. She was to take it back after a week. She did not know how much she needed. Divination, healing, is about intuition not about precision – it is in fact the opposite of scientific. Her intuition, responding to her need, told her to take as much as she could. She was careful to refrigerate the can each time she added to it, clearing a shelf where it sat on its own, away from the carefully chosen cheeses and cold meats that her man liked to snack on.

Once established, the pattern continued for six days: baths followed by food followed by drinking followed by what she insisted in thinking of as the necessary first step in the treatment that would restore her man to her. She drank more and more. Having finished the rum, they moved on to Blue Label whisky. She mixed it with Fanta.

She became expansive, confiding. When the electricity went out on the third night, she did not trouble to fire up the generator, but lay in the darkness with him.

'I got my man', she said, 'through a love potion.' Just saying it seemed like a form of release. She told him of the mother who had left her drunken father. The man her mother married, who had gradually ignored his wife and directed his attentions towards her fifteen-year-old daughter until, at seventeen, her mother had asked her to leave home, the thrill of getting a university place so that she never had to go home again, her first job. Meeting her man, falling for his sleek car, his deep laugh. The herbalists she had visited to secure him. Her fear that she was not enough to hold him, that the charms no longer worked, that she would be replaced. The measures she had taken to prevent that happening. The love potions, the supplications, the prayers, the intercessions. And now, this desperate stratagem.

On the fourth night she became maudlin, confessional.

'I am not a bad person,' she said. 'Am I bad person?'

'I want to shoot some birds,' he said.

His eyes were on *Top Gear*.

'Look what I have done for you,' she said. 'You have this nice bed, you have good food, really, and if I wasn't sure you would not know what to do with it, would not throw it away, I would give you money, lots of money, I would give you even a hundred dollars.'

He did not answer, but watched as one Richard tried to outdo the other Richard in escalating excitement over the latest Maserati.

On the fifth night, she inquired about his life. 'Do you have a home?' she asked him, then catching herself, 'Did you have a home?'

'I am going to shoot some birds now.'

'Did you have a woman of your own, were you married?'

'I want to shoot some birds.'

On the sixth night, she danced to a Don Williams song. 'Oh,' she wept, 'I love you desperately.' He kept his eyes on the television. On the seventh night, she brought out her photo album, and showed him the pictures.

The trouble began on the eighth night. This was the night she had decided she would take him back, as her man was to arrive three days later. She would take him back, then drive with the can to Seke to get the final medicine made up. She began to plan what to cook on the night her man came to her. She wondered whether she would have to serve him the medicine, or bath him in it. The thought turned her stomach a little.

When the time came, he would not get into the car.

'Please, you have to go.'

She was panicking now, unable to breathe.

'I want to shoot some birds.' He said it with a flat insistence.

'Okay, okay,' she said. 'Let's go to shoot some birds.'

The next night came and she still had not thought up the most effective way to get him out. She considered going to the gate, and asking the guards to take him out. If all else failed, that is what she would do. Her man would be home in two days, there was enough time. That night, he came to her room, something he had never done.

She was woken by a sharp pain and the taste of a metallic liquid in her mouth. She had dreamt that her man was standing over them, but saw that no, it was not a dream, and he was not standing over them but was being held back by his brother, and it was morning and in the bed next to her, the mad man had a gash across the forehead where a broken bottle of Blue Label whisky had cut him. She screamed and as she did so, the blood, his blood came rushing out of her mouth and on to the sheet they lay on, his essence mixed with hers.

The trial that followed was a short formality in which she confirmed her name, her address and her guilt. Her man was charged with attempted murder, then, the full details out, it was downgraded to assault, not even aggravated assault, said the Public Prosecutor because no man would have done less.

At Rotten Row, she pleaded guilty to sexual assault. An eager court reporter splashed the details all over the *Metropolitan* tabloid. Here was sex, illicit sex, here was magic of the darkest kind. 'SMALL HOUSE RAVAGES MADMAN,' said the headline,

'FOR CENTRAL LOCKING' continued the by-line. She was only knocked off the front page by a man who died in Gokwe but refused to stay dead.

Two months after leaving Chikurubi prison, she saw him, or she thought she saw someone very like him. He was outside the food court in Msasa. His hair was long and matted. His skin was so dirty it may never have once made contact with soapy Dettol water. But on his cheek was a scar that looked like it might be the faded result of an encounter with the jagged edge of a bottle. He looked straight at her and smiled. For a moment, she thought he winked at her blind eye before going back to rummaging through the bins in front of him.

In Sad Cypress

And I will turn your feasts into mourning, and all
your songs into lamentation; and I will bring up
sackcloth upon all loins, and baldness upon every
head; and I will make it as the mourning of an
only son, and the end thereof as a bitter day.

– The Book of the Prophet Amos –

Ndicashandura mitambo yenyu kuve kucema,
nenziyo dzenyu dzose kuve kurirakwokucema;
ndicafukidza zivuno zose masaga, nokuita
misoro yose mhazha; ndicaziita sepanochemna
mnanakomana wakazarwa ari mumne cete,
nekuguma kwazo sezuva rakaipa kwazo.

– Buku yaMuprofita Amosi –

PARIRENYATWA GROUP OF HOSPITALS
POST-MORTEM REPORT

Being an Affidavit in Terms of Section 278 of the Criminal
Procedure and Evidence Act
[CAP 9.07]

I, NGONIDZASHE LORDMORE GWATA, MBChB (UZ),
FRCPath (UK), being a duly Registered Medical Practitioner
and a Consultant Forensic Pathologist, do hereby make oath and
swear that:

On 11 June 2016, and at the request of the Zimbabwe Republic
Police, I examined the remains of PETER CHABURUKA
MUPONDA, which were conveyed to me under the authority
of SERGEANT PHINIEL ZUZE of Matapi Police Station,
Mbare. The examination took place over one and a half hours
at Parirenyatwa Hospital. The results of that examination are
contained in the memorandum below.

Memorandum of a Post-mortem Examination
by Dr N. L. Gwata

Name of Deceased   Peter Chaburuka Muponda
Sex   Male

Race	African
Age	65
National Reg. No.	Not available
Occupation	Court Interpreter
Address	27 72nd Avenue, Haig Park, Harare
Hospital number	Not applicable
Place of death	Rotten Row Magistrates Court, Rotten Row, Harare
Date of death	9 June 2016

EXTERNAL EXAMINATION

Deceased was a male of 1.68m in height. Appeared poorly nourished and skeletal. Clothes intact but in poor condition. Circumferential ligature mark around neck. Inverted 'V' indentation of skin apparent on right side of neck to match circumferential ligature mark and its mild vital reaction. Head flexed to the left.

Marked venous vascular congestion and central cyanosis above the ligature. Petechial haemorrhages on both eyeballs. No signs of recent of injury. No distinctive marks. No decomposition. Natural features. Skin intact. Position of limbs anatomical.

INTERNAL EXAMINATION

Not performed due to lack of resources.

OTHER SIGNIFICANT CONDITIONS

None detected.

SUMMARY OF AUTOPSY FINDINGS /OPINION

Ligature in-situ, inverted 'V' indentation on neck, perilaryngeal bruising.

As a result of this examination, I formed the opinion that the cause of death was:

a. Asphyxia
b. Hanging

Note found on body suggests self-strangulation.
Sworn before me ANTONIA D DENDERE, COMMISSIONER OF OATHS at HARARE this 15th DAY OF JUNE 2016.

ADDENDUM TO POST-MORTEM REPORT, DATED 20 JUNE 2016
(From previous page)

On 10 June 2016, I was asked to conduct a post-mortem on a deceased male, Peter Chaburuka Muponda of Haig Park in the surburb of Mabelreign, whose body was conveyed to Parirenyatwa Hospital in the charge of Inspector Phiniel Zuze, Officer Commanding Matapi Police station, Mbare.

On the same day, I sought to recuse myself from conducting the post-mortem on the grounds that I was aquainted with Deceased.

Deceased and I were born on exactly the same day, the 11th of November in the year 1950. We grew up as boys together in a village on the banks of the Devure in Masvingo Province. We herded our fathers' cows and goats together, played together and went to school together until Deceased failed to pass his Standard Six.

On the same day, having realised that I was acquainted with Deceased, I sent a memorandum to head office asking to recuse myself and transfer the responsibility for the post-mortem to Midlands Province. That afternoon, I received a directive by telephone from the Permanent Secretary in the Ministry of Health who stated that I could not to recuse myself as I am, at present, the only government pathologist in service.

I was informed that this was because my colleague, Dr T. V. Mubako, who covers Mat North and South Provinces had left the country for further training, while my second colleague, Dr Ananias Rixon Ngabi, who covers Midlands and Masvingo provinces, had had a nervous shock on the previous day which had necessitated his immediate admittance to Ingutsheni Mental Hospital. It was not known when his treatment would be completed.

The permanent secretary informed me that government has urgently sent for at least three pathologists under the health co-operation agreement signed with the government of Cuba. Even if those pathologists arrive, it is unlikely that their English will be of a level such that they can work without direction.

I honoured the directive and the next day, 11 June 2016, I completed my post-morterm examination in spite of my own discomfort. It is a matter of extreme repugnance to me to conduct post-mortems on persons otherwise known to me.

My medical conclusions are contained in the first page of this report. I emphasise that my conclusions are based on an external examination only. I took no samples for toxicological or other tests. Even if I had, the truth of the matter is that government hospitals are simply not equipped with the necessary chemicals or equipment for full toxicological screenings. In any event, I do not believe that further tests would have had any effect on my conclusions.

As I was aquainted with Deceased, I was able, unusually in

such cases, to confirm my diagnosis with further information that I gleaned about Deceased at his funeral wake.

In this memorandum, I explain why the most competent verdict for the coroner to reach should be death by suicide.

I need to explain that as a pathologist, I am not normally privy to any information about the subjects of my investigations, and indeed, once my subjects are off my table, I give them no further thought unless I am called to testify in court. In this case, I was driven by a combination of curiosity and, I must admit, pity, to establish what it is that might have caused Deceased to take his own life.

My curiosity arose particularly with respect to the meaning of the note that had been found on Deceased and that said, 'Come away death, and in sad cypress let me be laid.'

Twenty days after my post-mortem was completed, and after I had made the initial report above, the body was released to Deceased's family for burial. When I learned about the funeral arrangements, I made certain to attend said funeral and in the process acquired fuller and further particulars of his life.

Deceased may have been alone in death, but no man is ever alone in leaving life. As at all other funerals, his wake was attended by a large crowd of mourners who included his own relatives as well as those of his wife, his workmates and employers.

I spent an entire night at the funeral wake. From talking to various persons connected to Deceased, I managed to piece together a chronology of his life.

As I said above, Deceased and I were in school together until Standard Six. While I passed and went on to St Stephens Gokomere before proceeding to the University of Rhodesia and Nyasaland where I completed my medical studies, Deceased found work as a clerical assistant in a government office in Fort Victoria. From Fort Victoria, Deceased moved to Salisbury just after UDI where he continued in government service, but this time, not in a government office but *kwamudzviti* where he became a court interpreter. After independence in 1980, he remained with the Public Service Commission, and was eventually based at Rotten Row Magistrates Court. There, he spent the rest of his working life.

It was his job to translate the excuses, the lies and the sorry tales fabricated by accused persons seeking to escape responsibility for their actions and to translate also the accusations, sometimes truthful but occasionally spiteful of their accusers.

I have gathered that Deceased never rose higher in his profession than Senior Interpreter, Grade 8 Step 2. Modest as his salary was, it secured him a modest mortgage to buy a house in the suburb of Haig Park, in which he resided with his wife Hester Muponda, of Chitsa Village in Masvingo Province.

Deceased and his wife had three children. Neither his wife Hester, nor his three children survived him. It would appear that I conducted the post-morterm on two of those children, one who was killed in a road traffic accident that was declared a National Road Disaster, and another who drowned with other schoolchildren in the Darwendale Dam disaster.

Having lost his wife and three children, Deceased then moved in with a Ms Gertrude Chinakira of Sunridge, also in Mabelreign, a woman variously referred to by Deceased's relatives and neighbours as his small house. She herself disputes this characterisation of their relationship and considers herself to have been his second wife.

Shortly after this, the Public Service Commission put him on early retirement. Ms Chinakira says the strain on their finances ended the marriage. Shortly after he was thrown out of Sunridge by Ms Chinakira, his wife Hester died from an unknown illness.

Their house in Haig Park was taken over by his wife's relatives who refused him access to the house on the grounds that he had abandoned his wife. There were, from all accounts, several unpleasant scenes between all parties concerned. Deceased was blamed for what was considered his wife's madness and her subsequent death.

Deceased spent a considerable amount of money battling to regain his house. He used his dwindling resources to hire a lawyer to whom he paid the usual retainer. Lawyers, it appears, are the only professionals who are paid handsomely even before they have undertaken a jot of work. Unfortunately for Deceased, soon after he made over most of his golden handshake from the Public Service Commission, his lawyer was declared unfit and improper to practise law and thus struck off the roll of legal practitioners after being caught in a public affray with a prostitute.

This left Deceased in some considerable financial distress. With nowhere else to go, Deceased hired a room in Kuwadzana from where he went to town daily, to his old workplace. There he sought to re-establish contact with his former colleagues, and occasionally filled in for one or two, all without being paid. He was then evicted from Kuwadzana which is when he moved into the Rotten Row Complex. His presence went unnoticed at first as he would hide in the toilets at closing time before occupying an abandoned courtroom at night.

He was, however, eventually spotted by the complex security guards who then banned him from re-entering the complex. A few days following this ban, Deceased was found dead at dawn hanging from the sign outside the Magistrates Court that says, 'Justice is Free. Don't pay for it.' His body was moved by the security guards. A note that fell from his pocket was handed to the police.

On my enquiries at the funeral, I learned that the note was a line from a play by William Shakespeare. 'Come away' is in fact an invitation to death, and it would appear that 'sad cypress' is a long-winded way of talking about wood from which coffins are made. I must say that I was surprised that Deceased would have known this as he had always struck me as something of a dull fellow who had, after all, not passed his Standard Six. However, as I had not seen him for a number of years it may well be that he turned into the sort of fellow who read poetry and the like.

That, in a nutshell, is the story of Deceased. He had had a wife and three children, none of whom survived him. He lost his job, his house and his money. By the end of his life, he had as little as that with which he had come into the world. If his death could be attributed to one cause, I would say that he died from grief. As that is not a medically recognised cause of death, however, I refer to my conclusions in the first page of this report. Deceased died of ligature strangulation occasioned by use of his own belt. It was, very unfortunately, a painful, and in my view, entirely unnecessary death. May he find in the life hereafter all that he failed to find on Earth.

'Ladies and Gentlemen, Bob Marley and the Wailers!'

Finally, brethren, whatsoever things are true, whatsoever things are honest, whatsoever things are just, whatsoever things are pure, whatsoever things are lovely, whatsoever things are of good report; if there be any virtue, and if there be any praise, think on these things.

– The Epistle of Paul the Apostle to the Philippians –

Pakupedzisira, hama dzangu, zose zazokwadi, zose zinokudzwa, zose zakarurama, zose zakachena, zose zinodikanwa, zose zinorumbidzwa, kana kunaka kupi nokupi, kana cingarumbidzwa cipi necipi, fungisisai izozo.

– Nwadi yaPauro kuvaFiripi –

Saturday morning, 05:49

As Samson reached for Deliwe and she stretched her arms to touch him, she screamed loudly that she was tired of this nonsense and something had to change. Her voice deepened as she said, no, it was not nonsense and nothing had to change at all because all they needed to do was to be patient. Her voice became louder and deeper until it mutated into the voices of his quarrelling landlady Makorinde and her husband, Father Abraham.

Disoriented from the abrupt end to his dream, Samson reached under his pillow for his mobile phone. It was not yet six. It was not unknown for Samson to fall asleep to quarrelling voices and wake to them again, but the voices could not have interrupted him at a more inopportune time. He found with no surprise that he had a raging hard-on.

He closed his eyes and tried to go back to his dream. But neither sleep nor Deliwe came back on command. He knew why he had dreamt of her. He had read her message the night before. She had sent him a WhatsApp message, probably sent to everyone in her Contacts, in which she asked for his vote in the People's Choice vote of the Miss Sunshine City Beauty Pageant she had entered. As it was, he had a press ticket for the pageant, and he fully intended to go to the Rainbow Towers later that evening to see her on stage. A beauty pageant is not how Samson would normally have spent his Saturday night, but he belonged to that edifying profession that hopes that, if all goes well, the very worst will happen at any public event. Bad news made better copy than good news. Samson was a journalist.

As he listened to the quarrel outside, he found himself in the position of other eavesdroppers who had heard little that was good about themselves. The quarrel was about his good self. Makorinde was saying he had to go. Father Abraham was saying he should stay. Why, said Makorinde, should they look after a lodger who was late paying his rent? Why, said Father Abraham, should they chase away the only person at this house who actually had proper employment? He would pay when he had it. Makorinde said, well, in that case I will ask when he will have it. And Father Abraham said, Now, now, Chihera mine, we know what you can be like, let me be the one to talk to him, man to man.

Samson would normally have been gratified by Father Abraham's support, but he knew it came from pure self-interest. He had already paid two weeks' rent directly to the man. He had only been at this house in Mbare a month and two weeks, and had paid the first four weeks' rent directly to Makorinde. He had not thought twice when Father Abraham came to collect the next two weeks' rent directly from him at work. But just two days later, Father Abraham had confided that he had spent all of Samson's money on his chief passion. As it happened, Father Abraham's chief passion was to put down certain sums on the uncertain outcomes of sporting competitions.

Thanks to that Dutchman Van Gaal's incompetence, Father Abraham said, an incompetence that had seen him start the wrong players compounded with playing the wrong formation given the weakness in the midfield, Manchester United had lost to Sunderland, can you believe it, Samson, Sunderland of all teams, surely Van Gaal knows by now that captain or no captain, you simply don't start with Rooney, you start that young one, *uyu mpfanha uyu*, what's his name, Memphis then you bring on Rooney as added arsenal just before the second half.

But Van Gaal did not do that and now Father Abraham was finished, well, not finished but in a bit of a pickle actually, so could Samson just play along a while and tell Makorinde the rent was on its way, and better still, could Samson give him an advance on the next week's rent, just a twenty would do, maybe even a *gumi chete* to put on Federer on his match against Djokovic so that he could win back the money that Van Gaal had lost him?

Samson had given him ten dollars just to shut him up. It was then that Samson had realised exactly how the economic power lay in this household, and that he was not the tenant of a proprietor and his wife, but of a proprietress and her husband.

Father Abraham had that nickname from their lodgers because his children seemed to pop up like mushrooms. Any random child who appeared at the house was likely to be one of Father Abraham's many offshoots with different women. Tired of going to the maintenance courts at The Stables and getting nothing, because Makorinde held on to the purse strings with the same tenacity the president clung to power, Father Abraham's women ended up bringing their children to the house and leaving them there. His name came from the hymn in celebration of his prolific namesake: 'Father Abraham has many sons! Has many sons has Father Abraham! I am one of them. And so are you!'

His wife Makorinde's name was more obscure. She was a big and loud woman with a carrying voice, particularly when she was on her mobile phone. Samson had wondered why she was called Makorinde until one of the other lodgers at the house said, 'Well, Makorinde is Corinthians in Shona.'

'I know that,' Samson said. 'So why call her that?'

'*Akakoraka*, she is big, so she is Makorinde.'

An active member of the ruling party's Women's League,

Makorinde's life seemed to afford no greater pleasure than going to kneel at the airport to welcome the president on his many returns home. In the six weeks that Samson had stayed with them, she had gone to the airport once every week, the president's bespectacled face jiggling a benign benediction from her bottom as she walked, her voice booming out to anyone who greeted her on her way, 'I am going to welcome the president, they are expecting me now now', as though she alone had that distinct honour.

Samson hoped that Father Abraham would not make it hard to stay here. He had a history of lodgings, having known all too well the Great Migration of the Common-or-Garden Variety Lodger at the end of every month when the rent became due but there was no money to pay it, and they had to leave, a migration slightly eased by the necessity of leaving some belongings behind in lieu of rent.

He was happy here, at the corner of Chaminuka and Sixth Street. Like many Harareans, he had thought of living in Mbare with some dread. But once there, he realised it had its own charm. The rent was reasonable, the other lodgers congenial. He was a short right from Cripps down to Rotten Row, and from there, a short walk to his offices to pound out his copy. And Makorinde and Father Abraham were relatively prosperous, so there were none of the usual problems here about leaving his meat in the fridge of a landlord who did not have his own meat and thus eyed him sourly when he went to collect it.

Mbare was a place where something was always happening. Close to Makorinde's place on Chaminuka lived AmbuyaVaDudley, a curvy and vivacious woman who liked to dilute Chibuku beer with Cherry Plum and wore skintight trousers. When she was possessed, she became the grandfatherly Sekuru Muchabaya. She was a traditional healer who divined misfortune, threw bones and diagnosed and treated illness. From hanging out at her house, Samson had learned startling things about potions and magic, but more profitably, about the people who visited her, many of them well known. For though she claimed powers to heal that were equal to doctors of Western medicine, she did not consider herself unduly constrained by the latter's vows of confidentiality. Among the many things she promised her clients, discretion was not one of them.

'You just missed the MP for Harare South East, Samson,' she would say. 'And before that, the Minister of Public Works was here. So many problems in his life. And the permanent secretary of that Ministry was here, you know the woman who is sleeping with her boss, the minister. I gave her a charm to use on him, she asked for *chipotanemadziro*, lizard's tail, but he also came here for a protection against all love charms, so who knows. *Hodo! Zvichasotana zvega!'*

Also on Reverend Machingura Street was Manyara, who had become a fast friend of Samson. She needed very little inducement to entertain him with stories of the clients that she saw, men just as well known as AmbuyaVaDudley's, including a man who tried to persuade the girls not to use condoms they insisted on as he was just an 'old madhala with no disease.' The next time Samson saw the gentleman was at the opening of the Trade Fair, and he grinned to himself thinking 'Old madhala, no disease.'

The paper Samson worked for was the *Metropolitan*, a paper that specialised in salacious gossip and crime. So these tips were particularly welcome to him, and a few had come in handy. He was desperate to get out of the court reporting he was currently doing and move into Celebrities and Showbiz. It paid better because you could always make something on the side by getting people to pay you not to publish something about them, or accept payment to write favourable reviews and puff pieces. If he managed to find the right story, a hot story, he knew that he could move from Court to Showbiz.

The quarrelling voices grew louder as they approached his room. He hoped that he had remembered to lock the door. Yes he had, and he had taken the key out of the lock. Sure enough, there was a loud knocking at his door as the handle was tried from the outside. If he lay still, he could wait to leave after they had left. He simply had to escape Makorinde's awkward questions and evade Father Abraham's importunate begging. The president was coming back from Addis Ababa today at about 12 p.m., so Makorinde would leave to go and wait with others at the 'usual pick-up points', wherever those might be. Father Abraham would be off to town as usual.

Samson kept still, not daring to move even an eyelash. Luckily, he had remembered to draw the curtains closed the night before. The steps went back into the house. He turned his thoughts to Deliwe.

He flicked to the photos on a folder in his Samsung phone. He rather hoped she would do well in the pageant. She did not have to win it, she just had to do well enough to reach the final three. Her doing well was a golden opportunity for him. This was a potentially hot story, the kind that the Showbiz desk loved. He turned to the other folder, as though to reassure himself, and there they were, his other pictures of Deliwe, Deliwe as nature had made her, in all her glory. He had taken these photos on one of the nights they had spent together and she had fallen asleep without knowing what he did. She still did not know that he had them. He had not planned to use them at all other than for his private enjoyment, but now, if she did well in the pageant, he knew that his editor would pay a fortune to have them.

He had known Deliwe from childhood, together with her brother Dumisani and sister Velile. To Samson and the rest of the township, this family had been imbued with an exotic glamour because they were one of a handful of Ndebele families in the area. A gawky girl, with legs like a new-born giraffe, Deliwe had been known mainly for her high jump at school. Then she had disappeared and returned six years later from England, where she had lived with Velile, who had become a nurse. Trained as a beauty therapist, Deliwe was no longer the gawky teenager, but a leggy beauty who turned heads and dreamt of becoming a model.

When they reconnected, they had initially bonded over their desire to be anywhere but where they were. Her return had not been a willing one: she had been deported for overstaying her visa in England and he had come from a similar disappointment. After his stint at the Poly studying for a 'Diploma in Mass Communications', a Soviet-inspired title which made what they were learning sound more like studies in propaganda than journalism, he had seized gratefully at the opportunity afforded him by a generous brother who had offered to pay for him to do another degree, this time in Singapore. But alas, the brother had married while Samson was in his second year, and his new sister-in-law had decreed that a Singapore degree was a waste, so Samson had come back with no option but to use his MassCom qualification.

Then his brother had died in a car accident and his sister-in-law had told him that Samson was now responsible for his younger sister who was at boarding school. The fees increased monthly, and, in the meantime, it was all he could do to keep a roof over his own head.

Deliwe, for her part, had the responsibility of looking after her brother Dumisani's daughter. She had a job at the beauty salon in the ZB Life Towers complex. So the two had bonded over family problems when they saw each other for the first time after many years, in a *kombi* that dropped them both outside the Aquatic complex. They had met again. He found it surprisingly easy to talk to her, even about the embarrassing things concerning his finances and family that he kept from his other friends. They found so much to talk about when they met that, often, Samson found himself walking her back to her house, then she walked him back to his, and then Samson walked her back again to hers, until they eventually agreed to part at a point that was halfway between their homes.

Samson could no longer remember how it was that they had drifted into sleeping with each other. She had a sweet honesty that made him smile. He liked her best in the morning, her make-up gone, she had a vulnerability that caught at him. It would never have been a relationship, she was simply not deep enough for him to consider being serious about. And she had, on her part, been characteristically candid about his chances as her long-term prospect. 'I like you a lot, Samson,' she said. 'If you had a bit more money, I would like you even more.'

He had laughed out loud at that but it had not bruised his ego.

They had seen less and less of each other after Samson had moved out of Chitungwiza. She had become established on the pageant circuit, performing well enough in the lower ranked titles to become Miss Summer Splash Third Princess, Miss Aquatic Complex First Princess, as well as Miss Personality in the Miss Chitungwiza final. The last accomplishment won her a contract to advertise a soap. She called him up with the news that her face was on a large billboard near Newlands shopping centre. Unfortunately, the very next week, it was covered over by a large picture of the president, accompanied by a birthday message congratulating him for his thirty-six years of visionary leadership.

Whenever he saw her about town, she seemed happy to see him. 'I am with this guy now,' she said one night at the Book Café. 'He is very well up. In fact, he has friends who are the children of ministers. And he even has one or two white friends.'

She was fated, Samson thought, to become a rich man's bauble.

They were no longer sleeping together but he had those pictures. If she won, they would be his meal ticket. Not only would a promotion come his way, his editor promised a thousand dollars for every picture of a naked celebrity that they could get. And their definition of celebrity was elastic enough to include beauty contestants. And she would never know that it was him. They could have been taken anywhere and if she could do this with him, she could probably do this with everyone.

The thought came to him that this was unworthy, but he was desperate. He replaced that thought with another. Any of her new boyfriends could have taken it. Thus trying to ease his conscience, Samson drifted off to sleep.

Saturday afternoon, 12:37

When Samson woke up again, he found he badly needed to piss. His phone indicated it was just after twelve thirty. Then it died. He had put it on the charger when he got in the night before, but clearly, there had been no electricity for more than twelve hours. He listened and there seemed to be no one in the house, not even the other lodgers. From the house next door came the loud sound of Ijahman blasting, 'Are We a Warrior'.

The house belonged to Jah Teurai, also known as Jah T, a Rastafarian market trader in his late sixties whose grey hair fell in increasingly diminishing bunches from his balding pate. So loudly did Jah T play his music that the windowpanes rattled. If any neighbours dared to complain about the noise, Jah T simply said, 'But that is not noise. It is reggae.'

Jah T was a Mbare institution whose company Samson particularly enjoyed, particularly going through his records while they smoked a joint of Malawi Gold and Samson listened to Jah T's reminiscences. The highlight of Jah T's life had been his presence at Rufaro Stadium the night Bob Marley played the Independence

Concert. It was also the night of his conversion: Jah T claimed that it was the combination of the tear gas fired by the police to dispel an excitable crowd and the music of the Wailers that had set him on the path away from the Methodist church and on the way to being a Rastafarian of the Twelve Tribes of Israel.

It appealed to Samson's sense of the absurd that after Prince Charles had lowered the old flag and a new flag waved in its place, the first words said in independent Zimbabwe had been, 'Ladies and gentlemen, Bob Marley and the Wailers.'

Taking his soap and towel, he went to the outside bathroom. There was no sign of Jah T. He was probably in the house some-where. As there was no electricity, Samson had no choice but to give himself a bucket shower in cold water. Halfway through the shower, the music switched to Misty in Roots. 'Oh, I'm lost,' he sang happily along. 'Wandering! Wanderer!'

As a boarding school survivor, it was no hardship for him to wash in cold water, and in fact, this was part of his theory of why the country was truly unredeemable. Take a group of men and women who grew up in the rural areas with no creature comforts then went to mission boarding schools run on Calvinist lines, where they ate beans with bits of stone and caterpillars in their boiled cabbage before spending a good chunk of the seventies living lives of deprivation in the Bush as they fought the independence war, then give them a country to run and see what happened. No wonder that hot water and sanitation and good roads and regular supplies of occasional electricity came to be seen as luxuries, and a hunter-gatherer lifestyle to be perfectly normal.

Getting back to his room as Jah T's music changed to 'Ride Natty Ride', Samson wolfed down six slices of bread spread with Sun jam, washed it down with Mazoe and Marley and dressed to go out. Singing to himself, 'And it's the fire, fire,' he waved down a *kombi* and was soon on his way. At the traffic lights on Remembrance Drive, he read the newspaper headlines. Ten MPs had been fingered in some plot or another. They were now the fourth group to be 'fingered' in different plots. Samson was convinced that news editors simply kept the same headlines, changing the name as the circumstances demanded.

It was not the headlines but in the fine print that the full tragedy unfolded. It was in the stories that unfolded at Rotten Row that the fate of the nation was written large.

A man at Chitubu had been knifed because he had taken more than his fair share from a container of opaque beer. A woman who lived with her stepchild had cut long thin marks into the little girl's arms because she laughed in her sleep. A *kombi* tout accused of stealing a phone had been beaten to death by a crowd at Copacabana. A man accused of having a pet snake that rested under his car had been beaten unconscious on Leopold Takawira. A hairdresser knifed by her boyfriend at Northfields Penthouses had died from her wounds. A victim of political violence had refused to stay dead and buried in Gokwe. A 'small house' had seduced a madman to harvest his semen. An unidentified corpse had been found at Golden Quarry. A fight had broken out in Mbare over the rumoured news of the president's death.

These were the stories Samson listened to and wrote up every day at Rotten Row, the same road down which he had first come from Masvingo to Harare as a boy, with his mother and older brother and his sister just a baby. He still remembered the journey on the Hungwe Dzapasi bus from Masvingo, the recess at Pfugari to buy boiled eggs and bananas, the peanut butter rice and groundnuts they ate as the countryside moved past them, the music of the Bhundu Boys filling the crowded bus, and the drivers hailing each other with blasts of the horn as they passed each other. Most of all he remembered his mounting excitement as he spied the buildings of the city approaching and on the right, large black puffs of smoke rising from the giant chimneys. The chimneys were still there, but no smoke issued from them.

Rotten Row was now his daily stamping ground. He spent every working day at the court complex walking up and down the stairs of the circular building, moving from court to court to listen to tales of unravelling lives that he then reduced to copy of no longer than six hundred words, seven hundred if sub-editor Nixon Nhongo was generous.

His favourite teachers, Mrs Samupindi and Mr Makwarimba, had both taught him that the beauty of the English language lay in the elegance of its simplicity. At the Poly, he had spent a memorable afternoon listening to Stanlake Samkange, a veteran journalist who had urged his group of trainee journalists to follow George Orwell's rules of plain writing.

But Nixon Nhongo had very different views from his favourite teachers, Mr Samkange and from Orwell on what constituted good writing. He disagreed with all four as strongly as it was possible to disagree with someone you have never met. By the time Samson saw his own copy, now in the paper under his by-line, he found that it had been turned into more florid language. His modest reference to 'a male organ' had become a 'venomous one-eyed trouser snake', the rape victim who spoke with a low voice appeared shaking, her voice reduced to 'tremulous quaking', the elderly woman who had been beaten by her inebriated son became the 'grandmother clobbered and whacked by drunkard' and the magistrate who cautioned that the accused was in danger of contempt of court positively 'thundered' by the time the story appeared, and any person imprisoned was 'caged'.

Nixon Nhongo was currently enrolled as a first-year law student at the University of Zimbabwe. Samson did not want to imagine what would happen, if in addition to his journalistic Zimnglish, Nixon also added legalistic Legalese to his linguistic arsenal. Mercifully, that day was at least four years away, and by then, Samson was sure, he would have moved on to bigger, and, he hoped, better things.

Saturday afternoon, 14:44

Samson was tempted to walk across Africa Unity Square to the calm tranquillity of the Meikles Hotel, one of his favourite places. It was not just a hotel for him, but a sentimental place that was tied up with the childhood that he had begun again when his mother moved him and his brother to Masvingo. He had had just one wish then, to sit astride one of the two lions that stood sentinel at the entrance. But of course, he had never done it. He had known the hotel from its backrooms and kitchens, because his mother had worked in the hotel in Housekeeping. She made and stripped beds, and occasionally brought home treats in white boxes that had that distinctive yellow-gold 'M' logo on the lids.

He thought of his mother whenever he entered the Meikles. Its hushed grandeur no longer intimidated him, but he found himself as reassured as always by the sense of tranquil order within. He could not really afford it, but the Wi-Fi at the Meikles' Business Centre more than made up for the three dollars he had to pay for tea. As he placed his phone on the charger, he remembered that he had left his pageant ticket at work. He groaned as he realised that he would have to go into the office. As his phone charged, and he drank his tea, he listened to the conversations around him. A man dressed in the pristinely new khaki clothing that screamed 'New Farmer' shouted into his phone: 'I am here in Harare just this weekend, but I go back to Centenary on Monday. Monday. I said Monday. I go back to Centenary Monday.'

As soon as his phone was charged to sixty per cent, Samson made his way to work. At Century House, he greeted the security guard and walked to the lift.

'No lift today, Chef,' the security guard said cheerfully. Samson walked up the five flights to his office. He found himself in a large open-plan office filled with desks and computers and three large television screens mounted on the walls. The screens were permanently turned to the BBC, Al Jazeera and CNN. He passed the Showbiz desks where two men were huddled over a computer as they copied pictures of a half-naked Kim Kardashian from the UK *Daily Mail*.

Samson found it fascinating that whenever his countrywomen and other African women were pictured in the nude, they looked much more naked than white women and black women like Beyoncé or Rihanna. This, he suspected, was why there was such a stampede whenever nude pictures of a local celebrity popped up, like Deliwe, if she did well enough in the competition to become a celebrity. Before he could go over to join the two guys, he was greeted loudly by Ndomutenda, the women's columnist at the paper.

They had brought her in to give the Gender Perspective on news stories. The only women's issues she was interested in, however, were her own – she seemed to believe that she was contractually obliged to deliver to the *Metropolitan* a series of self-regarding, solipsistic reflections on her hair, her menstrual cycles and what she called her journey to 'She Spirit of her Inner Goddess'. That was also the name of her column, 'The Inner Goddess'.

It was all deadly serious, there was no humour or hint that other people outside herself might also exist. On Twitter, she described herself as 'Beautiful Non-Conformist, Sensitive Controversialist, Passionate Lover of Ideas' but it was clear that she loved only her own ideas. Her Tweets consisted of a series of trite quotes about inner beauty supposedly written many centuries ago by a Sufi mystic called Rumi interspersed with talk about her hair and intermittent scolding. The country, she had decided, and, indeed the world, needed to be scolded severely for its various flaws.

Just as, on the surface, Deliwe was not the person for him because she was shallow and vain, Ndomutenda appeared, on the surface, to be the kind of woman he should have been attracted to. Not only was she educated and bright and not at all bad-looking, she liked to read and travel. And she was a Salad who had grown up in the suburbs, a life that Samson envied and that he wished he had had himself. At this stage in his career, it was something that he could get only by association.

Having spent time with Ndomutenda, he found almost immediately that he had made a mistake. She proved to be far less than the sum of her parts. Within seconds of sitting down, she had begun a thirty-minute monologue about herself, most particularly, about her journey to her Inner Self, her Inner Beauty and her hair. Then she had looked at the next table and delivered a long sermon on women who wore hair weaves.

To Samson, there was nothing particularly exceptional about a woman who wore her natural hair, it was the hairstyle of every schoolgirl in the country, and, having grown up among the poor, natural hair was never in short supply in the townships and the rural areas, but for a middle-class woman like her, it necessitated endless self-scrutiny. As she went on about how natural she was, he did not bother to point to the artifice of her heels, her make-up or the push-up bra that thrust her breasts before him like an offering. By the end of the evening, he had decided he found her pretentious and judgemental. He thought her insincere and un-original. He had made his excuses, he had to take his *kombi* to Chitungwiza. He did not miss the dismissive look in her eye when he mentioned the *kombi*. He had walked her to her car, then went on to the Book Café where he joined Deliwe and her friends. Since that ill-fated date, Ndomutenda put on an ostentatious show of ignoring him, particularly when others were around.

So when he saw her on his way to his desk, he did what he

always did: he greeted her cheerfully, and was pointedly ignored. He walked to his desk, unlocked the top drawer, took out his pageant ticket and left.

Saturday evening, 18:07

From his office building, Samson walked down Josiah Tongogara Avenue, crossed Mazowe Street and walked on until he reached State House. He was in time for the changing of the guard, such as it was. Two camouflaged guards marched together in lockstep, until they reached their two comrades who were marching in similar fashion but in the opposite direction. On meeting, the four saluted each other, then turned smartly back to stand where they had been standing moments before they started the march. There seemed to be no rhyme or reason to the proceeding: Samson suspected they did this merely to relieve their boredom.

From State House, Samson crossed the road to the Keg and Maiden. He worked his way through the crowded bar to the long veranda that ran the length of the building. He stood for a minute to drink in the sight of the pristine and manicured cricket ground. Ahead in the short distance, he could see the Northfields penthouses. What he would not give to live on the top floor of that building and wake up every morning to the best view of Harare.

At a table at the end of the veranda, Samson spotted his friend Jimalo, who waved him over. If it had been later in the evening, Samson would have found a reason not to join him. Jimalo suffered the affliction of *marambadoro*, that condition where alcohol disagreed with a man to such an extent that he became a nuisance to others.

There were three types of drunks, Samson decided. There were happy drunks who were fun to be around and for whom alcohol was simply the sparkle to their fireworks. Then there were the morose drunks who became more and more morbid and talked endlessly about death and all the dead people they had lost, but were otherwise harmless. And then there were the *marambadoro* drunks like Jimalo who got more and more aggressive with each drink until they ended up picking fights, vomiting or pissing over themselves or, usually, doing all three.

At this time of evening though, Jimalo was safe. He was sitting with a couple of Rasta men that Samson did not know. He went across and greeted Jimalo and his companions as he sat down.

'*Ari sei m*alevels,' Samson greeted them.

'Sharp sharp,' said Jimalo.

'*Uri sei wangu*,' Samson said to the other fellow.

'Sharp *m'dhar*a,' the fellow responded.

'*Ko, shasha*,' Samson said to the third man.

The other simply nodded without saying a word.

Jimalo said, 'Samson, this is Bhidza, and this is Tonderai. Bhidza was just telling us his usual theory about the currency.'

Samson said, 'Oh yes?' It was one of the things that amused him the most about the ruling party, that for all its talk of sovereignty and independence, theirs was the only country in Africa that used a currency printed in a Western country.

Bhidza was the man who had not responded to his greeting. He looked to Samson like he might turn out to be a drunk of the morose variety. 'You know the problem with this currency?' Bhidza said.

His voice was low and urgent, as though he was imparting a great secret. 'I'll tell you what the problem is with this currency.'

'It's printed elsewhere so there is not enough money circulating,' Samson said. 'That's why we have these dirty dollars.' He fished out a dirty five-dollar bill and indicated to the waiter that he wanted a beer.

'*Ndipoo chibhodhoro*,' he said.

The waiter nodded and hurried off.

'No *mhani*,' Bhidza said, 'The problem with this money is that it is controlled by the Illuminati.'

'Sorry, what?' said Samson.

The waiter brought him his Black Label beer.

Bhidza continued, 'The Illuminati is trying to take over the world, together with the Freemasons. There are Illuminati symbols everywhere. Look at this. Look at this.'

He shuffled into his wallet and took out some dollar notes. 'The Reserve Bank *yeku*States, *inonzi chii*, Federal Reserve what-what. They are part of the Illuminati. Look at that. What is that? What is that?'

He held up an uncharacteristically crisp one-dollar note.

Jimalo said, 'That is George Washington.'

'No *mhani*,' Bhidza said. 'George Washington what. What is *that*, on the other side?'

'The pyramid?'

'Above the pyramid, what is that?'

'Oh, that eye.'

'No *mhani* that is not an eye. It is not just an eye. Look at it! Look closely! That is no ordinary eye. That is the symbol of the Illuminati. They are everywhere, these symbols, they are simply everywhere. My son, he is nine, I have banned all this Disney nonsense, Cartoon what-what Nickel this-that *zvimapopayi zviya izvi* because everywhere you look *mhani*, you find Illuminati symbols. Myself, as soon as I find myself with one-dollar notes, I get rid of them as quickly as I can.'

Once Bhidza began, there was no stopping him. 'Do you know why they are everywhere? Do you know who controls the world? I'll tell you who controls the world. It is the Illuminati, that's who controls the world, the Illuminati working with the Freemasons. And the Jesuits, yes, they have two secret societies, the Knights of Columbus and the Knights Templar. They have infiltrated the IMF, and the double, what it is it called, the double you T O, you know those ones that do trade and shipping what-what. And the European Union and African Union and Asian Union and all those unions. They all make up a secret government, it is global, I tell you, completely global, and they will use a social engineering technique that they call Secret Weapons for Quiet Wars. It is all in this book.'

Bhidza dug into the satchel next to him and held up a book in triumph, before slapping it on the table. Samson reached for his beer before the book could knock it over. The cover showed a naked woman in the grip of a grinning skeleton, both astride a winged white horse. Samson flicked through to the epigraph page and read: 'And I looked, and behold a pale horse: and his name that sat on him was Death, and Hell followed with him.'

'Why has no one told me that this bar has been turned into a library?' The four men looked up from the grinning skeleton as they were hailed by a loud voice. It belonged to a short but well-padded man who approached their table. Samson knew him well. Keen to escape the skeletal grip of the Illuminati, Samson hailed him with more enthusiasm that usual. He was an opposition party Member of Parliament who had been his senior at school. Then as now, his permanent cast of countenance was the gently lacerating look of a benign yet desperate man plotting to start a Prosperity Church. As he sat down to join them, Samson remembered that this was the same Member of Parliament claimed by AmbuyaVaDudley to have approached her looking for a lucky potion to advance his political career.

The men at the next table to theirs also recognised him, and in five minutes, the Illuminati was forgotten as the two tables gathered around this uniting force. Smiling and laughing, the Member passed greetings around the joined tables as freely as he had given out buckets of donor maize seed in the last election. '*Muripano zvenyu vadhara vadhara. Baba murisei.* Ah, *muzukuru, ndiwe uyu.* Ah, Tommy! *Chibababa!* How is it going with the business? Samson, *ari sei ma*levels?'

The man called Tommy said, 'You know how it is, life in Sosibheri. It's like being in a prison where you are fed on a diet of daily buggery.'

Jimalo said, 'And all you can say is, boys, just please be gentle.'

The Member chuckled as he added, 'Or you bring your own soap!'

Both tables burst into uproarious laughter.

Turning to Tommy, the Member said, 'So you were given a visa tonight. I thought you were under sanctions.'

Tommy said, 'The wife gave the visa *baba* but the visa is conditional. She said I can go anywhere as long as it is not to see those naked dancers that are all the rage. I am the only man in Zimbabwe who has not seen them dance live.'

The Member said, '*Pane nyaya paya*, I tell you, when they dance, there is not a soft member in the house. Not even this Member! But what is the worst your wife can do, and besides, how will she know?'

'My wife has relatives from here to Chitungwiza,' Tommy said. 'I can't misbehave without bumping into some unemployed *muzukuru* or *tezvara*. And they all gossip like market women in that family, *saka* tight. Even if I wanted a small house, I have to go all the way to Kwekwe or Gweru, *ndinotorova* out of town because Harare *yakatorohwa* embargo. Just as well, I can't afford a small house even if I wanted one.'

'Speaking of small houses and wives,' said the man opposite Tommy, '*Komurungu wenyu*, what's happening with your party leader, what's all this talk that he did not want to marry that woman?'

The Member became agitated. 'She is a lunatic. What sort of

woman claims to be married to a man who clearly says he did not marry her?'

'He should just accept the inevitable,' said Tommy.

'Accept what inevitable? Can a man be forced to marry when he does not want to?' the Member said.

'Of course a man can be forced to marry,' Tommy said with indignation. 'What man ever wants to marry? Do you know any man who got married willingly? Did you yourself get married willingly? No one ever does. A girl just turns up pregnant at your house and says now you have to marry me. So you marry and there you are. No two ways about it. It can only be marriage by ambush, by force or by *ginya*.'

The men burst into laughter. The Member feebly defended his leader before conveniently spotting a familiar face across the room, and making a hasty departure. As soon as he left, Tommy said, '*Ko muchinda uyu adzoka futi*? I thought he had left with the other guys who split from the party.'

'*Unotamba nezhara iwe*,' Jimalo said. 'My friend, hunger has no allegiance. It drives you to whoever pays the most.'

As the talk became general and political, Jimalo began to get more and more agitated. Another three rounds and he would be at the *marambadoro* stage. Samson took that as his cue to leave. From the veranda he walked out the way he had come in, through the crowded bar. The screens were now showing a tennis match; it was Federer playing Djokovic. This must be the match from New York on which Father Abraham had wanted to put Samson's rent advance. As Samson stepped out from the veranda and into the bar, Federer missed a volley. The room roared with howls of pain interspersed with cheers.

'*Musamutyire*,' yelled a loud voice. 'Don't fear for him. It's Federer, he will escape this one, *anopunyuka chete. Musamutyire, ndi*Federer.'

Federer missed a drop shot.

There was a universal groan.

Samson's way out was blocked by two men who were well in their cups and who were talking animatedly without listening to each other. The first said, 'They wanted to raise the price of beer. *Manje ipapo ndipo paanga avakuda kuirasa manje ipapo.* There would have been a revolution, I tell you. *Ndaitora gidi chairo.* Revolution.'

Without listening, his companion said, 'So I said to him, if you can do that, I will shake you by the hand, I swear on my son's life, I will shake you by the hand.'

His companion said, 'You know that shit that happened in Tunisia, that Arab Spring. Well, that would have been nothing in comparison. Myself, I would have led from the front. If they had raised the price of beer, I would have raised hell.'

Samson pushed his way past as he chuckled to himself. He was still laughing as he reached Rotten Row.

Saturday evening, 20:45

The Rainbow Towers stood at the no man's land where Speke Avenue met Rotten Row. Samson walked through the lobby. It was packed with what Nixon Nhongo would call revellers. The women wore outfits of varying degrees of tightness. The men were dressed in differing interpretations of formal wear, at one end, lounge suits worn with rakish bow-ties, African print jackets worn over lurid open-necked shirts, and, at the other end, imitation Sean John t-shirts worn with fake FUBU jeans and Michael Jordan sneakers.

Samson was pleased to see that he had timed his arrival so well that he would not have to spend any money on the over-priced beers in the hotel bar. As soon as he made his way to his seat in the Conference Centre, which was the pageant venue, the proceedings began. On stage stood the mistress of ceremonies, a pretty, dimpled and effervescent radio personality who had herself been a pageant winner.

She introduced Killer T, a dancehall singer, and asked him to serenade the twelve contestants as she called them one by one to the stage. They walked out in bikinis and high-heels that made it impossible for them to walk with any comfort or grace. Samson had his eyes on Deliwe, who wore a hot pink bikini and a beaming smile.

'Hotty property,' Killer T sang. 'Everything you want I will do for you. Yes, you are hotty property.' At the end of their parade, the contestants stood in formation and turned their backs to the crowd, which roared its approval.

The contestants left the stage, and were replaced by Winky D who gave an energetic performance of his two most recent hits. Next came the Evening Dress segment. During the parade, a contestant stumbled on the hem of her dress and almost fell over Deliwe. The crowd booed. As more performers took to the stage, the judges conferred and eliminated four contestants. To the mockery of the crowd, the young woman who had stumbled during the Evening Dress segment burst into loud sobs. Samson was delighted to see that Deliwe made the cut,

Then came the question and answer session. The questions focused on national beauty spots and monuments, for the pageant was supposed to help to promote tourism. Quite what the link between tourism and a beauty pageant was, Samson could not work out, apart from the obvious: come to Zimbabwe where the women are 'hotty property'.

The contestants were eliminated until only five were left. They were then required to show their talent. The first contestant came back to the stage in a costume of faux leopard skin that left little to the imagination. She danced a Jerusarema solo. In this rendition, the Jerusarema became, not a harvest festival dance with protected world heritage status, but something that would not have looked out of place in a strip joint. The next contestant sang a Beyoncé song with competence but no flair. The next two contestants were also singers, and both off key. The crowd became restless. The last contestant was Deliwe.

'I am going to sing,' she said.

Samson's spirits sank.

'Are you are a singer?,' the mistress of ceremonies asked.

'Not yet, but I want to be a gospel singer.'

Samson groaned. With the exception of the Beyoncé imitator, every contestant who sang had sung gospel. Badly.

'But today I am going to sing Chris de Burgh. Carry me like a flower in your heart. Sorry, fire, like a fire in your heart.'

As Deliwe sang, Samson realised just how little he knew her. She had offered to sing for him once, but he had declined partly because he had assumed she was not very good, and he would not have known what to say. But her voice was pure and true. The mawkish sentimentality of the words was redeemed by the purity of her voice. After she finished, there was a hushed stillness and then, a second later a roar of applause and whistles. He found himself with a tight chest and a feeling he had never known before, a combination of happiness, pride and possessiveness.

He barely noticed the rest of the ceremony. He felt a moment of tension when Deliwe made it to the top three, together with the Jerusarema pole dancer and an off-key gospel singer. The gospel singer was announced as the First Princess and still Deliwe stood there with another girl. When the Jerusarema dancer was announced as the winner, Deliwe gave a squeal of joy as she threw herself at the winner. She might have won herself, such was the radiance of her joy.

Still in her leopard skins, the Jerusarema dancer shouted 'Ebenezer!' and gave a loud prayer of ecstasy. Deliwe's beaming face was enlarged on the screen above him. Her joy was infectious. He had to remind himself that this was, after all, just a beauty pageant. As Killer T returned to the stage to sing 'Hot Property', and the Jerusarema dancer gyrated to the delight of the crowd, Samson made his way out. On his way back home, he stopped at Tipperary's and proceeded to get thoroughly and absolutely trashed.

Sunday morning, 07:45

Through his drunken haze, the voices of his landlady and her husband came. But they were not quarrelling: Makorinde was urging Father Abraham to get ready because there was no excuse, he had to come to church today. After that, Makorinde said, they would go to get some chickens with Samson's rent money. Samson smiled. It looked like Federer had come through for Father Abraham after all. From Jah T's house, the Wailers lamented that they had made their world so hard. Samson looked at his phone. It was a quarter to eight. The windows shook as Marley pleaded for the teachings of His Majesty and the Wailers rejected the Devil's philosophy.

Samson opened his folder of photos. He looked at his mobile to check his messages. Without opening the folders, he moved all of Deliwe's photos to the trash folder. Then he moved to the trash folder and emptied that too. As Makorinde hurried Father Abraham along because they would be late, and he knew she hated to sit at the back and Father Abraham said, 'I am coming, Chihera mine, let me just tie my tie,' Samson went back to sleep and this time, he had no dreams at all.

A Note on the Text

Four of the stories in this volume have been published previously as follows:

'The News of Her Death' was first published on the website of the *Sunday Times* newspaper on 28 February 2016.

A version of 'Copacabana, Copacabana, Copacabana' was first published by Amnesty International in the multi-author anthology *Freedom: Short Stories Celebrating the Universal Declaration for Human Rights* under the title 'An Incident At Lunchtime' (2010).

A version of 'Miss McConkey of Bridgewater Close' first appeared in the *Guardian* newspaper in December 2009.

'The Lament of Hester Muponda' was first published on the website African Writing Online (2009).

The lyrics from the songs 'Totutuma' by Oliver Mtukudzi, 'Njoka' by Mokoomba, 'Umuti WabuFyashi' by the Mulemena Boys, 'Simudza Mawoko' by Tocky Vibes, 'Chinamira' by Jah Prayzah and the Third Generation, 'Makomborero' by Fungisai Zvakavapano-Mashavave, 'Ziso raBob Marley' by Sniper Storm, 'Ebenezer' by Reverend Chivaviro and Friends and 'Chikwama' as arranged by Kapfupi are all used with the kind permission of the artists.

The quotations used at the beginning of each story are taken from the King James Version of the Christian Bible, as finalised in 1611, and from *Bhaibheri: Magwaro Matsvene aMwari*, the first full translation of the Bible into 'Union Shona', finalised at Morgenster Mission and published in 1949.

Acknowledgements

I have, as always, a million 'gratitudes'.

I am grateful to the Open Society Foundations (OSF), for a significant fellowship in 2012. I used that time to travel as I ruminated on the two large questions that propel this book: what is the content of justice, both procedural and social, in an 'open society', and what is the place of religion in such a society, particularly as expressed in the uneasy mix of Christianity and the traditional pre-Christian beliefs that still claim a hold on Zimbabwe. I know that this is not the non-fiction work that the OSF had hoped to see, but I hope that this book shows that the imaginative freedom afforded by fiction can reveal truths that the necessary caution of non-fiction may be hesitant to trumpet.

In particular, I wish to thank the following current and former OSF staff: Leonard Bernardo and Stephen Hubbell for their kind support and the Zim 'Quad' of Tawanda Mutasah, Deprose Muchena, Glen Mpani and Siphosami Malunga.

Writing this book was made a painless delight by the unshakeable confidence of my editor Lee Brackstone, and the faith of Stephen Page and Mitzi Angel. I also wish to acknowledge Sophie Portas and Donna Payne for their thought and care, Kate Murray-Browne for whipping the book into shape, Alex Russell, for rousing me from my bronchial bed on a significant day, and Kate Ward for her forensic search for the perfect 'Emojis'. At William Morris Endeavour, I am grateful to Eric Simonoff, Raffaella De Angelis, Siobhan O'Neill and for the abiding friendship and continuing support of my former agent Cathryn Summerhayes.

Thank you to my wonderful first listeners: Charity Strässle, Regina Gapa Chinyanga, Farai Mauchaza, Priscilla Sadomba,

Vimbayi Gapa and Naomi Mapfumo, and my first readers: Uchi Gappah, Ratiel Gapa, Angeline Kadzirange Gapa, Donald Chinyanga, Helliate Rushwaya Hay, Mary Majoni and Silas Chekera. To Kushinga Gappah, thank you for the supremely heroic effort of reading and editing one whole sentence, and to my soul sisters Chipo Chung, Paula Hawkins, Marina Cavazza, Lauren Beaukes and Marie Darrieussecq thank you for taking me as far as you did.

Thanks are due as well to my Languages Team: Douglas Rogers and Brian Latham who checked that my Rhodesian was fluent enough to pass muster, Takawira Mubako for help with medical language, Hawa Jande Golokai who checked my Sierra Leonean Krio and Brian James who perfected it, Albert Chimedza for help with Zambian Bemba and Tawana Kupe for help with Zimbabwean Kalanga. I also wish to thank Dominic Muntanga for the beautiful gift of the Tonga language, shared by Zambia, the land of my birth and Zimbabwe, the land of my being.

Asi zvokwadi zvingashata ndikasavuchira Nyanduri Tinashe Muchuri, my incomparable Shona editor. *Makaita hombarume. Zvigare zvakadaro Mazvimbakupa.*

Rotten Row is a book about the relationship between the law and justice. I wish to thank the many friends I met at the UZ all those years ago, twenty-five years in fact, who enriched my life then and continue to do so today. I am especially grateful to the inspiration of Nancy Chauraya Samuriwo and the wise counsel, friendship and support of Tatenda Mawere, Munyaka Makuyana and Tendai Biti. And to Brian Kagoro: though we were unable to squeeze water out of a rock, you have shown me what is possible.

I want to thank the entire squadron at the Advisory Center on WTO Law in Geneva, colleagues past and present: the Dream Team of Carol Lau, Pascale Colombo and Sandra Roethlisberger, the Old Timers Hunter Nottage, Tom Sebastian and Fernando Piérola

and the Next Wave (from the post-Roesslerite, Meagherean era)
of Kholofelo Kugler, Vitaliy Pogoretskyy, Leah Malabonga and the
Latin Quarter of Maria Alcover, Tatiana Yanguas-Acosta, Christian
Vidal-León and Alejandro Sanchez Arriaga. Alejandro, you were
always the patient recipient of my endless wittering. Thank you for
your friendship.

I want to thank the 'Senior Friends' who have advised and men-
tored me at key stages: Pieter-Jan Kuijper, Ambassador Amina
Mohammed and Ian Donovan. Thanks are due as well to Tony
Gubbay, for the precious gems from his library, to David Coltart
for the Ultimate Dream Job and to Ambassador James Manzou
who sold me to the world.

I am also grateful to all my former supervisors and bosses: Kevin
Laue and Beatrice Mtetwa at Kantor and Immerman; Debra
Steger, Nicolas Lockhart, Peter van den Bossche, Valerie Hughes,
Werner Zdouc and Hyung Chong Kim at the Appellate Body Sec-
retariat; and Niall Meagher, Jan Bohanes, Cherise Valles, Leo Pal-
ma and Frieder Roessler at the ACWL. I am grateful, too, to all
the Appellate Body Members I was privileged to serve, particularly
Claus-Dieter Ehlermann, Mitsuo Matsushita, A. V. Ganesan, Yasu-
hei Taniguchi and Jim Bacchus.

I want to honour three departed teachers whose memories I
have invoked in a story in this volume: Lawrence Tshuma, Kempton Makamure and Pearson Nherere. Lawrence taught me *Introduction to Law* and opened the gateway to a new world; Kempton
taught me both *The History of Roman and Roman-Dutch Law*
and *Jurisprudence*, instilling in me a love for Cicero, legal theory
and everything Rome. Pearson, who was born blind and achieved
first class law degrees from both Cambridge and Oxford, taught
me *International Law* and inspired me to reach both for those
dreaming spires and a bigger world.

My final 'gratitudes' are what in Zimbabwe we call *kutyora muzura*; they are genuflections or very deep curtsies to four exceptional writers. Without Helen Garner's *Joe Cinque's Consolation* and *This House of Grief*, this book would have been much poorer, as it would have been without the example set for me by Friedrich von Schrirach. Without P. D. James, I would not have found the courage to come to writing at my wizened age, and to find myself moreover, with a well-appointed room within her publishing house. And having found that room, I am grateful to John Coetzee, for the words that opened the doors to even more, and for *Summertime*, for *Youth* and for *Boy*.

Thank you all.